Brenna Lyons

Night Warriors

Night Warriors
Warriors, Book 1

FIREBORN
PUBLISHING

Fireborn Publishing Copyright Statement

Night Warriors
Copyright © 2004/2009/2015 by Brenna Lyons
Print ISBN: 978-1-943528-10-3
First Fireborn Publication: October 2015

Cover Artist: Brenna Lyons
Photo Credit: 123rf
Editor: Kathryn Lively
Logo copyright © 2014 by Fireborn Publishing and
Allison Cassatta
Licensed material is being used for illustrative
purposes only. Any person depicted in the licensed
material is a model.

This book is written in US English.

PUBLISHER

FIREBORN
PUBLISHING

**PO Box 5216
Haverhill, MA 01835**

Dedicated to...

My husband for getting me hooked on Blade.

Lisa, who usually hates anything about vampires but apparently not this series.

Beth, who compared this book to David and Leigh Edding's work.

Marlis, who provided the German translations for the updated version of the series.

Note from Brenna:

To those of you who have read the earlier novellas from this series, I beg your indulgence this far. As you know, I believe in souls meeting again and again. In this story, Jörg is decidedly the villain, but though his madness has won the day—temporarily, this is not the end for Jörg. Please, keep in mind that there is *always* another chance, even when it seems hopeless. On the other hand, this book will be a homecoming for those of you who've read the novellas. Unlike Corwyn and his brothers, you'll have no problem recognizing what Jörg's motives are, the source of his madness, or his fight to hold on, even when he knows it would be best to walk away.

Happy reading,
Brenna Lyons

Glossary of Warrior Terms

Beast- Beasts are what humans erroneously refer to as vampires. The stories humans tell are obviously not correct, but you can't expect a human to get everything right.

Blutjagd- The "blood hunt." Warriors crave battle with the beasts, as the beasts crave blood. Warriors are tied to beasts in that they sense many of the beasts' special powers. A Warrior can feel the use of coercion, feeding, and other controls of humans. They also feel other Warriors engaged in *Blutjagd*, the death of beasts and Warriors in their range, and the presence of nearby beasts that are not fully ghosted. Rigorous battle training will quell the *Blutjagd* for short periods of time.

Elder- One of the original beasts, the Stone stealers who were damned for their crimes against the Stone and the Warriors. The elders are gifted with powers turned beasts are not, including the ability to reproduce with a *Blutjagdfrau*, the ability to turn other beasts, and the inability to be killed by anyone but a Warrior.

Endspiel- The point in printing when a Warrior must either seal printing or go insane. A Warrior who feels printing may not progress should break printing long before this point. Note that they are rarely smart enough to do so.

Fluch- The Warrior's curse, passed from father to son or daughter. The *fluch* may be removed from a daughter but never a son. If the *fluch* is not removed in the *Zeremonie der Freiheit* by the time the menses begin or the *Zeremonie des Schutzes* is performed before freeing, the daughter is cursed to become *Blutjagdfrau*, a female Warrior. Because elders target *Blutjagdfrau* as mates, Warrior fathers will go to any lengths to free a daughter not marked by the Stone.

Ghosting- A talent that both beasts and Cursed Warriors learn to harness. Ghosting can hide the physical form of Cursed Warriors or beasts and all they hold or carry from each other and humans. In a lesser strength, it can "blur" the image of the user so that humans do not note the passage in particular but still see a person there, which avoids accidental collisions. Even a ghosted beast cannot hide uses of power that a Warrior can track. Warriors sometimes ghost in tandem to remain visible to each other but not other Warriors or beasts.

Krankheit- The "sealing sickness." In the final stage of the transformation between human and Cursed Warrior, at or about the sixteenth birthday in males and a year after the start of menses in females, the sickness strikes. The young Warrior will suffer nausea, vomiting, a high fever, disorientation, dizziness and may become incoherent. It is usually the only time in a Warrior's life that he or she becomes ill, save morning sickness in a *Blutjagdfrau.*

Printing- Like imprinting, a Warrior becomes tied to his mate for life. He cannot choose another if she's lost, cannot be unfaithful while she lives, and cannot ever divorce or otherwise dissolve the union. A printed Warrior is the most stable of men, unless his mate or children are endangered or lost. Then, he will suffer the printing madness and may have to be killed by his house. Likewise, a Warrior who breaks printing, even early printing, will suffer for it. A Warrior who breaks printing too close to Endspiel will face the madness.

Veriel- The Mad Elder. The Destroyer of Lives. The Mad Deceiver, who led the traitors and freed the elders from the Stone. The most hated and hunted of all the beasts. Fixated on one woman, he would destroy the world to own her. Or... At least, that's what the stories say of him.

Warriors- Also called Cursed Warriors, Krieger der Nacht, Soldat der Nacht or Sons of the Stone. The Warriors were an ancient race of protectors who spawned the beasts and now are driven to hunt their former brothers to extinction.

Zeremonie der Freiheit

Bei den Göttern, die uns alle geschaffen haben, erbitte ich, dass diese einer zur Sicherheit aller die menschliche Form erhält. Blut meines Blutes; sei frei von meinem Fluch für jetzt und für alle Zeit.

Ich befreie dich von der Schuld meines Fluchs und nehme die Pflicht, die die deinige gewesen wäre, auf mich zurück. Ich schwöre, dass ich an deiner statt und für deine Ehre kämpfen werde, bis der Tag kommt, an dem ich die Ruhe der Krieger finde.

Translated:

By the gods who forged us all, I ask that this one be transformed unto Human form for the protection of all. Blood of my blood; be free of my curse for now and all times.

I free you from the obligation of my curse and accept back into myself the duty that would have been yours. It is my oath that I shall fight in your stead and for your honor until the day that I join the Warrior's Rest.

Zeremonie des Schutzes

Bei den Göttern, die uns alle geschaffen habe, stelle ich dich unter den Schutz des Hauses [Name]. Ein jeder unserer Art und Sippe wird sein Leben geben um deines vor dem Bösen, das unter uns weilt, zu bewahren. Wandele nun gesegnet in unserer Mitte.

Translated:

By the gods who forged us all, I grant you the protection of the House [name]. Any and all of our kind and kin shall lay down life to preserve yours from the evil that walks among us. Walked blessed among us, now.

Swordbearer Reborn

Schwertträger Wiedergeboren

Chapter One

December 16th, 1976
Year 1476 of the Second Beast War

"What do you mean, dead? What the hell happened?" Corwyn Hunter demanded in two parts anger and one part fear.

At twenty-eight, he would be the youngest house lord in centuries. In the beginning, when people died young and there were less Cursed Warriors, it wasn't unusual for a man to become house lord at twenty, or gods forbid, sixteen like Andris Lord Crossbearer had.

But now? In this century? His father Jonas had only been Lord Hunter for six years, having taken his place at a respectable fifty-five, when old Grandfather Carter died.

Honor demanded that he not admit it, but Corwyn wasn't ready for this. Stone lord, yes. He was ready for that. Carrick Armen, the Lord Swordbearer, was ancient, and Corwyn had been born with the blood mark of Syth. When Carrick died, the Stone would pass into Corwyn's care, and every Warrior knew that. He had been trained for that task since he was in diapers, lectured on the importance of his place until Corwyn felt he might go mad from it.

But, house lord? No. He hadn't been prepared to be the oldest living Warrior of *Haus Jäger* for many years to come.

Kord Maher sighed harshly. "It was Veriel. You know that beast has never left a Warrior alive. Your father couldn't just walk away because it was Veriel. Honor demanded more from him than that."

"No," he affirmed in a sick voice, "he couldn't do that." With no older brothers or uncles, that left Corwyn in the hot seat. "What the hell was Jonas doing there? Why was he in your range, Kord? And without informing us he was going?"

"Or us that he was coming into our range?"

Corwyn winced. That was a major breach of trust with the Mahers. One did not poach on the range of another house. Jonas must have felt strongly about what he was doing.

"I don't have all the facts yet. I do know that he was protecting a young woman from your range. When she left, he followed."

"Protecting? She has his blessing? Which woman was it?"

His mind worked furiously. If one of their protected thought she was responsible for a Warrior's death, she would be distraught. Corwyn's first priority should be putting the woman's mind at ease. Warriors knew the risk they took, and she wouldn't be protected if they weren't all willing to accept that risk on her behalf.

Kord reached into the inside pocket of his long, black leather jacket and drew out a notebook. "She wasn't under his blessing. I'd say he was using her as bait, but that wouldn't be accurate. He wasn't hunting Veriel, per se. Jonas seemed to realize that the beast had formed a fixation on the woman and was trying to figure out why. Why her and for what reason? If Veriel simply wanted to take her, he would have taken her."

Corwyn nodded in understanding. "Is that Jonas's notebook?" He put out his hand, sure that he was right.

Kord passed it over. "Her name is Anna Louise

Jameson. She's a bookkeeper for a small electronics repair company. Jonas has quite a bit of information about her. He hadn't reached any conclusions yet about why Veriel would fixate on her, though."

Corwyn nodded uncertainly this time. "If my father felt it was that important, I'll check into it. Will you stay for dinner, Kord?"

He shook his head sadly. "I wish I could, but my lord calls. He allowed me to bring you the notebook, because he felt it might be of importance, but you know my grandfather."

Kord shrugged, and a wide smile sent shards of light through his midnight blue eyes. His shaggy black hair was like a dark mane around his narrow face. He rose to leave with a clap of support on Corwyn's shoulder, off to return to his lord with his senses open to the night for a possible kill on the way.

Yes, Corwyn knew Jason Lord Maher better than he needed to. He knew him well enough to know that, while the physical appearance a young Warrior kept was not something he needed permission for, Kord most likely took abuse, verbally or in trial by the old bastard, for balking his grandfather's will. Lord Maher was of the old school that included all of the house lords—except Hunter, now that Corwyn was her lord.

Corwyn sighed. It came in cycles, he supposed. Every few centuries it changed from a harsher regime to more autonomy and self-responsibility then back again, a never-ending pendulum. Corwyn was glad the change was coming. It couldn't come fast enough for his tastes, but for now, the old ways were still enforced in most of the world.

In the other ranges, trials of young Warriors often

ended in scars to teach them a lesson and involved pitting neighboring Warriors against each other, as he and Kord had often been pitted against each other as teens and young adults. Corwyn fingered the scar under his chin that Jason Lord Maher had gifted him— *with Carter's permission, of course*—bitterly.

The old ways were barbaric. There were better ways to train young Warriors. Luckily, Corwyn's rise to power meant that his own children could be trained the way he wished he had been, if he ever found a woman who would accept this life and want to stay with him despite it.

Corwyn was the oldest of three.

At nineteen, Stephen was the youngest and most like Corwyn: intelligent, cool-headed, and introspective. Still, Stephen lacked the drive of a truly great Warrior. Research and problem solving were more his forte than brute battle, though as a Cursed Warrior, he had the skills and used them well. Despite Stephen's blood and his training, he lacked a bit of the heart—the pride, perhaps, in what they accomplished. He was also sloppy in his ghosting, and no amount of trial seemed to break him of it.

Twenty-three-year-old Colin, on the other hand, was a veritable throwback to the outgoing regime. Hot-headed and mired in duty, honor, and glory, he was Stephen's opposite in every way.

Their constant rivalry was proof enough of that. Like the pups they were often compared to when their curse was new, it wasn't unusual to see Colin and Stephen tussling about.

The three brothers were outwardly similar, with their black hair and deep brown eyes. Jonas always said that was the mark of a true Cursed Warrior, but it was clear that the old prejudices about the Maher blue eyes still held root in many of the older Warriors.

To Corwyn's mind, the color of a man's eyes was immaterial when compared to his curse and skill. Mahers had those in abundance. The fires of battle and of love ran deep in them. Though only three years older than Corwyn, Kord had been mated for nine years and had a son, Lewis, by his mate, Julia.

His mind wandered back to his own brothers. Corwyn was the tallest at almost six and a half feet and was broad-shouldered, like most Warriors were.

Colin was shorter, barely topping six feet—*short for a Warrior*—and stocky. Somehow, the picture of an angry ape came to mind when Colin was in full *Blutjagd,* the blood lust that drove the kill.

Stephen looked the bookworm he aspired to be as much as a Warrior could. He was just shy of Corwyn's height but lean and wiry. Stephen moved like the wind in battle. At times, blades seemed to move right through him as he ducked them. His speed made him little more than a dark blur in the face of beasts.

Still, they looked like nothing less than brothers, with features so similar that, with them separated, the occasional Warrior couldn't tell them apart at a distance in their full-Warrior wear: jeans, armored boots, black T-shirt and/or black long-sleeved button-down shirt, a long black leather coat, and weapons belt. With their ability to mask their appearance from humans in general, few found it necessary to resort to any other form of clothing in their lives.

Outside, they were alike. Inside, it was amazing that they had been sired by the same man and pushed from the same womb.

And now, his brothers owed him duty as their new lord. Corwyn hissed in annoyance. It wasn't going to go smoothly. He sighed as he removed his own blade from its sheath and sheathed his father's blade—*my blade now.* He glanced at the lord's seal of *Jäger* in its hilt as he slid it home.

"I'll tell them in a few minutes," he decided. In the meantime, Corwyn opened the notebook and started to read what his father had discovered about Anna Jameson.

* * * *

Anna snapped awake, willing her heart to slow. This arousal was maddening. Every night, it was the same thing—or rather a similar thing. The man was always the same, though the encounters were always different—*and stunningly real for dreams.* She shuddered as she recalled how interactive the dreams were. If she didn't find something pleasing—*and that is strange for a wet dream, isn't it?*—it changed to something pleasing almost immediately.

The man in the dream was beyond handsome to downright sinful. His medium brown hair was longer than Anna typically liked, and his gray eyes glowed silver in the dim candlelight or firelight that was a staple in the dreams. Anna's head didn't reach his shoulder; at five feet five, that would make him well over six feet tall.

His age was impossible to gauge. At times, he looked like he was eighteen; at others, he seemed close to thirty. His body was perfect: strong and broad-shouldered, with sparse dark curls over a well-muscled chest and endowed well enough to keep any woman happy, she was sure. There was an intriguing scar on his chest, just above the right nipple, and a red tattoo on his shoulder, some sort of a symbol or glyph that made no sense to Anna but drew her hands and mouth like a magnet.

"*Geliebte. Regana,*" she whispered into the dark room.

Of all things he whispered to her while he made her his own, both in lightly accented English and in several smooth, foreign tongues, spoken as if he'd been born to them, those two words assaulted her over and over. They melted her, and Anna had no idea what they meant, only that they were spoken with tenderness and passion.

All told, the situation was driving her insane. Anna woke every night, feeling the comfortable aches of having accepted a lover but still aching for him as if she hadn't—which of course, she hadn't.

Anna groaned as she realized that that, more than anything, drove her to accept Matt's invitation out. Matt Collins wasn't typically a man she would go out with on a dare, but he was funny and attractive, just the kind of man to help her get rid of this pent-up frustration. If he was a little too full of himself, all the better. That just meant Anna would have no problem at all convincing Matt to engage in something hot and mind-blowing that would cure her of this aching need. Twenty-four was far too young to be committed, she decided.

* * * *

Corwyn heard Colin coming and glanced at his watch in shock. Two hours had passed while he read and reread his father's notes. It was obvious that Veriel had some need for or interest in the woman, but there was no clue what it was in his father's observations.

"Still here?" Colin questioned. "Sitting down on the job while I'm off hunting," he teased. "You're more like Stephen every day."

"Actually, I'm working on a problem for Father. Your hunt was successful." It wasn't a question. Corwyn knew a beast died in Hunter range, and Colin still had the faint smell of it on him.

"Just a low-level named Belanger. Is Father home or gone again on one of his secret forays?" Colin dropped into the chair opposite the desk and smiled at him.

Corwyn felt his jaw tighten reflexively, and Colin's smile disappeared.

"He met Veriel in battle two days ago. He followed a trail—a problem he was working on, and the beast didn't want his interference."

"Impossible. We would have sensed it," he raged.

"He was outside our range. In Maher, actually. Kord brought his notebook and weapon to me tonight after you left."

Colin went a shade of pale Corwyn had never seen on him before. "Did Veriel feed?" he asked woodenly.

"No. Calvin sensed Jonas's distress and sent Veriel to ground with the help of Kord. It was good that they were together and sunrise was fast approaching, or we could have lost more. You know Veriel has never lost to a single Warrior."

Colin nodded uncertainly but with an easing of his muscles.

Corwyn understood his upset. On the rare occasion a Warrior was killed by an elder, feeding was always a concern. While any turned beast could access an unprotected human's thoughts, it took an elder to read the thoughts of a Warrior. If the elder fed, all their safe houses, protected professionals, and strategies were forfeit, especially if it was the house lord who fell; they would have had to start from scratch. For that reason, more than any other, the houses shared information only when it was absolutely necessary. At least if someone was lost, he couldn't betray everything.

Elders rarely came within miles of Warriors. They fed, took their pleasures, and went to ground, moving on before reprisals could come. Only once in fifteen hundred years had an elder been killed, by the infamous Pauwel first Lord Crossbearer, but the elders were new then and unaccustomed to their powers. Regardless, they avoided the Warriors for fear of their lives and sent turned to keep the Warriors busy— except for Veriel.

Veriel was an enigma. He was The Mad Deceiver who'd released the beasts from their imprisonment within the Stone and turned his back on his life as a Warrior to go beast in the process. He was known as 'The Destroyer of Lives.' Unlike the other elders, he'd often sought out confrontation with the Warriors, especially the early Warriors of Hunter. For a time, it seemed that he was trying to exterminate the house completely. He was vicious and thorough, and more than once, Veriel had fed on Warriors.

Veriel had even done the most foolish thing imaginable, turned a Warrior and almost cost himself his life in the bargain. While all elders turned humans as a distraction to the Warriors, Veriel trained his turned vigorously to do the most damage they could. It was rare to find a beast turned by Veriel who was less than a high-level. He simply did not permit any less. When a Warrior died, it was often Veriel or one of his turned at work.

"Corwyn, with Father dead..." Colin began uncertainly.

He nodded stiffly and unsheathed his weapon, placing it on the desk more forcefully than was necessary. Colin stared at the seal in resignation. Crossed arrows superimposed over a bow and crested by the howling wolf head shined silver against the dark metal.

"I am *Jäger*, now," Corwyn growled the ritual words.

Colin met his eyes and straightened his spine proudly. "My blade is yours, my duty at your whim. I stand, a Warrior of Hunter, yours to command." He rose to leave.

Corwyn smiled stiffly. For once, that overactive sense of duty was going to work in the older brother's favor. There wouldn't be an argument or balking Corwyn's place in things. It was Colin's duty to accept it, and he would do so with no scene—publicly, at least.

"Colin, send Stephen down here. I may as well finish this now."

"What will you do after that, Corwyn?" he asked quietly.

"Solve this mystery of Father's, if I can."

"But what if Veriel takes your life, too?" Colin protested.

"Then you'll hold the seal sooner than you counted on."

"Can't it wait? Shouldn't you start your family as a safeguard?" This was the Colin he knew and sometimes loved. This was the Warrior who would try Corwyn's patience.

"This can't wait, but I swear to keep my eyes open for a mate while I work on it," he promised grimly.

Corwyn had never put much thought into his duty to marry and produce heirs until now. He'd always thought there would be more time.

Unlike Kord, few Warriors married younger than thirty. In the early days, they routinely married as soon after being blood sealed as they could arrange, but that had fallen out of practice as the bloodlines had grown.

Worse, most protecteds were professionals they needed and not suited to wandering around after a Warrior. Now every woman, bait and saved, would have to be evaluated as a potential mate. Corwyn grimaced at the thought of it.

Chapter Two

December 17th, 1976

Corwyn followed Anna from the company she worked for the next afternoon. He'd awoken suddenly that morning, realizing that even with his father's description, he might not recognize her unless he eyed her at her house to be sure.

He was wrong. With her long, red curls brushing over her back in a simple ponytail, Anna was hard to miss. He couldn't see her eyes thanks to the dark sunglasses she wore, but Corwyn was sure they were glittering, captivating.

He shook himself mentally. Anna was a mystery he had to solve and nothing more. Taking on a woman Veriel wanted was a sure-fire death sentence, whether Corwyn took her to mate or used her for release. Veriel wasn't like other beasts, but even Veriel had never fixated on a woman like this. That alone was enough to make Corwyn wary.

Typically, beasts weren't territorial. If they lost prey, there was a whole world full of others.

No, Veriel wanted this woman in a way Corwyn had never encountered before. He was single-minded.

If he didn't know better, Corwyn would have sworn she was *Blutjagdfrau*, but that was impossible. If a Warrior daughter hadn't been freed of the curse, if they were ever foolish enough to tempt fate—and the beasts—like that, the entire race of Warriors would know she existed. They would have to.

Still, there was something about Anna Jameson that Corwyn couldn't define. She drew him to her in some strange way he had never encountered before.

Cursed Warriors had fierce needs, which they were trained to control, weaker than the urges that drove the damned beasts and not as destructive, but occasionally the urges became overpowering and required purging. The hunt where they killed the beasts satisfied *Blutjagd*, the blood lust that became the urge to feed when perverted by the beast inside the damned ones. Training helped release that tension as well. Physical release with a woman satisfied the rest.

Printing stabilized a Warrior as nothing else could, but the *Blutjagd* involved in protecting a mate was some of the most dangerous there was, the most difficult to control. All Warriors took simple release with women until they found the woman who would accept them as mate—and after, if she died before her husband. They'd always been concerned with a woman's timing, even in the earliest days, sensing her to make sure they didn't produce children with a woman not their mate, but the advent of barrier contraceptives had made taking release a simpler matter.

Until he took a woman to mate and she granted him permission to give her children, Corwyn could chance no children. It was both a practical matter—the inability to properly guide, protect, and train a child who wasn't within your walls—and a matter of law.

The rules of sanction from the *First Book of Texts* made a Warrior's limitations clear. He could take no woman, even an enemy as many soldiers did, unwilling. He couldn't seduce an unwilling woman to his bed nor convince a woman to become his mate. He could never chance a child outside of mating and never without his mate's permission to create a life.

The rules of sanction were many and on varied subjects, and they alone stood between the Warrior's curse and the evil they could do with it unrestrained. Theirs was a life of controlling the curse fate had dealt them.

Ein Krieger, der den Fluch nicht unter Kontrolle hat, ist nicht besser als ein Biest.

A Warrior who cannot control the curse is no better than a beast. So spoke the sanctions, and it was true. Humans were essentially powerless before them, and it was a sacred trust that the Warriors protect them and do no harm. That was their way.

Still, Anna called to Corwyn in a way that made his body hum in anticipation. His entire being ached to take release. It wasn't her slim, graceful body or the way her hair burned red as embers in the sunlight. It was something else, and he was sure it was part of the mystery of her, of what drew Veriel to her.

Either way, Corwyn had decided in the dark hours of the night that he needed to do the one thing his father never had to solve the mystery. He had to get close to her, to learn whatever secrets only someone close to her could learn.

He willed his mind to overpower the pulsing need that thought shot through him. This wasn't sexual. Close didn't mean he had to bed her to find what he needed.

When Anna turned into a small diner, Corwyn followed. He'd left his weapons belt in the car, knowing that nothing a beast could send at him during the high point of the day would require anything but his bare hands to dispatch. He'd also left behind his armored boots in favor of a comfortable pair of leather tennis shoes, something his father had never understood his love for.

For the first time since shortly after first night, he was truly frightened about something. Corwyn grumbled to himself in annoyance. He was unsure about himself over a woman. He found himself considering and rejecting ways to introduce himself to her. Ridiculous! With as many women as he'd bedded in his life, the situation was comical. He took the table next to hers and steeled himself to start up a conversation.

"Anna," a woman's voice called.

Damn! She's meeting someone.

Still, Corwyn could gain information if he just kept his mouth shut and made himself unremarkable in the crowd for a bit. Maybe they would say something that would clue him in. It was a long shot, but if it failed, Corwyn could find a way to introduce himself later.

"Hi, Debbie," she purred in a voice as smooth as silk.

Her voice sent a shiver down his spine, and Corwyn listened intently while they ordered their meals. Anna ordered baked chicken and a salad with milk while Debbie was a junk food fiend: cheeseburger and gravy fries with a chocolate milkshake.

He ordered a rare steak, baked potato with butter, a salad, and black coffee. Caffeine was the bane of Warriors, he decided. Corwyn settled back to take in their conversation, satisfied that he already knew more about Anna and her friend than his father ever did.

"So, tonight's the night, huh?" Debbie asked in giddy excitement. "The big date with Matt Collins?"

Corwyn fisted his hand then forced himself to relax. Matt Collins sounded a little too mundane a name for a fifteen-hundred-year-old beast elder to affect in conversation.

Still, the way Debbie said it sent a spike of jealousy through him that was completely uncalled for. Corwyn didn't even know this woman. Why was he reacting this way to her? Was this what Veriel felt? This mad drive to insulate and protect her? No, beasts didn't think that way. They would be possessive, not protective—and usually not possessive either.

"I'd hardly call it a date, Deb. It's more like..." She sighed.

"A means to an end?" she teased.

"I swear, I shouldn't have told you," Anna answered miserably. "But, if I don't end this somehow, I'll lose my mind."

"Why can't you just enjoy a good fantasy like the rest of us?"

"Fantasy is one thing. This is more like an obsession, and it's killing my sleep patterns," she complained.

"So, take a sleeping tab and enjoy yourself. And if you ever meet someone who looks like him, drag him to a bedroom and find out if he's as talented as he is in dreams."

"You're hopeless," Anna accused.

"No, but my sister Susan is truly hopeless. Do you know what her opinion is?"

"You told Susan?" she asked in disbelief.

"I didn't mention names," Debbie protested. "I said it was an old college friend in Ohio."

"What's her opinion? It can't be any crazier than

anything else I've considered, and I've considered having myself committed. Now, that's crazy."

Corwyn heard the crunch of her biting off a piece of carrot from her salad.

"She thinks it's a past life intrusion on present reality."

Anna groaned. "You're kidding."

"Well, this is Susan, after all. But, look at the evidence. She has a point. Stone fireplaces, old-fashioned clothes, foreign languages—"

"Not always."

"Often enough. She suggests research into the life you're seeing."

"What kind of research?"

"Into the clothes you saw or that word. What is that word you keep hearing? The one you said he says in almost every dream?"

"*Geliebte*," she answered softly.

Corwyn felt his blood run cold, and he almost dropped his coffee cup in shock. What kind of a game was Veriel playing? This was obviously part of the beast's work. It had to be.

"Fine," Debbie responded. "Find out what it means. We'll find a book for translations or a linguist and find out what it means."

"What language?" Anna complained. "I have a word, but where do I start? I don't even know how it's spelled."

"German," Corwyn interjected without thinking of the consequences. He turned slowly, as Anna whirled to face him. *Green. Her eyes are green.* "I'm sorry. I didn't mean to eavesdrop, but the word caught my attention. It's German. I thought it would save you time..." He felt his cheeks flush.

Anna stared at him, her lips parted slightly, her eyes wide, exuding a heady scent that assaulted his nerves. *Heat.* She was in heat, and it was drawing Corwyn even from a distance and without his knowledge. Up close, it was heart-stopping. He could feel Anna's needs burning in her with an intensity that rivaled his own.

"What does it mean?" she asked quietly, her breath warm and sweet on his face.

"It means 'beloved'."

* * * *

Anna took in the man behind her. His black hair was cropped close in back and fell a little longer across his forehead. His matching black shirt was open at the neck, and she could see his racing heartbeat clearly in the vee of the opening. His lips looked soft and inviting. His broad shoulders and strong jaw hinted at immense strength. But, his eyes held her longest. Their dark depths spoke of a need she recognized immediately. No, this wasn't the man in her dreams, but he had something about him that was dangerous and compelling at the same time.

She licked her lips and considered this new arrival. Some senseless part of her screamed at Anna to have Debbie tell them she got sick at lunch and cancel Matt for the night while she took tall, dark and handsome home. Something told Anna she wouldn't regret it for a moment, and she pushed the thought away almost painfully.

Was she *that* hard up? She didn't even know this

man...or that he wanted her. At least, she knew Matt Collins. Maybe not well enough to do what she was planning to do with him, but he wasn't a stranger.

This man was just some guy sitting next to her in a diner, eavesdropping on her private conversation. A linguist, when she needed one? Anna furrowed her brow in confusion. When had her life come so unglued?

"See," Debbie yelled in triumph. "Everything considered, that's the last straw for me. Would you join us?"

Anna swung back to look at her in shock. "Deb, we don't know—"

"Corwyn Hunter," his voice rumbled from beside her as he pulled his chair over next to Anna and settled into it.

Her eyes widened at his height. He was beyond tall. *Like the guy in the dream.* Anna shook her head slowly as he met her eyes. *No, definitely not.*

"And you are?" He smiled a little too familiarly, leaning his elbows on the table.

"Debbie Wilks," Deb commented, offering her hand.

Corwyn shook it distractedly and raised an eyebrow at Anna.

"Mortally embarrassed," she admitted. Anna sighed and offered him her hand. "Anna Jameson. How do you know German, Mr. Hunter?"

He held her hand just an instant too long, and Anna blushed at the arousal she couldn't seem to control when he touched her. When he pulled his hand back to take his cup of coffee from the waitress, she shivered.

He smiled. "Call me Corwyn. Mr. Hunter was my

father. I learned German from my grandfather and French from my grandmother—and a few other languages here and there as I needed them."

"You must have been a blast in school," she mused.

He swallowed a mouthful of his coffee and shook his head. "I was privately tutored. My family moved around a lot, so conventional schools were out."

"Business?"

Corwyn nodded.

"How sad. So, you had no friends?"

"A few," he admitted. "I have two younger brothers and a bunch of cousins, so I had playmates."

Debbie's eyes widened. "You mean there are more like you?" she asked, fanning her short black curls with her perfectly manicured hand.

Corwyn shrugged. "I don't know that I'd say they're like me. They look a little like me. Anyway, back to the discussion at hand. Do you remember any other words?"

Anna smiled in amusement. "You believe in past life experiences, Corwyn?"

"I believe in a lot of strange things," he assured her. "Tell me. What other words do you remember?"

"Well, the only other one that comes to mind...that I hear often is *Regana*. What does that mean?"

Corwyn furrowed his brow. "It's not a German word," he mused, deep in thought.

"Oh, damn," Deb said in annoyance. "I was hoping."

"But, you know what it does mean, don't you?" Anna asked suddenly, unsure of what gave her that impression but knowing she was right as the words gushed forth.

He looked at her and nodded in something akin to shock. "It's— Actually, *Regana* is a name."

"German?" Deb asked.

"Yes. Very old," he confirmed.

Chapter Three

Corwyn shifted his weapon next to his hip. Lunch had yielded little more in the way of helpful information. After his announcement about Regana being a German name, Anna had said little. Deb had filled him in on some of the details, though she'd quieted when Anna shot her a dirty look.

It seemed Anna's current upset stemmed from nightly dreams of herself with a certain man. Corwyn was laying money that the man in question was Veriel. But, why would the beast go through with something this complex when taking a woman he desired was so simple for an elder like him? Veriel could take sex easily, as he had countless times over the centuries. What was his purpose?

Veriel was drawing Anna into a mindless heat for him. But to what purpose? Anna wasn't *Blutjagdfrau,* so she couldn't bear children for Veriel. No human woman could. The chasm between human and beast was simply too wide to provide more than release.

As it was, the chasm between Cursed Warrior and human was close enough to allow viable offspring. Since Cursed Warriors weren't eternal like beasts, the gods had designed it that way; they were born as human offspring who would develop from their cursed genes at sixteen unless they were freed in the *Zeremonie der Freiheit.*

Their boys were to remain cursed, but their girls— the few precious girls born to them were allowed to be freed. A cursed female would become *Blutjagdfrau* when the change came to her. She would be the female blood Warrior, a Warrior like any man was, but close enough to mate not only with humans and male Warriors but also beast elders. Turned beasts were sterile, one of their many weaknesses compared to elders, but the five remaining elders could produce children with a *Blutjagdfrau* mate.

Those children would be a dangerous hybrid of the two species the Warriors could never allow. In addition, their baby girls were so scarce that they were prized above all else. The Warrior with a freed daughter was the luckiest man alive, and the brothers of one had many responsibilities and quite a bit of jealousy. No Warrior would choose to condemn his daughter to the life of being sought by the elders for their depraved use in producing their damned heirs. No matter that children from a *Blutjagdfrau* and a Warrior would mean disaster for the beasts, it was simply a matter none of the Warriors would ever chance with their own daughters.

And so, it was a stalemate. The elders couldn't produce their higher plane and crush the Warriors, nor could the Warriors produce their high plane and destroy the beasts...without a *Blutjagdfrau*, and only the Warriors could make a female blood Warrior. Since they wouldn't, neither side could produce the ultimate Warriors.

There could be no offspring from Anna, and sex wasn't the sole object of Veriel's quest. What else could he want? As a beast, he had no kinder emotions. He couldn't feel love. Humor was dark and depraved. Sadism, anger, and hate were at the center of his dark soul.

A sudden thought occurred to Corwyn. Could Veriel want to keep Anna as a pseudo-mate? As a possession?

They'd learned early that turned human females were impossible to control and unwilling to be used as mates for the other beasts, even the elders. In the end, all but one had been destroyed by the elders themselves.

But if Veriel could convince Anna to stay with him willingly, he could have her indefinitely—until his darker side took over and wrecked the illusion he'd spin. After that, he would have to coerce her to stay or feed on her to build elaborate memories. With that much work involved, Corwyn had no doubts the beast would simply kill her and begin again.

Corwyn swore fluently in several languages at the thought of it. It was coercion on a whole new level, and he had to find a way to stop it before Anna was lost to the beast for as long as he let her live. If Veriel ever took her, it would be over Corwyn's dead body.

He sighed in the realization that if it came to that, the beast probably would have Anna over his dead body. Veriel didn't lose.

He watched the club doors sadly. Inside, Anna was enjoying her evening with Mr. Collins. Corwyn sensed no beasts in the area, but that would change. Now or later, Veriel would be coming for her.

* * * *

Anna looked off across the dance floor to where Matt would be coming back from the restroom. She was a bundle of nerves, but after the revelation at lunch, she was more determined than ever to sleep with Matt tonight. If she still had the dreams, Anna would have serious concerns. If not, she might just give Matt a second helping as a thank-you gift.

"May I buy you a drink?" a rich, velvety voice asked.

Anna felt her heart take up a choppy, frantic non-rhythm. Even before she turned her head, she knew what she'd see. His hair had the look of fine silk, shiny and soft, and she longed to run her hand through it right there at the bar. His eyes were molten silver in the dim light.

The only surprise was his choice of clothing. She'd expected something old-fashioned and uncomfortable: scratchy wool and linen perhaps, but he was dressed in a dark turtleneck that hugged his broad shoulders and outlined the contours of his chest and arms. His jeans were snug across his hips and crotch.

She shivered in the realization that she knew every inch of the body beneath those clothes from the red tattoo on his shoulder to... Her gaze settled in his lap, and Anna felt a warm sensation pooling inside her as she did. The familiar ache of needing that body was hard and insistent.

"Like what you see?" he whispered.

Anna felt her cheeks burn at the erotic invitation in his blatant stare. "What if I do?" she managed hoarsely.

For the second time in less than a day, she was considering ditching Matt—*not a bad plan overall*—for a complete stranger—*a very bad plan.* The problem was Anna was having trouble convincing herself that it was a bad plan. Some part of her mind and all of her body was demanding she take him up on his offer quickly.

"What would you like? We could take it slowly. Give me your number, and I will take you out— Or we could just go somewhere and see where it goes. I promise you can trust me. I will always be a gentleman."

The stark hunger in his gaze told Anna which alternative was his favorite, and she wasn't sure she wanted to disagree. It was her favorite, too.

"I know you will," she breathed.

"Which would you prefer?" His voice was soft, seductive.

Anna was being drawn in utterly. She leaned toward him, memories...visions of his arms wrapping around her and his lips closing over hers—

An arm slid around her shoulders, and she jumped in response, breaking the moment.

"Ready to go, sweetheart?" Matt asked in a strained, possessive tone that grated on her nerves for some reason.

For an instant, she shot her gaze back and forth between the two men. Finally, Anna met the strange man's eyes. "Maybe I'll see you here again," she decided suddenly. Until Anna knew what just happened, she wasn't about to commit to more than that.

His eyes hardened as he took in Matt's appearance, and Anna found that she was abruptly afraid of him. "As you wish. Ask for Jörg. I'll be around." He locked gazes with her, and the invitation returned. "Until then, *Geliebte mien.*"

Anna scrambled off of the stool and smoothed her

mini-skirt over her thighs reflexively. Her hands were shaking, and she couldn't meet his eyes. "It was nice to meet you, Jörg," she managed cordially.

She followed Matt through the thick crowd, glancing back when they reached the doors. Anna expected to see Jörg stalking after them, but he was still at the bar, watching her in what she could only assume was amusement.

Anna shivered as she followed Matt out into the night, more determined than ever that he was going to get lucky. Dreams or no dreams, Jörg frightened her on some elemental level that she couldn't explain, even to herself.

* * * *

Corwyn tensed. He felt the beast appear. The charm The Mad Deceiver exerted started almost immediately.

Neither of them would act in the club. Not even Veriel was that crazy—he hoped. So, Corwyn waited for them to appear, biding his time and praying to several ancient gods that tonight was not his night to die.

He could have entered the club, weapons and all. Any Warrior, even a first night, was capable of screening the human mind to what he was. It was one of the first things they were taught before the change was complete, but unless he went full ghost, Veriel would know Corwyn for what he was. Everyone inside was potentially in danger if that happened, so he waited. Tricking an elder was much more difficult than a human or a turned. The risk was too high.

When Anna exited the club with her date, Corwyn

was completely stumped. He considered it as he followed them. Veriel hadn't given up. He was sure of it. The beast had staked a claim. Tonight or tomorrow or the following night, the beast would come for her again.

At her house, he watched Mr. Collins walk Anna to her door. Corwyn's body tightened as she allowed him to kiss her passionately. Her hands skated up his chest, and she pulled him closer, inviting his attention. She took his hand to lead him inside...and Corwyn froze.

Veriel was close. A spike of coercion struck like a thunderbolt, lighting up Corwyn's senses in a brilliant flash.

Damn! The beast is powerful.

The man on the stairs paused, seemingly in a daze. He eased his hand from Anna's and backed away, shaking his head and making some conversation that seemed to concern her.

Anna watched him walk to his car and drive away, tucking a stray curl behind her ear in confusion. Corwyn shared that confusion. He couldn't sense Veriel anymore. If the beast intended to strike out, he wasn't going to do it in front of Anna.

Corwyn hesitated for a moment. Would the beast follow the man to exact some revenge or stick close to Anna? He sighed raggedly. Anna was the one he had to be concerned about, and the beast would return to her soon, even if it wasn't tonight.

He wished he had brought one of his brothers along. Corwyn could have covered them both, but he hadn't foreseen this atypical reaction from Veriel. Besides, if anyone died at Veriel's hands, it would be

Corwyn alone...or so he hoped.

* * * *

Anna punched her pillow in annoyance. She still wasn't sure what went wrong. She had been wildly attracted to two separate men, and she'd turned both of them away. She had been intent on a third man, who'd seemed just as interested, up until the second he walked away from her.

And his excuse? Good God! Matt actually begged off because he was tired? He hadn't been tired five minutes earlier. Five minutes earlier, he had been making all sorts of intriguing promises that had Anna hot and bothered.

"Dammit!" she spat. She wrapped her blanket around her shoulder. "What does a woman have to do to get laid in this city?"

If only Anna had taken Corwyn Hunter's number when he'd offered it. Of course, Debbie had taken it, but it was almost three o'clock in the morning. Anna couldn't call her to get it, and she wasn't about to call Corwyn and offer him the time of his life at this hour. "Dammit!"

She had tossed and turned for over an hour after Matt left, but she was getting very tired. Anna knew what was waiting for her in her dreams—*who is waiting for me there*—but she was powerless to stave off sleep any longer. She slipped into the warmth with a hopeless sigh.

Jörg was waiting for her. As she took in the stone walls and the roaring fire, she spotted him. Nude from the waist up, she watched his muscles ripple as he crossed the room to her. He didn't so much walk as he sauntered like a lazy cat after a big meal. He lay down on the thick furs next to her and ran his thumb along her jawline, sending pinpoints of pleasure through her.

"Here at last, *Geliebte*," his voice purred like the cat she'd just compared him to. His hand traced her throat and shoulder to cup a breast.

"Who are you, Jörg?" she managed. "Why are you here?" Anna wanted her words to show her conviction. She wanted to throw his hand off, but her body demanded consummation. She needed this, needed him. Anna wondered vaguely if Jörg would show up at her home if she asked him to in the dream.

"I am yours," he breathed. "I will ask nothing of you but that you give yourself to me. In return, I offer my love, my protection—and pleasure."

"Who am I?" she asked in a haze, as he bent his head to run his tongue along her breast, causing her to close her eyes to it just to think...or try to.

"You know who you are," Jörg whispered, moving his mouth to her other breast and teasing it to a peak expertly.

He sucked at the peak, and Anna arched into his mouth hopelessly. How could she fight this? Jörg knew exactly how to touch her to make her want him more.

"I'm not Regana," she breathed. Her hands moved to play in the silk of his hair. It was even softer than she'd imagined it would be at the bar.

"Your name is immaterial. My name is immaterial. I am yours. You are mine—always mine." As if to prove the point, his hand slid over the flat plane of her stomach to tease at the slick heat pooling between her legs. "So warm," Jörg mused, sucking at the other peak slowly. "I forgot how warm you are."

"What do you want from me?"

"Just this. Let me lose myself in you for all time."

Anna groaned as his fingers teased at her, coaxing her toward mindlessness that she fought, desperate to know how he invaded her mind and body so effortlessly. "Why me?" she breathed.

"You are mine," he repeated. "You will belong to no man but me."

A sudden image of his eyes, cold and hard as she left the club with Matt, assaulted her. The amused look on his face... Jörg knew she'd end up here with him despite the fact that she'd left the bar with Matt. He arranged it somehow.

Anna pushed him away. "What have you done?" she demanded.

Jörg smiled a mouthful of perfect, white teeth. "Why are you so upset? I have done nothing but make this lovely place for us." He started punctuating his words with strokes of his tongue, working down her abdomen. "Together. All alone. Apart from the rest of the world." Jörg swiveled his tongue in her navel for a moment, smiling when Anna moved restlessly beneath him.

He was suddenly over her again, his pants gone and the tip of him resting in the hollow of her body's juices, tickling just between the labia and teasing with the possibility of entering her. "This is all I want. Tell me you want it, too," he crooned, moving slightly to dip a fraction of an inch into her waiting body and pulling back to tease her again.

She forced her mind back to the subject. Jörg did have a way of making her forget her concerns in the face of what he was doing to her. "No," Anna breathed, holding him at arms length. "You've done something to Matt, haven't you?"

Her mind was suddenly clear, and the entire scene turned sinister: the fire too close and hot, the furs too rough, the shadows too deep, his hands keeping her body locked to his. His eyes were abruptly hard, and his caressing hands bit into her hips painfully.

Sharp nails—

"You belong to me," Jörg growled. "No matter what you have done in the past, you are mine now. You will give yourself to no man but me."

Anna struck him hard across the cheek—and woke up. She took several deep breaths as she surveyed her room in the dim light.

Her hip ached, and she pulled up the gauze nightgown she wore fearfully. There was a nasty-looking scratch where the dream Jörg had gripped her. A glance at her aching hand confirmed bruised knuckles.

Anna shook her head in shock. "What the hell is going on here?" she breathed.

"That was cruel of you, *Geliebte*," a disembodied voice teased. "Now, I have to start all over. Such a shame, but I do enjoy arousing you. It is not such a hardship to arouse you again."

Anna launched off the bed toward the doorway, but the door swung shut before she reached it. "What are you?" she asked hopelessly, backing to the wall.

"I am yours, just as you want me. I have learned your likes and dislikes."

"I don't want you." She shook as she said it and realized that in the last few minutes, that statement had become very true.

Anna jumped as hands brushed by her skin, still sensitive in her arousal.

"Oh, but you do want me," he affirmed in a rough voice. "Tell me what you want. You have only to say it, and it will be done for you."

"I want you to leave," she demanded. "I can scream." Anna realized how ridiculous that would sound to whoever answered her screams. They'd lock her up. She sobered. Maybe, she needed locked up. Would she be free of Jörg, then?

His fingertips touched her lips gently. "You do not want to do that," Jörg whispered, his breath brushing her cheek and his teeth grazing at her ear. "It would be an unwise choice."

She jerked her head away. "Why not?"

"I will not hurt you."

But whoever shows up—

"Let me please you. Let me take away the ache in you, in us both."

Jörg's voice was calling to something deep inside her, and Anna's body responded. Her eyes closed, and her head rocked back as the need she thought had left her flared up stronger than ever. His hands touched her body again, drawing out her pleasure and drowning whatever thoughts had been plaguing Anna mere moments before.

"Jörg, I need..." she began, struggling to remember what concerns she had.

"I know," he breathed, taking her mouth urgently.

The heat inside her exploded as he devoured her, demanding her response.

His mouth left hers. "I need, too."

He pressed himself to her, lifting Anna to fit his body. She gasped at the feeling of the hard length of him holding her hips to the wall. His hands roamed her, and her nightgown seemed to fall away from her body.

There was something in the back of her mind, something important that she couldn't quite reach, no matter how hard she tried. Anna wasn't sure she wanted to reach it. Where she was, she was warm and comfortable, virtually enveloped in a cloud of passion and safety. What she was reaching for was dark and dangerous. Anna knew that, and she turned her mind back to the sensations assaulting her with a groan of acceptance.

Jörg swept her back to the bed, covering her body with his own. Somehow, they were naked, and she smiled at the feeling of the rough hair of his body brushing hers. "So real," she breathed. "What a dream—"

Jörg's laughter tickled her cheek. "I am as real as you will let me be," he assured her. "Tell me how real you want me to be. Tell me how much of me you want to fill you."

Anna froze as the full force of that statement hit her. Jörg was real. He was here. This wasn't a dream, was it? "What are you?" she demanded, trying to edge away from his body. Jörg was visible now, and he seemed real enough, but Anna was frightened despite his inviting eyes. She couldn't seem to reconcile the shattered bits of reality in her mind.

"I am a dream, dear one—your dream," he whispered, lowering his head to kiss her again.

She pushed at him roughly, all too aware of her

position, her legs spread wide around him and his body pinning her to the bed, poised to take her. "My nightmare," Anna shot back, trying to land a punch.

He caught her hand easily, then the other as she swung it at his head. Jörg kissed them gently before he pinned them to the mattress above her head. He sighed raggedly. "I did not want to take you this way. I wanted you to come to me as willingly as you will next time."

"Never," she promised.

"I must have you tonight. If I do not, I will lack the control to be gentle with you. I can erase what I must do to gain your approval and leave only the pleasure for you. It was not what I wanted, but if I sacrifice this time, it will be what I want the next."

"What are you going to do to me?" she asked fearfully. Her breathing was strangled, her voice high and strained.

"It will only hurt for a moment," he promised.

Her gaze locked on his smile, as his perfect teeth elongated into fangs. Anna fought against his grip on her wrists and screamed, but the scream was cut short in shock as the teeth sliced through her neck. The burning pain dissolved into a haze then into orgasmic bliss. Anna arched beneath him, and she could feel Jörg's satisfaction at her response.

His voice echoed in her mind, a warm caress that intensified the pleasure until she felt she might climax from his—*kiss?*—alone.

This is nothing compared to the pleasure I will give you. You have my vow. You will see.

A flood of memories passed through her mind, culminating with Corwyn Hunter's face inches from her own.

Jörg's laughter settled in her mind. *The young Lord Jäger has taken his father's place. It will be my pleasure to remove him for you after he learns that he has already lost you.*

He pulled back, and Anna stared at his red-tinged teeth with a sort of detached awareness. She knew that she should be repulsed, angry, fearful...some emotions that she couldn't seem to feel.

"Now," Jörg began, "I will make you mine."

He shifted suddenly, but when Jörg lunged forward, he didn't penetrate her. Instead, he threw his head back and roared in pain and loss that struck her to her soul. He turned off of Anna, striking with what looked like claws at a shadowy figure behind him. A foul smell filled the room, choking her. Jörg howled a second time and seemed to dissolve into smoke.

She furrowed her brow. He was dressed, wasn't he? Anna reached out her hand to where he had stood a moment before. "No," she breathed in confusion.

Anna tried to move, but a burning pain in her neck assaulted her, burying what little consciousness she thought she had recovered.

A face swam before her eyes, calling her name, trying to pull her back from the red haze of unconsciousness. Anna recognized him—vaguely, but her mouth couldn't form the words to talk to him, to ask him what was happening.

He was beautiful. A halo of dark hair framed even darker eyes, wide in shock or fear. His hand pressed to her neck, and Anna groaned in discomfort.

Something heavy fell against her chest, and a confusing rush of words shot at her, making her head spin worse. Anna felt a kiss, a gentle brush over her lips, and she jerked from the sudden burning at her neck.

His words followed her down into the darkness. "You're safe now. I'll protect you."

* * * *

Corwyn shook lightly as he threw clothing into a bag for Anna. He realized that he should take more for her, but he knew more beasts would be on the way soon. He wrapped Anna in the blanket she lay on, sorry he couldn't take the time to dress her—and glad he didn't. Corwyn didn't think he could stand it.

The memory of Anna beneath the beast almost did him in. *So close—* He was almost too late.

Whatever Veriel started at was so subtle it hadn't registered at all. Corwyn had sensed nothing until the coercion started. He'd scrambled to her door, ghosting himself fully from human and beast alike. He had used his blade to break away the wood over the bolt and made his way to them as the beast stopped ghosting.

Corwyn had felt Anna escape Veriel's grasp. It was amazing. Either she was a very strong woman, or the beast hadn't put much energy into the coercion. Corwyn's heart sank as he felt the beast begin to feed; her chopped-off scream had nearly shattered his resolve. Veriel had been intent, so intent that he didn't see through Corwyn's clumsy attempt at full ghosting.

When he saw the beast's head come up, fouled with her blood, Corwyn's heart had stopped until he saw Anna move. He'd understood immediately. The only reason the beast fed was to calm Anna for what he'd intended to do next. That in itself was outside any experience Corwyn had of them. Veriel really did want to keep Anna as mate, but Corwyn still had no idea what motive he had for it.

Whatever the reason, Veriel had been ready to move on her, and that final abuse was something Corwyn could not allow.

Corwyn had faltered in his ghosting as he struck his blow, and Veriel had time to move as a result. The beast could have dematerialized or even skated away from the blade. What he did was more surprising. The beast had moved into the blade, taking it out of the kill zone but still taking the blow himself—to shield Anna.

Had Veriel avoided it entirely, Corwyn might have struck her accidentally. It had happened in the past that a beast had escaped a blow, leaving a helpless human victim in its path. Veriel had taken the blow rather than risk her that way, knowing he could go to ground and heal.

Why is he so damned intent on her?

Corwyn had moved quickly once his first blow missed its mark. The beast had bellowed in pain as he turned, suddenly clothed and claws extended. Veriel barely drew blood with his wild swing, but every instinct had told Corwyn that the next blow the elder threw would finish him. With nothing left to lose, he had taken Veriel head on.

The beast's claws had moved to protect his heart, as Corwyn knew he would, so the blow he delivered was already placed for the throat. If the beast had stayed long enough, he would have bled to death between the two wounds. All Corwyn had to do was survive long enough—

Against Veriel? He felt sick at the thought that he'd

even attempted something as foolhardy as staying close to an injured Warrior-killer.

He needn't have given it any thought. Veriel knew his position very well. He'd looked at Anna before turning on Corwyn with a glare that promised a slow, painful death for his interference. Then, he'd dematerialized.

Corwyn had held his ground for a long moment, anticipating another attack, but Veriel hadn't been ghosting. He could feel the beast as it fled to ground. Veriel did it on purpose, he realized. He'd wanted Anna cared for immediately, and Corwyn had obliged him on that point.

She was confused and in pain, and he shuddered to consider what her reaction would be when she regained her bearings. The bleeding had been considerable, since Veriel hadn't tended to her himself. Corwyn had held pressure on the punctures for a moment then decided that her protection had to come first.

He'd fished for an amulet in his pocket then paused in consideration. Corwyn had moved his hand to a second pocket and removed an amulet etched with his personal seal. Colin was sure to have a fit about this situation. It would have to be his personal protection for her and not a general promise of his house. Corwyn wouldn't drag them into it unwilling, even though it was within his power to order their compliance. Only in an emergency would they have to protect Anna. Any other time, she was Corwyn's responsibility alone.

Corwyn had looped the amulet over her head and let it fall against her chest. He'd given his blessing quickly, and his heart had ached for her as he sealed it.

Corwyn had recoiled slightly as Anna jerked away, but he'd soon realized that it was a good sign. His blessing was undoing Veriel's handiwork. The bleeding had slacked off to a sluggish flow that would be easy to stop, and Anna had looked at him in a detached sort of understanding before she surrendered to the unconsciousness her body and mind demanded.

Corwyn had knelt next to her for a moment, letting the rush of *Blutjagd* wear off. He'd scanned his eyes over Anna miserably.

Her red hair was snarled, and her neck was already swollen and enflamed beneath the blood staining her skin. A deep scratch marred the creamy skin of her hip.

Still, he found the swollen, sex-bruised breasts and the unmistakable smell of her arousal worse than the physical damage. Corwyn had stormed to the crumpled nightgown with the thought of dressing her again but he'd fisted it in his hand in frustration when he found it torn to shreds.

Corwyn pushed the memories out of his mind and packed for her. When he threw Anna's bag over his shoulder and cradled her to his chest, he made one last check for approaching beasts and ghosted them both for the trip to the car.

On the move, Corwyn considered the possibilities. Veriel might have somehow hidden the encounter from the other beasts, perhaps to protect Anna from his unscrupulous brothers.

The alternative was that the lesser beasts were avoiding the Lord Hunter. Like it or not, Corwyn had joined the ranks of the elder hunters by attacking Veriel. Only Pauwel first Lord Crossbearer, the elder killer, was more elite. Corwyn laughed nervously as he realized that he'd obtained his new status by virtue of a lucky shot, a quick duck, and a desperate move that he shouldn't have survived, coupled with Veriel's inattention to his surroundings. Under normal circumstances, Corwyn would have ended up like every other challenger to The Mad Deceiver. As it was, had he not slipped in his ghosting, he would have ended the night as Pauwel's equal.

Corwyn drove until well after sunrise, watching the mountains rise before him. By the time he pulled into the training house, he was exhausted. He carried Anna to the lord's chamber and settled her beneath a second blanket on the wide bed. Finally, he cleaned her neck and shoulder and bandaged her wound carefully. Confident that she would sleep for several hours, Corwyn sought out the phone downstairs and dialed home.

Colin answered on the first ring. "Where the hell are you?" he demanded without waiting for Corwyn to identify himself.

"It's safer for all of us if you don't know that right now."

"Okay, what the hell was that? I was checking out a pretty gruesome kill—"

"A man named Matt Collins," he guessed, cutting his brother off. Corwyn had felt the kill, but it was far from where he he'd been, and he couldn't abandon Anna to investigate.

"You're connected to that one, too?"

"I'm afraid so. It was Veriel's handiwork."

"What did the poor guy do to piss *him* off?" Colin asked in awe. It must have been a really bad scene to put that tone in his brother's voice.

"Showed interest in the wrong woman."

"Beasts aren't territorial. Women are a dime a dozen to an elder like him."

"Not this one. She's special."

"How special?" Colin asked suspiciously.

"Not that special. She's—for lack of a better word, his chosen mate."

"They don't mate."

"Don't you think I know that?" he snapped. "Look, Veriel is acting, for all the world, maddening as it is, like a mated man. He took my blade rather than risk her to it. He let me feel him go to ground, so I'd render medical aid to her without delay. It's nuts to watch him with her."

"Time out! You just took on Veriel?" he demanded.

Corwyn sighed and felt a blush come up. "Yeah. I'm still shaking. He's pissed off, and it's only going to get worse very quickly. He'll be to ground for a few days, but when he comes up—"

"What did you do to him?" Colin interrupted.

"Um... I stuck a blade in his back and slit his throat."

Colin groaned.

"I missed my mark, and he was protecting the goods," Corwyn grumbled miserably.

"What's worse than that? What is he going to find when he comes back up?"

"I've stolen his mate and given her my personal protection."

"Are you insane? Why didn't you kill her?"

"You think that's better?" Corwyn asked in disbelief. "She hasn't been taken yet, and she didn't seek this out. She's not a minion; she's a victim, like any other victim. I could feel her fighting him. She's a strong woman, Colin. She doesn't deserve to die."

"So, you've just injured an elder, stolen his woman, and given her your personal protection. What's next? Planning on taking her before he can?"

Corwyn froze in shock, staring out the windows into the trees but not seeing anything. Colin's bold statement had raised more than his interest, and Corwyn couldn't seem to sort out how he felt about that idea.

It wouldn't be right, he decided. The heat was an unfair advantage. It would be the same as taking a woman unwilling. He couldn't be sure it was the woman and not the heat talking if he took her under that influence, but...

Corwyn shook his head in confusion. Why couldn't he sort it out? Maybe it was because he'd never known the woman outside of that framework. Maybe getting to know Anna without that influence would clear his head.

"Corwyn?" Colin warned, when he didn't answer.

"Of course not," he snapped. "But, I do need answers, and I need them before Veriel recovers."

"What do you need?"

"Contact the other house lords. Now. Wake them if you have to. I need any information you can get on Veriel. I know he didn't leave many survivors to tell the tale, but I need whatever we have. I need to get inside his mind and find out why Anna is so important to him."

"Anything else?"

"Yes. While you have them on the line, find out if any of them know a woman named Regana. I think he may be transferring from one woman to another."

"Transferring what? He has no emotion to transfer."

"I don't know...yet."

"I'll get on it. When will I hear from you?"

"Before nightfall. I'll call you then."

"Corwyn—"

"Yes," he invited acidly.

Colin sighed. "Are you sure this scheme is worth it?"

Corwyn considered the woman asleep upstairs. "She's worth it, Colin. Trust me. She's worth it."

"Oh hell," he breathed.

"What?" Corwyn demanded.

"Nothing. Never mind." He sighed again. "Safe rest, Corwyn. Call me tonight." He hung up the phone before Corwyn could question him further.

Corwyn deposited his on the cradle in exhaustion. He headed for a bed before deciding that he owed Anna better than that. Corwyn pulled a pillow and blanket off of the bed he'd used as a child and collapsed with them in the corner of the lord's chamber. At least when she woke, he'd be there to handle the fallout.

Chapter Four

Anna tried to open her eyes, but the room was too bright. She groaned, squeezing her eyes shut. She started to raise a hand up to her aching head but froze and ran it over her naked stomach a second time instead. *That's wrong.* She didn't sleep in the nude.

She swallowed hard and tried to piece the night together, but the scattered images wouldn't gel into a complete whole. Matt left, and she'd gone to bed. After that, it was a mess. She'd dreamed of Jörg—or was he there in person? The things Anna remembered were either highly arousing or terrifying and completely unbelievable. She felt sick, but she couldn't seem to work out why she would feel sick. She was afraid of what happened but more afraid of not knowing what happened.

Anna squinted against the bright light in the room and searched for some sign of Jörg. She stifled a sob in the realization that she had no idea where she was. Did Jörg bring her here?

No. What little Anna did remember seemed to indicate that he'd left her. But, could she trust anything she remembered?

She drew the blanket closer around her shoulders and struggled to sit up.

"Need help?"

She froze at the sound of a male voice and looked up fearfully. *Corwyn? I can't reconcile anything.*

"Can I help you?" he repeated in a calming voice, moving to grasp the foot board of the wide bed.

Anna dropped her gaze and shook her head. "How?

Why am I—wherever this is?" She flicked an uneasy glance at him and looked away again. "Did we..."

"No, we didn't," Corwyn answered quickly. "Look, I can see you're uncomfortable. If you need help, I'll help you. If you want privacy while you clean up and dress, I'll go. I'll explain everything while we eat."

"What will I wear?" Anna forced out the words slowly. She was at this man's mercy until she figured out what was going on and found a way to get home.

"Your bag is there on the dresser. The bathroom is through there. Do you need my help?"

"No. Thank you."

Corwyn nodded and pushed off of the bed toward the door stiffly. "I'll be getting cleaned up in another room. I'll meet you downstairs. If you need anything, call. I'll hear you." He stopped with his back to her. "Anna, the amulet—the necklace you have on—don't take it off."

"Why?" Her hand sought out the heavy metal disc next to her skin.

"It's important. I'll explain downstairs."

"All right," she decided.

Corwyn nodded again and stepped into the hall, closing the door firmly behind him.

Anna hesitated, willing herself to move. Finally, she decided she was being childish. Whatever was going on, she had to get to the bottom of it, and she couldn't do that hiding in bed. Besides that, she needed the bathroom, a shower, and clothes. Unless she wanted Corwyn Hunter insisting to help her, Anna had to get up and get moving. Of course, if he got her this far, he'd already seen all there was to see.

She swung off the bed and stood. Anna wavered for

a moment, dizzy and disoriented, and placed her hand on the wall to try to find her center. She made her way to her bag and pulled out jeans, a peasant top, underwear, socks and shoes. She grimaced at the lack of toiletries and hoped Mr. Hunter had things she could use in the bathroom.

She dropped her clothes on the sink and turned on the shower to let the water heat. She used the toilet and started to untangle her hair with a comb she found in the bathroom, grimacing again and hoping it was clean.

She was stiff and sore. Anna shuddered as she considered the probable reason that her breasts were so tender. Her lips felt bruised, and she wasn't comfortable with not knowing for sure how they got that way. She still couldn't separate reality from her nightmares.

Anna stepped under the hot spray of water and yelped as it ran over a cut on her hip. She looked at it in confusion for a few long moments, trying to reconcile anything that would logically explain it to her. Logical seemed to be her problem. She sighed and started to soap up.

She stopped as her hand encountered a thick bandage on her neck. Anna rinsed off quickly and spun the water off before launching to the sink. She wiped at the steam-fogged mirror frantically with one hand while the other ripped at the bandage on her neck. She winced as the surgical tape pulled at her flesh.

Anna caught sight of herself in the mirror, unnaturally pale and frightened, holding back tears...and with love bites on her neck and chest. She did sob at that. Bites were not her thing at all. Anna never let a man leave marks on her. She tilted her chin up to inspect the injury beneath that bandage.

The puncture wounds were red and raised, and her stomach turned as she looked at them. The fractured images danced before her eyes, solidifying at last into an unbelievable but true whole. Anna staggered to the toilet and brought up what little was in her stomach.

She dressed woodenly, praying that she was dreaming, that everything was a nightmare and she would wake up alone—or even with someone, anyone as long as he was human.

Anna dropped down the stairs, grasping at the railing like it was a lifeline. Corwyn met her at the bottom.

She sought out his eyes miserably. "It wasn't a dream, was it?" she managed hoarsely.

He put his hand out to her. "No, it wasn't," he assured her.

* * * *

Corwyn followed, as Anna circled his outstretched hand warily and wandered further into the house. At the living room, she made her way to the couch and curled into it. He sat across from her and watched her nervously. She looked ready to bolt.

"Anna, I need you to talk to me now," he prodded, reminding himself to be gentle.

"What are you?" she asked quietly. "I know what Jörg was. I figured that much out on my own, but you're not— I mean, if the stories are right, you can't be. Right?"

"Some of the stories are true, but not all of them. Sunlight is true. I'm not a beast—what you would call a vampire." Corwyn sighed. "I hunt them, and I protect humans like you when it's possible."

"Our meeting at the diner was no accident, was it?"

He shook his head. "I was following you. My father found out Veriel was shadowing you. I had to know why. Beasts, even elders like Veriel, typically don't act that way. I'm sorry. He was doing something I didn't pick up on right away. If I had, he never would have gotten as far as he did."

"Veriel is..."

"One of the original six, the elders. There are only five now. Resten was killed early, before they were comfortable with what they are. That leaves Carstol, Cerran, Draden, Lorian, and Veriel. He called himself Jörg with you?"

She nodded uncertainly. "If he's—that's what you saved me from."

"I'll have to check that name. I wish I had it this morning. It would have saved time to make all my inquiries at once."

"Is he dead?"

"No. He escaped, but it'll take him several days and a feeding cycle to recover from my attack. He can't even begin looking until then."

She smiled grimly. "I guess it's a good thing that you're good at what you do."

Corwyn darkened, and her smile faded. He couldn't let her develop a false sense of security, but he hated to burst her bubble.

"We both got lucky," he admitted. "Veriel has never left a Warrior alive before in single combat. If I face him again, there's a very real possibility that I won't survive it."

Her face turned a sickly shade of gray.

"You'll still have protection, though."

"Your father?"

He sighed raggedly. "No. Veriel killed him four days ago," he admitted. "I believe you took a trip."

She nodded shakily.

"There are others, my brothers and other houses. More importantly, you have your amulet. Never take it off. It renders you invisible on their radar, but it also means that they can't touch you. If you remove it—"

"Will it work?"

"Have I been wrong, yet?"

Anna rubbed her head roughly. "I'm sorry. I'm probably not handling this very well."

"On the contrary, I expected much worse, considering the night you had."

"I'm sure it will be. I don't think it's all sunk in yet. I mean— Vampires, Corwyn!" Her face was tortured and she waved her arms hopelessly.

"I told you I believed in a lot of strange things," he offered weakly.

"I wasn't counting on this strange."

"I know. Look, if I'm going to get inside his head, I have to know some things. It can wait until after we eat, if you prefer."

"Thanks, but I'm not sure I'll ever be able to eat again."

"You have to eat. You've lost a lot—" He chopped it off as he realized what he was saying and to whom.

"Blood," Anna whispered, burying her face in her hands and rocking forward slightly.

Corwyn reached out to lay a hand on her shoulder, but she wrenched away. "Okay, I won't touch you unless you ask me to," he promised. "Now, will you please try to eat something?"

Anna looked at him and seemed to consider an important dilemma. "Don't say that," she requested.

"Say what? Anna, be reasonable. You have to eat."

"Not that. Don't promise not to touch me unless I want you to. Jörg—it made that promise to me several times. Obviously, it didn't keep that promise."

Corwyn felt his jaw tighten reflexively. "I'm not a beast. I keep my word, but if it bothers you, I won't say it. I'll just do it." He stood and headed for the kitchen. "I'm cooking now. I won't ask if anything sounds appetizing. I'm sure it doesn't. Do you have any allergies I should avoid?"

"No, I don't."

He nodded and started to leave the room.

"Corwyn?" she called after him in a low voice that was choked with emotion.

"Yeah?"

"I'm sorry. I shouldn't—"

"Don't be. It's what I expected."

Corwyn headed to the kitchen before he could open his mouth again. It was what he expected, but it wasn't what he'd hoped. He'd hoped she'd need a shoulder to cry on and strong arms to hold her.

He slammed the pots around harder than was necessary in his frustration. Touching her was a stupid idea all the way around. Not only was Veriel sure to take it out on each of them if he did, but Corwyn wasn't sure how much self-control he could boast.

It was madness! Logically, he knew that he needed

release—not self-release, but release with a woman. Veriel had drawn Anna into a heat that would knock a human man off his feet and was having a similar effect on Corwyn in close quarters. Hell, it was having that effect on him when he was following her and was a block away.

And now? Now that she'd been knocked out of that mindless heat, he still ached to touch her. Corwyn still needed release, and he was turning his concern for her into an excuse. Wasn't he? He wished it was that simple, but he was afraid it wasn't.

When Colin had suggested that Corwyn could only screw up worse if he took Anna before Veriel did, he'd tried to dismiss the idea, but that was exactly what he wanted. He had risen to the thought with an intensity that still shocked him to his core.

The real problem was that he didn't want her for simple release. Corwyn wanted Anna as wife and mate: in his bed, by his side, and wearing his ring along with that amulet. Too bad that was impossible. She'd be lucky to ever trust a man again after Veriel. Trusting a man who was so close to what she feared most was sure to be impossible.

* * * *

Corwyn had searched the library in the training house all afternoon, but he'd had little luck coming up with information about Veriel. Overall, the Hunters had had few encounters with that particular beast aside from the early Hunter Warriors he'd slain, and they hadn't been around to give any answers when the other Warriors reached them.

He'd used his research as an excuse to send Anna away to rest. After hearing her version of her encounter with Veriel, he'd needed the space.

He'd felt his blood screaming in *Blutjagd*, and the response frightened him. It was the response of a Warrior in defense of a mate. Humans—other humans would make Corwyn feel pity or sadness, make him plan, make him angry for what they'd endured. Only a mate should make him feel the rush of the hunt for revenge.

Corwyn was printing on her, and that was dangerous. If he printed fully on Anna, and she chose another, he could never mate. Worse, the reality of not having her would drive Corwyn insane, and by the rules of sanction, once he lost his control, his brother Warriors would have to track him down and kill him before Corwyn could do harm.

By the time he called Colin, Corwyn was thoroughly disgusted with himself. He had to either know she was willing to print or get away from Anna before the pain of breaking printing gave way to the point of no return when he could no longer end the process and try again.

His brother answered on the second ring, and Corwyn was already annoyed with him. "What have you learned?" Corwyn demanded.

"I have four houses lending me volumes that deal with Veriel. I'll let you know what Stephen and I learn when they arrive."

"No. I want to do that myself. When you have them, I want them all. Maybe I'll even find out why he's calling himself Jörg," he added sarcastically.

"Even I can answer that one, Corwyn. Haven't you

read the *First Book of Texts*?"

"Several times. You know I have," he protested.

"You didn't pay much attention to it," Colin grumbled.

"I know the rules of sanction by rote, and you know it," Corwyn countered acidly.

"What about the history of the elders and first cursed? Do you remember any of that?"

"Sure. The first cursed, their professions, how they were chosen, their sanctions— What's your point, Colin?"

"When the elders chose their path, they were forced to relinquish all things human."

"Including their human names," he breathed, reaching for the *First Book of Texts* on the table in front of him and flipping to the history pages that dealt with the early years, pre-first days, and the fall of the beasts. "Veriel was Jörg before he went to the Stone."

"Bingo, buddy."

Corwyn groaned. "Then, Regana is probably pre-text news. Dammit!"

"Not so fast, Lord Hunter. Two houses knew who your mystery lady was—unless there's another Regana pre-first days."

"Tell me."

"Regana was Pauwel first Lord Crossbearer's wife— the first Lady Crossbearer."

"Elder killer?"

"Is there any other?"

"Okay, what is she to Veriel?"

"Damned if I know."

Corwyn growled in frustration. "Great. So, I still have no idea what a Crossbearer protected mate has in common with The Mad Elder."

"Uh. Not quite."

"Not quite what?" he snapped.

"She was Crossbearer's wife, but she wore Swordbearer's personal seal."

"What? Why?" Corwyn demanded.

"She was Gawen's sister. He gave her his personal protection just after first days. There was some talk of her having..." He paused for a moment as if looking for something he had written down next to the phone. "Sacred protection of the Stone, as befits a mother, whatever that means. She married Pauwel later, but Gawen retained his personal protection of her, even when she was out of his household, though it doesn't say why that was."

"She obviously didn't marry Pauwel much later," he spat.

"Obviously. As befits a mother," Colin mused. "She did provide Pauwel's heir rather quickly...less than three seasons after the battle. Anyway, because of Pauwel's—situation, their child, Andris, wore Crossbearer's personal seal but had Swordbearer's blessing."

"What a mess? Couldn't they get anything right back then?"

"They had only one per house to deal with. No leeway. Well, I guess that blows the air out of Crossbearer's base, considering their second lord was trained and first nighted a Swordbearer. They let him claim the lord's seal that very night, though."

"He actually made a kill on first night?" Corwyn asked in shock.

"Yeah. A high level turned that was already badly

injured, but that's still amazing for first night. Elder Killer's blood was strong stuff. Those men were cursed hard."

"So...Regana was Gawen's sister and Pauwel's wife. We have to assume she knew all the elders and first cursed. The village wasn't that big. But, what was Veriel's connection to her? Think he was lusting after her while Pauwel was bedding her?"

"Who knows? Unless these texts give us a clue, only Veriel knows for sure."

"I don't want to know that badly," Corwyn stated.

"I don't blame you. Speaking of which, how's your houseguest?"

"Shaken, weak, untrusting. Much better than I'd hoped for after last night."

"Does she have any clue what he was after?"

"Her. It was that simple. He offered pleasure, protection, anything she desired for her to take him willingly. When he couldn't convince her, he fed."

"So, he reverted to normal patterns," Colin decided.

"No, he didn't. He fed only long enough to pacify her and he planned— He promised to wipe her memory of everything he did to force her and leave her only pleasant memories. I interrupted that."

"Why? What was his plan?"

"With only the pleasant memories, he believed she'd come to him willingly, over and over."

"I don't understand. Was this just some sort of experiment? Why the sudden urge for a willing woman?"

"Your guess is as good as mine, but I think it goes deeper than that. I think he wanted it to be Anna willing. Not any woman but Anna. I think he's printed—"

"He can't," Colin stormed.

"Dammit, Colin! I can only call what I see. Let me know when those books arrive, and I'll meet you somewhere to pick them up."

Chapter Five

December 22nd, 1976

Anna watched Corwyn from beneath her eyelashes. He made her nervous when he was like this. The first two days, he had seemed aloof, and she had spent most of her time sleeping and trying to regain her strength. For the next two, Corwyn had been poring over the old books he'd picked up in town—from one of his brothers, he'd said. Since then, he had been tense.

Every day, he was clean and dressed, but Corwyn hadn't shaved since they'd arrived, and he had a rugged look about him—almost wild. Every muscle in his body was tense, his jaw tight, and his eyes hard as onyx, making that wild look verge on dangerous.

Corwyn growled out answers to questions that he considered non-essential until Anna decided talking to him when he was in this mood was nerve-wracking. She hated when Corwyn was like this. It made her feel like she was living with an animal pacing in a cage.

With a faulty lock, she amended.

She watched him, because she couldn't help feeling that there was something else beneath the surface. The problem was, if it was there, Anna couldn't seem to reach it. She could have that first day if she had been less shattered. She was sure of it, but no amount of change on her part seemed to break through the barrier he'd erected between them.

Corwyn growled in annoyance at something he was reading, and Anna sighed.

"Something wrong?" he asked.

"I could ask you the same thing," she replied

pointedly.

He favored her with a hard look.

"You're tense, irritable, and downright anti-social."

"I'm busy trying to find a way to get our butts out of this mess," he countered. "You have a problem with that?"

"Not offhand," she admitted. "I just wish you'd relax a little."

"Why?"

"You're making me jumpy."

"Sorry," he grumbled and went back to his book.

Anna sat the novel she was reading down and started to leave the room. She paused as she passed his chair and turned to knead his shoulders.

Corwyn wrenched away as she touched him. "Don't," he ordered gruffly.

"Sorry. I just thought—"

"Just don't touch me," he whispered.

Anna felt her throat close over, and she bit back tears as she backed away. "I see," she whispered. "Don't worry. I'll keep my distance, Corwyn." She turned to go.

His voice stopped her at the doorway. "What do you see?" he asked honestly.

"Veriel. I guess I can't blame you for that one."

"I'm not afraid of Veriel."

"Yeah, right. You're no fool," she spat back.

"Okay. I'm terrified of fighting him, but I have to face that regardless. You're right. I'm not a fool."

"Thought so."

"What I said has nothing to do with Veriel—not with fear and not with what he did to you, so forget that crazy idea."

"Then why does the idea of me touching you send you through the roof? What's wrong with me that being in a room with me makes you so tense?"

"There's nothing wrong with you," he assured her.

Anna looked at him in disbelief. "Sure," she answered sarcastically as she turned to the stairs.

"I've spent five days not touching you, because you didn't want to be touched, Anna."

"And if I rescind that order, you'd suddenly calm down?" she countered.

"I can't answer that," Corwyn growled.

"Because you're bullshitting me," she decided.

"Because I'm not sure which would be harder," he countered.

Anna furrowed her brow. "I don't think I follow you."

Corwyn sighed raggedly. "Never mind. I'm just going insane."

"No. Not okay. I want to know what you're talking about." When he didn't answer, she cursed under her breath. "You can touch me, Corwyn. The ball's in your court. Figure out how you feel."

"You don't mean that."

"Of course, I do. Why wouldn't I?" she asked in confusion.

He stared at his hands miserably. "I could explain it, but I don't think you'd appreciate it."

Anna crossed to the chair next to him and perched on the arm. With his height, it put her just above eye-level with him. "Try me," she invited. "I'd give just about anything to find out what's on your mind."

He looked at her uncertainly.

"Look, whatever it is, work it out."

She started to stand, but Corwyn touched her cheek, and she stilled. Anna met his eyes and shivered as he moved toward her. His lips brushed hers lightly, and she tilted her head to give him a better angle. He caressed her jawline with his fingers while he moved his lips over hers, barely touching skin to skin and making her ache for more.

Corwyn pulled back and met her eyes. "My problem isn't in not wanting to touch you, Anna. It's in wanting you too much."

"Who says?" she managed.

"I don't understand."

"Who says it's too much?"

She leaned toward him and met his lips more purposefully. Corwyn responded eagerly. His tongue parted her lips, and he explored her mouth intimately and thoroughly. When he backed away, he averted his eyes as if he expected her to be angry with him for some reason.

Anna brushed her hand over the soft beginnings of his beard and smiled. "I like it," she murmured. "I never thought I'd like a beard."

Corwyn caught her hand and kissed the palm gently. "I shouldn't do this," he breathed.

Anna shivered as he kissed again.

"I can't turn back, Anna. I can't not touch you again."

"Is that why?" she asked breathlessly. His gentle kisses were doing wonderful things to her body, and when he scraped his tongue over the sensitive spot his lips were creating she almost jumped.

"Why I couldn't let you touch me?"

She nodded, as he brushed his beard over her

palm and pressed his lips to her wrist.

"Yes. I'm losing myself to you. If I go much further, I'm not sure I'll ever be able to let go."

Another kiss graced her wrist, and her knees felt weak. "Is that a bad thing?" Anna asked quietly.

"That's your decision," he breathed, tracing his tongue over her pulse.

She gasped at the sensation.

"I think I'd be happy to be there," he continued. "Would you?"

Corwyn met her eyes and pushed to his feet, setting Anna's hand back in her lap. He grabbed the volumes he'd been working with and started toward the doorway. "I'm asking for forever, Anna. It's all or nothing for me. I can't sit there with you and not touch you."

He left the room, and Anna watched as his back disappeared from view. There was no plea. There was no pressure. There was no mind-numbing seduction, which, gauging the state of her body, would have worked admirably. Corwyn had stated what he hoped for, given her a choice, and left her to make it.

Some part of her screamed that she should go after him. The more rational part wondered how much time he would give her to decide. All or nothing— All scared her to death, but she couldn't live with nothing after feeling that kiss. He was gentle and attentive, and no one—not even Jörg and his damned mind tricks—ever made her feel what Corwyn did with a simple kiss.

Chapter Six

December 25th, 1976

Corwyn watched Anna while she ate. For the last three days, she had been strangely withdrawn. He'd tried to convince himself that she was still deciding, but a dark surety that her choice had been made and made against him plagued him night and day.

He avoided asking. Corwyn didn't want to spook or push her if Anna was still deciding, but it was more than that. He was scared to ask her. Every moment that he didn't know for sure was a moment he could still harbor hope that he was wrong.

Anna was getting stronger every day. Her color was still weak but was returning slowly. The bite had all but healed except for the scar it would leave when the scab flaked away. She'd had no problems with it, save the intense itching that assaulted her as it healed.

If only Anna would smile, she'd be beyond beautiful, he decided. Corwyn felt as if he were trapped in a nightmare. Every time he looked at her, he wanted to run his hands through the wealth of fiery curls over her shoulders. He wanted to taste her mouth again. He wanted to take her to bed.

He wanted too much. He'd moved too fast. He'd almost moved much too fast. Corwyn had to stop himself or he would have convinced her into bed, and the last three days proved that he had called that one right. It would have been convincing Anna to willingness, and he couldn't have lived with that.

But, he had told her the truth. For him, it was all or nothing now. There would be no simple release.

Corwyn was printing, and it was probably already too late for him.

Just as she had the previous three nights, Anna cleared the table and washed the dishes quietly before disappearing upstairs. Corwyn watched her go and clenched his fists.

His blood was screaming as it had been for days, ever since that first kiss. He needed release, and he knew he was far beyond self-release. Corwyn needed a woman, but he was printing on Anna. He wasn't sure another woman would do. He understood now how a Warrior could go insane this way. Corwyn wasn't far off that. He felt as if he were riding the edges constantly now.

Corwyn tried to concentrate on reading, but the sound of the shower upstairs had his mind wandering. He found himself considering ghosting in to watch her and rejected it immediately—*well, almost immediately.*

It was underhanded. Beyond that, it wouldn't help his slim chances at survival much. It was bad enough that Corwyn could pull up the memory of how perfect her body was beneath her clothes, based on that hellish night he'd brought her here. Seeing it again could only make it worse.

He tossed the book aside and headed up to bed. It was early, but Corwyn couldn't concentrate anyway. He might as well spend his time staring at the ceiling as anything else.

Corwyn nixed the idea of a cold shower. Cold showers wouldn't do any good in the condition he found himself in.

He startled as a light knock came at the door of his room.

"Corwyn, can I come in?"

His mouth went dry. He couldn't seem to think clearly. "Sure," he managed. He scrambled up, leaning against the headboard with the blankets pooled around his waist.

As the door opened, Corwyn realized his position and bit back a groan. He should have taken the time to pull his jeans back on. He'd left himself at a distinct disadvantage. Short of coming up off the bed in the nude, he was trapped until Anna said what was on her mind and walked away.

Anna looked at him uncertainly, and he was afraid she was about to bolt. "Oh, sorry," she stammered, backing toward the door.

"Don't. If it bothers you, I'll get dressed and meet you downstairs," he offered. At least then, Corwyn would be on even ground with her.

Who am I kidding? She's not printing. There is no even ground.

She met his eyes and shook her head. Better, she stopped backing away. "No, it's okay. I just didn't expect—"

"Anna?" he prodded.

"Well, it's Christmas, and I wanted to give you a present."

A present? Some rational part of his mind was trying to figure that out. Yes, it was the twenty-fifth. Corwyn supposed she did celebrate Christmas. Most people did. Even Warriors with human mates adopted the custom. But, where would Anna find a gift for him? How?

"Oh. Thank you. I didn't get anything for you. I'm sorry. I really wasn't thinking about it."

Anna moved to sit on the bed next to him. "Actually, my gift is one we can share." She leaned toward him. "Is the offer still open?" she breathed onto his lips.

Corwyn's heart took up a wild cadence. "All or nothing," he reminded her. "If I take you to bed, it's forever. Do you want forever?"

She nodded, brushing her lips lightly over his.

"Are you sure?"

Anna leaned further forward, brushing her lips along his cheek. Corwyn felt himself harden as her breath left hot trails over his skin.

"I'm sure," she whispered, planting her lips near his ear.

Corwyn ran his hands through her hair and guided her mouth to his own, drinking in the silk of her beneath his hands and his tongue. He reigned in the fire inside, determined to take her slowly, but when she swept the blanket back to nestle her body to him, he groaned at how difficult it was not to fall on her like the animal raging inside him for release demanded.

His hands found the knot at the front of the robe she wore and he peeled the terry cloth from her shoulders. Without missing a beat, he pulled Anna's oversized nightshirt over her head, cupping an ample breast, running his fingers over a hardening nipple.

"I like your gift," he teased as he bent his head to capture the nipple in his mouth. Corwyn teased at her and drank in her excitement, as her hands brushed through his hair and she pressed against him.

Her hand moved to stroke the aching length of him, and he stilled, willing himself the control not to take her hard and fast.

"You're still working on the wrapping," Anna mused. "I want you to see what's inside." She leaned to capture the length of him in her mouth, and he watched in a mixture of shock and pleasure as she returned the teasing.

"It's our first time," he managed. "Don't you want a slow discovery?" Gods! There was nothing slow about this. If she didn't stop, it would be over very soon.

Anna lifted her head and pulled lightly at him, straining his control. "We can discover later. I want to feel the passion I know is there. Your gift, remember?"

"And yours?" he questioned.

"Oh, yes."

Corwyn parted her lips urgently, soaring into mindless possession as she responded with equal passion. His fingers found her wet and ready for him, and he groaned as she rose against his hand, seeking out his caress.

Anna pulled away slightly and watched as he sank his fingers into her. She panted out small cries of pleasure as he quickened his pace, drawing her up to the brink of release. "Please," she begged hopelessly. "Please come with me."

Corwyn eased his hand to her waist and smiled as he lay back. He pulled her over him, sensing Anna quickly to make sure he didn't need to put the entire experience on hold in hopes that there were condoms somewhere on the premises. His smile widened when he realized he didn't need to do anything of the sort.

"Can I see what's inside now?" he teased.

Anna shot him a crooked smile and reached to guide him into her. She dropped her hips to him. Her eyes closed and her muscles gripped around the length of him. Corwyn arched beneath her in pleasure, driving himself deeper into the tight, accepting depths of her.

Self-control forgotten, he guided her as he took her in fast, sure strokes, meeting her fully, over and over, until he found release like none he had ever experienced before. Anna collapsed over him, panting in the aftermath of her own climax.

He wrapped his arms around her, feeling the fire in his blood as glowing embers now that he had finalized his choice. All the conditions had been met. Corwyn was in *Endspiel*. Anna agreed to take him forever as hers. He took her to seal the pact. He laughed lightly in relief. The release of the printing tensions that accompanied his physical release was beyond anything he'd ever imagined.

"I take it you enjoyed your Christmas present?" she teased.

"I may have to start celebrating it."

Anna was suddenly very quiet, and fear settled in the pit of his stomach.

"Anna, talk to me," he urged her.

"I'm just wondering if I gave you a present you'll regret," she admitted.

Corwyn smiled in understanding, glad he'd checked before he took her. "You're worried about a baby," he guessed.

"Well, the timing wouldn't be the greatest," she agreed. "Someday, sure—"

"But not with Veriel after you?"

She nodded.

"It's not your time," he assured her.

"Are you sure?"

"It's one of the easiest things to check. I checked

before I started. I couldn't have taken you without asking, if it had been possible. It's—one of our laws. I promise to get protection. Unless you want to try for a baby, we'll use it whenever you're fertile. I give you my word."

She slid up his chest to brush a kiss over his jaw, and Corwyn froze. "What's wrong?" she asked fearfully.

He slid his hand over her chest and neck frantically. "Your amulet," he managed.

Anna's eyes widened. "I had it on. Honest, I had it on." She launched from him and dragged her nightshirt up from the floor. She pulled the amulet free from it miserably. "The buttons. It was stuck on the buttons." She pulled it back on and wrapped her arms around her chest. "He's coming, isn't he?"

Corwyn came up off the bed immediately. "You have five minutes," he shot at her. "We're clearing out."

She looked at him in dismay.

"Five and counting," he repeated. Corwyn cupped her head and planted a fierce kiss on her lips. "Hurry, Anna."

She nodded and bolted from the room. Corwyn was armed and dressed in two minutes. At four, he had thrown groceries and the borrowed books in the back of his car. When he pounded on her door at the five-minute mark, Anna slipped into the hallway with her bag over her shoulder and followed him out into the night.

Corwyn relaxed, as the miles fell behind them. Finally, he reached over and squeezed Anna's hand. "It'll be fine," he assured her. "The further we get, the safer we are. He had a long distance to come if he was still in Kansas."

"He's at full power now, isn't he?"

He sighed raggedly. "Yes. Colin said he stayed grounded for three days then he fed. He's ready to fight now."

"I'm sorry."

"For what? It was my fault. I was enjoying myself so much I left you unprotected. If you're apologizing for helping me enjoy myself, don't. Apologizing would mean you didn't intend to do it again, and I'm definitely not comfortable with that idea."

"We're going to die, and you're worried about having sex?" she questioned him in disbelief.

"First of all, I have no intentions of dying anytime soon. Second, if you thought that was just sex, I've got to try harder next time. Third, that is most definitely a one-time type of mistake. Fourth, if—and this is a really big if—I do die, I'm damned well going to die a happy man."

Anna shook her head in amusement. "On your second point—"

Corwyn smiled and raised an eyebrow at her. "Yes?"

"You can do better?"

He raked his gaze over her suggestively. "You didn't let me take my time about it," he reminded her.

"And if I had?"

Corwyn shuddered. "I might have died a happy man before I was done with you," he whispered miserably.

* * * *

Corwyn stretched his back as he rolled out of bed.

He smiled at the sight of Anna sleeping. They were too tired after their midnight run to do more than curl up together in bed, but he had every intention of showing her what a slow, thorough job he could make of driving her insane, sexually speaking—preferably very soon after she woke up.

He wandered down to the phone nude, with a quick pit stop on the way, and dialed Colin. His brother answered on the second ring, and Corwyn greeted him cheerfully.

"Oh, so you're still alive after all," Colin answered sarcastically. "I was starting to think Veriel carried you out of our range and ditched you in a shallow grave somewhere."

"Fill me in. There's a story in that comment."

"The training house is wrecked. You probably figured that was coming. Want to tell me what happened?"

"Her amulet was caught on her shirt and peeled off with it."

"And no one noticed? Ah, that's right. You were probably too busy provoking him by sleeping with his mate by then," he shot back acidly.

"She's mine, Colin. I've printed. I can't turn back now."

"Are you nuts? Of all the women in the world, you decide to print on the one the great mad elder wants?" he demanded. "He destroys lives, brother. Yours next, I'd wager."

"You've never felt the burn, Colin. You've never reached *Endspiel*. Trust me, it's not as simple as you think. Once you turn the corner—"

"Nothing is ever simple with you, Corwyn. So, now

you're sleeping with Veriel's woman? This just keeps getting better, doesn't it?"

"Out of a morbid sense of curiosity, how did you know Anna and I were sleeping together?"

"Well, let's see. Veriel made sure I got the message."

Corwyn's heart sank, and he dropped into the chair behind him woodenly. "Veriel came after you?" he asked. He hadn't considered that possibility. The fight was supposed to be between Veriel and himself—no one else.

"Not exactly. He sent a few of his goons with the message. He was too busy destroying the training house and trying to track you to send a personal message. I sent them home two short. I'm sure you felt that much. A high-level named Polero slipped away from me."

"I'm sorry, Colin. I never intended for this to spill over. What was the message?"

"He doesn't appreciate you handling his property. He wants her returned to him, now."

"He has to know we won't agree to that."

"*You* won't," Colin shot back, then he softened. "I won't either. You've chosen her now. I just hope she's worth all the trouble."

"She is. You'll like her, Colin."

His brother grunted in response. "I'll warn the other house lords. Veriel could get nasty about this."

"They're going to love this one," Corwyn mused.

"Don't worry. I'll water it down some—make it sound less like you're thinking with the wrong head."

Corwyn grinned, picturing the teasing glint in Colin's eyes. "Gee, thanks—I think."

Chapter Seven

January 3rd, 1977

Anna watched the approaching car nervously.

Corwyn wrapped his arms around her to comfort her. "Calm down," he soothed her. "They'll love you."

She smiled weakly. "That's good to hear. I wish I could be so certain." She had known the other Hunters were coming for almost a week, and she only got more nervous as time went on.

"Colin has been after me to chose a wife ever since Dad died." He shrugged. "He can't complain too loudly that I listened to him, for once."

"So, what? Two or three whole weeks?"

"In earnest," Corwyn admitted.

"You don't waste much time, do you?" she teased.

"Not with you." He released her and opened the door for his brothers.

Anna sucked in her breath as she got a good look at them. Corwyn hadn't been joking when he told her that Colin and Stephen were younger versions of himself. Colin was a good four inches shorter and stockier, and Stephen was a leaner, less-muscular version. Still, no one could mistake them for anything but brothers. Anna only wished she could count on Colin possessing any of Corwyn's good humor. Her husband's description of the middle Hunter boy as 'difficult' had her concerned.

As she expected, Colin spared his older brother barely a handshake and glance before heading for her.

"So, you're Anna," he commented brusquely.

"Yes, I am. You would be Colin, right?" Anna

managed with something that might have passed for confidence if you didn't know her well.

"That's me." Colin reached a hand up to her chin. "May I?" he asked.

She looked at him in confusion.

Colin sighed. "The bite. May I check it?"

"Oh, sure." She raised her head to give him a clear view, and Colin ran his hand over it critically. Anna shuddered at the memory of those teeth piercing her neck.

"You're right, Corwyn. We can camouflage it, but it's going to scar—worse than most. She must have jerked as he bit down, and without him sealing it—" He shrugged.

She furrowed her brow and ran her hand over the indented ovals. "Sealed? You mean Veriel could have healed it?"

"Healed is too strong a word." Colin guided her toward the living room with a hand on her lower back. "He could stop the bleeding and cause it to leave only a slight discoloration as a trace of what was done. But you would still be able to see it if you were looking for it."

"Why didn't he?" She shuddered. "I mean, if he really wanted to keep me around, why let me bleed out?"

"Control," Stephen spoke up from behind her. "As long as he kept the link open, Veriel had your complete acceptance. Most likely, he would have rewritten your memory while he took you—or right afterward, but he wanted to start first. Your memory rewritten, he assumed you'd let what was happening happen without any reason to question it."

Anna felt the color drain from her face. "Oh. I think I'm sorry I asked." She sank to the couch. "I don't understand. What Veriel did to me was unusual. I know that. Why would a beast have that power at all? Why be able to heal? Why stop someone from dying?"

"Several reasons," Colin assured her. "If he's creating a turned beast, the elder beast doesn't want him to die before he's infected with beast blood. Veriel accessed your memories, right?"

She nodded. "But what does that have to do with anything?"

"From time to time, beasts decide not to turn a minion. Sometimes, they recruit humans to do their dirty work during daylight hours. It's risky, since they don't directly control an unturned minion once the bite has been closed. They only have the ability to track them then. But, if something needs done during daylight, an unturned minion is their only hope of accomplishing it. Examining a human's thoughts by feeding is much more comprehensive than simply sensing them."

"So, if the memories are clean, he knows he can trust the human?"

Stephen smiled. "Or thinks he can. The human can still change sides suddenly, which means they check their minions fairly often."

Colin cleared his throat. "I—um think you can clear something up for me, but I don't want to upset you by asking."

Anna looked at him miserably. "Veriel killed Matt, didn't he?"

Colin snapped a startled look at Corwyn.

"I hadn't confirmed that for her," Corwyn admitted.

Colin darkened and looked away. "Sorry, Anna," he mumbled. "I'll drop it."

"No," she decided. "Obviously, Matt wasn't your question. What was? I'll answer if I can."

"Veriel has been on a killing spree. I need to know if it's somehow connected to you."

"Shoot."

"Do you know a man named Brian Barnett?" he began.

Anna blushed deeply. "That would be safe to say," she admitted. "We dated for a year in college." She flicked a glance at Corwyn, but he seemed undisturbed at the idea. Of course, he knew she wasn't a virgin on Christmas, if not before.

"How about Dillon Scott?"

Anna stared at her hands intently. "Guilty," she admitted.

"Roger MacReady?"

She groaned. "That should about end the list," she joked weakly, avoiding Corwyn's eyes studiously. If he changed his mind based on her past mistakes, she wouldn't be able to stand it.

"Not nearly," Colin drawled.

"But I haven't," Anna started to storm. She met Corwyn's eyes and looked away in embarrassment. "That should end the list," she repeated miserably.

"Just let me throw out the names. Maybe he didn't stop with strictly intimate encounters."

Anna groaned again. "Shoot," she whispered.

"Charles Stone?"

"Prom," she admitted.

"Jeremy Talbot?"

"A few dates in high school."

"Did you care for them?" Corwyn asked.

She looked at him in a mixture of shock and dismay, but there was no anger or hurt in his features—only curiosity. "At the time, I guess I did. I haven't seen any of them in years."

"Then, Veriel will see them as competition," he decided.

"A guy who took me to the prom seven years ago is competition? How?"

"They had hopes. A man with hopes could decide to try again, or you might decide to." Corwyn shrugged. "Or maybe it's not that at all. If he had you in his hands, Veriel might not care. He's frustrated because you're with me, so he's lashing out the only way he can. He's using your memories."

"So, you're not upset?" she ventured.

"Because Veriel is killing off men from your past? Why?" Corwyn asked in confusion.

"Because I have a past to kill off," she qualified for him. "I mean, you have some clue, but we never really talked about it."

Corwyn smiled, and his brothers chuckled openly. "Is that what's bothering you?" he teased.

"Well, the killing part isn't helping much."

Corwyn pulled Anna into his lap and wrapped his arms around her, nuzzling her neck with his beard. "Do I look upset? Have I ever been?"

"I suppose not," she admitted.

"If you're not sure, maybe I should go prove it to you," Corwyn suggested in a low, hungry voice.

"Down, boy," Colin interrupted him.

"Sheesh! These Warriors print on a woman and think of nothing but bed. Promise me you'll kill me,

Colin," Stephen pleaded.

"Gladly," he assured his younger brother. "Don't sweat me. Unless Corwyn screws this up, I'm never printing."

Corwyn glared at them, and they both regarded him with wide smiles. "You two will learn your lesson when you print," he warned.

"So I can turn soft like you?" Colin teased. "Uh-uh, buddy. Not me."

"I'm thinking he couldn't fight his way out of a paper bag right now," Stephen added.

Corwyn smiled crookedly. "I believe, my dear, that the Lord Hunter has to prove who he is."

"Can you?" Colin asked in mock innocence.

"That's it," Corwyn decided. "As Lord Hunter, I demand a trial of both of you."

"Which one first?" Stephen asked. "The fast, wiry one or the brute?"

"Nay, nay, little boy. I said both of you and I meant both. You want to embarrass me in front of Anna? We'll pile on the embarrassment, but it won't be mine."

Colin was suddenly serious. "You're kidding, right?"

"I'm not laughing."

"Corwyn, we were kidding," Stephen protested.

"With the wrong man, apparently," Corwyn assured him. "Now, are you scared?"

The two younger men looked at each other and shrugged. "No," they decided in unison.

"You should be."

Anna felt a stab of fear. Somehow, the situation struck her as wrong. "Corwyn, is this really necessary?" she asked quietly.

"Yes, it is. Don't worry. I won't kill them. I'll even endeavor not to do anything that breaks bones or causes stitches."

"What if they hurt you?"

He captured her in a fierce kiss. "I want to teach these pups a lesson, Anna. I want to show them what a printed man is capable of. Make me a promise that you'll go to bed with me right after the battle if I come out without having my blood drawn or bones broken and set me loose on them."

She shook her head in shock. "I'm not sure I'm comfortable with that," she protested.

"Sleeping with me?" he teased.

"Of course, I'm comfortable with that."

"Then what?"

"Being the catalyst for people hurting each other. I mean, isn't that what Veriel is doing?"

"All right, then," Corwyn decided. "Don't promise me. You're out of the loop. I still owe them this thrashing as a reminder of who is the house lord, and they'll still get it. Maybe, you'll allow me to take you to bed after the battle for your own reasons."

Anna took in his sad smile and speculated a little. "Well, since you're going to hurt them either way, come back to me in one piece, and I'll show you the time of your life."

"What's your reason?" he teased.

"You're good in bed. Do I need another reason?"

"Maybe someday you'll figure one out."

"Oh, you must mean that love thing," Anna mused. "That is another consideration, I suppose."

"Good start. Okay, the ground rules are set. Time for you to see what a Warrior is trained for."

"She's already seen that," Colin noted.

Corwyn glared at him.

Colin put a hand up for peace. "I meant Veriel," he explained.

"I was barely conscious for that," Anna assured him. "I'm still trying to sort out all the disappearing and reappearing clothing and weapons...and people. Nothing made much sense that night."

Stephen smiled widely. "Well, then this will be a real treat for you."

"I doubt it."

Despite her fears, Anna found the display amazing. Corwyn took on both of his brothers at the same time, and it seemed they were evenly matched that way.

The blades made her nervous at first, but she soon learned that they anticipated each other so well blades never landed. The damage invariably came from a foot or a fist. Those attacks came so fast at times that Anna had trouble tracking the movement. More than once, she only knew a blow had been struck at all by the reaction of the person who'd been hit.

When Corwyn finally decided the trial was over, Colin and Stephen were still on their feet. How they were was a mystery to Anna, but they were. Colin had a split lip and was moving tenderly because of a few gut shots. Stephen had two black eyes and sore ribs. Corwyn was fresh as a daisy. He'd barely broken a sweat in the frigid air.

"Okay, you've passed trial—barely. I suggest you put in some training hours before you face me again." Corwyn turned toward the house and sheathed his weapon. "Oh, and get mated please. It does wonders for convincing a man to survive the battle unscathed."

The younger two men groaned as he walked away.

"Was that an order?" Stephen asked seriously.

Corwyn smiled as he swept Anna up into his arms and kissed her passionately. "Yes, it is," he assured them. "Oh, and losers cook dinner. We'll see you then."

* * * *

Corwyn smiled, as Colin set plates before them. Overall, he was pleased with the trials. His brothers would heal in just a few days, and they got serious quickly enough when they realized he was really holding trial and not just showing off for Anna. He had no doubts that Colin wouldn't open his midsection again, and Stephen would make a greater effort to protect his face in the future. Best of all, there were no scars as a reminder.

Anna grimaced at the sight of them close up. "Was all this really necessary?" she asked.

Corwyn smiled. "You don't know how fast we heal. There won't be a trace of this left in four or five days."

She furrowed her brow. "That?" she asked, staring at Stephen's black eyes.

The young man smiled and dropped into the seat on the other side of her. "This is nothing," he assured her. "A love tap."

"Love tap?" Corwyn inquired. "Do we have to squeeze in round two before dark? If so, we'd better eat quickly."

"No. I do not require further instruction," Stephen assured him.

"That remains to be seen," Colin interjected.

"I only meant that beasts have done worse to me,"

Stephen explained. "After all, I'm not our great Lord Hunter. I can't take on Veriel and dance away unscathed."

Corwyn darkened. "I never said that. You assumed—" He chopped it off as he caught sight of the horrified look on Anna's face. "I'm in one piece. You never even realized. That should tell you how minor it was."

"How minor was it, Corwyn?" she asked quietly.

"Just a scratch. It didn't even need stitches. Okay?"

Anna nodded, but he noticed that she spent a good bit of time pushing her food around her plate instead of eating. Stephen watched her with a worried expression, and Colin furrowed his brow. Corwyn could hear the unspoken concern that Anna may not be suited for the life of a Warrior's mate. It was too late for Corwyn if she changed her mind, and all three men knew that all too well.

"So," Colin began suddenly. "Have you two decided when you're going to start having little Warriors?" he teased, though Corwyn could tell he was fishing for the answer that they already were—just in case she changed her mind or Veriel killed the new Lord Hunter.

Corwyn almost cringed to consider how they would have to handle custody of a young Warrior, if things went sour in a marriage. It had never happened before, so it was a non-issue. There had been theories for centuries that the printing somehow affected the woman as well as the man, but how that would be was a mystery, and the Stone loved a good mystery.

Anna cast a startled look at Colin. "We're— I mean..."

Corwyn squeezed her hand. "Not yet, Colin. When we're ready, we will."

The younger man darkened, but he held his tongue.

Stephen cleared his throat. "I suppose that's a good idea," he decided. "Even if Veriel wasn't breathing down their necks, Anna's still healing. She should build her blood up before she tries to carry a child. I brought ferrous sulfate with me to help with her anemia. I figured you'd need it."

"Thank you, Stephen," Anna said in relief, more from the saving comment on the baby issue than anything, Corwyn was sure. "That was a good idea."

"Yes, it was," Corwyn added. "I was so concerned with diet that I overlooked formulary cures."

"I consulted Jules," Stephen admitted. "She...liberated some from the pharmacy for me."

"She stole it?" Anna asked in disbelief.

Corwyn chuckled. "Our medical specialists sometimes get a little underhanded for us, but usually we have a doctor actually write a prescription for what we need so we don't risk things like that," he remarked pointedly.

"Don't blame me," Stephen protested. "I just told her we had an anemic victim we were caring for and asked her advice. The next thing I knew, she was at the door with the pills. You know Jules," he shrugged.

Anna looked at him in confusion.

Corwyn sighed. "Jules was bled pretty severely before my father and I killed off the beast who attacked her. She has a soft spot for other survivors," he explained, "but I'll talk to her. Getting fired for stealing vitamins is an unnecessary risk when we can get them legally—sort of."

"She sounds like a good person," Anna noted.

"Tough as nails," Colin assured her, "and she'd do anything for us."

"I meant to ask you something. You said a vampire—beast can track someone after they've fed on them, that link remains even after the wound is closed?"

"Your amulet breaks that," Colin explained. "Anyone who's been fed on that survives and wants our protection is granted it. If they weren't fed on, they have the same chance as anyone else out there. Still, we protect some—professionals like Jules and our doctors, even if they weren't fed on. It's a mutually beneficial business arrangement."

"You don't protect everyone?"

"We can't," Corwyn explained. "There would be too many. Besides, a beast isn't territorial. Even if he survives the battle and missed his kill, he won't go back for that same prey unless it's marked for easy tracking. He'll take the next opportunity that comes along."

"Except for Veriel, when it comes to me. Why? What makes me so different?"

"We don't know yet," Corwyn admitted.

"But, we'll find out," Colin promised.

Stephen nodded his agreement. "It's the least we can do for the new Lady Hunter."

"I have a title?" Anna laughed

Corwyn shrugged. "The mate of the house lord is always referred to as the lady of the house. She's sort of like a mother or older sister to the other women and children of the house."

"Which means you'll never have anything extra to do," Colin noted, "because Stephen and I are never going to print."

Anna's eyes glittered. "Bet me."

Chapter Eight

April 1st, 1977

Anna dropped into his lap so suddenly that Corwyn barely had time to catch her before she'd wrapped her arms around his neck and met his lips in a demanding kiss. Corwyn sensed her and groaned, setting her away from his body slightly.

"We can't," he breathed in disappointment.

Anna unveiled an impish grin and shifted to wrap her legs around him. "Of course, we can," she teased him.

"No, we can't," Corwyn corrected her. "When we moved last night, we left our protection behind. It's after dark, which means I can't go get more without endangering you, and you, my dear wife, have just entered high cycle. This you well know, because I started using condoms two nights ago. I'm sure you noticed that. So, this is out of the question," he decided.

Corwyn tried to set her off his lap, but Anna tightened her legs.

"Let me get this straight. You won't make love to me, because I might get pregnant."

"That's the general idea. Yes," he confirmed.

"You said we'd use protection until I wanted to try for a baby. What if I said I wasn't adverse to the idea?"

Corwyn found it hard to breathe and harder still to think. "Not good enough," he managed hoarsely. It wasn't good enough. She had to want a baby, not just be agreeing to a baby. It was too much like seducing a woman into willingness for his tastes.

"Really?" She considered it carefully. "What if I said I wanted you to make love to me all night long every night with no protection until whatever magic tells you I'm fertile tells you I'm carrying your baby? Then I want you to make love to me half the night every night so I get enough sleep to support the baby?"

"Are you saying that?" his breathing was already ragged in his need.

"I'm saying it. What do you say?"

Corwyn met her lips with a searing kiss that took her breath away. "That worked. You realize Warriors are potent men," he cautioned, already pulling her shirt up over her head between kisses. "There is every possibility that you'll be pregnant within a few days, even tonight. Are you sure you want this?"

She nodded solemnly. "Just make me one promise."

Corwyn stilled with her shirt clutched in his hand. "What promise?" he asked warily.

"If your magic tells you I'm pregnant in the next few days, don't tell me for a week or two."

"Why?"

"I don't want to give up you making love to me all night long that soon. At least give me that long."

"You have my word on it." He pitched her shirt away and captured her mouth again, devouring her mindlessly while he started working her bra off. "I'm sorry," he apologized. "I can't take this slow."

Her smile widened and her hands moved to the buttons on his shirt. "Take me as hard and fast as you want to," she invited. "Take me over and over. If your clothes aren't off the first time—if mine aren't, who cares? We'll get further the next time...and the next. I want to see how much you want this baby. Show me."

Corwyn groaned as he slid off the chair to his knees with her wrapped around him. He laid her beneath him. "Put your legs down," he requested. "I'm not going to make it as far as the bed. If I don't have you now, I'll go insane."

Anna dropped her legs and raised her hips to help him slide her sweat pants off. He ran a finger over her and groaned at how aroused she was.

"You want this," he mused. "You really want me to give you my baby."

She smiled and moved against his fingers. "Again and again," she assured him. "How many would you like?"

Corwyn dragged his jeans down and took her fast and hard while she held to his arms. "I want this, Anna. Can't you see how I want this?" He'd barely started when he was lost to the world in a release that seemed to draw his very soul into her. He could visualize his seed finding an egg within her, and he tightened again and immediately started soaring to another release.

Afterward, he lay still inside her, brushing his lips over her cheek. "Are you sure you want to try again?" he breathed as he nipped at her ear.

"I want to see how dedicated you'll be," she teased. "Just think of a little piece of you inside me for nine months. I want you to want it as much as I do." Anna moaned as he lengthened and thickened inside her again. "And you do," she panted. "Make sure I'm pregnant, Corwyn."

He pinned her to the floor and plundered her mouth as he surged into her again. "You'll be carrying my baby by the end of the week or I'll die trying," he assured her. "I promise, I'll take you to bed next time."

"Overrated," she decided. "I want you inside me forever."

Chapter Nine

April 15th, 1977

Corwyn wrapped his hands around Anna's waist and snuggled closer to her.

"Going to sleep?" she teased him.

"Yes, I am."

"So much for dedication," she mused.

"Nope. I'm dedicated, all right. You need sleep."

"Your magic told you I need sleep?"

"Yes, it did," he murmured into the side of her neck.

"Corwyn, I've never been more awake," she protested. "I think you're just making excuses."

"You made the rules, Anna."

"What rules?"

"All night for two weeks, then half the night so you get enough sleep," he reminded her.

"No, it was all night until—" She broke off in shock, as Corwyn raised his head and smiled wickedly.

"You're about due for a little something that's not on its way," he crooned as he ran his hand over her damp red curls and lower to cup her thigh, sending shards of pleasure through her. "A little something else is on the way."

Anna placed her hand on her abdomen lightly. "How long have you known?" she asked in awe.

"For a week. Are you mad at me?"

She laughed nervously. "Mad? How could I possibly be mad?"

"What do you think?" he prodded.

"Erin Allison, if it's a girl," she breathed. "Please,

Corwyn."

"If you give me a daughter, you can choose any name you like," he crooned.

"You want a girl?" she asked in surprise.

"Any Warrior would kill or die for a baby girl. Most of our babies are boys."

"So, I guess I shouldn't plan on pink?" she guessed.

"I said it was unlikely, not impossible. If it's a boy, do you like Andrew?"

"Andrew Hunter. It sounds very strong. It's a Warrior's name. Okay, it's Erin for a girl and Andrew for a boy," she agreed.

"You really are happy, aren't you?"

"Ecstatic." Anna smiled coyly. "Know what else I think?" she asked.

"What?"

"The night isn't half over yet," she invited.

Corwyn grinned and leaned to kiss her. "I was hoping you'd notice that."

Chapter Ten

May 6th, 1977

Corwyn saw the telltale signs that Anna was being overpowered by her morning sickness and blanched. That wasn't quite the way he'd wanted to announce their news. He hadn't realized that she'd show signs so quickly when he'd agreed to wait the three weeks until Colin and Stephen's next visit to tell them about the baby. He'd have to intervene quickly, or their announcement would consist of his wife losing lunch.

"Stephen," he barked, cutting off his youngest brother mid-story.

"Yes, Corwyn?"

"Remember that my wife is not a Warrior, please," he instructed. "Your descriptions are a bit—vivid."

The young man darkened. "I'm sorry, Anna," he mumbled, though Corwyn could tell he was uncomfortable with the idea that a Warrior's wife was so squeamish.

"It's all right, Stephen," Anna managed weakly. "I'm just feeling a little washed out today."

Colin furrowed his brow. "She's still not anemic, is she? She's awfully pale. Does she need more iron pills—or a doctor?"

Corwyn shook his head. "We could probably use more vitamins, but I don't think she needs a doctor yet."

"Corwyn, if she's sick, she has to go to a doctor, whether she likes it or not," Colin protested.

"I'm fine," Anna stated dryly, settling into Corwyn's shoulder.

"Oh, yeah. You look great," he replied acidly.

Corwyn pulled her into his lap. "She *does* look great," he countered in a soothing voice, "for a woman carrying the newest Warrior of *Haus Jäger.*"

Colin's jaw dropped; then he threw his head back and roared in laughter. "Damn you, Corwyn! That was not kind of you. You had me convinced that she was dying, and I'd have to print."

"You have to anyway," Stephen reminded him. "Corwyn ordered you to."

"He ordered you, too."

"I'm too young to marry. You're getting old."

Colin glared at him then smiled at Anna indulgently. "Congratulations, Mama."

"Thanks guys." She settled her cheek to Corwyn's chest.

"So, what's the plan, Daddy?" he continued.

"Erin for a girl and Andrew for a boy," Corwyn answered comically.

Both of his brothers chuckled.

"How do ya like that?" Stephen drawled. "First, he could only think about sex. Now, he can only think about babies. Promise me you'll kill me."

"Not true," Anna defended him quietly. "Corwyn still thinks about sex." Her lips curled in a wicked smile and she snuggled into his lap purposefully. "Luckily for me, he thinks about it often. Oh, yeah, and didn't you want to take them to trial again now that the weather is warming up, honey?"

Corwyn smiled. "Give me the word, and I'll prove it on either of those offers." He laughed at the scowl on Colin's face. "Now, just to show you I'm not mired in my cock, I need two houses prepared for delivery. I've made lists of what we'll need at each house."

He nodded to a piece of paper on the coffee table, and Stephen scooped it up.

"I want the Cedar Rapids house and the Minneapolis house. Contact Alan and Mark. Let them know not to make plans for the month of December. One of them is delivering a new baby Hunter that month."

"There are no clothes on this list," Stephen noted.

Anna blushed. "I have to be allowed to have some fun," she countered. "And, the first person who buys my baby black clothing answers to my husband."

Colin stifled a harsh laugh.

"This better be good, Colin," Corwyn warned.

"I was just considering— With that warning, I'd sooner face you in full *Blutjagd* than your wife after buying black baby clothes."

Corwyn grunted his approval. "Good. Keep that in mind."

Chapter Eleven

May 30th, 1977

Anna paced in front of the bank of windows. She felt as if she were waiting for the other shoe to drop. Corwyn had tried to convince her that she was just antsy, but she was convinced something was very wrong, despite his assurances that his 'senses' were picking up nothing.

They had moved four times in the last five months, and every time the beasts got closer. That, more than anything, had convinced her to have a baby now— before the beasts killed one or the other of them and left the survivor with nothing. With her amulet, it was almost certain she would be the one left behind, and Anna had been desperate not to be left with nothing of Corwyn. His child would be enough for her.

By the time Corwyn bolted into the room and started leading her away from the windows, she knew it was too late. "They're coming," she said in a flat voice.

He nodded as he led her back to the living room. "Yes. Veriel must have ghosted them in."

"He's here, too?"

"I think so."

"Let's get out of here," she pleaded. Corwyn said he wouldn't survive facing Veriel again. For all her protestations that his child would be enough for her, it wouldn't. Anna wanted to share the baby with him. It was supposed to work that way. "Now."

"It's too late." Corwyn led her to the corner by the stone fireplace and pressed one of his spare blades into her hands. "Take this."

"Corwyn, I don't know..." she stammered.

He ran his thumb over her cheek and kissed her gently. "They can't touch you if you keep your amulet on. No matter what happens, don't take it off."

"Corwyn—"

"No matter what, Anna. Promise me."

She nodded uncertainly, and he kissed her again—fiercely, this time.

"Please, don't get desperate on me," she pleaded.

"Maybe, he should," a strange voice called out to her from the opposite side of the room. "What Veriel will do to him for laying hands on you will break him."

Corwyn met her eyes and nodded as he drew his weapon. He turned toward the voice and nodded again. "Show yourself, beast," he ordered.

Two men—*beasts*, she reminded herself—appeared before him.

Corwyn smiled a predatory smile. "Ditero! How nice to see you again," he noted.

Anna was glad to see the smaller of the beasts, a man barely larger than she was, flinch and take a single step back at the sight of Corwyn.

"Who's your friend?" Corwyn continued.

"Chase," the larger man stated simply.

"Where's your master, Chase?"

"Not far."

"He does like to send in cannon fodder to slow a Warrior down first."

Chase smiled a crooked smile that said he thought much more of himself than Corwyn thought of him.

Anna pressed her back to the wall. "Be careful, Corwyn."

"The Lord Hunter careful?" Chase spat. "If he were a careful man, he would have kept his hands off of what isn't his."

"She is mine," Corwyn countered quietly. "She's my wife."

"Taken despite a prior claim," he dismissed.

"She didn't choose Veriel. Her choice is the only one I have to honor, not the whims of a beast."

"So, you honor a woman who throws herself into any bed she chooses?" the beast asked acidly.

Anna felt her temper start to rise. She was hardly a slut. Even Corwyn had made her feel more at ease by explaining the lifestyles of the Warriors before they chose mates. Surely, with their urges, the beast had been through hundreds—maybe thousands of women.

"When were you turned, Chase? This is 1977, not 1957," Corwyn answered in amusement.

Anna finally understood the game they were playing. Chase was trying to make Corwyn angry for the edge it would give him, and he was failing utterly.

Chase smiled tightly and advanced on Corwyn. She locked on the predatory look on her husband's face and shivered at how alien it seemed. Anna sucked in her breath in shock as the beast's fingernails lengthened into six-inch claws that looked as if they could rip a man to shreds. Chase shot a dark look at Ditero, and the other beast moved in slightly behind with a weary look.

Anna let loose a titter of nervous laughter. "That one has faced you before," she noted.

"Yes, he has," Corwyn replied. "I'm surprised your master managed to talk you into this, Ditero." When the beast gave him a sour look, Corwyn laughed.

"Didn't give you a choice, I see. Fight or die, huh? Okay, die either way."

Chase shot forward and swung his claws at Corwyn, but the Warrior was already gone in a flash of movement. Anna held her breath as he stopped between the two beasts. She prayed he was baiting them purposely. It wasn't until the foul stench struck her and Chase pulled his hand from his ribs, covered in a dark liquid, that she realized Corwyn had landed a blow.

Her husband's smile spread as the beast looked at him in confusion. "That's your best, Chase?" he taunted. "Veriel's obviously lowered his standards."

Both beasts moved at once. Corwyn swung at Chase, driving him back before planting the blade firmly in the center of Ditero's chest. He danced away, leaving the wound soaking foul blood over the smaller beast's chest. Ditero looked at the damage in shock and backed away. He collapsed to the floor unceremoniously, and Corwyn faced Chase again with a cocky shrug.

"Maybe he hasn't dropped his standards after all," he mused with a raised eyebrow.

Anna looked at the strange swirling disturbance behind Corwyn, but he was already in motion before the warning left her lips. The beast was barely materialized when Corwyn's blade planted in his heart and ended his attack.

Corwyn looked at Chase again. "Name him," he requested firmly, his eyes hard and his jaw tight.

"Rathe," he replied quietly.

Chase jerked toward Corwyn in a way that made Anna wonder if he'd been pushed. The beast's eyes showed a hopeless determination, and though he fought earnestly, she could tell he knew that Corwyn's next blow would be his end.

When all three beasts lay dead around him, Anna started toward him.

Corwyn waved her back. "Will you show yourself, Veriel? Or do you intend to send your turned slaves at me to tire me out half the night?"

A black cloud materialized slowly into the beast elder. "I do not need to tire you, Lord *Jäger*. I simply use you to dispatch my more disappointing pupils," he answered evenly.

Veriel turned his eyes to Anna; his smile faded into a dangerous scowl, as she backed to the wall. He swung his gaze back to Corwyn, and his eyes suddenly burned with something between hatred and malice. "You have turned her against me," he spat. "Do you have any idea how hard your interference will be to undo?"

"My— You think she enjoyed being controlled by you?" Corwyn asked in disbelief.

"I know she enjoyed the pleasure I gave her."

Anna blushed in shame at that. She did enjoy it, but she never wanted his hands or mind on her again.

"I never would have harmed her," he continued.

"You took her blood. You fed on her," Corwyn exploded.

"It was necessary, thanks to the interference of you and your father. I would never have done it again. Now, I will have to. It is the only way to undo what you have done to her."

Anna shuddered and cupped her hand over the scars on her neck. "No," she breathed in a shaky voice.

That was worse than the rest put together.

Veriel glanced at her sadly. "I will leave you only the pleasant memories, *Geliebte*," he promised her. He glared at Corwyn in challenge. "The pleasant memories of *me*. She is mine. You took what was not yours to take. By your own code, I call you to pay for that."

"She's not chosen you. No claim is valid without that step. You know that."

"She chose. Long ago, she chose me." Veriel's eyes softened as he glanced at her again.

Corwyn looked to her for some answer. "Anna?"

She shook her head in confusion. "I don't know what he's talking about," she assured him.

Corwyn nodded and shrugged at Veriel as if he was sympathetic, but Anna knew he was trying to gain an edge by either anger or confusion.

Veriel's features darkened. "I will remind you later, dear one. You cannot hide from me what you hide from him. I can see inside your soul."

Corwyn moved to place himself between the elder and Anna. "She's mine, Veriel. She made her choice."

"The fickle choice of a woman," he spat. "Why, when any woman in the world could be yours, did you pursue the only woman who can be mine? It is always that way with your kind. You always seek to rip the one shred of peace I might have for myself from me.

"You seek to destroy us. Look at our history. Every Warrior killed was killed in self-defense or defense of another. You cannot claim that of every beast you have killed. You cannot even claim defense of the humans. You hunt us endlessly. I am never permitted a moment of peace."

"You are incapable of peace," Corwyn reminded

him hotly. "You have no kinder emotions."

"I have proven a Warrior wrong once on that point. Would you like me to prove it to you?"

Corwyn dropped back a step and crouched to a more defensive position.

"No, I thought not," he dismissed the idea. "You believe that, because it is easier to believe that I am soulless. It frees you from the sin of my slaughter."

"Lies! Why can't you simply admit what you are like the others of your kind?" Corwyn shot back in disgust.

"There are no others like me." Veriel sighed. "You have printed on her. The kindest thing I could do for you is kill you now. Leaving you burning for her would be a far worse fate."

"I won't allow you to take her from me. She's my wife and mate. I cannot let you have her."

"Not while you live," he agreed.

"Not while you do," Corwyn countered.

Veriel moved suddenly, and their battle began. Unlike the lesser beasts, Corwyn couldn't seem to land a blow. At first, Anna hoped they were evenly matched, but when Veriel landed a bone-jarring blow that caused Corwyn to sink back, holding his free hand over his ribs, she cringed at the knowledge that her husband was barely staying on his feet.

Veriel speculated on his opponent for a moment. "You will not yield," he noted without inflection.

"Never," Corwyn breathed dangerously.

Veriel sighed and nodded. "As you wish, Cursed Warrior."

To Anna's amazement, the beast didn't attack again. He stood his ground and waited for Corwyn to come to him.

"What's your game, elder?" Corwyn ground out as he recovered his wind.

"I will take your life in defense of myself and my wife. Though it is my right—my duty, since you raised a hand to me—to destroy you, I will take the other path. That way, none may doubt my right to take it."

Corwyn nodded and backed toward Anna. "And if I don't attack you? If Anna and I walk out of here without a fight?"

"She is not yours to take. Lay one hand on her, and I will kill you where you stand in her defense."

"But, I pose her no threat," Corwyn countered.

"Neither did I. Still, you wounded me and stole her from me. You turned her against me. I gauge my wife's dangers for her. You are a danger to her peace of mind, her safety, and to my claim."

Corwyn fished in his pocket and tossed the car keys to Anna without looking her way. She caught them and tucked them into her pocket.

"And, if Anna leaves on her own? If she leaves without either of us?"

"She stays under my protection. If she leaves at all, she leaves with me."

Corwyn took a deep breath. "Then, we stand here all night. When the sun rises, two of us will still be standing."

Dark hate pooled in Veriel's eyes. "I cannot allow that. I will not leave her in your care and let you disappear with her again."

"Then you'll have to attack, won't you?"

"Then I will do my duty and kill you for your trespasses. Either way, my honor is unblemished in your death."

"You have no honor," Corwyn reminded him.

Veriel shrugged and closed the distance between them to strike a blow at Corwyn. As gifted a Warrior as he was, he lasted even less time in the second round. Veriel stunned Corwyn with a blow to the face and rendered him unconscious with a blow to the head before he could collect his bearings.

The beast sighed and reached down, grabbing him by the collar. As he raised Corwyn easily from the floor, he met Anna's eyes. "Leave," Veriel ordered gently. "Wait for me in another room."

"No! You can't—"

"*Geliebte.*"

She shook her head and tried to blink back tears.

"As you wish, dear one. I can erase your memory of what you will see. You do not understand now, but you will. It is kinder to kill him. You would not wish me to cause him undue suffering. You are too kind for that."

The nails of his free hand lengthened, not into claws but into blades the length of a sacred weapon. He turned his attention back to Corwyn with a sigh.

She fisted her hands, as his intention became clear. Anna's eyes widened as her hands closed around the hilt of Corwyn's weapon. She wasn't completely powerless, she realized. Anna launched at him before she could come up with a reason not to.

Veriel turned at the last moment and struck her, as she drove the blade into his side. His blow never quite landed, but a force like unseen hands shoving them apart knocked her to the floor. Corwyn landed next to her, and Veriel recoiled.

Anna stared at the beast in shock, as he grasped

the hilt of the weapon and pulled the blade from his body. For a long moment, he stared at her across the blade, and she scrambled away from him in fear.

A pained expression settled on his features, and Veriel threw the weapon over his shoulder. "I would never use that on you," he soothed her. "You are frightened. I know that. I handled our last meeting badly, and he has made you afraid of me. He is wrong, dear one. Please, let me show you."

Anna groped along Corwyn's arm until she encountered the blade still in his hand. She pried it loose and turned to face Veriel. His outstretched hand stilled then wavered.

"You can't kill him. I won't let you."

The beast stared at her in shock; then he grasped the wrist holding the weapon firmly. The force the amulet exerted made Anna scream, feeling as if her arm would shatter. Still, Veriel held on, his face a mask of concentration.

When he released her, he met her eyes miserably. "You carry his child," he whispered. "She is beautiful— like you. She has your spirit. She shares your soul."

Anna moved closer to Corwyn in shock. She watched Veriel pace back and forth across the room. He looked troubled, but she couldn't begin to guess the reason for it.

Would this development get them both killed? If Veriel could hold on like that, the amulet was useless. He could kill them both easily. He turned back to her, and Anna jumped at the intensity in his silver eyes.

"This baby means everything to you, does it not?"

"Yes," she admitted quietly.

Veriel sighed. "I cannot protect you yet. There are

things that must be done to protect you both, if you are to be mine as you should have been." He frowned at Corwyn. "Here with him is the safest place I can leave you...for now. The other elders will not interfere with you while the Lord *Jäger* protects you," he ground out in distaste.

"You're going away?" she asked suspiciously. "Willingly walking away?"

"I will return when the time is right." Veriel sank into a chair and regarded her over steepled fingers stained in his own black blood.

Anna felt her heart sink. "Why? Why can't you leave me in peace?"

"Because my only peace is in you," he answered simply. "You can and will find peace with either of your husbands. That is the way of it. I will give you the life you should have had, that we should have had together."

"If you're going to go, go," she replied nervously.

"In a few minutes. Lord *Jäger's* brothers will arrive soon. I cannot leave you unprotected, even that long. They will protect you for me, and when the time is right, I will bring you home where you belong."

"I won't go," she decided.

"When you remember, you will come willingly," he repeated.

Anna looked toward the hallway as the pounding feet headed up the porch and the door swung open. "They're here," she breathed in relief.

Veriel stood to face them. "Yes, they are. This is the hardest thing I have ever done, dear one—leaving you in his care again, but I will come for you."

"Don't."

Colin stormed through the doorway with Stephen close behind him. "Move away, beast," he commanded.

Stephen skirted behind his older brother, looking more intense than Anna ever thought possible for the easy-going young man. When he reached them, he dropped to one knee by Corwyn's head and felt for a pulse with his free hand, never taking his eyes from Veriel. "Strong," he reported to Colin.

His older brother nodded and took another step toward the beast in challenge. "I said step away," he repeated.

Stephen wrapped his arms around Anna and pulled her gently to the floor behind him. "Stay there," he breathed in her ear. He didn't wait for her nod to turn back to Veriel.

"Or what, Colin of *Jäger?*" the elder asked in a weary voice.

"If you don't stand down, I'll finish what my Lord Hunter started," he growled.

Veriel laughed. "Your precious lord has nothing but pure luck in his corner. I chose not to kill him because I have need of him."

"You expect the Lord Hunter to do you a favor? To serve a beast?" Colin asked sarcastically.

"This is a favor he will offer willingly, without my asking it."

"Then, why ask?" Stephen inquired in confusion.

"Because I will give you my oath, my warning for your lord. If he allows anyone to harm my wife before I return for her, he will wish I had killed him tonight."

"Your what?" Colin asked.

"You heard me," Veriel countered. He smiled at Anna weakly. "You will be safe. What you do now is of no consequence. You will come to me with your true memories. All of this will seem only a dream to you."

"Never," she breathed.

Veriel nodded and dematerialized.

Stephen stared at the place he had been for several seconds before nodding and sheathing his weapon. "He's gone," he assured Anna as he set about checking over Corwyn more carefully.

Colin strode to her and put his hand down for Corwyn's weapon.

Anna handed it over and pointed to the room behind him. "Mine is over there," she told him. "We should probably take it, too."

"Yours?" Colin asked pointedly, turning to retrieve it.

"Okay, the one Corwyn handed me," she shot back.

Colin picked it up, chuckling at the idea of a woman wielding one of their sacred weapons, she was sure. He looked from one blade to the other several times before turning back to her with a quizzical look. "Did Corwyn use the blade he handed you?"

Anna felt her cheeks darken, and she cleared her throat. "No, I did."

"Really? Which one?" Colin scanned his eyes over the three dead beasts speculatively, settling on Ditero as his likely candidate.

"Veriel," she informed him.

Colin looked up at her in something between shock and fury, and she shrank back.

"He was trying to kill Corwyn with those...those claw things he has," she protested weakly.

Colin shook his head and offered his hand to pull her to her feet. "That is one crazy elder. You stab him, and he still wants you."

"Don't ask me why. I've done my level best to dissuade him. That's for sure," she commented.

Stephen smiled his boyish smile. "Woman stabs me, I'd think twice," he joked. "He's not driving for a few days or breathing easily for a week or two, but he'll survive."

"Good. I'm too young to run this mess," Colin grumbled.

Stephen retrieved a plastic bag from his jacket pocket and tossed it to Colin; the other man caught it easily, without looking his direction.

"Get that blood off her hands before it starts to burn," Stephen instructed.

Colin started to run one of the gauze pads soaked in alcohol over her hands brusquely; he stopped and stared at her wrist in concern, turning it to inspect it slowly. "What the hell is this?"

Anna looked at the purple ring on her arm and nodded. "He grabbed my wrist and wouldn't let go. I wouldn't be surprised if my entire arm turned that color."

"With the amulet on?" Colin asked urgently.

Anna nodded her agreement of that, the terror at that fact returning like a punch in the gut.

He looked to Stephen in concern, seemingly as much at a loss for words as she was.

"I didn't think they could do that," the younger man confirmed.

Chapter Twelve

May 31ˢᵗ, 1977

Corwyn tried to move and groaned at the spikes of pain in his head and ribs. For the first minute or two, he couldn't seem to pull it together. Why the hell did he hurt so bad?

An image of Veriel suddenly flooded his mind, and he jerked awake. The room was quiet and dark. His muscles relaxed as someone placed a cool cloth on his cheek.

"Oh, honey," he grumbled. "Thank you."

"You're welcome, sweetheart."

He froze as the voice and the chuckling registered. "Stephen?" Corwyn asked in a panic, trying to sit up.

His brother's hands pinned Corwyn down easily in his uncoordinated state. "Knock it off. Just lay there," he ordered in a fierce whisper.

"Anna?"

"She's asleep next to you. She finally gave up waiting for you to open your eyes an hour ago. I wanted her to give up three or four hours ago. Now, stop trying to wake her up. She's had a rough night."

Corwyn ran his hand over her arm in the dark, assuring himself that she was really there before he sank back into the bed. "Is she okay?"

"Bruised and exhausted, but fine."

"Bruised? How the hell did he manage that?" Corwyn knew a beast could cause bruises by hitting with enough force to make the amulet push the victim into something, but it was rare that they wanted to take the pain to do that. Did he strike Anna? Had

Veriel's solicitous act turned to violence after all?

"Grabbed her wrist and held on. Did you know they could do that?"

"No. No, I've never heard of the amulet failing."

"Oh, it didn't fail. I'm surprised her damned arm's not shattered. He just refused to let go."

"Why did he do that to her?"

"It might have had something to do with her planting one of your blades in him," Stephen suggested. "Apparently, the beast made a move to finish you off, and Anna didn't care much for it, so she ran your blade into the side of his ribs. Bled him pretty well, actually."

"Dammit! Is she crazy? He'll be out for her blood, now," he fumed.

"Uh... I don't think so. I think it turned him on."

"It what? Explain."

"Veriel stayed until we arrived to—protect her. And, he only left her with us with a warning for you."

"What?" Corwyn asked sarcastically. "Let me guess. Hands off."

"No. His parting comment to Anna was that he didn't care about that. What she does until he comes for her again is immaterial to him."

"He's going to kill her," he decided.

"You're not listening to me. He's coming back to take her, not to kill her. He's calling her his wife, and he's talking about her true memories— I thought the elders and first cursed were all supposed to be unmarried. Wasn't that one of the early sanctions for the Stone-Chosen?"

"Yes. It was. What was the warning, then?"

"You're to make sure no one harms her until he

returns for her. Anything else is—well, anything goes as far as I can tell."

"Does that make sense to you? I think I have a concussion."

"You do have a concussion, and no, it makes absolutely no sense to me. If he wants her so badly, and it seems he does, why leave her with another man? Especially when he was so furious that you were sleeping with her? Why give her carte blanche to sleep with you now?"

Anna's voice came out of the dark, sounding barely awake. "To prepare a safe place for me and the baby. He says he can't protect us from the other elders yet," she finished miserably.

"He intends to take our baby, too?" Corwyn asked. A panic settled in his stomach like a swarm of angry bees.

"That's what he said."

"Why? Why take our baby?"

"Because he knows the baby is important to me."

"If he thinks he's taking my wife and son," Corwyn raged.

Stephen's hand closed on his arm, bringing Corwyn up short. He forced back his *Blutjagd*. Anna didn't deserve this reaction, and he knew it.

Anna covered her ears in the dark and murmured something that he didn't quite catch but that was surely not a plea for him not to yell so loud.

"What did you just say?" he asked.

"Not a son," she managed, yawning and already half-asleep again. "A daughter, a beautiful baby girl. Erin Allison— I get my pink, Corwyn." He could almost see the content curve of a smile touch her lips as she said it.

Corwyn felt his heart sink. "*Blutjagdfrau*," he breathed. Ignoring the pain in his ribs, he rolled to gather Anna into his arms. Corwyn kissed her forehead before he tucked her beneath his chin. "He won't take you from me," he promised solemnly. "He won't take either of you."

* * * *

Corwyn stared at his brothers, his expression no doubt as stony as his mood.

"You need your rest," Stephen reminded him for the third time since he'd finally peeled himself off of his sleeping wife and made his way down to the office in the manor house.

"Rest? That beast wants my wife and my daughter. He wants to take them both. My child isn't even born yet, and he's already planning to use her to produce his damned children. How can I rest?"

"What are you going to tell Anna?"

"Nothing. She'd miscarry from the stress for sure. All she can do is keep wearing that amulet and hope that grabbing her wrist is the worst he can do with it on. If that's all she can do, that's all I want her concerned about."

Colin shook his head angrily. "You have to tell her."

"Not until it's necessary. Not *unless* it's necessary."

"What's your plan?" Stephen asked.

"What else? Stay low. Stay mobile. What else can I do?"

"Maybe—" Stephen shook his head and met Corwyn's eyes with one of his patented 'I have a brilliant idea' looks.

"What are you thinking?" Corwyn asked suspiciously.

"Veriel will be looking for you here, in our range."

"And?"

"Texas— The whole southwest is a damned big place, Corwyn. I'd bet even old Jason Lord Maher would agree to hide you until Erin is born if he knew Veriel had plans to force a *Blutjagdfrau* for his use."

Corwyn smiled at the thought. "I'm impressed, Stephen. The houses are so unaccustomed to working together that it wouldn't be expected for us to ask for help, and it's definitely in the best interests of all not to allow him to take my daughter. Call Kord. I want to get Anna out of Hunter range as soon as I can. Who knows how long he'll be to ground, and who knows how long it will take him to 'prepare' for them."

Chapter Thirteen

June 3rd, 1977

Anna recoiled slightly from the heat outside the plane. It took her breath away.

It had taken three nerve-wracking days to set this move up. Veriel had only stayed to ground for two of them, a fact that Corwyn and his brothers found profoundly amusing and she did not. All three of them had stood watch over her for the remaining night, and Anna hadn't slept at all for fear of Veriel's return.

Corwyn took her hand and led Anna down to the tarmac. She could pick out the man waiting for them easily. It was hard to miss another tall, dark-haired man in the telltale black shirt and leather jacket, though she was amazed that he could stand the extra layer in this heat.

"Makes no sense," she mused, letting Corwyn balance her for the few steps to the ground.

"What's that?" he asked, moving gingerly for the three broken ribs Veriel had left him with.

After seeing how fast his bruises healed, it still amazed her that his ribs would be knit in seven to ten days, by Stephen's estimate. She'd be lucky if the bruising on her arm was half healed by then.

"I can spot you guys a mile away. How is it that no one else does? It's not like you're inconspicuous. You're a rather striking group of men, you know."

Corwyn smiled. "There are several reasons, actually. The first is that we make ourselves 'blur' to humans most of the time, but your amulet helps you see us. We don't want people noticing us, but our protected need to see us clearly. The other major reason is that you know what you're looking for now."

Anna shook her head. "I don't buy it. I didn't know what you were in that diner, but I sure noticed you, even before you opened your mouth. Did you want me to see you?"

"No, not really. You noticed, huh?" he teased.

"You have no idea how close I came to inviting you home right then and there. God! That makes me sound like such a slut," she decided.

"He worked you into an intense heat. It wasn't your fault. I'm surprised you could control it, at all."

"No, you don't understand. I wasn't going to bed with Matt because I couldn't keep my hands off of him. In fact, I was kicking myself for even considering it. I was just desperate to stop what was happening and he was..."

"A means to an end?"

"Yeah. I guess he was."

"And with me?" Corwyn prodded.

"Oh, I wanted you! I wanted you immediately. I can't even explain it. The worst part is, I was convinced that you wanted me too. I mean, I was sure that you did, even when my mind argued that I was insane."

"I did, but I wouldn't have gone home with you."

Anna stopped and met his eyes in shock. "Why not? Veriel?"

He shrugged. "Yes and no. I knew what he was doing, not how but what. If I'd taken you in that condition, I'd've raped you. I wouldn't have known you had a choice, that you were really willing." Corwyn shook his head. "I could never have done that, no matter how much I wanted you."

Her smile returned. "I did have a choice, and I wanted you." She started walking toward the car again.

Corwyn wrapped an arm around her hip. "Well, I'm glad you liked what you saw," he teased.

Anna faltered and forced herself to breathe deeply. She shuddered. Corwyn tightened his grip slightly and turned her chin up to examine her expression. His eyes darkened and his jaw tightened at what he saw there.

"Tell me," he ordered quietly.

"It's—nothing. It was just something Veriel said to me."

"You didn't tell me anything like that."

"You only asked about my place. That was earlier."

"The club?"

She nodded.

"Tell me."

"He approached me at the bar when Matt was gone and offered to buy me a drink. You can probably imagine what the walking dream syndrome was like in that state."

"Powerful," he mused.

"Heart stopping. He asked me if I liked what I saw." Anna felt a blush creep up her neck and cheeks. "I did. I think that's the worst of it, really. I can still remember that it felt good. It was arousing." She shuddered. "How could I be attracted when every shred of common sense screamed at me to run the other direction?"

"He was controlling you. I could feel it when he started. The heat you were in and the dreams he'd arranged for you gave him an edge."

"It almost worked," she admitted. "If Matt hadn't touched me— Even after, I was confused. It wasn't until I saw how cold and hard his eyes were that I was afraid of Veriel."

They had finally reached the car, and Corwyn released her hip to clasp the other man's hand. "Hello, Kord," he greeted the shaggy-haired man.

"Nice beard, Hunter. That's new."

"Anna likes it. Anna, this is Kord Maher. He looks dangerous, but the beasts are the only ones who need to fear him."

She smiled and shook the hand he offered. "Hello. Thank you for all you're doing, Kord."

His smile turned puppyish. "The chance to meet a legend? I couldn't possibly pass it up," he assured her.

"Legend?"

"The idea of Corwyn sticking a blade in Veriel and coming away with a pulse was a surprise. A human doing it is a miracle."

"No. Veriel didn't kill me, because he didn't want me dead. If he had—" Anna pushed up her sleeve to bare the deep bruising on her arm, now an ugly purple and green. "If he wanted me dead, I'd be dead," she assured him.

Kord whistled a long, low note as he touched the mark. "I see it, and I still can't believe it. Veriel really did this with the amulet on?"

Anna nodded weakly. "The heat is getting to me," she pleaded. "Can we talk in the car?"

Kord startled. "Of course. I'm sorry. I should have realized." He opened the door and motioned them into the new Caddy. "The a/c should help."

She sighed as the cool air washed over her.

"Better?" Corwyn asked as he slid in beside her.

"Much," she murmured. She sank into the hollow

he provided beneath his arm, trying to keep her eyes open for the trip, though she was beyond exhausted.

Anna heard the trunk shut, a sure sign that Kord had stashed their belongings.

Kord slid into the front seat and started driving. "So, explain how Veriel managed to bruise you like that. All I keep hearing is that he managed to hold on despite the amulet."

"I wish there was a better explanation, but there's not. He grabbed me and held on. I felt like my arm was going to shatter into a thousand pieces."

"I'll bet. I've seen a beast thrown ten yards by the blast." Kord met Corwyn's eyes in the mirror. "So, why don't you tell me why Veriel chose now? Why Anna? Why this baby?"

Corwyn cleared his throat, looking discomfited.

Anna looked at him, suspicion eating at her. "What does he mean, Corwyn? Veriel only wants our baby because of me, right?"

"Yes and no," he replied anxiously.

She sat up straight and hit his arm with her open hand. "Dammit! If you say that to me one more time, I'm walking away from the whole bunch of you. I swear it, Corwyn."

Corwyn grimaced then sighed. "Veriel has always had a hostile relationship with the Warriors, especially the Hunters. Where the other elders avoid us, he seeks out confrontation. From his point of view, I've injured him by taking what he owns from him."

"You mean taking me from him. What else?"

"Warriors usually have boys. That's why I assumed you were carrying a boy. I explained that we have more boys than girls. About eighty-five percent of our babies are boys. A girl is something very special. Few Warriors ever have one to protect. Taking both of you from me would be the end of me, worse even than taking you and a son. He knows it's the one and only way to start an all-out war, and he's intent on doing it."

"Your children are Warriors. What if it's a girl? Will our daughter be a Warrior?"

"Never. Women are never Warriors."

"Why?"

"They—just aren't." Corwyn was biting something back. She could see it behind his eyes.

"So, there's no possibility that there's something inherently special about our baby? Right?" Anna prodded him.

"None," he assured her, looking far too relieved.

Anna met Kord's eyes in the mirror and noted his crimson features. "Kord?" she asked pointedly.

"Nothing. There hasn't been a woman chosen by the Stone in fifteen hundred years, and she did her job. There's no need for another. Besides, if you were chosen, you'd have the dark features like we have and a blood mark. I can see that you don't have the features, and I'll assume you don't have a blood mark; Corwyn would have mentioned it."

"There was a woman chosen? For what?" Corwyn asked in sudden interest. "And why isn't there anything about her in the early texts?"

"There is," Kord protested. "*The Early Histories* written by Gawen talk about it. I don't remember it in any other book, but it is in that one. Jason has one in his protected collection. I imagine all of them, even the recopies, are protected. They're very rare, but surely you've seen one once in your life."

Corwyn shook his head in confusion. "I don't think I have. Hunter's copy must have been lost over the centuries. Fill me in. Why do none of the other books talk about her?"

"Gawen wrote *The Early Histories* long after first days, at the end of his life. *The First Book of Texts* and the other primaries were all old news by then. Apparently, he didn't want to mess with history by making too much public knowledge during the lifetimes of the individuals. Much of what's in the later book was known only to the first cursed, and Gawen didn't set it to paper until he realized that even his successor wouldn't see the end. He thought some tales needed told."

Corwyn nodded uncertainly. "Okay. So, who is she? This Stone-Chosen woman?"

"Regana, the first Lady Crossbearer," Kord supplied.

Anna felt the blood drain from her face. "Regana?" she breathed.

Corwyn wrapped her in his arms. "It's all right," he soothed her.

She pushed away and glared at him. "You knew about this," she stormed.

"I knew Regana was Pauwel first Lord Crossbearer's wife and Gawen's sister. I didn't know she was Stone-Chosen for any purpose. I swear it."

"What does this mean?" Anna demanded. "Veriel thinks I'm Regana reincarnated. You know that. So, what does it mean that she was Stone-Chosen?"

"He what?" Kord exploded.

"Veriel's crazy," Corwyn assured her. "Kord said it perfectly. If you were anything but a normal human being, the Stone would have marked you. It didn't, and you're not." He met Kord's eyes in the mirror. "And you! When I asked for information, why didn't anyone send me that volume?"

"You asked for volumes about Veriel, and there's very little in *The Early Histories* that's not already in *The First Book of Texts* about him."

"I also asked for information about Regana."

Kord sighed. "Maybe Jason assumed that you had a copy already. Maybe it slipped his mind. I can't say for sure, but Jason will let you read it. We'll stop by the manor house now."

"Fine," he snapped. Corwyn settled back into the car seat and rubbed his head roughly. "What was she chosen for?"

"She was Raga. She had the mark of Ani," he supplied.

Corwyn groaned. "Stone-protected, as befits a mother," he quoted miserably.

"If you knew, why the hell did you ask?"

"I didn't know it meant *that* mother," Corwyn protested. "How the hell does something like that get lost in the shuffle after all these years?"

"What mother?" Anna demanded. "If you don't tell me..."

"Raga was the mother of the greatest Warriors, the true elder killers, but Regana did her job. She had a son with her husband, Pauwel, elder killer."

"What does that have to do with me?"

"Not a thing. Veriel's crazy. For whatever reason, he's fixated on you. Maybe you look like Regana, except for the eyes and hair. I don't know how he chose you. The problem is, he believes you're Regana. That means any sons you give me will be elder killers. He has to keep you from giving me sons. He believes—I think." Corwyn shrugged. "I really need to read that damned book. But, this is all starting to make sense."

"Maybe to you," she replied in exhaustion. "To me, this keeps getting more surreal and demented."

* * * *

Corwyn settled more comfortably into the chair in Jason's office. He'd sent Anna to rest when they'd arrived. The delay meant that they wouldn't reach their destination until late night, if they traveled today at all.

The history was ancient. It was a recopy, still written in the ancient language of the Stone. Still, even with the time it took to translate, it only took him three hours to read the thin volume.

The book was more focused than *The First Book of Texts*. It dealt almost exclusively with the major events of the first few years after the elders went to the Stone, ignoring many of the facts already covered in the other book. It dealt intensely with Pauwel and Regana. The story was both eye opening and chilling, considering the current situation.

Jörg and Pauwel had been the greatest Warriors of the first cursed. They'd been closer than brothers, partnered for the coming battle by Sibold, the master trainer who'd taught the first cursed. But the most powerful Warriors have the most powerful curse. Jörg went mad and went beast. Pauwel claimed his mate without Gawen's permission and against the sanctions, long before he should have taken her to his bed.

Pauwel didn't know when he took her that Regana

was Raga. No one but Sibold did, and he had guided her development and protection in secret so that no struggle for her affections would cloud her judgment in choosing her mate.

Still, being Raga, the beasts were drawn to her. Resten killed Sibold to try to take her, and Pauwel killed the beast on his second attempt. Veriel tried to take her many times—and Pauwel's son. The Destroyer of Lives finally killed her, long after her husband's death.

Regana had fought valiantly, trained as a Warrior by Gawen and Pauwel for her own defense, if not from the beasts then from the villagers who'd feared her and tried to kill her while Regana still carried Pauwel's son. In her final minutes, Regana had succeeded in sending Veriel to ground for three days. That meant she was either very lucky or a better Warrior than Corwyn had ever met.

Regana seemed fearless. Long before Pauwel and Gawen had trained her, she took on Veriel with Sibold's blades in defense of the dying leader. Whether the elder left for the threat of her skill or because he had no wish to kill her, as he had no wish to kill Anna, was immaterial. She'd threatened, as an untrained human woman, with only her amulet to protect her—and carrying a child, to plant a blade in Veriel, and he'd left.

Corwyn wondered at the similarity between the women. Anna had planted that blade with no warning, but in a similar circumstance, she'd placed herself between Veriel and Corwyn as Regana once did for Sibold.

Veriel wanted Regana. As Raga, that was

inevitable. Suddenly the greatest two, one gone beast and the other a printed man, were wrestling for Regana's life. Perhaps, it was unavoidable that Veriel was the victor, though he'd paid dearly for it.

Overall, besting Pauwel was as advantageous as killing Regana would have been. There had only been one son of Raga to produce the true elder killers. Had there been more, the war might have ended long ago.

Corwyn sighed and rubbed his eyes. Veriel fixating on Raga was understandable, but he still had no idea why the elder pursued Anna. She wasn't marked. Corwyn was sure of it. Was The Mad Elder simply so demented that he believed Anna would recapture memories of the original Raga? The ancient tales of the first war between the beasts and the Warriors were sketchy at best, but they made no mention of any relationship between Raga and Veriel.

The clothing, setting, and circumstances of Anna's dreams would seem to indicate that Veriel saw her not as Raga, but as Regana, but Regana hadn't been Veriel's. He shook his head in confusion.

Perhaps Veriel's madness was in wanting Regana, and all the rest were psychotic ramblings. If so, his hatred for his Warrior brother would have to be intense.

He groaned at the inadequacy of the answers at hand. It seemed that only The Mad Deceiver knew for sure, and his perceptions and interpretations couldn't be trusted.

Finally, Corwyn pushed up from the chair and wandered off in search of Kord. He found him in deep conversation with Jason about a beast they were tracking.

Kord looked up as he entered. "And? What did you find, Corwyn?"

"Damned if I know what drew him to Anna in the first place, but planting a blade in him has only reinforced his belief that she is Regana revisited. Actually, I'm not really sure why he was fixated on Regana and not Raga...unless this is more a Jörg thing than a Veriel thing. He did use the name Jörg with Anna... Anyway, this incarnation of Veriel knew Regana as this incarnation of Raga, but there are just too many holes."

"But why the sexual interest?"

Corwyn dropped onto the sofa next to Kord and shrugged. "I've considered the possibility that the madness that sent Veriel to the Stone in the first place may have been caused by an urge to print, but there's no way to be sure."

Jason nodded. "But, what you're suggesting is that two first cursed printed on the same woman much earlier than sanctions allowed. Pauwel took her, and Veriel went mad...probably from finding out that waiting cost him taking her himself. We know that Andris was born a whole season before the other young Warriors. The book talks about the other lords seeking Pauwel's blood for taking Regana against sanctions. That means Regana was carrying well before either the choosing ceremony or the battle."

Corwyn grimaced. "That explains a lot of what he's said to Anna, but not nearly everything. Veriel claimed a woman's choice of mate was fickle. He claimed that Regana chose him first, and Warriors have always sought to take what was his from him. He calls her his wife and says he has a prior claim on her.

"Now, I see two possibilities here. Either he is truly mad and believes he had some connection to Regana that never existed, or Regana played a very dangerous game by baiting two Warriors. How Pauwel got her aside, I want to know how Veriel could choose to go beast in that case. *Blutjagd* alone would demand he fight to the death to keep her from another man's bed."

Kord grunted his agreement with that one. "Veriel would have had to touch the Stone willingly. With the battle looming, do you think Sibold may have settled the dispute rather than allowing the two to battle and losing them both? If Veriel was decided against—"

"No. By all accounts, Sibold was a genius. Either he would have allowed them to fight to the death or— more likely, he would have killed one of them outright. He knew what Regana was, and he couldn't risk losing all three by killing her. So, he would have killed one of them and allowed the other to keep her.

"Veriel said something to Anna. 'You can and will be happy with either of your husbands' or something like that. But, we still don't know if what he is saying is real or a demented dream."

"So, you think Regana was leading both men on?" Jason questioned. "If that's true, she caused the split."

"There is no way to know. She was headstrong and bold, but there was no indication that she was devious."

"Forget what you know about Anna for a minute. We've already established that his basis for making Anna over into Regana is faulty. If Regana led both men on, and if Veriel felt the decision was being swayed against him to give her to Pauwel, especially if he felt it wasn't Regana's choice to go to Pauwel, wouldn't Veriel feel justified in going to the Stone? And wouldn't he feel he had a prior claim?"

"If that is the case," Corwyn asked with a raised eyebrow, "whose bed was Andris of Crossbearer conceived in?"

"What a mess," Kord decided.

Jason grunted his agreement. "I don't suggest you bring that possibility up to Gunther Lord Crossbearer unless you want to make a powerful enemy. Maybe it's better if we don't examine the reason so closely. For one thing, we'll never know the truth now. For another, no matter what his reasons are, Veriel will not give up."

"Neither will I," Corwyn asserted. "Regana be damned! Anna didn't choose Veriel. She never chose him. She chose me."

"And that is why we must protect her. That and the possibility that Veriel is playing a dangerous game with us."

"What kind of game?" Corwyn asked.

"It's possible that Veriel is casting these suspicions just to sidetrack us, just to keep us off balance. What if his plan all along was to get you to print and take your daughter to mate?"

"Too complicated and impossible to predict," he decided.

"Hear me out. He drew your father in by playing with Anna in a way beasts never do. He killed Jonas to make sure you would take the seal, knowing you would continue your father's inquiry. You're a young lord, and you needed a mate. He worked Anna into a frenzy and created a situation where you would have to spend a great deal of time with her."

"I never took her in that mindless heat," Corwyn

protested.

"But, you wanted to. You started printing, and you took her after she recovered."

Corwyn groaned. "He can't have planned this. What about my daughter? He couldn't have known I'd have one. There hasn't been a girl in my family—"

"In five generations, eleven male births with no females," Jason finished for him. "Hunter was due for a girl. Overdue for one, actually. Veriel had all the time in the world. After all, if your first child was male, your second or third might be female. All he had to do was wait for the right pregnancy to steal her back from you."

"Even if it's true, he's not taking her back. Our daughter will be freed. It's immaterial what his plans were."

"Absolutely. It's too great a chance to take," Jason agreed.

Kord smiled. "And messing with you may just seal his fate."

Corwyn laughed. "I had almost forgotten about that. The book did say that Veriel was to be killed by a Warrior Hunter born. The Stone foretold it. That was why he was killing off the early Warriors of Hunter. I wonder why he stopped?"

"Who knows? He is mad."

Chapter Fourteen

October 30th, 1977

Anna opened her eyes and watched as Corwyn ran his hands over the tight swell of her belly. He had pulled her maternity top up to just below her breasts and was intent on playing a game of 'find the Daddy' with their rather active daughter. He was enchanted; his eyes glowed as an elbow or knee brushed under his fingers.

She sighed in contentment, and Corwyn startled.

"I'm sorry. I didn't mean to disturb your nap," he apologized. "I just saw—" He lowered his head and blushed.

"I know. You just saw her moving around and couldn't resist."

He started to move his hand, but she covered it with her own.

"Don't stop," she pleaded. "I love it when you play with her. You look so—loving and wonderful. I would give up all my sleep to see that."

Corwyn smiled crookedly and kissed a probing fist through her extended belly, brushing his soft beard over her skin in a sensuous caress that heated her blood.

"It's not just our daughter that I love," he breathed, obviously aware of what he was doing to her.

Anna ran her fingers through his thick, black hair. "I know, but there's something special about the love you have for Erin. It's sweet. I love to watch you talk to her and touch her."

"Wait until she's born. You'll have to be firm with me, or I'll spoil her rotten," he warned.

"Who's going to be firm with me?" she teased.

Corwyn met her eyes with a familiar gleam and crawled up between her legs slowly. "You called?"

Anna giggled at him. "I said firm with me, not firm in me."

"Is that a complaint?" he asked, laying feathery kisses over her lips while he splayed a hand over Erin.

"Never. Wanna rock the baby to sleep, Daddy?" she offered.

Corwyn groaned and pulled Anna onto his lap, capturing her mouth in a passionate kiss while she wrapped her arms around his neck. He stilled and dropped his chin to his chest, groaning in annoyance instead of passion this time.

"Dammit," he breathed.

"What is it?"

He pulled her shirt down and smoothed it over the baby gently. Then Corwyn set her off of his lap. "Someone's coming. We'll have to finish this later."

"Kord?" she asked.

Anna hoped it was Kord. She hadn't really cared for the other two Mahers. Corwyn had confided that he couldn't blame her. Calvin and Jason were what Corwyn called 'old school,' while Kord was more like Corwyn and Stephen. Even Colin was coming around, little by little. Kord's easy-going style, coupled with him taking out a turned that had come for Anna, had endeared the younger Maher to her heart.

He sighed, crossing the room. Corwyn pulled a shirt over his head, started to tuck it in then decided to leave the shirttails out to cover his obvious state of arousal. "I don't know, but there's an upset Warrior headed this way," he admitted.

Anna scrambled off the bed, as Corwyn strapped on his weapons belt. "Old school?" Corwyn didn't typically wear weapons in daylight unless he was facing someone old school.

"I think so." Corwyn headed for the living room, barefoot but prepared for any fight that was necessary.

Anna shuddered, watching him from the bedroom. Most of the Warriors she'd met were reasonable men, but the old school men...and the old traditions they upheld were vicious. They frightened Anna in their intensity and bloodthirsty nature.

At times, watching the Warriors was like watching snarling, territorial animals circling each other. At other times, they frolicked like playful puppies. They even called each other pups as an endearment. Maybe they saw the truth of it. An upset Warrior, however, indicated the snarling type of encounter was about to occur.

She heard Corwyn grumbling a variety of curses under his breath as a car pulled up outside. "It's the whole show, the house lords of North America."

"What? Why?"

"Damned if I know," he admitted, "but the gang's all here. Jason brought Gunther Lord Crossbearer and Carrick Lord Swordbearer, the Stone lord." He shook his head. "I want to find out what they're up to. Stay in there while I try, okay?"

"Sure. I don't think I ever want to get between two Warriors, especially upset Warriors." Anna pulled the door to the jamb so she could hear even though she couldn't see.

* * * *

Corwyn took several deep breaths to calm himself, while the other lords made their way up from the car. He was fairly sure he knew where this was going, and he was about to make a lot of enemies if he was right. If Corwyn was reading this correctly, he was surprised the representatives from the European houses hadn't traveled here with their North American brothers.

He opened the door to admit them solemnly. "Gunther, Carrick, Jason— What brings you?" *As if I can't guess? They won't buy that.*

Jason sat on the couch and leaned forward to place his elbows on his thighs. "How is Anna, Corwyn?"

He leaned against the wall close to the bedroom door in a defensive posture that they would all recognize. It was a silent threat. "She's fine. She's napping right now. We did some baby shopping this morning, so she's worn out."

Gunther smiled, a strange thing to see on him. Gunther wasn't a man who was accustomed to smiling, at least not since he became lord of his house. "Women do like to shop for a baby," he mused.

Corwyn decided to cut right to the chase. "And it's so easy to spoil a baby girl, don't you think, Gunther? You had Nancy. You must remember what the rush is like. I know Piers used to get really jealous of his sister. Carrick, you had a sister, didn't you? Grace? Did your parents spoil her, too?"

The old man nodded slowly. "Yes, Grace was spoiled rotten," he admitted.

Corwyn studied him carefully. In his mid-seventies, Carrick's hair was pure white and so brilliant that Corwyn wondered if he wore a black cap to hunt.

Gunther cleared his throat. "We need to talk to you, Corwyn."

"Who does? Do you speak for the Kaufmanns, Smiths, and Farmers? Or is this simply the North American lords who approach me?"

Jason sighed. "The European lords are in full agreement."

"Very well. I needed to know whom I face. It is only fair to know the name of one who challenges you."

Gunther blanched. "No one challenges you, Corwyn. The house lords have simply been discussing your situation, and we feel it's time—" he began.

"No. You're not using my child. She is going to have a normal life like all of yours have been gifted. She deserves no less than any of yours."

"Be reasonable," Jason chided him. "Look at the facts, Corwyn. She may never have a normal life. With The Mad Deceiver involved and so intent on Anna, he may decide to take them, even if you free her."

"I'll risk that."

"We won't," Gunther countered.

"What are you saying, Crossbearer? It's not within your rights to demand this of me. By our laws, you cannot order how I run my family. My own father, were he still my lord, couldn't do that. You cannot take my wife and children from me. You have no rights in this matter at all."

"You're right. We can't order it, but we can refuse to support your decision. If you go against the other house lords, we'll have to withdraw our protection."

Corwyn nodded stiffly. "We will leave for Hunter range tomorrow," he decided.

"No," Jason thundered. "Stand down, Corwyn. Think about this. If Veriel is intent on a *Blutjagdfrau*, freeing your daughter will only make him pursue ours more intently, every Warrior daughter until he succeeds in forcing the confrontation."

"It's the same threat that's existed for fifteen hundred years. Nothing's changed in that. Guard births jealously and free your daughters immediately. That's been our way all this time.

"We've never dared try this before, and I'm not willing to now. We knew we'd be sentencing the girl to hell for her entire lifetime. I won't do it. If you want one, talk some other Warrior into it. My daughter will *not* be cursed."

"It will end this," Gunther argued.

"Go home and tell Piers to have a younger sister for Talon. Tell him it's your wish as Lord Crossbearer that she be cursed. Will the dutiful Crossbearer give the only daughter he will ever have for you? I notice you didn't, when it fell to you. Will he give his daughter up for all of you?"

Corwyn felt his blood boiling in *Blutjagd*. Erin would never be theirs. She would never be Veriel's, even if it meant his life at the beast's hands to stop it, alone and unsupported. "I will not do that to her," he repeated.

"Carrick," Jason called. "You're the current Stone lord. What does the Stone say?"

The old man smiled weakly. "The Stone grows weary of fighting, but it won't comment on the subject of your daughter, Corwyn. It is still and silent."

"Then, the choice is mine to make," he asserted. "Erin will not be trained as a Cursed Warrior."

"The Stone says nothing?" Gunther prodded. "Isn't that unusual?"

"Not really," Carrick replied. "It's happened before. Not often, but it does happen. It typically means that there's a hidden secret or puzzle that must be unraveled before the Stone will speak. I believe it amuses itself this way," he decided ruefully.

"What does the Stone say about Anna?" Corwyn asked suddenly, unsure of what difference it would make.

Carrick smiled crookedly. "The Stone is amusing itself wonderfully."

"Nothing for her either," he guessed.

"On the contrary, it gives me a riddle. It says that she's the mother's daughter and the mother's mother."

"Never having met Anna's mother, I can't say whether or not Anna is like her, and the rest sounds like nonsense," Corwyn replied.

"No, Corwyn. Not *her* mother's daughter. The Stone said she is *the* mother's daughter," Carrick corrected him.

Corwyn spun around, as Anna touched his shoulder.

Her face was pale and pained. She laid a hand over Erin protectively. "He's saying that Erin is the one Veriel is looking for, isn't he? Erin is Regana or Raga or whatever you call her. Not me at all, but Erin." Anna shook her head and pulled back tears. "You promised,

Corwyn," she whispered. "You promised there was nothing special about our baby."

He gathered her into his arms and shot a murderous look at the other men in the room. For a long moment, he didn't speak. Corwyn couldn't tell Anna she was wrong. From what Carrick said, it sounded like she was dead on.

"If she is Raga, she'll have a blood mark. Is my daughter marked?" Corwyn demanded.

Carrick cocked his head and seemed to be listening to another conversation. He sighed. "Silent, Corwyn. I can't tell you that."

He growled in frustration and closed his eyes as he considered his options. "She can't be Stone-touched. Sibold knew who Regana was from the beginning. The Stone would tell us if she was marked. As long as she has no blood mark, Erin will be freed from the curse," he decided. Corwyn kissed Anna's forehead. "I promise you that. That promise, I can keep."

"You will not reconsider?" Gunther asked. "You will not allow your child to be trained?"

Anna shuddered in his arms.

"Never," Corwyn whispered.

"Then, Crossbearer withdraws its support."

Corwyn forced his eyes not to shut in grief, forced himself to witness their refusal.

Carrick sighed. "Swordbearer concurs," he added.

Jason nodded. "Maher stands with the other lords. If you do this, you do it alone, Corwyn."

He nodded. "I understand. One question— I will pose one question to you. If Erin is chosen— If she is Stone-Chosen to be *Blutjagdfrau*, will you chance not giving her every ounce of protection you can? Until she's born, we can't know for sure."

Gunther shook his head angrily. "If she's Stone-Chosen as mother, she's Stone-protected, as befits a mother."

"Then, we have nothing left to discuss. We'll return to Hunter range tomorrow."

Chapter Fifteen

December 15th, 1977

Corwyn snuggled up behind Anna and wrapped his hands around her to run them over their baby. He smiled widely. "She's busy in there," he commented.

Anna groaned in affected torture. "I thought you said your females were never Warriors? I swear your daughter is trying to fight her way out of me."

Corwyn sobered. "I shouldn't go," he decided. "Colin can handle this. It's too close. If you go into labor—"

"Don't be silly. I saw Alan yesterday. I'm not even due for a few more days, and most first babies are late." She ran her hands over his and leaned her head into his shoulder. "You were the one grumbling to me about how a Stone summons can't be ignored, right?"

"Yes," he sighed.

"Then, you have to go. Just do me three favors."

"Anything. Tell me." Corwyn buried his face in her neck and kissed her gently.

"First, come back in one piece. Be careful for me. I don't want to raise our daughter alone."

"I'll do my best. What else?"

"Second, don't be late for dinner. It's Swiss Steak. Please, promise me you won't be late."

"For Swiss Steak...and you, I'll be on time." He nuzzled her shoulder, edging her shirt aside with his chin. "What else?"

"Bring me ice cream. I'd kill for something sweet."

Corwyn roared in laughter. "You never ate so many sweets when I met you," he noted.

"I think our daughter has a sweet tooth." Anna groaned and moved her hands over her stomach. "She certainly burns off enough energy."

"I suppose the question is this— Does she get hyper from the sugar, or does she crave sugar because she's hyper?"

"She's no less hyper when she gets none."

"Yeah. You're just grumpier if you don't get any," he teased.

"So, humor the pregnant woman and bring me ice cream," she pouted.

"I will bring you ice cream," he promised. Corwyn sighed. "I'm still not sure I should go."

"Go. Carrick said it was an emergency, and he won't come here. You tried that. So, go. I can call Alan or Stephen, if something goes wrong before your brother arrives. I'll be fine, and you'll be home before dark."

"All right," he grumbled. "If you're sure, I'll go, but I'd rather be here."

Anna turned in his arms and planted a solemn kiss on his lips, while he soothed Erin. "We'll be fine, Corwyn. Find out what Carrick wants, and come home on time for me."

"With ice cream and in one piece," he assured her.

* * * *

Anna placed the last of the dishes in the cupboard and rubbed her back in annoyance. She looked at the clock and groaned. Stephen should have been there an hour earlier.

She looked at the door in exhaustion. Stephen had a key. He could let himself in when he showed up. A nap was what she needed. After battering her all night, Erin had been strangely calm since Corwyn had left. Napping while Erin napped sounded like a wonderful plan to her.

She tossed and turned under the heavy blankets, unable to fall asleep. Finally, Anna felt as if she had to use the bathroom—*for probably the hundredth time today.* She sat up and froze as a gush of fluid announced that Alan's determination of her unready state was a grievous error.

"Oh, no," she complained quietly. "No, no, no. Erin, honey, you can't do this to me. Your father has to be here for this." *Or at least his brothers—*

She swung off the bed and made her way to the phone without breaking to clean herself up. There would be time for that later. Anna dialed their number. After six rings, she gave up in frustration and slammed the phone down.

Anna ground her teeth and grabbed the phone again. This time, the phone picked up on the second ring. "Alan?" she asked before anyone could speak on the other end.

"Excuse me?" a female voice asked.

"I need to reach Alan," Anna breathed urgently. "Dr. Prentice, please. It's an emergency."

"This is the doctor's answering service. What is the nature of your emergency?"

"I'm— I'm Anna Hunter. Alan is my cousin. I need him. I think I'm in labor."

"Can you give me a number where the doctor can reach you?" the annoying woman replied.

Reading from a card! "Alan knows how to reach me. Just get him, please."

"He might not have your number with him, ma'am."

"He has it," Anna growled. She ran a shaky hand over her forehead. She was too tired to deal with this woman, and she was snapping like her in-laws. "I told you, he's my cousin. He knows the number. Just get him."

"How far—"

"Dammit! Just get me Alan. Tell him it's Anna." She slammed the phone down in frustration, wincing that she was going to break it, at this rate. She tried Colin and Stephen again with no answer.

Anna changed and cleaned up, watching the clock nervously. She tried the Hunter manor once more before collapsing at the table and waiting for someone to call. It had been more than forty-five minutes, and she was seriously considering wading through the answering service again, when the phone rang.

She launched to it and picked it up before the second ring. "Alan?" she asked urgently. Anna didn't care who it was. If it was Alan, she had her medical care. If it was Stephen or Colin, she had protection. Either way, she wouldn't be alone anymore.

"Anna? What's wrong?"

She bit back a sob. "Oh, Corwyn! Come home now. Please, come home," she pleaded in a pitiful voice.

"Calm down. What's wrong?"

"My water broke. I think I'm in labor. I can't reach Colin and Stephen. Alan hasn't called back. You're gone."

"And you're panicked," he finished.

"I'm terrified, Corwyn. When will you be home?"

"An hour. Two at the most. I'll try Alan before I leave. You try Stephen again. Where the hell could he be? He should have been there more than two hours ago. This isn't like him."

"Don't say that. Please, don't say that."

"It will be fine. I'll be there long before dark. Just keep locked up."

"Okay. I'll see you soon."

"Calm down. I love you, and I'll be there soon."

"Don't stop for ice cream," she managed weakly.

"I won't."

Corwyn hung up, and she tried Stephen again. No answer. Alan called twenty minutes later. Corwyn had reached him. His answering service still hadn't.

"How far apart are your contractions?" he asked gently.

"I don't know," she admitted, feeling foolish.

"It's all right. Let's time a few."

Anna found concentrating on the pain much worse than ignoring it, but it only took Alan three contractions to make his determination. "Sit down. Drink something cold. Better yet, chew some ice. I'll be there soon."

"Thank you, Alan."

"You'll be fine, Anna. I'll be there, soon."

Despite Alan's assurances, Anna knew she was in a desperate state by the time the doctor arrived. She opened the door wearily, and Alan's eyes widened as he swept her back to bed.

In all honesty, Anna didn't remember much after that. Apparently, she was further along than even Alan had counted on. By the time he placed Erin in her arms, Anna was so exhausted, she was barely holding onto consciousness.

Her daughter was beautiful. She had her father's hair and impossibly dark eyes above her slightly squished nose. Erin ate ravenously for what Alan proclaimed an inordinately long time, taking each breast in turn before staring at her mother with those curious eyes.

Anna ran a soft cloth over Erin to clean her then dressed her, while Alan prepared something for 'the new Mom' to eat to boost her strength. Her breath caught as her fingers traced a tiny red mark on the back of her daughter's shoulder. It looked like an irregular freckle—or a small birthmark of some sort. It wasn't like Corwyn's blood mark and it was hard to see, but it was something, and it concerned her.

She wished Corwyn or Stephen—even Colin was there. They would know what a blood mark was. It was a cinch that Alan wouldn't. It wouldn't do any good to show it to him, so she covered it with a sigh and decided to show it to one of the Warriors when they arrived.

Anna startled and looked at the clock. Even if Corwyn took two hours to get back, he should have been back more than an hour before. A cold certainty stole over her. Something was very wrong.

She called Alan in and had him try Stephen and Colin again to no avail. For whatever reason, every Hunter was out of reach. Despite Alan's promise to stay with her until one of the Warriors showed up, Anna was sure that the entire situation was out of control.

Anna succumbed to sleep only because her body and mind left her no other option. She woke several times to the sound of Alan cursing solidly as he failed to reach the other men. As the darkness dragged her down again, Anna worried about another darkness coming. This one would bring Veriel with it. She was sure of it.

* * * *

Corwyn stifled a groan, as the truck hit yet another huge pothole in the road.

"Are you sure you don't want me to take you to a hospital, buddy?" Bill, the trucker who had picked him up thirty minutes earlier, asked for the fourth time.

Corwyn squinted his eyes at Bill. He was a huge bear of a man with a rust-colored pelt and concern in his eyes. Under other circumstances, Corwyn would have laughed at a Warrior being dwarfed by a human man while he was injured.

"No. I have to get to my wife. She's in labor with our first. If I miss it, she'll kill me," he lied smoothly. It wasn't himself he was worried about. If his condition was any indication, there was every possibility that Colin and Stephen were likewise detained from reaching her. That meant Anna and Alan were unprotected. He had to reach them.

"She'll be at the hospital, right?" Bill countered.

"No. Natural birth at home—with a doctor, of course," he replied.

Bill grunted. "If babies ain't all he does, get him to check you over while he's at it."

"It's not," Corwyn assured the other man. "He will."

"That how you ended up in that ditch? Driving too fast to reach your lady?"

Corwyn sighed. "No. Someone drove me off the road," he admitted. "Hit and run." And, he had a pretty good idea who.

"You should report it," Bill fumed.

"I will once I know my family's safe. I will. I think I know who to blame."

Bill grunted again, and Corwyn closed his eyes.

Corwyn knew it would be a bad day when he was summoned to Carrick. The old man wouldn't come all the way to Cedar Rapids, demanding that Corwyn meet him on the other side of nearby Iowa City. The so-called 'emergency' summons meant only that the Stone had decided to impart information to Corwyn and demanded his presence to do so.

At the Stone's direction, Carrick slit a page cleanly from the back cover of a book where it had been pasted centuries before. It was a page in one of the Kaufmann histories that detailed a woman Veriel loved, that he kept as wife until the Lord Kaufmann of that era, Etienne, took her life. The woman had fought off the lord with a sword when he tried to rescue her from the elder.

Striking her down had been unintentional, but it could not be undone. Etienne didn't survive Veriel's wrath for long, only long enough to tell his tale to the new Lord Kaufmann, Rober, and to beg the gods' forgiveness for what he'd done.

Veriel had more pressing concerns than finishing off Kaufmann. While the old lord lay dying, Veriel did the only thing he could to save the woman. He created the first female turned, the only one the Warriors ultimately killed and the one who lasted longest before going

146

rogue, the fair Lady Caitrina. Servants had overheard Veriel calling Caitrina by the endearments Regana and Geliebte.

"He's done this before," Corwyn breathed. "Why didn't anyone tell me?"

"Until the Stone told me to look for this, no one knew. It was stricken from the Kaufmann history in shame."

"Dammit! Rewriting history this way is hurting us, Carrick."

"I agree, but the Stone assures me that much has been rewritten this way over the years."

"For what reason?" Corwyn demanded. "Is protecting a family name enough reason to hobble us?"

Carrick sighed. "I don't know," he admitted.

A sudden, sinking feeling assaulted him. "Why now, Carrick? Why did the Stone choose now?"

The old man shrugged. "I don't know," he repeated. "The Stone is amusing itself."

"Phone. I need your phone, Carrick."

His worst fears realized, Corwyn managed to find Alan before turning on Carrick. "Your damned Stone has left my child unprotected. Will you help me, now?"

"I can't. You know I can't. The Stone will do what it needs to do. It drew you here for a reason. Swear you'll train your daughter, and everything will change. I'll back you. The Stone will. All of us will."

"No. I gave Anna my word. Unless Erin is marked, I will free her. I must."

"You're determined not to raise a Blutjagdfrau?"

"What life would she have?" Corwyn raged. "She would be pursued endlessly."

"If there was a way for her not to be pursued, would you allow it?"

Corwyn *seemed frozen in shock.* Not pursued? If Erin could have a normal life and still be the blood Warrior to end the curse— *It was tempting, but he'd promised Anna.*

"Hunter," Carrick thundered.

"Not unless I'm forced," he whispered. "I gave my word."

Carrick nodded. "Go to her, Corwyn. Don't waste time with me."

Corwyn found himself shaken awake.

"We're here, buddy," Bill informed him, as he snapped his head around and took in his surroundings. "This is the address you gave me, right?"

"Yes. Thank you, Bill. Let me give you something for your trouble."

"Naw," the man laughed. "Just take care of your lady and baby."

"Thanks again," Corwyn threw over his shoulder as he launched from the cab of the truck and up the front stairs.

Alan met him at the door, and Corwyn could see the relief written on the other man's face. "Thank God," he breathed as he ushered Corwyn in. He eyed him critically and touched the deep bruise at his temple gingerly. "What happened to you?"

"Long story. Where are Colin and Stephen?"

"I don't know. I can't reach them."

"Still?" A cold certainty that they would show up, if at all, as injured as he was stole over Corwyn. Veriel had planned this ambush very well. But, how could he know when to plan it?

"Still no answer, but I couldn't leave Anna."

"How is she?"

"Doing well. Sleeping, actually."

"False alarm?" Corwyn asked in surprise, heading for the stairs.

"Not at all. Erin is lovely. They're both fine," the doctor assured him with a broad smile. "I won't tell you it was an easy birth, but Anna did well."

Corwyn's heart skipped a beat. He'd missed it. He'd missed it all. "The baby— Is there a birthmark?"

Alan furrowed his brow. "I didn't see one, but I wasn't looking for it. If there is, it isn't glaring."

Corwyn nodded gratefully. He glanced at the dimming light outside. "Go, Alan," he ordered as he launched up the stairs two at a time. "You have to leave, now."

"Corwyn! Your injuries," he protested.

"Tomorrow. You've done enough. This place will be swarming soon. Don't be here when they come."

He didn't wait to hear Alan leave. A protected, even the doctors with an overactive sense of duty, knew to follow a Warrior's orders, especially a house lord.

Corwyn opened the door to the bedroom fearfully, but Anna was asleep with Erin in the Moses basket on the bed next to her. He kicked himself for doing it this way. If he had warned Anna about what he had to do and what was at stake if he didn't free her, Corwyn could do it here, but he hadn't wanted to scare her. He still didn't.

Instead, he scooped up the baby and rushed her to the dining room. Corwyn pulled off her sleeper as quickly as he could and set a child's amulet on the table next to her. As soon as she was freed, her protection would have to be accomplished. If he gave his blessing first, he couldn't free her.

Corwyn drew his blade long enough to slice a long cut in his left palm. This was a blood oath, a sacred and honorable promise that he would accept Erin's curse back onto himself. He needed to draw no blood from her, only to paint the blood symbols on her in his own blood, as he would have painted it in beast blood at a first kill. After that, Corwyn would make the vow, perform the *Zeremonie der Freiheit* as every Warrior had done for a female child for fifteen hundred years.

Erin stared at him with a look he would classify as confused as he painted the symbols on her in his blood.

"It's all right, Erin," he soothed her. "You'll be safe very soon."

Chapter Sixteen

Corwyn snapped his head up at his wife's scream of outrage.

"What are you doing to her?" she demanded. "You can't—"

He sighed. Colin was right. He should have told her. "It won't hurt her, Anna. It must be done and done quickly."

She tried to pull the baby from him, but Corwyn blocked her with his body.

"No. Don't please," she begged, as he finished painting the blood symbol on her chest.

"I must," he snapped. "If I don't do this, the elders will take her."

Anna stilled, and her face drained of color. Corwyn felt a pang of regret for her fear. She feared the beasts, and he knew it. He should have warned her.

"Veriel?" she breathed.

"And others. What I'm doing won't harm her. It will save her from Veriel. She must be freed." He hoped it would save Erin. In reality, he didn't know for sure.

Anna nodded. "Freed," she mused. "Do what you need to."

Corwyn sighed in relief and hurried to get his daughter into a comfortable hold. He didn't take the time to bind his hand. Instead, the blood dripped from the fist under her onto his jeans and the rug around his feet.

He placed his free hand on Erin's forehead over the blood mark, and she met his gaze levelly, her dark eyes already so aware. Cursing himself, Corwyn started the ceremony. "*Bei den Göttern, die uns alle geschaffen haben, erbitte ich, dass diese einer zur Sicherheit aller die menschliche Form erhält. Blut meines Blutes; sei frei von meinem Fluch für jetzt und für alle Zeit.*" Corwyn pulled his hand to her chest. He had only to free her from her obligation, and she would be safe.

Corwyn opened his mouth to speak, but his inner sense warned him of the attack coming. He pushed Anna to the wall and swept their daughter into her arms, as the blur shot past his shoulder. "Hold her," he commanded, drawing his weapon.

Anna moved back to the far corner of the room, clutching her amulet as he turned to face his attacker. The beast looked young. With light blue eyes and long, sandy hair, he looked like he had been plucked from a beach movie. Yes, he was young—and cocky.

"Name yourself," Corwyn commanded.

The beast smiled, revealing his perfect, deadly teeth. "I am called Polero." He executed a stiff bow that spoke of another time. Perhaps, he wasn't as young as he seemed after all. His sandy hair fell across his forehead, and he shook it away.

"A turned? They sent a turned for me?" Corwyn asked in mock disbelief. He knew who Polero was. He'd already been bested by Colin.

"Not for you, Corwyn Lord Hunter. I come for the child."

Anna backed further into the corner, but Corwyn laughed. "You think you can take her from me?"

"No. That is for another. My brothers are coming."

"So are mine," he spat as he moved in to land his first blow.

Polero executed a fading dodge, but it was an old

trick, and Corwyn had encountered it many times before. His cut was solid, but it was not perfectly placed.

Polero backed away in shock. "How—"

"You face Lord Hunter, beast. You're cannon fodder." Corwyn felt them converging, beasts and Warriors both; he prayed that Stephen and Colin would arrive before the beasts.

Corwyn landed another blow and backed to his family. For now, he would incapacitate Polero.

He wasn't as easy as many of the beasts Veriel had sent at him. This one must be a favorite. Polero was better trained than even the best Corwyn had seen so far. Corwyn needed to weaken him.

When Erin was safe, he'd kill the beast. For now, he couldn't risk himself. There was no one else who could complete the ceremony. But, until Polero was incapacitated, he couldn't complete it.

Polero collapsed to his knees, and Corwyn clapped his hand back over Erin's heart. "*Ich befreie dich,*" he began quickly.

Corwyn never got to complete the ceremony. The blow to his head came from nowhere, and he barely registered Anna's scream as he fell. Corwyn forced himself from the brink of unconsciousness, as Anna bolted past Polero toward the door, Erin in her arms.

"No," he protested weakly. "Don't leave the house."

But, it was too late. She was gone.

From her reaction, Corwyn had no doubts who he faced. He swung his head around to sight Veriel, waiting for the killing blow to fall. Only Veriel or another elder could have ghosted in so perfectly, and only Veriel would cause such a panic in Anna. He tried to move his limbs to protect himself, but his body was heavy and unresponsive. Corwyn wondered how hard that head shot was.

Veriel watched his struggle in amusement. He smiled coldly. "Do not concern yourself, Lord *Jäger*. Now, is not your time to die.

"You took her from me once. I will take back what is mine, my wife and my child. Search for them, but you will never find them," he taunted. "And once I have proven that you have lost them for all time, I will kill you. I must go now. My family awaits me."

Corwyn tried to hurl his blade for a killing blow, but it passed through the phantom illusion Veriel had projected for him. He choked back a sob, as Veriel started laughing. The elder's next blow gave him blessed respite from the pain of his loss.

* * * *

Anna shook in exertion as much as from the cold. When Erin had been placed in her arms just a few short hours ago, she'd pictured a much different life. Now, still shaky from her daughter's birth, her husband was gone and the devil himself wanted them for himself, all for the birth of a Hunter daughter.

They are coming. Veriel would be here soon. Anna couldn't outrun them. She looked around, desperate for some way to save her baby. The market at the corner was closing, and there were still a few cars in the parking lot.

She looked at Erin hopelessly. Anna couldn't ask for a ride. The people in the car would become instant targets. Besides that, they would take one look at her, in her flannel nightgown and boots, carrying a newborn wrapped only in the heavy crocheted blanket and a diaper, and either turn her over to a hospital or the police. Either way, there would just be more victims for the beasts that would come for them.

Anna couldn't even shield Erin, *unless*— She pulled her amulet off of her neck and kissed it before she shortened the cord and placed it around the baby's throat. Then, Anna hurried to the dark parking lot.

She found an open car easily and nestled Erin into a pile of soft suitcases and bags. The car's plates were from New Hampshire. With any luck, they would be miles away before they discovered the baby hidden there.

Even if they returned to Cedar Rapids, in the light of day, Alan would be able to help Colin and Stephen claim Erin. They would find a way, make up some story. The amulet would assure that they could claim her. Erin would be safe with the amulet.

"Quiet, little one," Anna crooned as she closed the door and tripped her way painfully to the alleyway across the street.

She kept moving, alley to alley, sobbing and running her hand over the barren expanse where her amulet had lain for a year. Anna had no protection now, but if it was a choice, Erin had to come first. Maybe, Colin and Stephen would be able to find her first and they could go after Erin together.

She moved quickly, trying to put as much distance between Erin and herself as she could. Anna was openly crying now. It was her life for Erin's. She couldn't bear the thought of what Veriel would do to her without her amulet to protect her. Anna said a silent prayer that Corwyn's gods would protect her child.

"No one can hide her from me for long."

The voice stopped Anna in her tracks, and her shaking intensified.

"Yes, Veriel," he answered her unspoken curse in amusement.

Anna turned to face him, shielding her mind as Corwyn had taught her, hoping that it was enough. Her breath plumed before her face in the sub-zero weather. She tried to meet his eyes, but the glow of silver made her look away.

"Where is your child, *Geliebte*? I told you I would return for you both. The time has come for you to come home with me. Where is your daughter?" His voice was soft.

Anna shivered in the knowledge that he wasn't nearly as calm below the surface. "I told you we wouldn't go," she managed through chattering teeth.

"This is not the place for this discussion. Once we are home, I will remind you of your true past." He reached for her, but she jumped away before his hands could touch her.

"You can't have her," she decided. "You can't have either of us." Time— Every precious moment gave her husband's brothers time to get to Erin first.

Veriel laughed a harsh laugh at that. "I have waited all my life for this chance, the chance that was stolen from me. At an appropriate age, I will have her as my wife. She can bear my children. To think that the Lord *Jäger's* own seed has made me the mate I have waited so long for. How appropriate an end."

Anna shrank from him. Veriel was insane. She

always thought the moniker of 'The Mad Deceiver' or 'The Mad Elder' was an exaggeration, but he was truly insane.

He closed on her again, and Anna shook in fear. "Where is she? Where is my future mate?" he crooned. "With you as wife and Erin to mate later..." He smiled at the thought.

"She's not yours. She'll never be yours," Anna repeated. She was getting tired. The cold was winning.

Veriel grabbed her by the arm, and his smile spread. "I thought so. You gave up your amulet to protect her. If that is her only protection, the others can take her easily. Lord *Jäger* had no time to bestow his blessing. We will find where you hid her, amulet or no.

"In the meantime," he ran a hand up to cup a breast and moved his face to plant his breath on her cheek, "you may not be able to carry my children, but you are still mine, as you were born to be. I will torture Lord *Jäger* by having you over and over whenever I wish, and you will enjoy it. You remember the pleasure I can give you. I will give you that pleasure again," he promised.

Anna looked at him in shock, ignoring the memories of that pleasure as they threatened to overpower her. "Corwyn is alive?"

"He lives only so that I may torture him with taking his family from him. I think I will give him the same year he stole from me. You could have let me kill him when I had the chance last. That would have been painless for him. But, never mind that. Once you have your true memories, it will not matter to you."

"He will kill you and take us back," she asserted.

"Perhaps. I am supposed to die at the hands of a Warrior of *Jäger*, but not her lord. But, by then, I will have had you. Will he want you then?"

"He will always want me," Anna whispered.

Veriel sighed, nodding his agreement. "He will. I will have to kill him, after all, and not indulge in this revenge. But, you are newly delivered, dear one. It is not time for pleasure. Perhaps for now, I should simply take the information I need from you. Erin must be cold."

She grimaced at that. She could be cold. Erin could die. *No. Any chance is better than Veriel.* "I won't tell you where she is," she assured him. She wouldn't give him anything he could use.

"I said I would take it," he reminded her. "I can make that pleasurable too. You remember that I can." He moved his face around hers, inhaling her scent. "A woman newly delivered is so sweet. Her blood is rich and pure," he mused. "Her mind is so receptive—"

Anna panicked. "No."

She tried to pull away, but Veriel held her in his grip easily.

Anything but that! If he fed, she couldn't shield him, and Erin's location would be forfeit to him. Anna reached around, searching for any weapon she could find and came up with a beer bottle. She shattered it against the wall and swung it toward him.

Veriel laughed in amusement this time. "You know you can't hurt me that way."

His smile faltered as hers grew. Before he could gauge her intent, Anna turned the sharp glass on herself several times: her jugular, her abdomen, her heart.

The beast stopped her before she could strike again. "What are you doing?" he demanded. An edge of panic tinged his voice.

Anna laughed weakly as she collapsed against him. "For my family," she whispered. "Corwyn will kill you. Take my blood. Take my body. It's all you'll ever have of me, Veriel."

The beast smiled coldly and let her fall. "You are wrong. I will have my mate, with or without your help. Perhaps, you were never meant for me, but only to lead me to Erin. I will have her, and she will enjoy it. I can promise you that. I will give that much for you and for her."

"Don't count on it." Anna slipped away into the numb bliss in the darkness with thoughts of revenge. Corwyn would end it. He would bring Erin home.

Chapter Seventeen

December 16th, 1977

Corwyn came to consciousness slowly. His head ached, and he groaned against the pillow. His stomach clenched as a spike of nausea washed over him. He felt as if the room was spinning. No, not spinning. It was moving. He snapped awake and tumbled to the floor of the camper.

Stephen moved to help him to the bed again. "Easy, Corwyn," he soothed him. "Rest. It'll be days before you're ready for that."

He groaned and sank back to the pillow. "Anna?" he inquired, certain that the news was bad. The fact that she was nowhere in sight was all the proof of that Corwyn needed.

"I'm sorry, Corwyn," Stephen whispered.

Corwyn fought to focus on the battered face of his youngest brother. Whatever Veriel had planned for him had been no more kind than the scheme he'd enacted for Corwyn.

"Veriel took them," Corwyn spat.

His heart ached in the knowledge that he hadn't been able to protect them. Veriel couldn't hold Anna for long with her amulet on, but if she removed her amulet— With Erin to hold over her, Corwyn wasn't sure Anna would resist when Veriel demanded her amulet.

"No, Corwyn. I'm sorry. Anna is dead. We didn't make it to her in time."

Corwyn felt his blood burn in *Blutjagd,* even as he cried out in his loss. Taken he could have handled. He

would get her back. He'd faced that before. But dead—
There was no turning back death.

"How?" Corwyn demanded. "How did it happen?"

Stephen shook his head. "Her amulet was gone. We think she gave it to Erin. Without it, Veriel could track right to her."

"Veriel has Erin?" Corwyn wasn't sure which would be more painful to hear. Alive and with that beast or dead and out of danger.

"No. They're still searching, and so are we. All the houses are."

Corwyn closed his eyes wearily. *Of course, they are. They finally realize what they've done. They should help search. It's the least they can do after allowing the lapse that enabled Veriel to separate my daughter from me before she was freed. Their worst fear is realized now— or soon could be.*

He had to know about Anna. Painful as it was, Corwyn had to know how he'd failed her. "Did Anna— Did he?" He couldn't ask. Corwyn couldn't voice either of his worst fears, either of the things he'd promised Anna he wouldn't allow again.

Stephen didn't answer.

Corwyn glared at him. "Stephen," he warned.

"No, he didn't, Corwyn," he replied quietly. He stared out the window miserably.

"How did Anna die?" Corwyn demanded, knowing his brother was hiding something.

Stephen didn't answer.

"You didn't have to keep her from rising turned?" he asked in horror, remembering the Kaufmann diary.

"No. She—" Stephen bit back a sob and turned further away. "She killed herself. Probably to save Erin.

I hope she succeeded." He glanced back at Corwyn. "Was Erin marked? Is she Stone-protected?" he asked.

"I don't know," Corwyn admitted. "I hope not."

"What?" Stephen breathed in shock.

"When we find her, I'm freeing her, Stephen. I won't do this to Erin. It's the least I can do for them both."

Hunter Born

Jäger Geboren

Chapter Eighteen

May 12th, 2002

Jayde Marie Albright slapped on a coat of lip balm and surveyed her appearance in the bathroom mirror. Her long, black hair was pulled into the tight braid slung over her shoulder, and her deep brown eyes seemed impossibly huge in her pale face.

Puppy-dog eyes. That's what her mother had always called them. Her parents said she'd always looked sad and critical, even as a baby. They'd never added that Jayde had good reason to look that way, but she guessed that they thought it.

Long before they admitted that she was adopted, Jayde had guessed it. With a voracious appetite for learning that propelled her into reading at age four, she came across the fact that Ron—her blonde, blue-eyed father—and Pam, her red-haired, brown-eyed mother—could not possibly have produced a child that looked like Jayde did very early in life.

She had known she was adopted. Jayde hadn't been prepared for the truth of how she came to be with the Albrights. She'd expected a teenage single-mother or even a rape victim. She hadn't expected to discover that she'd been abandoned in the back of a car somewhere along the interstate, so newborn that no one but her birth mother and maybe someone who had helped her had ever seen her before her adoptive parents laid eyes on her.

Jayde had been ten when she finally learned the truth. As she dropped her medallion over her head, saddened by the sight of it even as she longed to feel it next to her skin, she remembered the day vividly. Drawn to the attic by something she couldn't name, Jayde had been tearing through boxes marked with her name when she came across the metal disc on a leather thong, wrapped in a heavy green crocheted blanket.

From the moment she touched it, Jayde had felt a connection to the piece of jewelry. She'd studied it carefully, that day and many days after. It was a beautifully-etched piece, crossed arrows superimposed over a bow with a howling wolf head at the top. A single word, *Jäger*, was etched above the design. She'd searched out the word later. It was the German word for 'hunter.'

She'd tripped down the stairs, shaking in a nameless rage, a rage that she'd felt the likes of more than a few times in her life since.

Her parents looked at her in concern. "What is it, Jayde?" her mother asked.

Jayde held the medallion, hanging from its leather cord, in a fist so tight she was white knuckling and driving her fingernails into the palm of her hand. "Tell me," she demanded.

Her father stared in shock at the medallion then at the jumble of green blanket thrown over her arm. "Where did you find that?" he asked weakly.

"You know where," she shot back. "I found them in the attic where you hid them."

"We didn't..." her mother began quietly. "No, you're right. We should have given it to you earlier. We intended to eventually."

"My mother gave me these things, and you never told me?"

"We don't know that for sure." She faltered on something more.

"What do you mean? If I came with it, you have to know something. There's always a story with something like this."

"Jayde, sit down," her father requested gently.

She hesitated.

"Please, honey. Sit down and let us explain."

Something in his voice knocked the fight out of her, and Jayde sat woodenly in the recliner across from them while they explained, in halting voices, the whole sordid story.

She had them repeat it over and over when she was older. She even came to appreciate the meager humor of her father running the car onto the shoulder of the road and digging through the baggage frantically to find the baby squalling unexpectedly from the cargo area of the station wagon. Her mother was fond of remembering how markedly her husband shook as he held the baby, now wrapped in one of his t-shirts and stripped of the soaked blanket and diaper she was abandoned in while her mother drove to the nearest hospital.

Abandoned in a car in the northeastern states in December— Jayde shuddered to consider what could have happened. Her parents maintained that she was a gift from God, but Jayde had her own opinion of that. If any god was involved, he just made sure she ended up with a caring couple, not like the ones who disposed of her in so cold and callous a fashion.

While she listened, Jayde fashioned the ends of the thong into a sturdy knot, studying the only link she had to the life that had tossed her out like so much garbage.

She didn't want that poor excuse for a family back, but something deep inside her longed for the medallion. It felt like a part of her, and she would never let it go.

When she dropped it over her head, her mother stiffened. "Jayde?" she asked fearfully.

"It's mine. It belongs to me, and I want to wear it," she replied stubbornly. Jayde bolted from the room with the blanket tucked under her arm and locked herself in her room to cry until her tears were spent.

It hadn't been her finest moment. She admitted that later.

They never had the explosive confrontations some adoptive families have after a moment like that. After all, there obviously wasn't a loving family waiting for Jayde somewhere. It obviously wasn't a mistake that she had been given up. She'd just been an inconvenience to be passed off. No, the only problem that came from the revelation was an uncomfortable awkwardness that surrounded them for six months or so, until Jayde came to her senses and decided they were all the same people they had always been.

She looped her medallion under her sweater with one hand as she collected her notebook and the computer disks from her desk with the other. Jayde pulled her brown suede jacket on and checked for the wallet and keys she kept shoved in the inside pockets.

Jayde left her apartment with one last glance around. At times, she regretted selling the house when her parents died. Then, she remembered how neurotic she'd been living there alone. It made no sense, but she'd found the sudden need to lose herself in a crowd. Jayde didn't like people much. She never had, but the need was crushing in its intensity, so she'd taken the apartment in the renovated factory building instead.

It helped, but it didn't eradicate the sense of danger she felt. At times, she would be walking down a street and feel a sudden urge to change course for no good reason save the rising panic driving her to do so. It passed. It always did once she changed her flight path, and the next day it would be gone. Jayde could walk down that same street without a problem.

On the bus to the college, she sat next to Terry. The younger woman shared several art classes with her and was probably the only person Jayde considered a friend. Terry often teased Jayde that she would end up as the world's oldest student someday. Having officially changed her major at least four times, Jayde had earned her BA in languages when she was twenty. Still, she kept taking classes in anything that struck her fancy.

In the four years since then, she'd continued to go to school full-time, taking classes in nursing, religion, history and art history, fine arts, psychology, computers, math, and science. Living off of the money she earned working almost full-time as a tutor and the proceeds from the sale of her parents' very upscale house, she'd spent most of her inheritance and insurance money on continuing her education. Jayde joked most recently that she should get her masters in teaching and be done with it. At over three hundred credits, she should find something more meaningful to do with her life than text translation and karate classes.

"How'd your workout go?" Terry asked, breaking the silence between them.

"Good. I'm up for black soon," she commented

evenly. Jayde went to the gym constantly, and Terry knew it. It seemed Jayde was jumpy and irritable if she didn't blow off some steam sparring on a regular basis, at least every other day if not every day.

"Maybe that's why you never have dates. You scare all the guys off," Terry teased.

A crooked smile softened Jayde's mouth. This was an ongoing joke between them. She didn't like people, and that seemed to extend to men. "I do fine, and the workouts clear my head."

"Sure. You do fine," Terry drawled. "You do fine with the occasional dinner and a movie and handshake at the front door. How about flesh and blood: sweaty, hot, mind-blowing sex?"

"Tell you what, Terry," she offered. "Show me a man who isn't a complete loser, and I'll consider it."

"I've tried that," she complained. "You're hopeless, you know that? You won't spend fifteen minutes in the same room with a man."

"Drop it. When I find him, I'll know."

"You're not staying late, are you?" Terry asked nervously. "I know you think you're invincible, but—"

"No. I just have some computer work to take care of after class; then I'm headed home. Eight or nine o'clock max. You know I'm careful."

"You better be. Another girl disappeared just a few nights ago."

"Yeah. I know." They got off the bus and started across to the arts building.

Jayde shuddered, as the sense of danger assaulted her full-force. She scanned her eyes over the deserted rose garden in unease. She came this way every day. She'd most likely come this way tomorrow, but today her gut reaction said to stay the hell out!

"You okay?" Terry asked in concern.

"Yeah. Just remembered I have to swing by the bookstore before class. Want to tag along?"

"No. I have to see Jinx about some paints before we meet. See you there."

Jayde stifled the urge to drag Terry back, as the younger woman turned onto the brick-lined path through the bushes. "Sure. Be careful, Terry."

"You too." She made her way across the garden.

Jayde held her breath until Terry reached the other side safely. She uttered several choice curses under her breath and started to step onto the path, but the panic only increased until Jayde pulled her foot back from where it hovered over the dirt. "What the hell is the matter with me?" she muttered. "There's no bogeyman coming up out of the ground after me." She turned on her heel and stalked around the long way, cursing herself solidly in half a dozen languages and promising to see a shrink the first chance she got.

Late for class, Jayde was annoyed with herself the entire time she spent indoors.

She drank in the cool evening air as she headed for the computer lab. There was just something invigorating about the night air, she decided. Even when the panic struck, there was something safe and comforting in the night.

* * * *

Talon Cross watched his bait from his ghosting place in the trees. Grelden was here somewhere, and the woman walking down the garden path from the library to the residents' hall and the street beyond was just Grelden's type. She was young, dark-haired, of moderate height, and slim yet shapely...just the type of woman Talon would love to meet himself, but this was business.

Still, that was how most Warriors met their wives, he reminded himself. As the last in the Cross line, his father and grandfather certainly wouldn't complain if Talon married and produced a few heirs to safeguard that line.

Talon's senses were humming. Grelden was moving in for his kill now that the woman was in sight. Considering what he knew of Grelden, the beast wanted more than just a meal and a kill. He pushed that thought away painfully. What the beasts subjected women to always made him angry, and Talon needed his wits about him for the coming battle.

For a split-second, Talon thought his plan would fail. The woman looked around nervously and backed off a step. She seemed to take a deep breath before squaring her shoulders and pushing on into the trees with a look that spoke volumes of her determination.

Is she a human sensitive? They were exceedingly rare. In fact, there were only three known to the Warriors now. They were prized women when they were found, pampered and revered for the strange curse that let them see the ghosted beasts, something not even a Warrior could accomplish.

Full sensitive or not, she felt something, and that indicated she might be a lesser sensitive, much as Colin Hunter's mate could feel the presence of but not see the ghosted beast. Talon would have to find out if she was a sensitive when the battle was over and offer his protection if she was, but destroying Grelden came first.

The fact that she ignored whatever she felt was lucky for both of them. At least this way, he would likely stop the beast. If she led it away from the ambush site, Talon might not be so effective.

The woman approached, and so did Grelden. When she was well within the trees, he struck. Talon was already in motion, so the full import of what he was seeing took a moment to sink in.

Grelden grabbed the woman roughly then froze in shock, his eyes widening. She took the opportunity to land a decent punch; not that it affected a high-level like Grelden, but it was a valiant effort. The beast's response was swift and painful. His blow tossed her like a rag doll into the trees, and he growled his annoyance.

So intent was the beast on his prey that Talon's approach was missed. Talon didn't take time he didn't have to consider what that meant. Instead, he struck hard and fast as Gunther had trained him to. In two swift blows, Grelden lay dead at his feet, and Talon turned his attention to the victim.

It was unusual for him to concern himself with a victim who hadn't been used to feed in so public a place when he should be making good his escape, but this was no ordinary victim. She'd felt the beast, and more surprisingly, Grelden had hesitated. He had to know why.

She was beautiful, even with the bruise coming up on her cheek. Her dark lashes made enticing crescents on her pale cheeks below the frame of dark hair.

He ran his hands over her, trying to be impersonal

while he looked for injuries. She seemed not to have more than the bruise and a bump on the head. As he ran his hand over her chest, he stilled in realization, outlining the heavy metal disc.

Talon groaned as he pulled the amulet from beneath her sweater. She was Hunter-protected, graced with the lord's amulet, to boot.

What the hell was a Hunter-protected woman doing in Crossbearer range without warning the Cross family that she was here? Where was her proper guard, either Cross or Hunter? Who was supposed to be watching over her? He raged at it. Had Talon known she was protected, he would have done that in the first place instead of using her as bait and allowing Grelden to touch—

His mind worked furiously. Grelden touched her. If she was protected, fully protected with her lord's blessing, the beast should have been blown away from her with a full measure of pain for his trouble. Grelden shouldn't have been able to hold onto her or to strike her down. So, she couldn't be fully protected. Why would a Hunter give an amulet...the lord's amulet, no less, but not finish the job?

Talon shook his head. He was wasting time. He had to go, and he had to take the woman with him. Whatever the circumstances were, he had to assume that she was protected and treat her as if she was. He sheathed his sacred weapon and cradled her to his chest. Talon moved silently off the path and through the dark woods toward his car, ghosted fully.

Once he had her settled inside, he swung into the driver's seat and left sedately. More than ever, Talon needed to be inconspicuous. He could ghost his way past most humans, car and all, but he didn't need the waste of energy or the delay right now. Talon glanced at her constantly while he drove. She was an enigma, and because of the evidence, he had no idea what her reaction would be when she woke to find herself in Crossbearer custody.

Talon didn't dare take her to a city house under the circumstances. He needed one of the cabins, so he headed toward Vermont. There was a little cabin outside of Ludlow by Mt. Okimo that would do nicely. Once he reached the mountains, he could relax.

In the meantime, Talon needed answers. He fished the cell phone out of his jacket pocket and dialed his grandfather's cell.

Gunther Cross picked up on the second ring. "Yes, Talon? I take it your night was fruitful?" he asked, though he surely knew that Talon had made a kill. As lord of the range, he would have felt it. Even another Warrior in range of it would have.

"Yes, Grandfather. More so than I counted on, though. I need your help."

"How so?" the Lord Crossbearer asked in amusement. "You never struck me as needing any help from others."

"I need information of a very serious nature."

Gunther sobered immediately, his voice lowering to the deadly calm Talon was most accustomed to from a house lord. "If I can, of course."

"I have a Hunter-protected woman with me. I've taken her into my custody."

"A Hunter-protected in our range?" Gunther fumed. "I'll have to speak to Corwyn. He knows better than this."

"Dammit! Then, you know nothing about her?" He grimaced in the realization that he'd secretly hoped it had been an oversight that no one had warned him about her.

"No, but I fail to see your problem. Protect her until I arrange her proper guard from Corwyn. Most likely, she's newly protected and forgot to tell Corwyn that she was leaving his range," he decided as the most logical explanation.

"My problem is that I'm not sure she has a proper guard. I'm not convinced that the Hunters know about her, at all."

"I don't understand. Explain."

Talon sighed. "She has the Lord Hunter's amulet, his personal seal, but she has no blessing. How could this happen? Why would she have an amulet and no blessing?" he asked in frustration. When a protected died, the Warriors were always careful to retrieve the amulet. These things didn't happen, especially not with a lord's amulet.

"By the gods! You're certain?" he asked urgently.

"Grelden struck her. He touched her twice with nothing more than mild discomfort or annoyance for his trouble. I'm sure of what I saw."

"She's still alive," the old man mused.

"Of course. He only rendered her unconscious." Hadn't Talon made it clear that she wasn't badly injured? If she had been, he'd have reported what steps he was taking first.

The Lord Crossbearer was strangely silent.

"Grandfather?"

"Are you somewhere you can pull over?"

"Yes. Why?"

"Give her your blessing. She must be fully protected immediately."

"She wears Hunter's seal," he protested. "I couldn't possibly—"

"The woman is young—perhaps twenty-five? Dark hair? Dark eyes?" the Lord Crossbearer asked urgently.

"Yes, but why—"

"Pull over and do as I say, boy," Gunther stormed. "The Lord Hunter will thank you for this trespass. Trust me."

"I'm not a house lord." And, that was a lord's amulet, not even a general Hunter amulet. "At the very least, I should—"

"Any may give the blessing in an emergency. This *is* an emergency if there ever was one. Right now, you're more important than the Lord Hunter, Lord Crossbearer, and even the Stone lord. You're there to give this blessing, and we're not. Do it, now."

"All right. I'll go now."

"No. Set down the phone and give her your blessing. Then I'll explain everything to you...when she's protected."

"Yes, Grandfather."

Talon set the phone down and pulled off the side of the dirt road he was traveling. He sighed as he cupped the young woman's face in his hands. Talon gathered his power and leaned close to her. "*Bei den Göttern, die uns alle geschaffen habe, stelle ich dich unter den Schutz des Hauses Kreuzträger. Ein jeder unserer Art und Sippe wird sein Leben geben um deines vor dem Bösen, das unter uns weilt, zu bewahren. Wandele nun gesegnet in unserer Mitte.*"

Talon said the blessing in German, because it was

the language Gunther preferred to use for it, though he knew it in four foreign languages, including the language of the ancients. Gunther was listening this time, and the old lord was already irked. Better not to needle him further about unimportant things, Talon decided.

Talon hesitated before he sealed the blessing with a gentle kiss. He wanted her, and few women affected him so markedly. "Duty," he breathed into her lips as he touched them with his own for the seal.

He sucked in his breath in shock, as a pulse of pleasant electricity coursed from her lips to his own and rushed through him, spreading warmth through his muscles until it pooled in his groin. Talon bit back a groan as he hardened under the force of that intimate caress of power. For several long moments, he argued himself out of doing something stupid, like kissing her again.

When he recovered enough to think clearly, Talon slammed the car into gear and swung out onto the road. He swore fluently in several languages before he scooped up the phone again. "Grandfather, this better be damned good! Who is this woman?" he demanded.

The Lord Crossbearer laughed heartily at his reaction. "Did the blessing go well?" he asked.

"Let's just say I'm not sure who just blessed who. Who the hell is she?" And, what the hell was the energy blast that had him aching behind his jeans? This was something more than a sensitive, though he couldn't begin to guess what she was.

Gunther's laughter ended abruptly. "You were a child at the time. Years ago, every Warrior in the world was searching for that girl. By the time you trained, we had all but given up hope of ever finding her. We'd assumed that she was dead or lost forever." He hesitated long enough that Talon opened his mouth to speak. "She's Erin Hunter, Corwyn Lord Hunter's daughter. But I don't know what name she's using now."

Talon pulled the wallet from the inside pocket of her jacket where he'd felt it while he carried her to the car, silently cursing himself for not checking that before he called in to report her. It was nearly a given that Gunther would have asked her name eventually.

He tried to recall any mention of Erin Hunter, but nothing came to mind on the subject. That fact bothered him...a lot, much more than he would like to admit. A sense of unease came with a secret of this size being kept.

He flipped the leather open and switched on the overhead light. "Albright. Jayde Marie Albright," Talon informed him. He switched the light off again and tossed the wallet on the dashboard, wondering how a lord's daughter could be 'lost' or why she would use an assumed name.

"This isn't going to be easy, Talon. She has no memory of her life as a Hunter. That is guaranteed."

"Why? What happened?"

"She was separated at birth from her family."

"Why was she not blessed?" he demanded.

"There was no time. Veriel and the other elders arranged for the Warriors to be detained when they knew her birth was imminent. By the time the lord returned, he was attacked. His wife fled with the baby. She gave her own amulet to save her child and hid Erin somehow. Anna lost her life to Veriel because she'd surrendered her amulet to her baby."

A sudden sick swirl assaulted Talon. "The ceremony? Surely, he had time to free her," he asked hopefully.

"Interrupted," Gunther admitted. "She's *Blutjagdfrau.*"

"Gods alive! It's too late now." Even if Talon hadn't given her the blessing, Jayde was more than sixteen. Her curse had been sealed in *Krankheit* by now, and it was too late to free her.

"Yes, it is. If Veriel finds Erin now, he'll force her to give up her amulet and then—"

"And then, Jayde will be forced to bear them an army of elite elders who can walk the day. What can we do?"

"I'll speak to Corwyn tonight. For now, we have to keep her in custody. If she's willing, begin her training. That is a given. She must be trained eventually. The sooner the better. I'll contact you tomorrow."

"Yes, Grandfather. Sleep well."

"Not until Erin is trained and safe."

"Jayde," Talon reminded him. "From what I saw of her tonight, Jayde will not take this lightly."

* * * *

Corwyn stared at Colin in shock. "Gunther Lord Crossbearer? At this hour? Why?"

"I don't know, but he swears it's urgent."

"Probably wants to ask the Stone lord something," Corwyn grumbled. He didn't mind being the Stone lord, but everyone expected him to be at their beck and call twenty-four-seven for answers to every question they thought the Stone could answer.

As far as Corwyn was concerned, the Stone was all but useless. It was an insult to place him in charge of the damned thing after the fiasco it arranged with Erin's birth, but his mark of Syth made it crystal clear that it was to be Corwyn's place after Carrick died. Still, it couldn't—or more likely wouldn't—tell him anything of use in locating his daughter after all these years. It wouldn't even tell Corwyn if Erin was dead or alive.

Corwyn sighed. He'd lost his wife and daughter because of an amused stone entity and a bunch of bone-headed lords who couldn't see past their own greed. He still remembered their refusal of aid in startling detail. Gunther had denied him support first. Then Carrick, followed by Jason.

Kord had been livid. If he hadn't been bound by duty to Jason, he would have fought with Corwyn alone against the entire beast army. Corwyn still owed his friend for admitting his loyalty at the airport as they left Maher range. He was sure Jason made Kord pay for his show of support later.

"I'll take it," Corwyn decided. Like it or not, he had a duty. If Gunther needed something from the Stone, he had to provide it. He moved to the desk and scooped the receiver to his ear. *But I don't have to like it!* "It's late, Gunther. What's so important?"

"Sit down, Corwyn," Gunther countered quietly.

"What are you up to old man? I am in no mood for your games," he warned.

"I said, sit down," he barked, seemingly rattled.

Corwyn furrowed his brow and sank into the leather chair behind him. "I'm sitting, Gunther. Tell me, but this better be important."

His voice softened to a near-plea. "You have my vow, Corwyn. I will make every wrong I've ever done you right. Just hear me out."

Corwyn rolled his eyes. *Yeah, right. Know any bridges for sale?*

"Does the name Jayde Marie Albright mean anything at all to you?" Gunther continued.

"No. Should it?"

"It's Erin's name, Corwyn. Your daughter is alive and under my grandson's personal protection."

Corwyn felt it hard to breathe. His head spun lightly, and he almost laughed that had he not sat down at Gunther's direction, he would surely have ended up on the floor at that statement. Still, his mind argued that such a thing couldn't be true. It couldn't fall to him so neatly, so cleanly, and without the fight to find her he'd waged all these years. "You're sure?" he asked in disbelief.

"She's wearing your personal seal, but she had no blessing. She's the right age and has the right coloring. And...Talon said the blessing was—unusual. Who else could she be, Corwyn?"

"You let him bless her?" Corwyn raged. His mind searched for clarity. Why would he protest that? She had to be protected. It was no longer a matter of freeing her first.

"I ordered it. The amulet alone wasn't enough."

"You can't be sure of that." Was it that she should be protected by Corwyn and no one else that bothered him so badly? Corwyn shook his head at that thought. The houses had their wish. Now, they all had to protect her, but Hunter most of all.

"We're sure. Talon destroyed a high-level named Grelden on site. He said the amulet was little more than an annoyance to the beast without the blessing."

"The beast laid hands on her?" Corwyn's heart beat frantically in the memory of Anna beneath Veriel. *Not my daughter. Please, not that.*

"Talon stopped him. Grelden knocked her unconscious. He struck her when he felt the amulet's meager power."

"Tell me where, Gunther. I'm coming immediately."

"No. Give it time, Corwyn. We don't know if she was targeted or if it was a chance encounter. Either way, they may have realized who she is now. If you make a move to come to her, they'll follow you in. They'll be watching for you to move."

"I have to come. Who'll protect her?"

"Talon will. For now, there's no safer way. Give it a week or two. Let the fervor die down. Then, come to her. At least, Talon will have the worst of it. He has to convince her of the truth. If you go now, she may never turn to you."

"I'll try, but you will keep me informed." Not going now that he knew where she was might well drive him insane in the meantime, but if it was the only way to keep her safe, he'd have to try.

"Daily, if you wish. I've told Talon to start her training when she's willing."

"Good. Tell him he has my gratitude, but if she's injured in his care, not even you will stand in my way," Corwyn warned.

"If she's injured, it will be because Talon has given his life," Gunther assured him.

"Tomorrow, old man. I will have an update

tomorrow, or I'll be on your doorstep before the following dawn."

Corwyn hung up the phone and stared at the antique piece in shock, memorizing the lines of the wood grain and the brass fittings as a means to order his scattered mind.

Erin was alive. After all these years, she was half a continent away with a past he had no knowledge of. Worse, she was past the change and ripe to Veriel's lecherous plans for her.

She was protected by an unknown quantity—a child Corwyn hadn't seen since he was a boy of seven, blessed by him, and about to be trained by him. Trained by Crossbearers— Corwyn would have to inform Gunther about the boundaries they would have with her. Erin wasn't Cross, and she would not be trained as Crossbearers typically trained.

Corwyn's hands were still tied in so many ways. He glanced at his hands, lying on his desk, and fingered the longer of the two scars on his left palm. Erin's freeing scar had always tortured him. It was a constant reminder of Corwyn's failure and of his loss. Erin and Anna were both lost to him, but now he had found Erin again as he'd always promised Anna in his mind he would do.

He smiled grimly. *Too late! Oh, Anna, I found her too late.* Corwyn dropped his head into his hands. He should be happy that he had his daughter again, stranger or not, but finding her could well destroy her.

"What was all that?" Colin demanded, reinforcing the gloom taking hold of his heart.

"Erin is alive. She's in Gunther's care." *The first to deny me the aid that cost me her? How could she be given to him? Of any man alive, he deserves to be her savior least.*

"When are we leaving?"

"We're not. Not until they've prepared her for what she's facing."

"You trust the Crossbearers to protect her?" Colin's face was a mask of something between terror and dismay.

"For now." *Not for long.* "Gunther is afraid they'll follow me in. I'll give them a little time and then—" He sighed deeply.

"You'll bring her home, of course."

"I'll meet my daughter. I'll find out what her wants and needs are."

"She *needs* not to be made into their whore, Corwyn. You know they'll try."

"But, she has choices in that. I'm going to find out what those choices are."

"Are you crazy?"

"Colin, do you know what her name is?"

"Of course I do. Erin Allison Hunter."

"No, she *was* Erin Allison Hunter. Now, she's Jayde Marie Albright. As much as I would love to order her life for her, she isn't mine to yank around anymore.

"I've had years to consider what it would be like to find her. Until she turned fifteen, I dreamed of completing the ceremony and bringing her home with us. After that, I had to face the truth that finding her meant her entire life would become a living nightmare for her. Whatever peace she has will be a miracle. She deserves whatever miracles I can give her."

Chapter Nineteen

May 13ᵗʰ, 2002

Jayde stretched stiffly, her mind mired in cotton batting. *How did I get to bed?*

She remembered finishing up at the computer lab and heading back to her apartment. It was late—eleven or so. She'd gotten sidetracked on a new program and lost track of time. The path was well guarded, so Jayde hadn't been worried about the walk to the bus stop.

It's typically well guarded, anyway. The man in the black turtleneck— Yes, a man had grabbed her, and Jayde had punched him. Her punch should have done something, but her hand ached from it while it'd had no effect on him. She had panicked, then.

Maybe I should have listened to that nagging voice that told me not to go that way instead of ignoring it. Well, arguing that would get her nowhere. How was she supposed to know she'd meet Mr. Psycho?

Her cheek gave a twinge as she ground her teeth.

He hit me, didn't he? Yes, he had. Jayde had never known someone could hit that hard.

Or that fast. Normally, Jayde could see everything coming at her, and her reaction time was one of the fastest her instructors had ever encountered. It hadn't helped this time. She'd barely tensed her muscles to move again before he'd knocked her flat.

The last thing Jayde remembered was the vision of the dark-haired man coming to her rescue, taking her attacker down and leaning over her.

Did he kiss me? Jayde smiled at the strange dreams her mind had concocted. Was she sick that she was coming up with such outlandish half memories?

Who am I kidding? Jayde hadn't been sick in well over a decade...which meant she was seriously overdue, but she didn't feel sick. She vaguely remembered the last time she was sick; it was a sensation that was impossible to mistake.

"What a dream," she whispered, stretching again. Still, the dark-haired man was someone she wouldn't mind meeting under other circumstances.

How did I get to bed?

She froze as her outstretched hand contacted metal above her head. Jayde squinted to look at it in the dim light. A metal headboard? This wasn't her polished wood sleigh bed. This wasn't her apartment.

Jayde scrambled to her knees and took in her surroundings. She was in what appeared to be a cabin, rustic but comfortable.

She took several deep breaths and tried to evaluate her situation. She wasn't tied up. Either her host expected her to stay willingly, or he thought she had nowhere to run. She was still dressed. That was a good sign.

She stepped off the bed quietly and pulled her shoes on before padding out into the main room. The sun was still a gray line on the horizon. If Jayde could sneak out now, she had a fighting chance.

She stared at the man on the couch in confusion. He was the man who came to her rescue.

Or did he? Were they in this together? If so, there was another one around here somewhere. That would be the red-haired man with the piercing, gray eyes. Jayde shuddered as she remembered how cold and predatory those eyes were.

Her gaze settled on the sheathed knife. A weapon couldn't hurt, though knives weren't her usual thing, she argued. It was long and looked heavy, but it was the only thing in sight.

Jayde bit her lip and looked at the sleeping man again; then she started edging it out of its sheath. When it was in her hand, she crept toward the door. The voice from behind her startled Jayde so much that she almost lost her grip on the knife.

"Put the weapon back, and sit down, Jayde."

His voice was rough and rich, and she stopped cold with her eyes locked on the door, so close to escape and so far with him behind her. She spun around with the knife out in front of her.

The man was sitting up and watching her, apparently amused. His dark hair was tousled and curled at the base of his neck. A shadow of a beard roughened his cheeks under dark eyes that glittered with the laughter that seemed just below the surface.

Is he mocking me?

He was lean and muscular, and the thick mat of hair on his chest disappeared into the top of his jeans.

No need to think on that too much!

Jayde could make out several scars on his arms and broad shoulders. This man was no wimp, and she had no doubts that he was powerful. She had no intention of testing just how powerful he was unnecessarily, but she still had to get out of here.

Jayde backed toward the door with the knife out as a warning.

"Where are you going, Jayde? We're in the middle of nowhere and we have to talk."

His voice was firm but low, almost calming. Did

she need calming? She almost laughed at that.

Jayde considered his words. She had surmised as much. She glanced through the window and saw the car on the dirt track. "Keys," she demanded. "Give me the keys to the car."

"Or what?" he countered. "Will you use that blade on me? Can you?"

Now, he's mocking me. She was sure of it. But, where was that blinding anger when she needed it most? Taking a holiday, it seemed.

"If it means my freedom, I damn well will. Why did you bring me here?"

The man sighed. "Let's start over."

"Let's not. Give me the keys and let me go."

"I can't," he admitted. "Your father wants you protected. I'm that protection."

"My father is dead," she growled, furious at the lie. "You should have done your homework better before you grabbed me."

Jayde bit back tears. At least if she did die here, no one would miss her except Terry. It would have killed her parents to find her missing this way.

"Your adoptive father may be dead. I'll admit that I don't know a thing about the family that raised you and haven't had the chance to check it either, but your father is alive and well."

"No. No one knows who my real parents are. I was abandoned."

"You were taken away for your own safety, and something went terribly wrong. Please, let me explain. My name is Talon Cross."

"I don't want to know your name," she shouted, her panic rising. If he told her his name, he couldn't let her go. "I don't know what game you're playing, but I don't like it. Give me the keys." Jayde backed another step toward the door. *The hell with the keys. I'll walk out rather than stay here.*

The man stood and faced her fully, keeping her pinned in his sights. Jayde shivered at that though she found it less than threatening.

"Please, let me show you something," he requested, his hands up in a calming gesture.

She shook her head.

"You wear an amulet."

Jayde's eyes widened then narrowed. He could have found that while she was unconscious, she reminded herself. "My medallion?"

He nodded. "It was left with you when...when you were lost. You should always wear it."

"Why?" she demanded. "It's bugged?"

"Call it a good luck charm. It belonged to your mother. She gave it to you before she died, the night you were born."

"And abandoned."

"Sent away," he corrected her.

"Away from whom? My father?"

He shook his head again. "Your father's enemies. You met one last night. You remember Mr. Happy with the mean backhand, don't you?"

Jayde stretched her jaw experimentally. It wasn't nearly as bad as she'd expected. It never was, she supposed. "Why should I believe any of this?"

"If you give me a chance, I'll show you why."

"I don't think so." *Not within striking distance, precious.* "I want to go back to school, back home to my life."

"Mr. Happy has friends who are looking for you or soon will be," he cautioned, taking another step toward her.

"I can't stay here. I have nothing." Jayde backed off another step, keeping him out of striking distance.

"I'll arrange for what you need...anything you need. Just—"

"I'm *not* staying. I'm leaving, with or without those keys." She started backing toward the door again.

The man—*Talon*, she reminded herself—threw up his hands. He walked toward her purposefully, grumbling out his response. "Enough of this. I've tried being nice."

The words chilled her. Talon had reached his breaking point, and a brown belt and a knife suddenly seemed like a pittance next to the brute strength coming for her. Jayde sliced the knife in an arc between them, and Talon jumped back in surprise.

"I told you I'll use it," she shouted. "Don't come near me." Jayde forced her hands not to shake.

"That wasn't bad," he mused. "Teaching you is going to be easier than I thought."

"Teaching me what?" she asked suspiciously.

Talon moved abruptly. Like the man the night before, he was almost too fast to track. By the time Jayde started her swing, his hand was locked around her wrist. He yanked the knife away from her with his free hand and tossed it back onto the couch.

"Part of my job is teaching you the right way to use that weapon." Talon released her wrist but stayed close.

Jayde was suddenly aware of how tall and broad he was—at least six feet four, she guessed. He seemed to dwarf her, overpowering her with his presence and the aura of his strength.

"Then, give it back and let me take another shot at it," she managed in a voice that could pass for sarcastic.

Talon smiled and shook his head, his Adam's apple bobbing in silent laughter, as if she was a child who'd told a really bad joke. "I don't think so. Not until you calm down. Now, if you'll come with me," he invited.

"I don't think so," she mimicked sweetly as she brought her foot down hard on Talon's bare instep, brought her hand up into his jaw, and shoved him backward with all her weight. The move should incapacitate him, she knew, but Jayde wasn't stupid enough to bank her life on it. She flipped the lock as he crashed to the floor and launched through the door toward the trees.

She didn't make it far. Jayde was only halfway across the open area, when Talon tackled her. She beat at him and tried to push him off, but in the end, he had her pinned beneath him with her wrists locked in his hands. Jayde seethed that he wasn't even breathing hard for all her struggling. He was simply faster and stronger than she was.

And better trained.

"Lesson two, Jayde. That doesn't work. Don't try it again."

"Get off me," she ordered, trying to fight back tears at how easily she'd been overpowered.

"Let's get a few things straight first. You aren't in charge here. I am, until Corwyn arrives; then he is. You are staying here, whether you like it or not. You can stay comfortably or you can stay tied to the bed.

Corwyn doesn't care how you stay as long as you stay. Which is it?"

"Who is Corwyn?" she demanded.

"Corwyn Hunter is your father."

"Who am I?"

"Jayde Marie Albright," he answered sheepishly.

No. He thinks I'm testing him. Dammit! "No. Did they name me? Did anyone—" Her voice broke, and Jayde swallowed before she started again. "Did anyone bother to give me a name?"

"Erin," he whispered. "Your name was Erin. Please, let me show you what I've been trying to show you."

She nodded. "Show me. Prove to me that I should trust you."

Talon eased off her, obviously watching for some sign that she would strike at him, but Jayde was too worn to try him again.

He helped her up and looked at her wrists uncertainly. His hands, still circling them, caressed her skin. She took a deep breath, trying to clear the lightheadedness that assaulted her at the move.

"No more escape attempts. Promise me."

Jayde looked away at the seemingly endless trees then met his eyes in resignation. "For now," she agreed, "but I want that proof. If I'm not convinced, all bets are off."

Talon nodded and drew an arm around her to lead her into the cabin. Jayde had to remind herself not to sink into his chest for support. She would not depend on him. She couldn't if she was ever going to get out of here.

He led her to a desk at the far end of the main room and pulled a scrapbook out of one of the deep drawers. Jayde eyed the other volumes inside. They were all old hand-bound leather books, the type she loved to find and translate. Maybe she'd get a look at them at a time when Talon wasn't around. She sobered. If he ever left her alone—

"What is this?" she asked, turning her attention back to the scrapbook on the desk.

He blushed. "The current houses."

"The what?"

"Story for another time. Let's take one step at a time, okay?"

Jayde nodded. "Okay. Give me proof," she invited.

Talon flipped the book to the first page. "This is my family. Gunther is my grandfather, Piers is my father, and me." He pointed out the three men in the pictures. Jayde noted that he skipped over several other people, and she wondered who they were.

"What's this?" She pointed to a rough drawing of a tipped cross with the word *Kreuzträger* beneath it at the top corner of the page.

"Crossbearer. It's my family crest."

"So, what does this prove?"

"This page? Nothing," he admitted. Talon flipped several pages back. "This one."

Her eyes shot to the crest, and she fumbled her medallion out from under her sweater. Jayde didn't really need to. She knew the crest anywhere. "Almost the same," she mused. She ran her hand over the picture in the book. "*Jäger*—Hunter. Corwyn Hunter, you said...his name..."

"It's just missing the wolf head at the top," Talon confirmed for her. "Only you have that on yours."

"Why?"

"It means you're of the lord's household. You have his personal seal, not just a general Hunter seal given to any protected. Only the wife and children of Lord Hunter wear that seal—or a very important protected, but that doesn't happen often. Corwyn is the Lord Hunter. I'm sure he had an amulet made for you, but your mother gave you hers."

"Why? How did she die? In childbirth?"

Talon darkened considerably. "No. She died trying to protect you from your father's enemies, trying to keep you hidden until Colin and Stephen could find you. They never did."

"Colin and Stephen? Who are they?"

Talon pointed out two men in one of the pictures. "They're your uncles, Corwyn's brothers."

"Where was Corwyn while this was happening?" she demanded. "He should have been protecting us, shouldn't he?" Her anger at it was bordering on uncontrollable. Her mother died at the hands of his enemies while he was nowhere to be found? Why would she want a father like that?

"Overpowered. He tried to protect you both, but he was outnumbered, outmaneuvered." Talon sighed. "Are you convinced?"

"It's a good start. Who are these other people?"

"Stephen's wife Gabrielle and Colin's wife Jannelle. Their children." He pointed to the picture at the top, an older photo. "These are your parents, Corwyn and Anna."

"She was very beautiful."

Jayde touched the picture, drawing her fingers over the image of her mother. Even in the faded photo, she could see the glitter in the woman's green eyes as her hands rested over her very pregnant belly.

Corwyn was smiling behind a heavy beard, but otherwise his looks were typical of the other men in the pictures. He was tall and broad with dark hair and eyes. He towered over her mother, wrapped her in his arms like a child and rested his large hands half over hers.

Her heart sank. Jayde had been wanted. She had been very wanted in this family. *No. Erin had been wanted.* Jayde pushed that thought away.

"Yes, she was," Talon decided. "You favor her quite a bit, you know. You have your father's coloring, of course, but otherwise, you might be sisters."

Jayde blushed deeply. "Was that a compliment?"

"It's a fact. Take it how you will." Talon stood and stretched. "I need a shower before I cook breakfast. I'll ask you bluntly. Do I need to restrain you, or will you stay here while I do that?"

She startled. He actually trusted her after she attacked him and tried to run? Or was Talon just confident that he could force her back, if she broke her word?

"I'll stay for now. I still have a lot of questions. I suppose I should stay until I get the answers, at least."

Talon smiled, and she looked away, swallowing a lump in her throat. Even with that rugged stubble, he was gorgeous. Too bad Jayde hadn't met him under other circumstances. This was one man she wouldn't consider a loser on sight. Too bad she couldn't be sure he wasn't actually an enemy.

His voice rumbled from someplace deep in his chest. "I'll hold you to that promise. But, if you cross me, I will tie you. Don't make me do that, Jayde."

"I know you will, Talon. I know." And, Jayde did know. *So much for trust.* He knew she had nowhere to go. If Jayde left, Talon would hunt her down and make sure she couldn't run from him again.

Chapter Twenty

Talon stepped under the hot spray of the shower and willed his body to unwind.

Being with Jayde was pure torture. He had never responded this fiercely to a woman before, and his body picked now to turn traitor? Now, with a woman he could never have? Even if she was willing, Corwyn would never permit his daughter—*the* Blutjagdfrau *no less!*—to take Talon as her own. A house lord, next in line to a house, but never the youngest member of a dying house. She was too important to waste on such a man, wasn't she?

When Talon had plucked his weapon from her hand, he couldn't back away. Being next to Jayde was exhilarating. He had been so intent on her and his reactions to her that Talon never saw her strike. He grimaced at the lesson Gunther would deal him if the old lord knew that. Talon left that thought behind as quickly as he could.

Subduing Jayde had been relatively easy, since she was untrained. Reigning in his natural inclinations and keeping her from feeling his fierce state of arousal had been much more difficult. Thankfully, she hadn't been looking that direction.

At least not after her perusal of me in the main room. The one that left him in the state he found himself—for the first time in his life—unable to control. If the rest of Jayde's time with him was anything like this, Talon might have to take to wearing his shirttails untucked to hide what seemed to be a constant need in him.

Wrapping his arm around her as he walked her in had been a moment of weakness for him, and skirting the edges of telling her how enchanting she was as she looked at the album had left him shaken.

This was not something he could enter into. Corwyn's right to his life if Talon gave into this madness aside, if he printed on Jayde and she left, he would be in agony—or dead. As fast as he was falling, dead would be a very real possibility.

Talon had to admit it. He was in over his head. He only prayed Corwyn would come for her quickly and take Jayde far away. Talon was the last of the Crossbearers. He had to take a wife and produce children. If Jayde stayed much longer, he would want no one else. He was sure of that.

He dried off quickly and pulled on fresh clothes from the bag he carried in the trunk of his car. Talon heard his cell phone ringing as he passed into the bedroom and opened the connection. "Yes, Grandfather?" he answered without looking at the caller ID. After all, chances were slim that it was anyone else.

"Is all well?" he asked urgently, slipping into the formal mode of speech he'd no doubt had to use when conferring with the other lords.

"Yes. Jayde wants answers, and she's content to stay put for now. But not forever. I may have to keep her in my custody by force soon."

"You've not had to use force yet?" the older man asked in disbelief. "If she lacks a fighter's spirit, we have serious problems."

"On the contrary, Grandfather. So far this morning, I have been attacked with my own blade, physically assaulted, and had to run her down and wrestle her to the ground. She has the temperament of a *Blutjagdfrau.*"

Gunther laughed in amusement. "Has she wounded you?"

"You must be kidding. I said Jayde was determined, not that she was highly trained. Had she been trained, she would be a formidable opponent, though. We're simply coming to terms with what foolishness I will or will not accept. Nothing more."

"You think she'll be easy to train?"

"It won't be difficult, if she's willing. I'd wager *nothing* is simple, if she isn't."

"She's handling this well?"

"Better than I'd anticipated, though I am glad I called you for more details last night. Without them, I would have nothing of interest to her to hold her willingly."

"Where is she, now?"

"In the main room while I clean up and dress."

"You left her alone? You did bind her, correct?"

"No, I did not."

"She'll run," Gunther replied in a panic. "You'll have to track her. If you lose her—"

"She won't. I have her word, and I believe her. Jayde does what she says she will, whether that's attacking me if I approach or staying put. She has honor."

Gunther grunted in disapproval. Overall, that was nothing new. His grandfather approved of few people and fewer actions. Talon could almost track his unspoken belief that Jayde had no honor because she hadn't been raised in their ways and had it driven into her by force.

"When will Corwyn come for her?" Talon asked, breaking the silence.

"When it's safe. We don't wish to lead the beasts to her. It may be several weeks until we're certain."

His heart sank. Weeks? Even a few days with Jayde would be too much.

"Is there a problem, boy?" he demanded.

"No, my lord. No problem at all." Talon ground his teeth at the lie. He couldn't admit this failing. A strong Warrior could control his blood better than this. Talon would have to do so. He wasn't a beast and never would be.

"Good. Corwyn has demanded daily updates in exchange for our trespasses, so I'll be checking in often. When it's safe for me to come there, what do you need?"

Talon nodded. The unspoken command not to leave her for an instant, even to restock, was evident in that question. "Things for Jayde. She has nothing but the clothes on her back. I'll have to improvise until then. Fresh supplies. The canned and dry rations will get old very quickly. Training gear for Jayde. My belts will be too long for her, but a boy's will do fairly well."

"I'll arrange it in the next few days. Corwyn sends you his gratitude."

"Knowing the Lord Hunter and this situation, that came with a warning," Talon guessed.

"If Erin is injured or taken, it will mean your life. I assured him that it would be your life to the beasts and not forfeit to him."

"It will. I'll give you Jayde's sizes this evening. I have to check on her now. Goodbye, Grandfather."

Talon closed the connection and sighed raggedly. He pulled on his boots and headed into the main room. "What do you say to some breakfast?" he invited, smiling at the blade Jayde had carefully sheathed.

The main room was empty. Talon's smile disappeared as he checked the kitchen and pantry.

He pulled his weapons belt on and cursed solidly. *Grandfather was right. She has no honor.* Jayde hadn't been taught it.

Talon may not be able to drill honor into her in a few weeks, but he'd give her another lesson—fear. Jayde would regret breaking her word to him so much that she would think twice before doing it again. Visions of her tied down to the bed as he'd threatened had him hard again; Talon pushed them away, his *Blutjagd* burning in a mixture of annoyance with himself and anger with her.

He pushed the front door open more forcefully than was necessary and strode out onto the porch, scanning his eyes around for any sign of her flight from him.

He stopped cold, his eyes blinking in disbelief in the gloom of the overcast morning. Jayde was sitting between several large trees that afforded even more block of the almost non-existent sunlight, her legs folded under her...reading. Talon reigned in his frustration. She needed education.

Talon crossed to her slowly, gauging her reaction, but she had none. Jayde was sitting in a vulnerable position, unaware of the danger she opened herself to, completely and blissfully oblivious. It was sloppy, and it could get her killed.

Finally, he stopped a few yards away. "Jayde," he barked.

She snapped her head up, and he was surprised to see fear in her eyes. Talon hadn't even seen fear when she'd awoken to find herself kidnapped to an unknown place by a strange man. Seeing fear in Jayde's eyes wounded him somehow, in some odd way he couldn't name. He wanted to soothe her.

Jayde pushed to her feet abruptly with the book locked to her chest, backing away from his outstretched hands as he advanced on her. Talon sucked in his breath as he got a better look at what she was reading. He put his hands up in a calming gesture, hoping that her fear was of him and not the book.

Like all the sacred texts the Cross family owned, this one was written in the old languages. If Talon remembered correctly, the *First Book of Texts* at this cabin was written in German, but it could be in French, Italian or Gaelic just as easily. If it was in the language of the ancients, it would be in a fire safe at the manor house or the one housed in the Stone room every range kept in case the Stone fell to their care.

Talon said a prayer to the old gods that she couldn't read German. It was an unusual language for an American to learn. Maybe Jayde was just looking at the illuminations. He cringed. They were bad enough.

He surveyed her as he inched closer. Her eyes were wide, and she was shaking. Talon cursed under his breath. Jayde understood it, all right. She understood much more than he'd planned to tell her in the next few days. He had wanted to ease her into the discovery.

"It's okay, Jayde," he soothed her. "I understand. It's a lot to swallow all at once."

"This is my fate?" she whispered. "I'm this

Blutjagdfrau?" Her eyes pleaded with him to deny it.

Her pronunciation was slightly off, but Talon nodded. *Damn! She speaks German.* How much had she read in the half hour he was gone from her? How much did she understand?

"I'm supposed to do this? To be some vampire's egg donor? I'd rather die first." She threw the book at him and tried to run for the perceived safety of the trees.

Talon let the precious book fall and drew her back effortlessly. She turned on him and grasped at his weapon, pulling back to unsheathe it. He pried her fingers from it when it had barely moved. This time, Jayde didn't plan using it against him. There was no doubt what she intended. He wrapped his arms around her and crushed Jayde to his chest, reducing her fight for freedom to twists of her body against his.

"Let me go," she sobbed. "I don't want this life. I don't want to be used that way."

"You won't," Talon assured her. "It's my place to make sure you aren't, until Corwyn arrives to take you home. I swore to give my life in defense of that one promise."

"Help me," she begged.

"I will. I'll teach you to protect yourself, and I'll protect you. I'll tell you whatever you want to know. Trust me. I won't fail you."

"The book talks about a *Zeremonie der Freiheit...*" Jayde's breathing hitched, and she met his eyes, hopeful for something he couldn't give her.

"I'm sorry. Corwyn was in the middle of it when he was interrupted, when they attacked. It's too late for that."

"Why?" she demanded miserably.

Talon sighed. She'd obviously skimmed through the section without reading it carefully. "You're past the change," he whispered.

"What change?"

"Come inside. I'll explain everything while I make you something to eat."

"I'm not hungry."

He smiled. That was pure stubbornness. She had recovered some of her composure, though not much.

"Come eat. You'll get sick if you don't. When the sun is high, we'll come out again. I promise that."

"But never at night," she guessed.

"No. Or even at twilight or dawn. We'll only come out when the sun is high, and you will stay with me when it is this darkly overcast."

"But, it's day," she protested.

"High-level beasts and elders can take a small amount of weakened sunlight. Enough to kill, if they must. We have to be careful. Come eat, and I'll answer your questions."

She nodded uncertainly, locking the book he handed her in her arms like a shield. Talon wrapped her under his left arm, carefully covering the hilt of his weapon with his right, unwilling to take the chance of her grabbing for it again. Inside, he seated her at the table and removed the book from her stiff fingers.

"We only have canned and dried foods for now, but supplies will be brought out to us. What would you like?"

Jayde shook her head sadly and remained silent.

Talon moved to the pantry. "We have soups, tuna, stew, pork and—"

"Beef stew," she interrupted him. "Please," she

added quietly.

"Good choice. I have some dried goods: crackers, breadsticks, and cookies—"

"Breadsticks."

"Coffee, tea, soda, or water?"

"Any caffeine-free soda?" she asked hopefully.

"Only rootbeer."

"Okay."

He loaded his arms with her choices and closed the cold pantry door. Talon set a rootbeer in front of her and started opening the large can of stew. Thankfully, he heard her open the can of soda and take a drink. At least, he wouldn't have to find a way to force Jayde to eat.

"What change?" she asked again. "You mean puberty? The ability to—"

He glanced over his shoulder and grimaced at the sick tinge of gray in her face. "No. You probably reached that change at twelve or thirteen."

"Eleven," she offered.

"The *Fluch*— The curse changes us at sixteen. We begin our training a year earlier, when the first signs appear. At sixteen, after the final stage of the change, our training intensifies as we accept our curse."

"Fighting them is your curse?" she guessed.

"Our curse. All the houses. Now that you've passed change, it's yours, too. It's too late to free you."

"I have to fight them?" Jayde groaned.

Talon shook his head. "Only to save yourself," he assured her. "You are *Jäger geboren* and not freed, but you will never be a Night Warrior. No one would risk you that way."

"*Jäger*— Hunter— I'm sorry. I'm Hunter born?

What does that mean?"

"You're a woman of house Hunter. Or a Warrior of house Hunter..." Talon paused as he considered that. What rights did Jayde have? He would have to treat her like a freed female until he knew for sure. He shook his head in annoyance. "I've never had to explain this before."

"If you're saying I belong to them, you're wrong."

Her voice was suddenly strong and sure, and a slight edge of *Blutjagd* burned in her. Talon was glad to hear it though he disagreed with her comment. Jayde had no choice in the matter.

She furrowed her brow. "I know what happens if—" Jayde motioned to the book between them. "What happens if I have children with one of you? Or a human man? I could do that, right? I mean, being *Blutjagdfrau* doesn't mean I can't have children with a human man. Right?"

Talon sucked in his breath. "You could choose a human, I suppose. That's how the Warriors marry...or have until you came along. You would have to grant him your protection and fight for him against the beasts. Our wives usually seek that, but I'm not so sure a man would—from a woman."

"Why?"

He looked at her in confusion.

"Why do they seek it?" she qualified.

Talon smiled crookedly. "Being cursed doesn't leave much time for a social life. The women we marry are typically saved from a beast while we hunt. They know exactly what they're seeking protection from."

"That's how my parents met?"

He nodded. "Corwyn saved Anna from an elder

named Veriel."

"So, since I won't hunt, I won't have the opportunity to meet human men. Is that it?"

"Actually, since your only freedom will be during the day—probably with a Warrior escort, you'll have the chance to meet human men. But, any man you choose will become a target at nightfall, and you won't be able to help him before he's married to you...while he's living apart from you, I mean."

"And?" she prodded, perceiving more to the story.

Talon sighed. She wasn't going to like this. "Corwyn will—discourage it highly," he admitted.

"He'll forbid me to marry? Why?"

"Only a human."

"He wants me to marry one of you. Why?"

Talon shrugged. "I can't say for sure what Corwyn wants. Since we've failed to keep you from becoming the blood Warrior— This is all new, Jayde. It's untried ground."

"What about children I have with one of you?" she interrupted him.

"According to the texts, children with us will mean the end for them just as children with them would mean catastrophe for the world."

He startled as Jayde launched to her feet and followed her as she bolted. This time, Talon caught her in the front room; he wrestled her down again.

"Stop," he ordered. "Stop this."

Jayde redoubled her efforts and almost succeeded in pushing him off. "I won't be used, Talon," she growled. "Not by their side and not by yours. No one is going to bed me unless I want to be bedded."

Talon pinned her beneath him and ground his

teeth against his instant arousal. He shifted away once he had her immobilized, shaking lightly. Jayde had to stop this incessant running. Every time Talon had to do this, it was harder for him to control his body's reaction to her.

"They won't," he assured her. "All of our men are sworn to keep the beasts from taking you. None of our kind would take an unwilling woman, not even you. As advantageous as it would be, no one will force you to bear children for us. We can't."

"Then I can choose who I want?" she asked suspiciously.

"You are *Jäger geboren*. You must secure your father's permission first."

"And if he disagrees?" she prodded. Oh, but Jayde did like to ask what he didn't want to answer.

"The man wouldn't dare cross the Lord Hunter. Not even his own house would protect him, if he did."

Talon shivered at the thought, grasping on the rules of sanction beaten into him since he was a young training pup. It was the only thing stopping him now, and that realization shook him. Talon was riding the edges of control and propriety.

"The Warrior who can't control his curse is no better than a beast, and it is the lord's right to destroy him as he would any other beast. If the Warrior who has committed the wrong raises a hand to the lord, it is the lord's duty to destroy him. It's what protects humans from our kind. It is the law that makes us safe to walk among humans. We have a duty. That is why we won't take an unwilling woman. Our sanctions say it."

Jayde stifled a sob. "So, my choice means

nothing?"

"If Corwyn values it, it does. Your father wouldn't deny you unless he felt he had good cause."

Like a union he sees as a weak alliance, his mind taunted him. Would Corwyn deny her then?

She isn't offering!

"So, I'm a prize," she decided, her arms relaxing under his hold in something resembling defeat. "If the great Lord Hunter and I come to an agreement, some lucky man can have me. If not, I'm doomed to be alone and unhappy, because my body isn't my own to give. I can't even offer, can I?"

Talon's groin tightened painfully in response, and he steeled his nerves. "You can offer, but only a fool would proceed without Corwyn's say, no matter how badly he may want to."

She looked at him with piercing eyes that she undoubtedly inherited from her father. Jayde ran her thigh up between his parted legs gently, prompting a shiver of anticipation from him. Her eyes widened as she brushed by his erection, and Talon bit back a groan.

"You want to," she mused.

"Of course," he retorted, angry with himself for his lack of self-control. If she complained to Gunther—or to Corwyn, his life was forfeit. "I'd have to be dead not to," he spat before he could reign in his tongue. *Gods, but that was the truth.*

Her look of amazement faded into hopelessness. "Because I'm the *Blutjagdfrau,* and the great Warriors could be your children?" she accused.

His shock at her assumption dissolved into anger. "Never. I want you because I've wanted you since the first time I laid eyes on you—before I knew who you were." Talon pushed away from her then lifted her to her feet. "Go in the kitchen before the stew burns," he ordered.

Jayde nodded uncertainly and moved back to the table. "Talon?"

"Yes?" he snapped, more annoyed with himself than with her. At least she could claim the rules were new to her. He had no excuse.

"Would my— Would Corwyn agree if it was you I offered?" she managed.

"I don't know," he answered honestly. "I don't know him well enough to answer that. Corwyn is grateful to me for saving you from Grelden, but he will be very picky for you. I'm not a house lord. I probably won't be one for twenty or thirty years, and I'm the last of my line." Talon's heart sped up that she was considering it even as he realized how unlikely it was for Corwyn to agree. "Is that your choice?" He kept his voice as unaffected as he could when he asked.

"I don't know what my choice is, but I know I'd rather give myself to a Warrior willingly to end this than let the beasts use me."

His heart sank. "Then, I would only be a means to an end," he decided.

"No. You wouldn't be that." It was a dismissal.

Talon didn't know what she would see him as, but it wasn't a love match.

* * * *

Jayde tried to normalize her breathing. Talon was right. Reading the old stories caused nightmares—bad ones. She relived her perceptions of the uprising the original elders staged, the escape of the elders from the Stone, and the centuries of fighting that had followed each. Until one side or the other was victorious, the curse would continue as it had for the last fifteen hundred years.

She went to the bathroom and returned to the bedroom, but just the sight of the bed made her uneasy. Instead, Jayde veered off toward the main room and the kitchen beyond. *Cookies.* Talon said there were cookies in the pantry. A midnight snack couldn't hurt, she decided.

She was halfway there when Talon's voice penetrated the darkness to her. "Jayde? Are you all right?" he asked quietly.

"Yes." She cringed. She had answered too quickly, too forcefully.

"What's wrong? Tell me, please."

Jayde shifted her weight and started back toward the bedroom. "Nothing. Never mind."

"Come here," he invited.

She hesitated. Jayde wanted to. Ever since she'd realized Talon wanted her and he'd told her it wasn't for the promise of some fabled children she could give him—

But, it would only get him into trouble with the Lord Hunter. *With my father.* She still couldn't wrap her mind around that concept without unease.

Or worse. If Talon does his duty and refuses me, I don't think I can face him again.

"Come here, Jayde." That time, it was an order.

His voice sent a tremor of pleasure through her. Here in the darkness, it was so easy to pretend that

Talon was calling her for something more than the brotherly talk he was sure to offer before sending Jayde back to her bed, where they were both safe from Corwyn's wrath. God, how she wished that wasn't what he was going to do.

She moved toward the couch on that thought. Jayde could see his outline in the faint moonlight filtering through the trees. She sucked in her breath as Talon's hands closed around her waist and drew her down next to him on the couch. He wrapped his arms around her, pulling her gently to his chest. The smell of him, the feel of his leg touching hers through his jeans and the shirt he'd lent her, the feel of the soft curls on his chest brushing her cheek... It was so easy to imagine something more.

"Tell me," he said again, reminding Jayde why she was really here.

"I just couldn't sleep." She sighed, drinking in the scent of him.

"Nightmares?" Talon ran a hand up her back to play with one of her curls.

"You were right," she admitted.

"Told you."

That spoiled it. It was so older brother of him.

"Talon, there was something I read today..."

"What is it?"

"Am I protected? I mean, I have an amulet, but if my mother gave it to me— I have no blessing. Do I?"

"You're protected," he assured her. "The blessing has been done."

"It's impossible. If Mr. Happy was a vampire— He was, right?"

"A beast," he corrected her. "He was."

"He shouldn't have been able to touch me. Is the book wrong?"

"It's not wrong. You already had your amulet, but that wasn't enough. You have my blessing. I gave it when I was ordered to, before my grandfather told me who you are."

She smiled. "You blessed me?" Jayde liked that idea far more than seemed warranted.

"It needed done. Without it, you were vulnerable to attack. For the same reason, I'll have to start training you with the sacred weapon as soon as possible."

"What's involved in the blessing? The book isn't very specific."

"That book isn't. There are others that are. I invoke our ancient gods and draw on their power to charge the amulet you wear. I pledge my life and the lives of all within my house to defend you." Talon cleared his throat. "And I seal it with a kiss."

Jayde licked her lips, wishing she had been awake for that part. "If I am blessed by your house, I'm yours," she theorized.

"This is unusual, Jayde. You shouldn't have an amulet of one house and the blessing of another. It's only happened one other time in fifteen hundred years that I know of. But, regardless of that, you are still *Jäger geboren*. Technically speaking, you're still Lord Hunter's."

"What if I wasn't?"

Talon sucked in his breath and his hand pressed against her back, bringing her into closer contact. He didn't answer.

"What if I was a Crossbearer? Or free?"

"If you were a Crossbearer, you would be under my

grandfather's rule. If you had been born a Crossbearer, you would have to get the permission of whatever man was your father, like my Aunt Nancy got Gunther's permission to marry even though his father was still Lord Crossbearer at the time. Free? I wish I could free you, but even as a freed woman, you would still need Corwyn's permission to marry, as Nancy did."

"How far does my autonomy stretch?"

"You don't have autonomy." His hand returned to the curl he'd been investigating.

"Wrong word, apparently. What freedoms do I have?"

"I don't understand."

"What exactly does my father control?" Jayde turned, straddling him neatly. She ran her hands over his chest.

His muscles tensed beneath her fingers. Talon placed his hands over hers, stilling them. His heart was racing beneath her palms and his breathing was strangled.

Jayde felt as if she was on fire. Her mind seemed to take a back seat to some mindless craving she needed Talon to satisfy. She shivered. She needed this.

"Please, don't," Talon begged her.

Still, Jayde could feel his fight to control his reactions. He was failing, and she wanted him to fail.

"You can't marry me. You can't make love to me," she murmured, reveling in the demands her body was making. Her body was slick and heated, and the heat washed over every muscle until the aching between her thighs was pulsing through her entire being. It would be so easy to forget the rules. It was so tempting to forget them. Jayde's body demanded to go as far as she could, as far as he would allow.

"You know I can't," Talon moaned. "Don't torture me like this, please."

"Can you kiss me?" she asked. "Is that allowed?" Jayde prayed it was. If she couldn't touch him, she would incinerate. She needed that, at least.

"I shouldn't." His voice was barely a whisper.

"Will Corwyn kill you if you do?"

"No, but—"

Jayde kissed him. Talon moved his hands to cup her face. He teased her lips until she was aching for more then parted them gently with his tongue. Jayde groaned as he sealed his mouth to hers and cupped her head to draw her closer to him.

This was what she wanted—what Jayde had always wanted when she'd sent men packing. She wanted to give herself to a man like this and give him children.

Her mind barely protested the thought. *Of course, children!* Had there ever been any doubt that she would want to give Talon children? The thought disappeared into a mindless need to have him give her those children, to have him with her always.

Talon broke off the kiss and held her slightly away from him, shaking lightly as he did it. "You have to go back to bed," he ordered hoarsely.

"Come with me," she invited, turning her face to nuzzle against his wrist. Jayde needed him to come with her. She couldn't remember why she needed it anymore. She just did.

"I can't."

"Just to hold me. Please." She needed to touch Talon, if nothing else. Jayde needed to feel his skin next to hers and smell his musk mixing with her own.

Talon grasped her hips and pulled her against him. Jayde moaned as the hard length of him, straining against his jeans, touched her through the single layer of his shirt tucked between her thighs. She bit her lip hard, faintly tasting blood.

"I can't," he growled. "For the love of all that's holy, I can't." Talon released her hips. "Please, go to bed, Jayde. If you don't, I'll do something we'll both end up regretting later."

Jayde nodded and lifted herself back to her feet in a sort of daze. What was she doing? What had come over her that she was acting this way? Was this what he meant about controlling the curse? Did it turn you into a sex-crazed maniac?

But, Jayde had been cursed since she was sixteen, and she had never had the least bit of interest in a man until now. She moved toward the bedroom, lost in thought. When the answer came to her, she stilled and forced her breathing to return to an even flow.

"Talon?" she called out softly.

"What?" he snapped.

"If the Lord Hunter agrees, would you marry me?"

"Jayde, please... You can't ask me this." He was tortured by the question. She could hear it in his voice.

"I have to know, Talon. If it's possible, would you?"

He didn't answer.

"I'm asking, Talon. It's my choice. If I have to bear children, I will accept nothing less than what I just felt from you. If Corwyn doesn't agree, there will be no children from me—ever. Now, if it's possible, are you willing?"

"Yes. I hope you know what you're doing," he

breathed.

She didn't, but Jayde wasn't about to confide that to him. All she knew was that no one but Talon would do for her. She was suddenly angry at the restrictions put on her. She was a Warrior...or soon would be. She deserved a Warrior's rights. Jayde had done a little reading about that. She would have to do more.

"If I'm so damned important, I deserve some consideration," she decided hotly. "They won't take me by force, and I'll only agree if I get my own way. As long as I know it's what you want, too..." She let it hang hopefully between them.

"It is, but you have to do something for me."

Jayde felt like she could fly. "Anything." She'd do anything Talon asked as long as she knew he wanted her as much as she wanted him. "What do you need?"

She sobered, remembering how tortured he was when she offered herself to him. It was his life on the line, if she gave in like that again. "I promise I won't make any demands on you that we can't— I'm sorry, Talon. I asked too much." Jayde felt horrible about it now. It wasn't her life on the line. She was too important to kill. Wasn't she?

"Thank you, but I need you to do something else. You have to start your training tomorrow."

"Training? You mean as a Warrior?" she asked in confusion.

"The Lord Hunter will not be impressed if he feels I'm neglecting my duties, for any reason."

"I understand. We'll begin tomorrow."

Chapter Twenty-One

May 16th, 2002

"How do you fight with this damned thing?" Jayde growled in frustration.

"You practice and get used to it," Talon answered patiently.

She swung the weapon, her hand wavering a bit in the arc.

He knocked it from her hand easily. "Hold it tighter," Talon instructed. "Don't be afraid of it."

Jayde glared at him and stretched her hand before retrieving his weapon from the ground. She turned it curved-side-up to show him the gap between her fingers. "Afraid of it, my ass," she spat. "It's too big for my hand. I may not be an expert, but even I can see that." She flicked it back in the dirt and walked away, rubbing her sore hand.

Talon sighed and sheathed his blade. He started after her. "I know it's too big, but until someone brings us supplies, it's all I have for you. Even if you have your own, with a smaller grip, you might have to improvise with whatever is on hand in an emergency. You have to be able to use a man's grip."

She glared at him again and kept walking. Talon knew she was frustrated. After three days, Jayde wasn't getting any better at this, and she was afraid of what the lords would say. Would they separate her from Talon because they believed she needed a teacher who could drill it into her faster?

In addition to that, the lack of fresh food and spare changes of clothes frustrated her. Talon had to admit that canned and dry goods for so long was wearing on him as well, and the clothes— He decided that he didn't need to dwell on that too closely right now.

He followed her into the cabin and stepped around her, as Jayde stopped at the couch. When he returned with the liniment, she eyed him suspiciously.

"What are you up to?" she asked.

Talon grabbed her hand, then grabbed it again and yanked it back roughly when she pulled it from his grasp. "Sit down and be quiet while I do this," he growled, annoyed more with the fact that he found touching her so disconcerting than at her for her frustration with him.

Jayde groaned as he massaged her sore muscles with the liniment, rubbing out each knot and hot spot with his sensitive fingers. Her hand relaxed, and he moved up over her forearm and bicep muscles. She sank into the couch, boneless in her relaxation, as he worked. Her eyes closed, and Talon half expected her to fall asleep.

"Better?" he asked, smiling at her reaction.

"Oh, yeah." Jayde sighed. "Don't suppose you can work that magic on my shoulder? Never mind," she corrected herself immediately.

"Why?"

She looked at him in disbelief, and her meaning sank in slowly.

"Oh. If I promise to be professional about the whole thing?"

"Can you?" She raised an eyebrow to make her point.

Talon sighed. Jayde had him pegged. He was aroused already, and she was still dressed. Still, he prided himself on self-control, and his body's reaction to touching her aside, Talon had a duty to care for her.

"Slip your arm out. I can be professional," he assured her as he moved behind the couch and opened the bottle again. Still, Talon found himself staring just a little too long as she unbuttoned the first three buttons on the shirt he'd lent her and slipped her arm out for him to work on.

They were doing a lot of laundry, trying to keep her in clothes. Since Talon had three full sets of Warrior wear, they were covered for him with oversized button-down shirts to spare for her, if he only wore the black T-shirt every day, but that still left Jayde with only one set of underclothes and one pair of jeans and socks. Those clothes had to be washed every night so that she would have something to wear the next day.

That meant nightly torture for Talon, knowing that the moment her clothes went in the wash, she wore nothing but the long shirt that reached almost to her knees—*my shirt.*

More than once, he'd crossed through the bedroom to the bathroom while Jayde slept and stood, riveted on a leg protruding from beneath the blanket or the swell of a breast pressed against the fabric of a Warrior's shirt.

Why does the fact that the shirt is mine make it more difficult to ignore?

Part of him desperately hoped for more while some rational part of him knew seeing more of her body would be Talon's undoing. Knowing that Jayde was nude beneath his shirt as she straddled him that first night had almost been his end. Anything more— Talon was honest enough to admit that he wouldn't survive long.

He reminded himself to be professional as the peach-colored fabric of her bra was so close to his hand. Talon rubbed liniment into his hands and started kneading her shoulder. "You're off balance when you fight," he commented as he rubbed out the first tight spot, searching for a neutral subject. "That's why you get sore along this line."

"Women perfect balancing the padding nature saddled us with. Changing that balance by adding five pounds of metal to the end of our arm after ten or fifteen years of working on it is a little disconcerting."

Talon ground his teeth. Admiring that padding was going to get him in a damn lot of trouble soon. "Well, we have to figure it out," he decided.

"Yeah. Correct me if I'm wrong, but you men start training at about the same age women are adjusting to our new bodies. If I had trained then—"

"You didn't," he cut her off. "And, it's too late to do it right, now. If we knew where you were at fifteen, we'd've freed you instead of training you."

"If wishes were horses," she muttered.

Talon smiled. He located another knot and reminded himself to be professional. *Who am I kidding!* Sighing, he pushed her bra strap aside, and she jumped slightly.

"Relax. Hands off, okay?" he assured her as he started working on her shoulder again.

Jayde laughed nervously. "You know how I feel. It's your neck on the line here. Like it or not, they won't kill me," she grumbled. "So, I try not to put you in these ridiculous situations."

"Let's change the subject," he decided. Thinking

about the penalty was a definite sinker for both his heart and for what needed sunk. That accomplished, Talon didn't need to dwell on it any longer.

"To what?"

Talon's eyes widened as he glanced at her shoulder again. "What is this on your shoulder?" he asked, staring intently. *Ani—* There was no mistaking the blood mark, if it was a blood mark. He'd never seen one up close.

"My birthmark?" she questioned. "Distinctive, isn't it? The doctors thought it might have been a tattoo at first, but being a neonate and having it? I mean, when would anyone have the time to give me a tattoo? It would have had to heal, and there was no time for that. So, they decided it was just a really strange birthmark and left it at that."

"Ah. I see."

Talon's calm outside masked his terror inside. It was a blood mark. All the Stone-Chosen had one, but no one since the first cursed and Regana first Lady Crossbearer had anything but the mark of Syth for a Stone lord. Regana was the only woman who'd ever had a mark, and it was the mark of Ani—the mother, the birth, the beginning.

Now, Jayde was marked, but everyone assumed that Regana had done her job by giving Pauwel his son, Andris. Was there something unfinished in her life that the Stone would choose another mother? He pushed away that thought with the idea of discussing it with Gunther at a later date.

"Tell me all you know about how you were found," Talon requested, changing the subject again. "The Warriors never understood how you made it out of

Iowa City."

"Iowa City? As in Iowa?" she demanded. "Dammit!"

"What's wrong with that? That's where you disappeared from."

"Needless to say, Mom and Dad discovered me a long-ass way from Iowa. When they found me, they were in New England—western New York, to be exact. I guess newborns sleep a lot. They aren't very hungry, I've heard. Anyway, they loaded bags in the back somewhere in Indiana, and Dad swore up, down, and backward that I wasn't there then. They never retraced his route as far as Iowa."

"Wait! Iowa to New York? That's a long way to carry a baby and not know she's there. They never realized in all that time?"

"Apparently not, until I started squalling. Dad damn near wrecked the car to find me. He was terrified that the bags shifted and landed on me or something, but I was just unhappy. I was soaked through, hungry, and needed to be held.

"For obvious reasons, the search was most intense in the northeastern states. They theorized that I probably wouldn't have slept longer than that, and since Dad said I wasn't there in Indiana—" She sighed.

"They let them keep you?"

"They were a foster family. Or I should say, they had qualified to be one in their state. They couldn't have a child of their own, and it was the quickest route to adoption. So, when they hadn't located my family by the end of my three days in the hospital... Under the circumstances, they were given permission to foster me. They were at the hospital more than most birth parents. They even got a hotel room and refused to continue their trip."

"Hospital? Why? Warrior babies are usually so healthy."

"I was a neonate who got dragged God only knew how far. I was dehydrated. I also had a mild case of jaundice, but with my condition when I got there, they didn't want to take any chances."

"Okay. So, they took you home. Then what?"

"Keeping me until my parents were found was what they were promised. Two years went by with no parents. They were the only parents I ever knew, and it was obvious no one else out there cared enough to try and get me back. By then, they were calling me Jayde."

"Why Jayde?"

"The amulet said *Jäger*." She shrugged. "Who cares. They picked a name. They had that right. I sure's hell had no other identification, so they picked a name that was close to the name on the amulet."

"Is that why you asked if you had a name?" he inquired gently.

"Yeah. What the hell," she grumbled. "First chance I ever had to find out. It was a shock, finding out someone wanted me after all. All my life, I thought I was a throwaway, someone's trash. Turns out I was wrong all that time."

Talon bit back a swell of compassion at the idea of Jayde being someone's trash—of her even thinking it. "So, what happened after two years?"

"The state relinquished parental rights on John and Jane Doe, parents of the now Jayde Marie Albright, and I was adopted by my parents."

"What about your amulet?"

"I found it when I was ten and demanded to start

wearing it."

His hands stilled as the full import of that statement hit him. "Gods alive! You were completely unprotected for all those years."

"I realize that now. Even at ten, I wasn't protected all the time. I took it off to bathe, swim, sleep, in dress clothes, for gym class— Until I read that book of yours, I never wore it all the time. Now I'm terrified to take it off." Jayde furrowed her brow. "Funny... I wanted nothing to do with that family, but the amulet called to me."

Talon nodded as he moved to another spot on her shoulder. "You knew instinctively that you needed it," he guessed.

"No, I mean it literally called to me. It called me to the attic. It called me to the box. It demanded I put it on. This thing magic or something?"

"Sort of. Every amulet is touched to the Stone when it's crafted. It's infused with the Stone's power. So, I guess the Stone could use it somehow."

"Good thing it did. If I hadn't been wearing that amulet when Mr. Happy struck—"

"I never would have known who you were, but he would have. He would have been the luckiest beast on the face of the Earth."

"For all of sixty seconds until you killed him," she corrected.

"Uh. Longer than that. You distracted him, so I had a clean shot at him. It's typically not that easy."

"Let me ask you something. How do the authorities explain the bodies you leave in your wake?"

Talon shrugged. "Never really thought about it. They're stabbing victims, I guess. Dead is dead. Their teeth extend for a kill and the musculature relaxes at death, so it's not so apparent."

The faint feel of a Warrior intruded on his senses, moving closer. *Gunther. At least, we're talking shop. I'll just have to keep it that way.*

"What about sunlight? Don't they—poof or something when the sun comes up? That'd be damned hard to explain, wouldn't it? Our corpse just blew up, Sarge?"

"You watch too many movies. Piercing the heart with a sacred weapon kills them because they can't regenerate fast enough to fix it. Plus, it immobilizes their nervous system somehow, so they can't continue fighting once their heart is taken with a sacred weapon. Taking their heart with anything else just means they lose a lot of blood fast, and they can still fight on top of it. That's bad news.

"Bleeding them out kills them just like it does a human, but you have to keep them from going to ground to heal or feeding to replenish before they bleed out. That only works well with two Warriors, since one blade has to be planted in his back where the beast can't get leverage on it to keep him from using his powers—like dematerializing and fading away. They can still fight that way, so unless you have another weapon hidden somewhere or can improvise something really fast, it's a bad situation to be alone with a pinned beast. The heart is a better shot.

"Sunlight will kill them. It burns in small doses, like a bad and very painful second or third degree sunburn. The effect of being killed by sun exposure is more like a shock to the system—maybe a heart attack or a stroke than bursting into flame like the movie industry likes to show, but dead is dead. And with a beast, dead is good. Once a beast is dead, it's over. If you kill it by a heart shot, the sunlight is a moot point.

"I suppose the hardest thing to explain would be that foul blood of theirs, but that's not my concern. I don't guess we've ever concerned ourselves with it, because if the humans ever found a way to fight beasts by analyzing that blood, we'd just have a new ally. Our blood is almost indistinguishable from human. If someone did notice a difference, it would be chalked up to an unusual blood chemistry."

"I take it the rest is a load of crap, too? Crosses? Garlic? Holy water?"

"A bunch of junk written by Christian novelists. You want a cross?" He flicked her amulet. "That's your cross. The Christians wanted to believe their God could banish any evil. Amulets of a totally different belief structure were a threat to that belief. As for the garlic, that one is a bastardization of an old-world fable. If it works at all, it's because the beast can find a meal that doesn't smell so bad," he joked.

The soft touch of tires on the soil outside confirmed that his grandfather had arrived.

"Is there anything else that works besides the sacred weapons?"

"You can attack with anything, really, but their recovery time is phenomenal. Don't try to hit them in the balls, the instep, or the solar plexus. You'll just piss them off."

"Got that one. My hand still aches. Punching Mr. Happy was like punching a brick wall, and his return fire was impressive."

"I've seen a baseball bat to the kidneys take one

down long enough for a heart shot, but that was a low-level turned, so don't count on it."

A change in the wind currents announced a large body in the doorway.

"Let me guess. It won't be a low-level turned coming for me."

"Not on your life."

"So, who took down the turned with the bat? Your father?"

"Nope. It was Gunther. Right, Grandfather?" Talon asked pointedly.

"Ah. So, you do know I'm here?" he replied acidly from the doorway behind them.

Talon yanked his hands away, as Jayde scrambled to pull the shirt back on behind the shield of his body. He could tell she was embarrassed.

He forced a stiff smile onto his face. "Of course, I did. I felt you from the highway. You taught me yourself, didn't you?"

"Explain yourself, please," Gunther requested evenly.

Talon turned to him with the liniment in hand. "Training woes. Did you bring the smaller blades? Mine are too large for her hands. Boys blades and gear should work well for her smaller frame."

Jayde turned to face Gunther with darkened cheeks and wide eyes.

"Erin," Gunther breathed, forgetting his annoyance with his grandson. His eyes brimmed with a deep emotion that Talon couldn't remember ever seeing before. "I'm sorry—Jayde. I forgot myself. It's just... You're so like Anna. Had I seen you on the street, I would have recognized you as her child immediately."

Talon startled at that. He hadn't realized that Gunther had ever met Anna personally. Corwyn had only been with Anna for a year when he lost her, and Gunther wasn't in the habit of traveling.

"Thank you, Lord Crossbearer, and thank you for your hospitality and your protection." Jayde gushed it out, looking very nervous at the prospect of meeting a house lord, especially one who held her fate in his hands.

"No need to be so formal with me, girl. If either of us should be honored, it should be me." He eyed her outfit critically. "That's the best you could do, Talon?"

"I told you she had nothing—just the clothes on her back, and her sweater is hardly what I would have her train in. Shirts are the only thing I can lend her, and those are outrageously oversized on her."

"I see that. Well, I brought her clothing in the sizes you specified, training gear, and a few things Sylvia decided a young lady might appreciate having. She should be in better shape, now."

"Who's Sylvia?" Jayde asked in sudden interest, probably hoping for a female companion.

"Our doctor," Talon explained. "It's been a long time since Gunther and my father have been in the company of a young lady for any length of time. I imagine they asked her opinion about what to buy for you."

"Not at all," Gunther objected. "I know how to delegate authority. After all, I am a house lord. I gave her your sizes and money and let her do the shopping. That reminds me; I dropped a run bag in the trunk of your car—for both of you."

"Thank you." Talon's gratitude was genuine.

Without that bag, he would be the one hurting for clothes if they had to run. He would literally give Jayde the shirt off his back, and he would have to fashion a toga or a bath sheet as clothing while his washed every night. Talon shuddered internally at the thought of that, but better him in the toga or the towel than Jayde. He wouldn't survive the first night of it if it was her.

"Well, at least a woman did my shopping," Jayde interjected brightly. "No offense to you gentlemen, but I'll be happy to wear something other than black again."

Gunther cleared his throat, turning a stunning shade of crimson.

Talon laughed at his discomfort. "What my grandfather is trying not to say is that he ordered Sylvia to buy you Warrior wear. Am I right?"

"Yes. I'm afraid so," he agreed.

Jayde blushed deeply. "Oh. I don't mean to sound ungrateful. I apologize. They're clothes that fit. I shouldn't ask for more. I imagine black is useful for fighting at night." She scooped her hands in her back pockets, looking very unsure of herself.

"How's the arm?" Gunther asked suddenly.

She smiled and rolled her shoulder. "Much better. That was my fault, by the way. I asked Talon to help me work out the spots I couldn't get to."

Gunther frowned at Talon for a long moment before returning a smile to Jayde. "I'm sure it was, Jayde. Talon knows his duty. Why don't you go out and try on your gear? Piers will keep you company while he unloads supplies for you." He said it all gently, and she left with a confidence that Talon didn't share.

Lord Crossbearer—when Gunther was like this, it didn't help to think of him as anything else—watched her go. Talon didn't. He steeled himself for what was surely coming after an innocent comment like that. When the door closed behind her, the older man swung back to Talon. All emotion was gone from his eyes now; they were killing eyes.

"Explain, and make it damned good," he ground out dangerously.

"She's worried."

"I'm listening."

"I explained how women—our women are expected to behave. Jayde hasn't been raised that way. It terrifies her that something as simple as my rubbing liniment in her shoulder could be misunderstood. She's afraid of getting someone—me—she's afraid of getting me killed over something so trivial."

"Swear it to me. Swear to me that you haven't bedded her against the sanctions."

Talon shook his head, relieved that Gunther had phrased it in a way he could answer with complete honesty. "I haven't. On the Stone, I haven't. I know my duty."

Gunther sighed and rubbed his hand over his mouth. "It's bothering her that much?" he asked honestly. He was showing genuine concern. This was new for Gunther.

"Yes. To make matters worse, I've been fielding questions for three days straight because of those damned texts," Talon spat. "She would have to know how to speak and read German, wouldn't she?"

"She needs to know these things, Talon. Her

training doesn't consist of simply teaching her how to use a weapon and what the killing blows are."

"I know that, but I can't answer what she's asking. I can't even argue her logic."

"About what?" he asked in sincere interest. This was a definitely new and disconcerting side of Gunther.

Talon crossed the room and flopped in a chair. "The rules for women—and you did say she had no autonomy—assume they are less. They've been freed from their curse, and they must accept the limitations placed on them by the Warriors of their houses."

"Don't state the obvious, boy. Get to the point." Now, that was the Gunther he knew.

"She's not freed. She's being trained as a Warrior. Jayde is a Warrior, more so than any of us are. She's Stone marked. Did you know that?"

"You're sure?" Gunther asked, visibly reeling.

Talon nodded. "I saw it when I was rubbing her shoulder. I'm pretty sure Corwyn couldn't have freed her if he tried."

Gunther looked far away for a moment. "What is her aspect?" he asked quietly.

"What's wrong?"

"A Stone prophecy when Anna was pregnant with her. What is her aspect?"

"Ani. I wondered about that. After all, Andris—"

Gunther waved his hand. "Let's not discuss that," he decided. "Corwyn had his own ideas about why there would be another Raga, but it hardly bodes well for Crossbearer, so—"

"Andris was born to Pauwel and Regana," Talon continued, ignoring his grandfather's dismissal.

The old man sighed. "We know he was born of

Regana, anyway. Corwyn seems to believe that Regana was already carrying Andris when Pauwel took her to wife and that Veriel turning Pauwel stopped her from producing the true beast killers to him. After all, if she did her job, there wouldn't be need of another, would there?"

"Then, who would have fathered Andris?"

Gunther cleared his throat and stared at his hands for a moment. "There has been conjecture that before he went beast, Jörg and Regana may have consummated a union. Perhaps with her agreement. Perhaps not. After all, he went to the Stone for a reason. If he took her unwilling and fled there to escape Gawen— He is mad." He shrugged. "At any rate, we can never know for sure now."

Talon swallowed a bitter lump at the thought.

Gunther glared at him. "Don't even think about it," he growled. "Even if it were true, he wasn't a beast yet."

"By whose standards?" Talon asked acidly. *No better than a beast*— Were the Crossbearers really descended from a beast that would take a woman in rape and run from his judgment to go fully beast? Talon decided not to think about it, after all. Maybe his shortcomings with controlling himself had some biological stem. Still, he would never stoop to using that as an excuse.

"Back to the subject, boy."

"Jayde? Yes. She's Stone-Chosen. She's our better—in the case of her father, his equal since he's Stone-Chosen himself. Equal pay for equal work, Grandfather. She doesn't understand why she should be treated like a freed woman when she shares the curse of the Warriors. How do I answer that? Tell me, because I don't agree with it."

"The texts don't cover this."

"She says they do. *Mehr als menschlich, weniger als verdammt.* More than human, less than damned. It doesn't say men that are, does it? Nowhere does it...and I checked twice to be sure of that."

"You know I can't make this decision. I'm not Lord Hunter. She is under my care, not my rule."

"I know. Can you approach Lord Hunter for her? She's angry, frightened. The first day alone—" Talon groaned and buried his face in his hands for a moment.

"What happened the first day?" Gunther asked solemnly. "I know she tried to run. What don't I know?"

"What didn't happen? The worst was when she found the texts. Jayde said she'd rather die than be a whore for either side. She—tried to use my weapon on herself when she found out. She begged me to complete the ceremony to free her and cried when I explained why I couldn't.

"In one single moment in time, she went from being an independent woman to having no control over her life, her body... Jayde lost every right she'd ever held dear. Can you imagine how difficult that has been to swallow for a woman like her?"

"Why didn't you tell me any of this?"

"I wanted to give her privacy. Jayde had nothing else left but that. But, as time is marching on, accepting it is not getting any easier for her. She's not suicidal anymore, but I can't promise that the lingering depression she falls into won't get worse again."

"I'll speak to Corwyn. I can't promise anything, and he'll likely seek counsel before he answers." He sighed.

"I'll do my best."

"That's all I can ask."

"Well, let's help Piers unload."

Talon nodded and headed for the door. On the porch, he stopped and smiled. Jayde was practicing the basic movements fluidly—with two blades. A blade in each hand corrected her balance problems, and the smaller grips and bracers corrected most of the control issues.

Gunther clapped a hand on his shoulder in a rare show of pride. "Good. She's doing well, but why dual-style?"

"She's female," Talon stated as if there never should have been a question.

"Come on. Let's help Piers."

"I'll be there in a minute."

Talon jogged over to where Jayde was training and got inside her swing to jar her wrist again. This time, she kept her grip.

Jayde smiled. "Told you I just needed a smaller grip," she informed him.

"Very smart, Ms. Expert. Let's see an arc."

She swung her arm smoothly, balancing her weight on the balls of her feet.

"Elbow up. Forearm parallel." He tapped her arm lightly to bring up her swing.

She backed off.

"What are you doing?" he demanded.

"Stay away for a second. I want to test my balance," she replied seriously.

"How?"

Jayde smiled secretively and met his eyes. She was suddenly a blur of motion. It was obvious that she'd had extensive training in martial arts. She incorporated the weapons into her movements, adding simple arcs and thrusts to the punches, kicks, and turns she would have studied. When she finished, Jayde walked back to him, looking happier than she had been in days. "I think I have balance back," she joked.

Talon swept her feet from beneath her and pushed on her shoulder to land her on her butt. He smiled crookedly at her scowl. "Don't get too cocky," he counseled her. Then, he offered his hand to pull her back to her feet. "Pretty moves, Jayde. Now, we'll make them functional moves."

She nodded quietly. She was learning.

Chapter Twenty-Two

May 20th, 2002

Corwyn stared out the window of his office and sighed.

"What have you decided?" Stephen asked, keeping a neutral voice.

"I have to do it," he answered.

"Are you insane?" Colin demanded. "You can't give her autonomy. You'll lose all control over what she does."

"We've argued this for four days, Colin. I won't make her wait for an answer any longer. I won't lose all control. I'll still be her house lord until she marries—if she marries. If Jayde was freed and raised with us, I'd agree with you about the outcome of this. She wasn't. This is the right thing to do."

"If she marries? If! She has to. Dammit, Corwyn. She has to marry and produce children now. Otherwise, what's the point of this? Besides, she's Stone-Chosen to—"

"Yes, she is," Corwyn cut him off cleanly. "Being Stone-Chosen makes Jayde the better of you and every house lord who condemned this move. Face it. We all inherited what we are, Colin. Even the mark of Syth is little more than a rubber stamp to announce who'll hold the Stone next. Who we are was a cosmic accident of birth for all of us, except for Jayde. She's truly chosen. Anna was chosen to bear her for me, and Jayde was touched by the Stone. I'm not sure that I have the right to deny her anything within reason.

"The point is, Jayde should have been freed.

Knowing now that it was impossible to free her, she should have been raised with us, and I screwed that up—me and all those idiots in charge of the houses and the Stone. I know what it's like to lose everything, Colin. Jayde had a good life and she had it ripped away, because when she was a baby, I screwed up. I owe her this one."

"The life she lost was a lie. She needs to accept reality now," Colin argued.

"Why do you think her reality has to be a harsh one? What is wrong with letting her find whatever happiness she can?"

"I'm not saying she can't choose. We can't force her, after all, but we can encourage her. We can introduce Jayde to our men. Someone has to be her type."

"You're talking about seventy men. Eighteen of those are far too old for her. Most of those are or have been married. Another twelve are in her age range but already mated. Four are still teens."

"That still leaves about thirty-five men. I don't see the problem here."

Corwyn growled in frustration. "You should have had a daughter," he cursed. "Where does it end, Colin? What if we introduce her to all of our young men, and Jayde refuses every one? Here's a thought! What if she's refusing them because she feels pressured? What if the men feel the urge to push themselves on her in hopes of catching her eye and push her even further away? Do you want that? Do you want Jayde to choose never to mate? She may. If she does, there's nothing I can do about it, autonomy or no."

Stephen put up a hand to still Colin for a moment.

"What if she already has a lover? Jayde had no idea what she was. What if she already planned to marry when her life was disrupted?"

Corwyn groaned. "It would fall to me. If the man was still willing to have her, I'd have to grant him my protection and bring them here. I can't ask the other lords to support it."

"Are you insane?" Colin asked again. "He'd be a target. What happens when an elder kills him? She'll be *very* happy then."

"If he would give her peace and happiness, I'd accept the burden. I'm more worried that Jayde has her heart set on someone who won't accept her now. That may be the last straw for her, if it happens."

Stephen cleared his throat. "Is there any possibility that she..." He dropped his gaze.

Corwyn looked at him in confusion. "What, Stephen? Spit it out. Let's get the worst case scenarios out in the open all at once."

"If we're going on the assumption that she had a full and healthy life, that Jayde took release as every Warrior does but with no knowledge of the repercussions... Well, accidents do happen, Corwyn. She most likely had no practice sensing, and there's an error factor to human contraception, even when you're careful. Add that to our rather overactive reproductive abilities. What if there's already a half-human baby to consider?"

"Then, the baby would be raised as one of our own. A cursed mother with a human father shouldn't be any different than what we deal with every day. The baby would be comparable to any other young Warrior.

"If the baby's father chose to marry her, we'd take

him in. If not—" Corwyn sighed. "If Jayde chooses one of our men and she carries a human man's baby, he would have to agree to raise her child as one of his own. The hardest part of this whole thing will be training our men to see Jayde as an equal."

"I don't understand you, Corwyn," Colin exploded. "She's to be a protected woman. She won't be a Night Warrior."

"She's a Warrior, and she's being trained as a Warrior. If you really believe she'll never kill a beast, I think you're deluding yourself. I think she'll see more action than most of our young men, and the beasts will be less willing to go to ground where Jayde is concerned."

"Being a target doesn't make her a Warrior."

"No, but being cursed does. This is my choice, Colin. It's the best I can do for her now. I'll let Gunther know tonight."

Chapter Twenty-Three

May 21st, 2002

Talon appeared in the doorway, and Jayde groaned in the realization that she'd screamed in her sleep again, shooting upright in fear. "I'm sorry, Talon," she whispered. "I don't know what's wrong with me."

He sighed as he sheathed his blade. She watched him cross the space between them in the dim light she'd finally caved in and started leaving on the previous night, feeling very exposed and childish.

Talon moved smoothly and silently as a cat. He slept in his jeans when she was staying with him, though she shivered at the thought that he probably slept nude when she wasn't. Jayde surmised from watching him move that he probably wore nothing beneath them in the way of underwear, and that thought made her want to know for sure.

His Warrior's wear of the black T-shirt and/or button down shirt had been discarded for the night. The same held true for his armored boots, and he hadn't bothered with the long, black leather jacket since he slew the beast that attacked her the first night.

As Talon came for her, barefoot and bare-chested, with only his weapons belt and the way he stalked the room as signs of what he was, Jayde closed her eyes and reminded herself for the hundredth time that she could not get him killed just to get him into bed with her. Still, she was afraid if she didn't, she'd never taste the passion he ignited in her again. If only the price wasn't so high.

As the days went on, resisting the urge to touch Talon was getting harder and harder. The only good thing was that Jayde had a name for it now—printing. She'd finally found what she was looking for two days ago under a description of the facets of the curse. Jayde was printing on Talon, and if she was denied him, she would go insane and have to be put to death. It was a frightening thought—death either way.

She opened her eyes as the bed shifted with the addition of Talon's weight. He ran his knuckles over her cheek lightly, and she sucked in her breath at the sensation, stifling the urge to kiss his hand as it neared her mouth.

"There's nothing wrong with you," he assured her. "I sleep better during the day, because I prefer to be awake when the beasts wake. We all have nightmares when we realize how real the stories are, when we meet our first beast. If we didn't need to practice outside, I'd suggest switching your sleep schedule, but then you'd never leave the house."

Jayde nodded. "I'd probably still have nightmares. Light doesn't seem to be my problem," she noted miserably, gesturing to the light filtering from the bathroom.

His hand moved to her chin and he ran his fingers over her neck. "What can I do?" he offered. "You need to sleep."

She closed her eyes again. "Nothing, Talon. I just need to work it out." It wasn't a lie. There was nothing he could do and keep his head.

His breath was suddenly on her cheek. Jayde resisted meeting his eyes, knowing what she wanted would be all too evident.

"Can I hold you?" he whispered close to her ear.

She shivered in anticipation. "No. If someone caught us..." The heat coiled deep inside her, where she wanted him to be so desperately.

"No one will come here at night. They'd be afraid of leading the beasts in. They'll only come in the day, unless a beast attacks." Talon wrapped his arms around her and lifted Jayde into his lap, pulling her head to his chest. "Can you tell me to stop? Will you tell me to?" he asked.

Jayde shook her head, brushing her cheek into the soft mat of curls that smelled of his musk. That musk made her body respond urgently. The throbbing between her thighs was punctuated by a warm wetness that made her dizzy with need. "I should stop you. This isn't safe." She brushed her cheek against his curls again as she said it, experimenting with the answering call from her body. God, it was fantastic!

He cupped her chin and turned her face up to his. "Open your eyes, Jayde. Look at me." Talon's breath left hot trails along her lips, and she found breathing difficult in the aftermath.

"I can't."

"Please. I have to see," he pleaded, leaving another fire trail along her sensitive lips.

Jayde opened her eyes and met his gaze miserably. "I can't do this," she repeated.

Talon lowered his head to brush his lips over hers. "Let me do it, then."

He took her mouth expertly, in a way she hadn't realized anyone could kiss. Jayde lost herself in that kiss. She wasn't sure when she wrapped her hands in his hair and pulled his mouth harder onto her own, but she was doing that, and her mind only had a momentary qualm about it before it was banished with so many other thoughts.

His movements became more fevered, but she found herself only vaguely aware of it, caught up more in how what he was doing affected her than the individual caresses of his lips and tongue that carried her there. She wanted him. She wanted him to undress her and make love to her.

What then? Some spoilsport in her mind demanded an answer to that question. *Corwyn will kill him. Will it matter then who was the aggressor and who allowed herself to be swept along?*

"No," she cried out, pushing his face away. If Talon didn't stop now, she wouldn't be able to tell him to. Already, Jayde didn't want him to stop.

"Please, Jayde. I have to touch you. Not touching you is killing me," he pleaded, burying his face in her neck and panting in his restraint.

"Corwyn will kill you. Don't you get it? No matter— I can't allow it, or you'll die for it."

"No matter what, Jayde?" Talon raised his head and locked onto her eyes. "Tell me that you want me, and I'll risk anything to have you."

"You won't risk it, because I won't let you. You won't take me without permission—my permission at least. You said as much. Even if they don't come here tonight, there will be proof of it later. I won't let Corwyn kill you."

"If I leave no proof—"

"There would be proof. You know there would. There are some things I can't hide," she pleaded with him.

"There are things I can do. I can give us pleasure without actually taking you."

"I don't..." Jayde sighed. Her body was demanding contact, demanding satisfaction of some sort, any sort. "What would happen if they found out?"

"I'd face Corwyn," he admitted, "but short of someone walking in on us, there would be no proof for anyone to demand judgment on me."

She hesitated.

"Jayde, if I don't find a way to touch you, Corwyn might as well kill me. Every night is harder for me. I can't take you. You won't allow it. Don't deny me this, too."

"No proof," she mused. "You're sure of that?"

"I'm sure."

"If I'm not," Jayde warned him.

"You will be," he promised.

Talon brushed his lips over hers in lieu of asking her permission. When she responded eagerly, he groaned deep in his throat.

Talon eased her to the bed beneath him, and Jayde stilled at the feeling of his erection pressing into her thigh. The aching need for him made her head swirl. She wanted to touch him. As if he was reading her thoughts, Talon rolled slightly to the side and drew her hand down to him. Her mouth went dry. If only it didn't mean his life—

Jayde started to unbutton his jeans, desperate to feel him cupped in her hand with nothing between them. He stilled her hand immediately and pressed it to his length again. Talon groaned as she ran it over him, cupping him and stroking him through the fabric of his jeans, tracing the outline of him and aching to feel his weight in her hand.

"Why?" she asked breathlessly, unable to draw her eyes from the rigid evidence of his arousal.

"We can't lie to the house lords," he managed. "We have to be able to say I didn't take you, I didn't see you undressed—or you me, I didn't spill my seed in you or even on you."

"What about the rest?"

"For that, I'm already damned. I was when I allowed you to kiss me that first time. I took great pleasure in that kiss, as I recall."

Her hand stilled. "Then, your life is forfeit, already?" Jayde asked hopelessly.

"No. Corwyn can strike me for that...and for this. He has the right to beat me solidly, and honor demands that I allow him to do it. He won't kill me for it."

"What about me? What's the punishment for a woman who acts like I'm acting?"

"Corwyn could strike you, but he won't. I guarantee he won't. Even if you weren't— Gunther told me how devastated Corwyn was when he lost both you and Anna in the same night. He would never physically harm you, and anything he did do, he would do to protect you."

"Why didn't you tell me this the first night?" she asked quietly.

"Because I thought I'd die if I didn't find out what kissing you was like. Corwyn can do his worst to me, and it will be worth a blow for every moment that you'll give me in your arms. I've racked up enough blows to die a very happy man," Talon joked.

"You won't die. I won't let you." Jayde met his lips

then pulled him back over her. "If you die, I promise you'll die very happy."

"Good."

Talon captured her mouth, and she sank to the bed beneath him, heedless of anything but the deep-seated need he awakened in her. He explored her, drawing Jayde into mindless pleasure. She moved against his hands, as Talon found every curve and hollow of her.

"That's right," he breathed. "Show me how to touch you."

Jayde startled as his hand cupped the wet center of her. "No. You can't. There'll be proof," she pleaded with him.

"Trust me. There won't. If you think there will be, I'll stop. I know other ways."

He ran his mouth over her breast through the fabric of her shirt, and she arched against him, longing for more.

"Let me show you what I have in mind?"

Again, Talon kissed her, seeking Jayde's approval by her reactions. She sank to the bed, holding his mouth to her, lost in the sensation of him claiming her gently and praying that he didn't think his fingers inside her safe enough. Jayde wasn't sure how deep in a woman the hymen was buried, but she was fairly certain it wasn't deep enough. Talon had large hands, and she'd read that the full depth of a woman's vagina, unstretched by a baby or sex, was only four inches.

Still, she was afraid to tell him what it was that she feared. As long as Jayde was a virgin, she could refute any charges that Talon took her, and as long as he didn't know it, he wouldn't stop. The punishment for this was sure to be higher.

Jayde gasped as his hand started moving over her, not in her and not at all like giving herself pleasure. The sensations were more intense, his touch at once coaxing and demanding. Talon sought out her mouth, his tongue plunging in mute promise of what he wished he could give her. He pulled away, letting her moan escape into the air around them.

"Someday," he whispered. "We'll find a way. You have my word."

"God, yes. I do want it when it's safe." *Not before it's safe. No matter what.*

The urge building in her was almost overpowering. Jayde wanted him to claim her properly. She wanted Talon's child in her, a piece of him growing in her. She squirmed further into his hand, seeking the answers to all her mind's fevered prayers.

"Please," she begged him, wanting everything spiraling just out of reach.

"It's coming. Let it come to you." His voice was rough and low.

"Come with me. Don't send me alone." Jayde grasped his arm, looking for an anchor, looking to pull him along where she was going, wanting to hold Talon to her as long as she could.

"I will when it's time." He drew her free hand to cover him again. Talon moved against her shaking fingers, matching her moan as he strained against the front of his jeans. "If only I could take you. I live for it."

Jayde cried out as the first shock wave washed over her, and Talon moved his hand and rolled to press the hard length of himself to her, rocking gently against her while she held him to her. She arched against the ridge of his cock and cried out again as the full force of her orgasm shook her to her core.

People say actual intercourse is better. I won't survive better than this.

The thought was ripped from her, as Talon's movements speeded. He fisted his hands in the sheets beside her head as he roared out a cry of release. He stilled over her, breathing in shallow gasps and looking as stunned as Jayde felt. Talon dropped a kiss to her lips, gently seeking affirmation from her, reassurance that she didn't regret a moment of letting him bring them both pleasure.

He smiled weakly. "I never dreamed it would feel this good. I must have you. Promise me, if it's possible—"

"You'll have it. You have my word."

Jayde understood his plea. The climax Talon brought her to gave her only momentary release from the ache building again for him. This ache was stronger, more insistent, impossible to ignore. If she didn't find a way to have him without risking him soon, she would go insane.

Talon started to pull away.

Jayde held him to her, already dreading the moment when he would leave her arms and leave her bed to return them to the cold existence of sleeping alone. "Please, stay with me. Don't walk away."

"I can't. If someone came in the morning and found me here like this, they'd assume—"

She bit back the response that she could prove them wrong. Jayde wasn't ready to admit that to Talon yet. She had to find out if she put him at greater risk first.

"For a little while," she begged. "If someone came before you left the bed, we could say you were protecting me and fell asleep. After all—" She ran her hand under his weapons belt and smiled suggestively.

Talon looked down in shock then laughed lightly. "That's a first. I've never forgotten to take that off before."

"You've probably never left your jeans on before."

He darkened and looked away.

"Okay, you've probably at least unbuttoned them."

"That's a fact," he muttered.

"Good. I'm special. I'm the first woman you've ever loved dressed and with weapons on," she mused wryly.

His eyes narrowed dangerously, and he cupped her chin to keep her locked on his eyes. "You *are* special, and I don't mean as a *Blutjagdfrau*. That can be damned. You make me want things no woman ever has. You make me want you like no woman ever has. You're no one's trash. You never were. You've always been wanted, wherever you were."

She smiled tightly. "A little too wanted sometimes."

Talon sighed and kissed her. "I'll stay. Not all night, but at least until you're asleep." He rolled himself until he lay next to her and drew her onto his shoulder before pulling the blanket over them. "Like this. I don't think anyone would believe I was guarding you like that."

Jayde nodded and nestled her face to him. She smiled then chuckled. Talon looked at her in confusion.

"You need a shower before we encounter anyone. You smell wonderful, but you smell of sex."

He nodded. "Thanks for warning me."

Jayde lay awake for a long time, running her fingers through the dark curls next to her face and thinking. If the price wasn't so high, she'd kiss Talon now and demand he make love to her.

It wasn't just the maddening aching in her anymore. It wasn't just that she wanted her first time to be with him, though she did—more than anything, it seemed.

She was terrified that the vampires would get her. Jayde had read about their ways, the ways they would use her with no pleasure and no dignity. She was terrified of facing that as a virgin, of having them take her virginity and not even having sweet memories of how it could be to strengthen her.

The beasts wouldn't have waited for Jayde to reach the change. Most likely, they wouldn't even have waited for puberty to start her degradation. They would have wanted her subservient by the time the change came and her body adjusted to let their seed plant.

Knowing they could still steal that precious experience from her would excite them, make some beast incredibly pleased with himself as he made her bleed. Or—whatever dark equivalent there was to that. Maybe some sort of dark humor? Jayde shuddered and pushed that thought away.

She considered telling Talon. Maybe if he understood what was a stake for her?

No. It wasn't that he wasn't willing, now. Whether or not it would benefit her, Corwyn would kill him for taking her, virgin or not. That was not something Jayde could risk.

* * * *

Talon swept the cell phone to his ear on the first ring, trying to clear his mind of sleep. "Yeah?" he grumbled into it, too bleary-eyed to check the caller ID feature to see who was phoning him.

"Still asleep?" the Lord Crossbearer barked. "Explain yourself."

"Nightmares," he yawned. "She's starting to fear the night for what beasts will come for her in the night. We all go through it, but most of us know we have years before first night. I know we need the day to train, but last night was bad. Jayde will get ill, if I don't let her catch up on her sleep somehow."

Gunther grunted his agreement. More and more, the old man seemed to soften when it came to matters of Jayde's health—or her feelings. "Do you have any ideas for combating this?"

"Little things. The winter drapes are up, so she doesn't imagine eyes in the darkness outside watching her. They're always closed after dark. A light in her room while she sleeps. Jayde's embarrassed by the childishness of it, but I have to do something."

"Any success?"

"Limited. Standing guard over her works better."

"How do you mean that?"

"Seeing me standing guard when she wakes gives her peace, even if it's nothing more than me sitting up asleep with my weapons belt strapped on. I've had to do that more than once. Knowing she won't face them alone is enough." Talon sighed. "She's almost never unarmed. She's taken to sleeping with her weapons hung over the headboard."

"She's becoming dependent on you. You realize

that?" Gunther accused.

"That may be best for now. When she's trained, it'll be different. If we were attacked tonight, I need her to follow me without question like a first night boy."

"I suppose that's true enough. She's not trained well enough to improvise yet." Gunther sighed. "I called for a reason, Talon. I don't know if this will help put her at ease or not."

"What is it?" he asked in concern.

"Apparently, Corwyn expected Jayde to have many of the concerns she does. I kept her privacy as much as I could, as she deserves, but I presented her requests to him and let him deliberate. He never wanted this for Jayde, and he does understand her upset. If he could, Corwyn would free her now."

"As would I," Talon muttered.

Gunther sighed again. "One of the reasons we've never tried this in the past was the life we'd be subjecting the woman to. It's simply not right that she must sacrifice all freedoms this way, especially when she's been raised to value that freedom. How wrong we were..."

"Wrong? Wrong about what?"

"We tried to convince Corwyn to let his daughter become *Blutjagdfrau*. He refused. Jayde was taken from him, because we withdrew our support. We left him wide open to attack, hoping he would change his mind and agree to give her up to training."

"That was outside your rights," Talon replied, shock warring with anger and disgust.

"Yes, it was. Believe me, I have regretted it every day I've lived since then. I was the first to withdraw my support. When she was lost to us— It almost crushed

Corwyn. He was little better than a madman.

"Frankly, I'm surprised that he's trusted me with Jayde this long. That's probably only because I'm not the one whose care she is in. Had it been me who found her and not you, Corwyn would have taken her from our range the first morning. I have no doubts. He only trusts you, because you didn't betray him.

"I never expected to meet Erin, you understand? Even if she was ever found, I thought she would be entrusted to someone else, never to a Crossbearer."

"Because you withdrew support first?" Talon asked.

Gunther grunted his agreement.

"Was that why you never told me about her? Because we would never be trusted with her? Or was it in shame of your part in it?"

Gunther sighed. "Both, I suppose," he admitted.

Talon took a deep breath. "What did the Lord Hunter decree?"

"Against the judgment of the other house lords, he has decreed that, as one of the cursed, she has a Warrior's rights."

Talon bit back a relieved bubble of laughter. "It will help," he assured his grandfather.

"Remind her that she still owes allegiance to her lord. If he forbids something within his rights to forbid any Warrior, she must obey his wishes to the letter."

"But in all freedoms a Warrior has, she has complete autonomy?" he asked for clarification. She had to have complete autonomy with no restrictions for him to take her as his mate.

"Jayde has Corwyn's word on it, but he asks questions of her motives. Corwyn has to know these things so he knows what he faces on her behalf."

Talon's heart sank. If the question was whether or not Jayde had made her choice of mate, he would have to answer honestly. Would the Lord Hunter renege on his word if he knew that choice? After all, it hadn't been presented to Jayde yet; it could still be undone.

"What does he need to know?"

"Does Jayde have a human lover she wishes to drag into this?"

"No." Talon grimaced. He'd answered too quickly, in too harsh a voice.

The question seared him. He hoped she hadn't taken a human lover, though as cursed, he could expect that Jayde had over the years, just as he had, just as every Warrior did. Talon hoped she wasn't just turning to him in her loss.

"I don't think so. She understands the danger," he continued more evenly.

"Has she decided never to bear children? While we all hope that small victory will come of this mess, Corwyn will support her decision if Jayde wishes not to mate. Perhaps, if she had been raised to the idea—"

"She hasn't decided." Considering the fact that they'd never discussed the possibility seriously, Talon hoped she was open to the idea. He was the last of the Cross line. He had to produce children for the sake of his house, and Talon wanted to have them with Jayde. "She only wishes any children she bears will be with someone she loves, whoever she chooses to love," he answered in a half-truth. "A Warrior has that choice. That's all she wants, the right to choose."

"Good." Gunther sighed in relief. "Corwyn will be most happy to hear this news. Now, comes the hard part. This will be a most unusual undertaking."

"Grandfather—"

Talon hesitated. How could he address this issue without tipping their hand? He had to be sure Jayde understood the ground rules she was playing by. Talon couldn't risk anyone taking her from him before they were secure in their commitment to the union he prayed she was as dedicated to making as he was. The lords could take her, he realized, if she wasn't sure and they moved quickly enough.

Worse, a misinterpretation could result in his end before Corwyn could sort it out, but probably not. Talon's life would be forfeit to Lord Hunter alone if the decision was against him, and honor demanded that Corwyn give Jayde the freedoms he'd promised her— including sparing Talon, since Jayde would be within her rights to give herself to Talon for release and take him to mate.

"Yes, Talon?" the Lord Crossbearer barked, breaking him from his reverie.

"Sorry. Explain to the Lord Hunter... Jayde refuses to be viewed as a prize or as a means to the end of securing children. If she feels pressured, he'll only push her in the opposite direction."

"Are you suggesting he coddle her?"

"Not at all. I'm suggesting he give her the freedoms he promised and not force her out socially. She's calmed considerably, but the idea of being used by either side initially sent her running. I don't want to spook her again."

"Running?" he asked in a panic, as if he'd forgotten that she had.

"She's never cleared the open area," Talon assured

him, "and she hasn't run in days. I'd prefer to keep it that way."

"Very well. I'll explain it to Corwyn. Take care of her, Talon."

"As is my duty," he answered, closing the connection.

Talon dropped the phone on the pillow next to his head and rubbed his hands over his face. Now that he had the freedom to pursue her, Talon found that he was more nervous than he'd ever been. So much could still go wrong. What if Jayde wasn't sure in her choice or wasn't willing to do what must be done? If she changed her mind, he couldn't bear it.

Worse, what if Jayde did have a human lover she was secretly pining for? What if she was already carrying that man's child? The thought of it sent Talon to his feet abruptly. He had to know for sure.

He entered the bedroom quickly but quietly. For several moments, Talon took deep breaths to calm himself and watched her sleep. His heart softened as he looked at the fall of dark hair thrown over the pillow and her cheek—*so soft beneath my hand last night.* There couldn't be another man for her, could there? Could Jayde give herself to Talon so completely if there was?

He sat on the bed beside her, and she stirred, opening her eyes and smiling as she spied him.

Jayde stretched luxuriously beneath the blanket. "Good morning," she murmured.

Talon placed his hand on the other side of her hip so he was leaning over her. "Jayde," he managed in a husky voice, "have you ever given yourself to a man before?"

She froze, and she looked up at him warily. What she saw in his face frightened her. Talon could smell Jayde's fear as she backed up the headboard with wide eyes, dragging the blanket up as a shield.

"You can't," she whispered. "Corwyn will kill you. Please, don't let him destroy you."

He shook his head. "He's granted you autonomy. The same freedoms any Warrior has are yours as long as you obey him in the same ways any Warrior of his house would."

Jayde furrowed her brow in confusion, no doubt trying to remember what rights a Warrior had.

"You have the right to choose mate and husband," he qualified for her.

"This is for real?" she asked. "You're in no danger?"

"There are rules. If you want this, it's forever...unless I die. In that case, you could choose again."

"Never," she assured him.

"Please, don't say that," he begged. "If I die—"

"What other rules are there?" Jayde asked, seemingly intent on not hearing him say it again.

"When the others find out, there may be tension. I cannot defend myself. It'll fall to you to demand your rights of Corwyn. Allow no one else to stand as judge in his place, even if it means he gets on a plane to deal with it himself."

"Judge? You mean he could still decide against you and take your life?" she demanded. "No. I won't take that chance."

"He won't. He can't. Honor demands that he keep his word and give you the freedoms he promised you. Others may disregard that, if you don't demand your right to face Corwyn. If you do that, the worst they can do is separate us until he arrives."

Jayde hesitated.

"I swear it's all true. As long as you demand Corwyn, no one can kill me. Knowing that, do you still wish to choose me?"

She threw her arms around his neck. "Oh, yes. Would you accept me? It's forever for you too, right?" she breathed.

"My choice was made when I gave you my blessing. It hasn't changed since then, and it never will."

Her hands left his neck, tracing those wicked tracks through his chest hair with her fingertips, driving Talon to the edges of restraint. He covered her hands, stilling them and trying to regain enough composure to think.

"Jayde, I must know. Have you taken a man before?" At the very least, he should be asking that for practical reasons, but he was honest enough to admit that this wasn't practical or rational.

She blushed deeply and looked away from his eyes to their hands on his chest.

His heart sank. "Jayde, please tell me. Is there— Was there another man you cared for?"

"No," she assured him. "There hasn't ever been— I've never..." Her blush deepened.

Ever? Never? Jayde's been intact all this time, and she's choosing to surrender her maidenhead to me, only to me.

Talon fought back the fire in his blood at the gift she was giving him. Jayde was intact, and she needed him to be gentle with her. A new surge of protectiveness washed over him. Intact—and she wanted him. This was a sacred trust. Talon would have to do everything possible to ease her into the experience.

He cupped her face back to his and kissed her solemnly. "Do you know what to expect?" he asked.

She nodded. "I know it's painful the first time or two. I know I'll probably bleed, but I've been told it gets better after that," she finished hopefully.

"Yes. If you're intact, there will be pain and blood. I can't stop that, but I can try to make you forget it quickly, if you wish it."

Jayde kissed him, trembling lightly. "I wish it," she whispered against his mouth.

Talon drew her into his lap, pulling Jayde free from the blanket that covered her. She roamed her hands over his chest, tracing his training scars.

"Have you seen a man fully naked?" he breathed.

Jayde bit her lip. "In movies and pictures, not in person," she admitted.

He groaned as he captured her mouth. *Completely uneducated—and mine.*

Talon moved her hands to the buttons on his jeans as he felt her passion grow. Her fingers shook as she undid them, but she didn't stop.

When Jayde ran her hand over him, breaking off the kiss to look at the length of him as she stroked him, he shifted her to the side to remove the jeans completely, giving her a full view of himself. Her eyes were wide and her breaths came in little gasps as she ranged her gaze over him. Still, her hand surrounded him, torturing Talon with the need to restrain himself. A blush came up, and she met his eyes uncertainly.

"Touch," he invited. "Get to know my body. I want

you to be completely comfortable with it. I will be with yours. Intimately so. Discover me. Experiment."

She nodded and looked down at him. She cupped the heavy weight of his testicles, gently teasing at the mat of hair that covered them, and they hardened in response. Jayde sucked in her breath and moved her hand to his leg in surprise. "They harden, too?"

Talon laughed lightly at her innocence. "Yes, they do. It's in preparation," he explained.

He didn't explain exactly what it was in preparation for, because he didn't want to spook her with the idea of a baby, not now when her sudden refusal would be painful, both physically and emotionally. If Jayde asked for protection, he was sure there was some around here somewhere.

Was it wrong to avoid the subject? What if she didn't think about it until later and it was simply an oversight in her inexperience? Would Jayde be upset that Talon knew and didn't say anything? But, bringing the subject up had far worse possibilities.

Should he sense her? No, if Talon knew she was high cycle, he would feel compelled to ask. *I am compelled to ask. The sanctions...* He shook his head slowly. Did he lack honor that he was arguing this?

Jayde ran her hands over him again, and Talon's mind refused to continue its internal argument. Only this mattered, only her hands on him.

She tested the feel of him. It was pure torture not to return the favor, but Talon wanted her to relax. Her shaking in his arms was unacceptable. He wouldn't take her as long as she was so frightened. It wouldn't be a satisfying union for either of them that way. He lay back fully, allowing Jayde free reign to explore until her fear was replaced by curiosity or overpowered by her need.

Her hands caressed him everywhere. Talon groaned at the feeling of her mouth tracing the muscles of his shoulder and chest and closed his eyes to the sensations pulling him along. He wasn't sure how long he could take this. It was glorious and maddening at the same time. Still, Talon sank into visions of her perfect body beneath him, crying out as she had the night before, climaxing for him—only for him in all her life.

Her hand returned to the length of him, and the vision Jayde sank over him, encasing Talon in the waiting warmth between her thighs. But, when the real Jayde took him into the warmth of her mouth, Talon balled his fists in the blanket beneath him and cried out harshly. It was too perfect, too close to the vision in his mind. For his sanity, he could do no less. The alternative would have been to take her hard, fast, and unready. He couldn't do such a thing. He met her eyes as she pulled away in shock.

"I'm sorry," she apologized, looking frightened. "I thought men—well..." She blushed deeply, and he regretted his reaction. Jayde thought he didn't like what she'd done.

Talon willed his muscles to unclench. "Jayde, come here," he invited.

She hesitated, and he cursed himself for startling her and undoing the ease he had obviously given her to try something so bold.

"Please. You did nothing wrong. Another time, when I don't have to take things slowly, I'll let you do that to your heart's content." Talon hardened further at the thought of it. "Right now, I don't have the ability to hold back if you do it to me. Please, come to me."

Jayde moved into his waiting arms. "I didn't hurt you?" she asked in confusion.

He laughed. "No, but I can show you pleasures so great you'll feel as if you'll die or shatter if it doesn't end soon," he assured her.

She pressed the length of herself to him with no fear or hesitation. "Show me," she whispered. "Please, show me."

That was all the invitation Talon needed. He kissed her, his hand seeking out the buttons of the Warrior's shirt she was using as a nightshirt—*my shirt*. He allowed himself to think it, to revel in it.

He swept it off her shoulders and cupped a breast in his hand. Talon met her eyes and rolled his tongue over her nipple slowly. Jayde's eyes widened, and she cried out softly.

"Did it hurt?" he asked, enjoying teasing her.

Jayde shook her head furiously, and he sank to continue his thorough exploration of her body. Talon lost himself in discovering how to pleasure her. When he pulled back and ran a hand over her panties, slick in her excitement, she rose to meet the embrace.

"Yes, Talon. Please make love to me," she begged.

"Your pleasure first," he decided as he pulled the silk and lace from her body.

"Not your hand, Talon," she whispered. "I want you." Her eyes were half-lidded and her breasts rose and fell in invitation—just for him.

"Not my hand," he agreed.

She watched as he lowered his mouth to take her. Jayde gasped, but she didn't move to stop him, and

Talon took her gently. At first touch, she tensed, but she soon relaxed and moved against him, groaning and running her hands through his hair as he used his lips and tongue to explore where no man had ever been permitted to explore. Her breathing became ragged, and her hands gripped his shoulders.

"Talon, please. I need..."

He increased his urgency in response to her plea, knowing Jayde wasn't certain exactly what she was asking for. Once she experienced her release, he'd take her maidenhead. If the gods were kind, the endorphins rushing through her system might dull the pain for her.

She came hard and fast, and Talon positioned himself over her. It would be kinder to take her while her own climax would mask the pain—or the pain might shatter her pleasure, he reasoned. He couldn't do it until he knew Jayde was prepared for the pain.

Jayde met his eyes, still glazed in the glow of her climax. "Talon, please," she begged again.

Talon eased in, just a little to allow her time to adjust to the feeling of his invasion. Her eyes closed, and she moved against him. He tried to stop her.

"Don't. Your maidenhead," he cautioned.

"Take it. Please, take it."

Talon nodded and surged forward, taking it in one swift motion. He froze as she stifled a scream and gripped his arms. Her body tensed completely.

"I'm sorry," he whispered, kissing her gently. "Relax. I'm told it will ease if you let it."

She met his eyes miserably. "Tell me," she pleaded with him.

"I love you. I'll make the pain go away if you relax

and let me," he assured her.

Jayde nodded and raised her head to meet his lips. Her kiss wasn't tentative as Talon expected. It was passionate, needing and searching for something. As he felt himself drawn in, her body unknotted beneath him and around him.

Talon moved slowly, carefully, afraid of hurting her again, but she moved against him, encouraging him onward. He groaned as he increased his pace and was rewarded by Jayde's voice panting out a request for him not to stop. Talon couldn't have asked for more than that.

He captured her mouth then released her and took her in sure, strong strokes. Her muscles clenched around him, drawing him further into her hot, silken embrace. His seed filled her; he cried out in a shattering release that only intensified as her gripping muscles contracted around him, welcoming his seed into her.

As a Cursed Warrior, Talon had taken release in human women before, when his body demanded the purging of sexual tension, but never unprotected, never with the chance of producing children. It was a totally different experience when you felt your seed leave your body, free to impregnate a woman you love. Talon couldn't imagine any other type of release now that he knew the pure joy of it. He shuddered under the force of that complete release, hoping that Jayde would welcome the possible outcome of it as he would.

Talon buried his face in her hair, drinking in the musk of them mixed on her body. It was a scent he wanted to smell every day until he died.

Her hand moved through his hair and her lips

brushed over his temple. "I could stay like this forever," she mused.

"No, we can't. We have to clean up and get training," he reminded her.

Jayde groaned. "Now?"

"Just because I love you doesn't mean I'll take it easy on you. In fact, we have to train harder than ever."

"Why?" she asked nervously. "Is something coming that I don't know about?"

"My life depends on you demanding your rights, physically if necessary."

"I have to fight someone? One of ours with the sacred weapons?" she asked in disbelief.

"If necessary. Don't kill him unless you have no other choice," Talon joked.

"Very funny. You could have warned me. I'm not ready for that."

"Which brings me to the cleaning up part. Whenever we sense someone coming, we'll have to eradicate any indication. Until we're ready to defend our choice—or until someone asks directly or oversees us, we say nothing."

"We can change sheets, but what if these stain?"

"You're female," he reminded her. "Bleeding is normal for you." *But maybe not for long.* "Sylvia did your shopping. I'm sure she thought of sanitary napkins. Speaking of which," he said as he slid from her slowly, shaking in the spike of pleasure the sensation of moving in her brought, "you may want to use one today."

Talon looked at his shaft and laid a hand on her thigh gingerly. He hadn't realized there would be quite so much blood involved, and she shed it for him. In a Warrior's life, blood was everything. Blood was life. Blood was death. Blood was release of *Blutjagd*, and it was pain of injuries. Jayde had shed her blood for him, and there was no greater gift than that.

Chapter Twenty-Four

Talon had to admit that he'd never seen Jayde train harder. He wasn't sure if it was having her autonomy, the release of sexual tension, the thought that his life depended on her training, or—he had never considered the possibility before—allowing herself to print on him as the male Warriors did with a mate? That thought made him smile. If Jayde was printed, she really was his forever. The force of her printing would have to be as strong as his was. Whatever her reason was, Jayde was more focused and fighting harder than Talon was accustomed to.

She was also focused on acting as if there was nothing between them. Talon knew she was nervous, because her ability to sense was still weak. He had explained ghosting to her days ago.

The older a Warrior got, the stronger his ghosting got. Even Talon couldn't sense Gunther when his grandfather went ghost, unless they went ghost together. The mental pathways of tandem ghosting nullified the effect on the participants so they saw each other clearly despite the fact that no one else—beast, human or other Warrior—could. Ghosted Warriors frightened Jayde, so she was taking no chances.

When Talon suggested they hide their relationship until they were ready to defend it, he hadn't realized how difficult that would be. Damned if she didn't make it look effortless.

While Jayde was busy experimenting with new moves and studying the ancient strategies, Talon found himself preoccupied with the underwear he knew lay beneath her Warrior wear. Sylvia may have been ordered to buy Jayde the basics in outerwear, but she was less Spartan with the more intimate details, knowing that she was purchasing for a young woman who would undoubtedly appreciate something feminine. As a result, Jayde's underclothes were a fine array of silks and lace that made Talon sweat to consider, especially since she had dressed in front of him and he had been allowed to undress her.

He had almost put off training to take Jayde again when he caught sight of her in the set she wore for training, but he held rein. Talon had backed off not simply for training but because he didn't want to hurt Jayde by taking her still-tender body too many times when she was adjusting to a man's invasion of her.

Strange that a man that could be calm and collected about facing a beast down could be so scattered by the mere thought of undressing a woman when he knew the little red lace confections that lay under her clothes.

By the time dinner rolled around, Talon was dying for her company again and anticipating sunset with a fervor unmatched since the night of his first hunt when he foolishly still thought it was 'cool.' When dark finally came, he swept Jayde into a passionate kiss. "Please, tell me you're not too sore," he begged.

Jayde smiled and wrapped her arms around him. "Showers first," she suggested. "I smell like a bear."

"You first. I'll hold down the fort."

She nodded and disappeared into the bedroom. Talon smiled as the water started running, imagining Jayde running soap over her skin. Someday, he would have to join her for a shower, if there was ever a time they could relax that way. Maybe during daylight hours, after they had defended their union. He suddenly realized that there were no sheets on the bed and dragged them from the dryer.

Talon dropped the pile in the middle of the bed...and froze. "Oh, no," he breathed. He could sense the faint trail of a low-level turned and prayed there weren't ghosted elders backing him. "A fluke. Please gods, let it be a fluke," he prayed as he moved quickly to the source.

Hunting a low-level was a simple thing any teen worth his salt could accomplish. The ghosting of a first night was better than that of the average low-level. Talon had dispatched him, cleaned his blade on Shorig's clothing, and sheathed his weapon before the shower turned off.

He pulled back the curtain with towels in his hands. Jayde started to make a joke, but one look at his face silenced her. She turned off the water and grabbed a towel for her body while Talon dried her hair.

"What's wrong?" she asked earnestly.

"We have to leave."

"They're coming?"

Talon nodded. Oh, yeah! They were coming. The entire range had lit up like a Christmas tree. Nothing was hiding, and everything was moving. Her eyes widened and she bolted for the bedroom to dress with her hair still wet.

Jayde was pulling on her weapons belt when Talon handed her a paper bag. She looked at him in confusion.

"Some perishables for the trip. I'm not sure we'll be able to stop tonight and I don't want to stick you with all canned and dried again if I can avoid it. Just getting there will take half the night."

She nodded, knowing not to ask where they were going. In truth, the route he would take to spirit them into Canada would probably bore her, and he didn't think Jayde would run, but it wasn't a Warrior's way to share information. Talon grabbed her hand and led her toward the car.

"What is that smell?" she complained suddenly.

Talon hesitated, not wanting to frighten her. "Beast."

"Close?" she whispered.

"Not close enough to hurt you," he answered in a half-truth.

He didn't sense anyone yet, but even if the turned was alone—which seemed likely now, the elders knew what Shorig sensed. If he'd sensed Jayde and realized her for what she was, they were on their way. Shorig had certainly sensed something, because every beast in Cross range was in motion and not bothering to hide himself.

Talon sped through the back roads, changing direction to another of the hundreds of dirt tracks he knew any time it seemed they were headed into a group of incoming beasts. The beasts didn't follow. They seemed intent on their path and passed by without notice whenever Talon changed course. It was almost two hours before he felt confident contacting Gunther.

"Where the hell are you?" the Lord Crossbearer demanded by way of his greeting.

"Didn't you always teach me to get away first and check in later?" Talon replied acidly, his nerves shot from the constant belief that the elders were around the next bend, ready to take Jayde from him.

"Is Jayde all right?" He rushed on without allowing Talon to answer. "Corwyn is up in arms. The entire beast ranks seem to have gone insane. It's not just here. It's everywhere."

"She's fine. Dammit! That means Shorig sensed her and knew what she is."

"A low-level? Alone?"

Talon didn't ask how Gunther knew Shorig. Maybe his grandfather knew the man at turning. Shorig couldn't have been turned very long. Talon would estimate twenty years, at the max. Barring that, he was an exceptionally inept beast.

"Yes. I think he may have simply stumbled on the wrong place at the wrong time. Maybe if they're close enough—"

"Then, why didn't Grelden sense her?"

"I don't know," Talon snapped. "None of us have dealt with a *Blutjagdfrau* before. Maybe, she was latent and her training has made her light up with a limited range. She's faster and stronger since she's started training."

"I hope not."

"I agree, but there's no way to know for sure unless you want to try to torture it out of some beast. Is there?" Talon shot back.

"We'll damn sure try to find out, won't we?" Gunther sighed. "Are you sure Shorig isn't following you?"

"Am I that sloppy?"

"Did Jayde see it?"

"No," he answered simply.

"Are you going to tell her?"

"Are you insane?" Talon demanded.

Jayde shot him a shocked look, and Talon squeezed her hand, giving her a tight smile in comfort. She nodded and stared out the window nervously. She could sense many of the beasts he could, he knew. Like him, Jayde was no doubt nervous about what she couldn't see.

"Is that wise?" Gunther continued.

"Yes," he snapped in irritation.

"Are you afraid of her emotional state or her lack of sleep?"

"Yes," Talon stated more calmly. He glanced at Jayde out of the corner of his eye, but she didn't seem to realize there was anything of importance going on—thankfully.

"I see. I agree. Piers and I won't mention your kill to her."

"Thank you."

"What else can we do?"

"Lay low. The last thing we want is anyone leading them to us. You know where I'm going."

"Understood. Will you need anything?"

"We'll make due. Once I'm sure we're clear, I'll arrange for my own supplies. Other than that, we'll be fine unless we run again. Let Corwyn know that everything is fine here."

"Immediately. Take care of her, and watch your back."

"Don't I always?"

* * * *

Corwyn paced the length of his office. Just after nightfall, every Warrior's senses lit up like a fireworks display. He had fielded calls from every American house lord and much of Europe so far. It was Jayde. They all knew whatever went wrong was Jayde, but no one knew what.

To make matters worse, Talon hadn't checked in yet. If they were running, he wouldn't do that until he felt they were secure. If she was taken and he was dead— Corwyn shook himself mentally. Better not to think about that possibility.

On the lighter side, the beasts' ranks were getting a good weeding. In a frenzy and with no way to expend the energy, the low-level turned were easy pickings for the Warriors. In Hunter range alone, there had been five beasts killed in the last hour.

The phone rang, and Corwyn pounced on it, every muscle tense. "Talk, old man," he barked without asking who it was. Anyone but Gunther would be up to his ass in beasts and too busy to call him now.

"She's fine, Corwyn. She didn't even see the beast that Talon destroyed."

"One? Alone? How?" he questioned in confusion.

"We don't know how—yet. Talon thinks he may have been in the right proximity to pick her up on radar. It was a single low-level turned, not even a challenge for Talon, but they know now. What the beast sensed has been transmitted through that damned hive mind of theirs, and they know she's alive.

"Talon has taken her underground. As far off the charts as he can reach tonight. In the meantime, we'll work on the how. I wish to the gods and Stone I knew."

"I want her delivered to me, old man. I want her

back under my personal protection, now," Corwyn shouted, cursing his trembling hands. They got too close.

"In this frenzy? Have you lost your mind?" Gunther demanded.

"When it's over then."

He sighed. "As you wish, but there are some things you must know before you make that decision for her."

"Like what?" he growled dangerously.

"Jayde is having problems right now...settling into the realities of what she is."

"We settled that. I gave her autonomy."

"This is another issue. Our boys are told the tales from the cradle. They train for an entire year before they first night with their lord to watch a kill. It may be many more months before they are allowed to make a kill."

"And?" Corwyn demanded.

"Jayde has had only a week, Corwyn. Talon is barely holding her together. The less upheaval in her life, the better. He hasn't even told her about the beast he killed, and neither will anyone else. Talon doesn't think she'll handle one so close very well."

"What is he afraid of?" he asked pointedly.

"She's not sleeping, unless he's guarding her. Her training is progressing well, but I'm not sure she'll follow orders from anyone but Talon yet. In a battle, that one thing may save her life. Her emotions are raw. Jayde talks to Talon; she confides in him. She's comfortable with him in what must be a terrifying situation for her. Right now, she's helpless, and she knows it. A first night boy is more prepared than she is, and you know how ill-prepared they are."

"What you're telling me is that it would be a mistake to drag Jayde here and take her away from the one person she trusts."

"I believe so, but even with autonomy, you control a Warrior's movements. If you order her return, she'll come to you."

"How dire is her emotional state?"

"At this moment, the nightmares are the worst," Gunther admitted.

Something in that statement bothered Corwyn. *At this moment...* There was something important he wasn't being told. Of that, Corwyn was sure. "At other times?" he prodded.

"The morning she woke in our custody was the worst. Jayde was uncontrolled to the point that Talon almost had to tie her hand and foot."

"Uncontrolled how?"

Gunther sighed. "Talon was trying to preserve her privacy. He left it to me to explain the situation, if it came to this."

"Explain what?" Corwyn demanded. "You're not inspiring confidence in your handling, Crossbearer."

"Jayde tried to use Talon's weapon against him. Amusing, you can imagine. She tried running several times, though she never made it. She begged him to complete the *Zeremonie der Freiheit*. She bounced back and forth between anger, despondency, and hysterics. She—" He cleared his throat nervously.

"She what?" *Here it comes. He saved the worst for last.*

"She tried to use his weapon on herself. In less than twenty-four hours, Talon turned that around into her current state of mind. Don't ask me how he managed it. From my point of view, it was a damned miracle."

Corwyn sat heavily and stared at the window in misery for her suffering. "Why didn't anyone tell me this?"

"Several reasons. Jayde wants to pull herself up and function. She doesn't want everyone thinking she's either weak or insane. Most of all, she doesn't want you thinking it. And, we didn't want to concern you, if it would eventually pass."

"She cares about what I think of her?" The thought struck Corwyn as strange. He cared about what she thought deeply, but Corwyn had thought of almost nothing but his daughter and Anna for the last twenty-five years. Jayde didn't know him. She had no reason to trust him or his motives. Corwyn had resigned himself to that long ago. Still, Jayde cared what he thought of her. "Why?"

"She thought she had been abandoned as a newborn. How did she put it? She felt like her real parents thought of her as trash. Jayde wants to make a good impression on you, especially now that she knows she wasn't... She can't accomplish that if you think every little thing is a problem for her."

"Did she have a good family? The ones who raised her?" The files Stephen had pulled up on them didn't tell Corwyn much. It didn't tell him the many things he *wanted* to know about the people who'd raised his daughter.

"From what I overheard, yes. They sound like they were good people. Lots of love and laughter in that house. They're dead, now—for the last five years or so. Car accident, I think Talon said."

It was a car accident. It was one of the few things that had relieved Corwyn about the situation. He couldn't imagine the pain they would have felt, had they been alive when Jayde went missing. He couldn't even claim he would have told them that she was all right, if her safety depended on them not knowing it. The guilt of that realization hadn't done much for his sanity.

Gunther went on, probably assuming that Corwyn wanted more information. And, he did. He wanted to know everything about her, everything he'd missed.

"They named her Jayde, because it was the closest girl's name to *Jäger*. She wanted to know her real name. She wanted to know that she had one, Corwyn. It was the first question she asked Talon about herself."

Corwyn stifled a sob at that. "Gods alive! She really thought she was unwanted. Does she know how it happened? Why we couldn't find her?"

"They were searching for her parents in the northeastern states only. We would have missed it, because they made no mention of the amulet, and they weren't looking anywhere near you for a home."

"I don't understand."

"Anna tucked her into a car. Erin— Jayde slept quietly all night and for part of the day before she woke. They had reached New England, Corwyn."

That part, he'd known...New England and nothing else. "She told you all of this?"

"No, none of it. She talks to Talon. I overheard bits and pieces of it. Talon filled in the rest. Anything you want to know, ask me. If anyone can get answers for you, it's Talon."

"Speaking of which..." He hinted for the answers he'd already requested. Corwyn tried to convince himself that it wasn't a test, but it was something of a test, if he was going to be honest.

"There is no human man, and she hasn't decided whether or not to bear children. Jayde wants a husband she can love, and she doesn't want to be hounded to latch onto one."

"Just to put some other factions at ease, is there any possibility that she's already pregnant to a human?"

"Little early to answer that, but we'll let you know when we know."

"Thank you, Gunther. Jayde can stay with Talon for now, though I want a progress report on her training soon. I also want to meet her soon.

"From now on, I expect you to tell me everything, Gunther. Jayde is my daughter. I don't want secrets between us. This is too important."

"You have my word. Tomorrow."

Gunther broke the connection, and Corwyn stared at the phone, tightening his hand reflexively. She didn't deserve this. He hadn't wanted this for Jayde, and if Gunther and the others had supported him, this might not be necessary now.

Talon was the only saving grace for Crossbearer. If his daughter trusted him, if Jayde depended on him, she would have him. If Jayde wasn't safe on Cross land, Talon could come with her when she came to Hunter range—if Gunther would allow it.

Corwyn didn't trust Gunther as far as he could throw him, but for whatever reason, Jayde had latched onto Talon in a situation where she likely shouldn't have trusted anyone. That said something about the young man. Maybe Talon hadn't been poisoned by the old-school Cross ways like the rest of them.

Chapter Twenty-Five

May 22nd, 2002

Talon turned to throw his arm over Jayde. He knew the sun was getting high, but they both needed the sleep more than the training. Jayde had stayed awake for most of the drive, but Talon had been forced to carry her to bed when they finally arrived. Stress and exhaustion had finally overtaken her, and she was nearly impossible to rouse. He'd removed their weapons belts and shoes before collapsing beside her.

Jayde turned further into his chest, and he smiled sleepily. For a moment, he wasn't sure what she was doing. He groaned as he realized that she was undressing him.

"What are you up to?" he asked with a crooked smile.

"Making sure you die happy," she teased.

"We're not dying." He moved to undress her. "Are you sore?" he asked urgently.

Jayde moved her hands from his shirt to his jeans. "No, I'm not," she assured him.

"Good, because I want you."

Talon took her mouth as he finished undressing her. He teased at Jayde's body while she finished divesting him of the last of his clothing. Naked at last, he plunged into her, reveling in the fact that Jayde was ready for him with barely a touch.

"So sweet," he breathed as he moved inside her warm and willing body.

He guided her legs around his hips, and Jayde tightened them, urging him on. Talon smiled, as she made an inarticulate sound of longing and pleasure.

"That's right. Hold me in," he crooned as he quickened his motions. "So ready for me..."

As if proving his point, Jayde arched up as she cried out in release. The contractions that gripped her drew him up and over into a free-fall in a vacuum of swirling lights and pinpoints of pleasure. Talon cried out as his senses deserted him, and he lost himself as he exploded into her, the very essence of himself becoming part of her.

Talon shuddered, knowing that was exactly what was happening, what he wanted to happen, figuratively but also literally. He wanted his child in her, not for some damned prophecy the Stone spat out but to know she had accepted him so utterly.

Carrying a child they made together, feeding that child on nutrients from her own blood, suddenly sounded like the most erotic thing he could imagine. Running his hands over Jayde and knowing his child was sheltered there would make Talon the happiest man on Earth, as if part of himself was there even when he had to leave the warmth of her.

He ran his hands over her body, already regretting the moment when he had to separate himself from her. "Forever," he mused.

"Forever what?"

"If I could hold this moment forever, I'd do it." His hands stilled, as the light left her eyes. "What is it?"

She shook her head and tried to look away, but he cupped her face back to his.

"Tell me, Jayde."

"I thought knowing what it was like would make it easier, but I think I'm even more terrified now."

He furrowed his brow in confusion.

"I was afraid of being captured by them without ever knowing what loving you was like. They won't allow me pleasure. I've read what they—"

"And now?" Talon prodded, unwilling to hear her put her fears of the beasts' tactics into words.

"I'd rather die than submit to what they'll do. I thought that before. I know it now. I can't even bear the thought of..." Jayde shook her head hopelessly.

"We won't allow it. Never take off your amulet. Promise me. Even if they kill me and every other Warrior that gets within a hundred yards of you. Never let that amulet leave your body. I'd rather die than let them touch you."

Talon cupped a hand under her navel. "And if you carry a child when they come for you, your amulet will protect him, too. If it comes to a choice, your only duty is to that child. He's the one you have to protect. The beasts will kill him. Without your amulet, you can't prevent that. Promise me you'll let me die to save you and our child, if the choice is posed to you."

"Don't make me make that choice, Talon."

He smiled crookedly. "If it's my choice, this is it. It won't be my choice, if it comes to that."

Jayde nodded. "I promise," she managed miserably. "I hope it doesn't come to that."

"So do I," he admitted. "In the meantime, I have to leave this luxurious, sensual, glorious—"

"Get to the point," she ordered in amusement.

"Good. You can still smile. I have to get up and get showered."

"Training," she cursed.

"You have the rest of the morning off unless you

want to practice alone—inside. I have to run to the nearest store and pick up supplies."

"You're leaving me?" Jayde asked, her hands tightening on him in a near-panic.

"For two or three hours in broad daylight," he soothed her. "The only thing that could come here would be human, and you can handle any number of humans. I doubt that will happen anyway. Trust me. Just keep those weapons on you."

"Should I wash the sheets while you go? After all, I'm still not proficient at seeing the Warriors coming."

"No. None of them will be coming for several days. I told them to stay away until we know we're safe here."

"Have you?" She smiled an impish smile. "Then it would be safe to..." She let the invitation hang between them unspoken.

Talon kissed her. "After training, when we wake— I intend to take you every free minute you give me until we have to be careful again. Is there anything I can get you while I go?"

"I'm dying for something sweet. If they have cream horns or Ho-Hos—"

Talon grimaced. "You eat that stuff?"

"You don't? Women like sugar and chocolate, especially when we're exercising enough to work it off."

"Are you saying I'm working you too hard?" he challenged.

Jayde laughed and shook her head. Then, she arched to move herself around him. "Not hard enough," she teased.

"Really?"

She nodded.

"What do you want?"

"Give me a baby to protect." Jayde ran her hands up the expanse of his chest. "Give me a piece of you to hold onto, no matter what else goes wrong."

Talon felt a warm surge of love and protectiveness. His blood burned to grant her wish. He had a fleeting thought that her printing was talking for her, and his was answering, but he decided that it didn't matter if it was. If Jayde's printing made her daydreams of his child in her womb as enticing as his were, she really meant what she was saying.

His softening member went stiff inside her again, and her eyes widened then closed as she rose to meet him. Talon surged into her again, and her legs wrapped around his thighs. He took her fast and hard, unable to control the wild need in himself that her proclamation let loose.

Panting from a shattering release, he ran his lips over her forehead as he actively searched out her body's rhythm, something he had purposely avoided until that moment. Her fertile time was almost upon them, Talon noted. Already, Jayde was preparing to accept him. If the gods were kind, they could produce a child very soon. Aftershocks wracked him at the knowledge that she was so close.

"I promise it," Talon breathed against her ear as he wrapped himself around her protectively.

* * * *

Talon scooped the cell phone from his jacket pocket with a smile on his face and checked caller ID. "Yes, Father? What's the news?"

"They've gone to ground all over the world, and the

other Warriors are shocked into exhaustion."

"The hunts went well?"

"We lost Richard of Swordbearer, and there were quite a few treated injuries, but the beasts lost almost two hundred of their number world-wide. Most were low-level but not all," Piers reported.

Talon whistled a long, low note. "It was a frenzy. Is it over?"

"We won't know until nightfall. So far, it's still quiet in the far ranges of the world where night has fallen again, but the test will be our range come nightfall. It might be better if it's not over. We could knock them to their knees."

"Two hundred is a good start."

"Better than we hoped when it all went crazy."

"Do we know what started it?" Talon asked hopefully.

"Not yet. We imagine something drew Shorig, but we don't know what. How is Jayde?"

"Very well this morning—afternoon. She wouldn't be if she knew how close he got to her."

"Is that wise to say? What if she overhears you?"

"I'm picking up supplies."

"You left her?" Piers asked in disbelief.

"She's more than safe until nightfall. Jayde's deadly to anything they could send at her now. I've only been gone two hours, and I'll be back with her in twenty minutes or so. Gunther complained that she's too dependent on me. Look on this as a test. She let me leave her with no complaint. I imagine she'll be nervous as a cat when I get back, but she'll adjust."

Piers grunted his agreement. "At least, I have good news for Corwyn," he decided.

Talon's breath caught in his throat. If she could let him leave— Corwyn couldn't take her now. He willed his voice even before he started talking. "Her letting me leave her?" Talon asked.

"No. The fact that she bled."

Talon tried to reign in his panic. "Explain," he managed in a tight voice. They might not know. Piers certainly didn't sound upset, so maybe they didn't know what the blood meant.

"Her monthly. I saw the stains and the discarded napkin."

Talon's heartbeat took up a sick pounding. If they asked directly—

"Corwyn had—concerns that she might have come to us carrying a half-human child."

For a moment, he considered his options frantically. Talon decided on a half-truth. If he didn't confirm or deny what they said, there was hope. "No, Father. Jayde didn't come to us carrying a child," he assured him. A sudden revelation left him cold. "Oh gods, no," he breathed.

"What is it?"

"Her blood. Why didn't I think of it? Could what she is be broadcast as a pheromone in her blood? If that's the case—"

"Any beast close enough to sense her would pick up on it while she bleeds?"

"If that's the case," Talon agreed. "In fact— If it is a hormone, she may have a spike for a day or two at high cycle. I wish I knew how this worked. Can Corwyn get the Stone to tell us anything?"

"She would be running half the month," Piers mused then seemed to snap back to himself. "No.

Corwyn tried the Stone. It's dead silent, as usual when something important lies to be discovered. Strange how it refuses to take sides, when we need it most."

"Of course, I could be wrong about this. If the Stone won't help, there is no knowing for sure what the problem is," Talon admitted.

"I'll discuss it with Gunther. Keep your eyes open."

"I will."

Talon hung up with shaking hands, considering an even worse possibility that he couldn't admit to Piers. Maybe, what they'd sensed wasn't her blood but the loss of her maidenhead. Jayde had bled monthly for the last thirteen years, and though there were beasts around her—even one stalking in and around her campus—none had ever sensed her.

The Stone was silent for something important that lay hidden. They were certainly hiding the fact that they'd consummated a mating. But, why would the Stone not tell Corwyn that Jayde had printed? There was no anticipating the whims of the Stone, but maybe it was showing them mercy by granting them time to be solid in their union before raining trouble on them from the houses.

If he'd activated her by taking her— Talon groaned. If she were to breed, it had to happen eventually, but he would have waited if he had known. He would have waited until Jayde was better trained and more prepared for what she faced.

No, I wouldn't have. Madness would have taken me first.

The question was, was it a one-time event type of beacon or one that was permanently engaged now? The beasts continued to stream to where she was deflowered. Were they sensing her or the act?

Talon thanked several ancient gods that Jayde hadn't taken a human man to her bed before she met him. Two images filled his mind, one sad and the other frightening.

The sad one involved a human man, sated and happy after his lover left his home. The beast that came for him would have stopped at nothing to gain the information he wanted about the woman whose blood still stained the human's skin. He'd have fed if necessary, though with most humans that was hardly necessary as a means to information.

He would have fed, all right. The beast would have fed for the killing rush and the ecstasy of the sex memories the man had of their *Blutjagdfrau*...and the pain the beast would have caused him for presuming to touch her would have been an even greater amusement for the damned thing. It would have been agony for the man left to face it. After that, the beast would have gone for her. That was the frightening part, what the beast would have done to Jayde when it found her.

Worse, was the idea of the beast coming upon them mid-coitus or in that hazy afterglow. The man still would have paid his price—during or even after the beast had taken Jayde as his reward for delivering her to the elders. If there were more than one beast, they might all have been granted that reward as a means to punish her before the elders took her to mate. The elders would have enjoyed her fight while it lasted and continued to use Jayde to please themselves and to produce their children until she died.

Talon shuddered at the image. That was what

awaited Jayde, if they took her from him. That was what would become of her, if he failed and she was not able to escape to death after him.

They would find a way past her amulet. Veriel had such a plan for Anna. He would use it to take Jayde. Of that, Talon had no doubt.

"Never." Talon swore raggedly, pushing back the rising rage before it registered to Piers and Gunther. "I'll never let that happen to her."

But, had he already set it in motion again? Was it her maidenhead or each time she mated? If it was the latter, the beasts would be on their way to her as soon as the sun set, and they would always be running. Talon prayed it was just her maidenhead.

"Corwyn is going to gods-damned kill me for this," he cursed.

* * * *

Jayde went out to the car and grabbed two of the bags from the back. As she turned back in the kitchen to go for more, she caught sight of Talon's expression. He was drawn and nervy.

"What's wrong?" she asked, a spike of terror racing through her.

"Nothing," he lied.

She grabbed the bags from his hands and thumped them on the countertop before turning back, her fists on her hips, to glare at him. "Don't ever lie to me, Talon Cross."

He nodded miserably. "I'm sorry for that. The truth is, I'm not sure."

"You sense something? Now? In broad daylight?

It's not even overcast."

"No. Nothing like that."

"Then what?"

Talon hesitated.

Jayde sighed and lifted herself onto the edge of the table. "I'm sitting down, Talon. Hit me with it."

"The next few nights will be tense," he began.

"Why? What's going on?"

"I think I may know what led them in, but I can't be sure, yet."

"Sex?" she guessed.

"If it is, they'll be showing up here. I'm praying it was just losing your virginity," he whispered. "If that was it, they won't be coming here."

She groaned. "Are you sure it wasn't just a chance encounter?" she questioned.

"I can't be sure of anything, right now. It could have been pure luck on their part, but that would be damned long odds," he admitted.

"Did you just come up with this out of the blue?" she demanded. "Or was there some catalyst that brought it together for you?"

He blushed and shuffled from foot to foot nervously.

"Talon," she ordered.

"Piers saw your blood on the sheets and in the trash," he whispered.

For a moment, Jayde wasn't sure her heart was still beating. "Then, Corwyn is on his way, and I'm not ready," she managed weakly.

"No, he's not. They assumed it was your monthly."

"You lied to them?" Her voice raised in panic. He couldn't lie to them, he said. The penalty for that was a bad one. "You'll get yourself killed," she accused.

"I didn't lie. I just didn't correct them."

Jayde glared at him. "Humans call that a lie of omission," she noted.

"They thought a monthly was good news. It meant you didn't come to us pregnant to a human. I simply assured them that the blood they saw confirmed that you didn't carry a human's child. It wasn't a lie...exactly. Everything I said was perfectly true."

She hit him. Some irrational part of her demanded it, though Jayde felt she might cry when she saw the raised mark of her hand on his cheek. He closed his eyes, as if the sight of her tortured him. That freed her to vent on him.

"Corwyn will kill you. Don't you get it?" she stormed. "If they see this as a lie, they will kill you for it."

Talon stepped further into the vee between her knees, but he didn't touch her. "If taking you brings them down on us in force, whether or not you're taken in the battle, he will kill me," he admitted. He dropped his chin to his chest. "I didn't know this was a possibility, Jayde. Forgive me, please."

"Forgive you for what? You weren't flying solo. I wanted it too, and neither of us knew."

"We still don't know," he reminded her. "For the next few days, we're sleeping part of the day and spending the night awake. If they're not led here in three days, they won't be—at least by that. That means half-days of training for those three days, but we'll make it up later."

"You forgot a step in there," she noted.

"I did?"

She nodded.

"What step?"

Jayde wrapped her legs around his hips and drew Talon to the edge of the table. She pulled his hands to her chest and leaned back on her elbows. "Bait," she whispered. "Lots of bait."

Talon's eyes locked on his hands for a moment then followed the path of them as he traced her body down to the scissor of her legs around him. The throbbing between her thighs rose and a liquid heat answered his touch.

"You really want to piss them off," he managed in ragged gasps as his body hardened and he pressed it to her in a daze.

Jayde shook her head. "I want you, here and now, forever," she invited. "Will you take me, here and now?"

Talon nodded his agreement as he caressed the warmth pooling between her thighs. "Here and now, forever." His hands moved to open the button and zipper on her jeans. "If Corwyn kills me, I'll die happy."

Chapter Twenty-Six

May 26ᵗʰ, 2002

Jayde tossed the sheets in the washer, raising the window to air the room out. While Talon finished his shower, she pulled fresh sheets on the bed. He launched out as she slid beneath the spray, granting him a quick kiss on his way past. By the time she was out, he had dressed and retreated to the kitchen to start breakfast. If all went well, Lord Crossbearer would assume they were simply going through a normal morning routine.

Jayde felt Gunther arrive while she dressed. Now that she knew what she was looking for, she realized she'd been feeling the presence of Warriors for years without knowing what they were.

She walked to the table just outside the small kitchenette, yawning from their recent lack of sleep. It had been four days, and the beasts hadn't shown up again. Talon had grudgingly pronounced them safe only last night.

"Good morning, Lord Crossbearer," she managed sleepily.

Gunther raised a mug of coffee to her. "Want some?" he offered.

"No. I haven't taken up caffeine—yet. I may have to soon."

"Probably better if you don't. It's a nasty habit, one of the few addictive habits Warriors allow themselves."

"Better than cigarettes," she replied, taking a seat and accepting a glass of milk from Talon. "Thanks."

"Beasts smell the smoke on clothing and breath,"

Talon informed her. "No smart Warrior goes anywhere near the stuff. Sausage and eggs?"

"Either that or a cream horn," she teased, sipping her milk.

His usual scowl rewarded the joke. "I still can't see how you can eat those things," he complained.

"You use caffeine. I use a sugar rush. Don't knock it till you try it."

"Tried it. Made me fat," he answered from the stove.

"You obviously weren't working hard enough to burn off the extra calories."

"Ah. Well, training today will show you what work is," he promised.

"Damn! Gotta learn to keep my big mouth shut." She raised an eyebrow at his back. "What? No sarcasm?"

"Just agreeing—and calculating the odds."

"Slim to none."

Talon set a plate in front of her and sighed. "That's what I thought. Figures. Breakfast, Grandfather?"

"No thanks. Just coffee," Gunther replied. "Never thought I'd see you cook."

Jayde laughed. "That's why I'm in charge of dinner and he's in charge of breakfast. He gets to cheat and use cereal or toast sometimes."

"You complain, and you're on your own," Talon shot back.

"Me? Complain?" Jayde replied innocently.

Talon turned from the stove, raising an eyebrow at her, his own plate in hand.

"Okay. I complain when I land too hard for comparative comfort."

"Better that than dead. How's that for comparative comfort?" he asked pointedly, as he speared his eggs and started eating.

Jayde chewed the mouthful she was working on while she considered it. "Ask me that after my tailbone heals," she muttered.

Gunther shook his head in amusement. "How is her training progressing?"

Talon nodded, swallowing a mouthful of sausage. "Better than I was at first night already," he admitted.

"Already? How?"

"Jayde has had training—not our training, but being cursed made her seek out training that the humans could give her. Most of what I've had to do so far has consisted of teaching her the basic movements, incorporating weapons into what she already knows, clean-up of her existing form, strategy—and motivation."

Jayde scowled at him. "Pain is a great motivator," she accused.

Gunther chuckled. "It usually is. Ask Talon about pain."

She raised an eyebrow at her husband.

Talon shrugged in response, though he darkened. "You can get over leaving a hole in your defenses if it's made painful enough often enough."

"Where was this hole?" she asked.

Talon studied his plate intently.

"I see. Guess I better not try that one."

"That would be a smart move," he muttered. "Besides, there isn't a hole there anymore."

"Bet me," Jayde warned.

Gunther laughed heartily. "That's one I'd pay to

see."

"Remember what I said about cocky?" Talon reminded her.

Jayde shrugged, popping another bite of sausage into her mouth.

"Besides, that won't work on a beast, remember?"

"No, but it will work on you if a beast does it," she replied quietly.

"Well," Gunther interrupted, "I wanted to get an update for Corwyn. He's decided to let Talon continue to train you for now."

Jayde nodded solemnly. "For how long?"

"I don't know. He wants to give you time to settle in, but he does want to meet you very soon."

Jayde gaped at him. She pushed away her plate and launched to her feet, grabbing her weapons belt and pulling it on as she headed for the door. Talon called out her name as she reached for the knob.

She stopped with her back to them and worked at the buckles for a moment. "I'm not ready, Talon. You know I'm not. Not yet."

"You'll do fine, Jayde," he soothed her.

"Fine isn't good enough."

Jayde pulled open the door and dragged the bracers from her back pocket as she walked into the sunlight outside. Fine wasn't good enough at all. She had to be flawless before she fought someone to protect Talon from Corwyn's wrath. There could be no chance of failure.

* * * *

Talon pushed his plate away and rubbed his

forehead roughly.

"What was that?" Gunther demanded. He had to know what Corwyn would find when he came for her.

"Nerves. That's a light case of them. You should see her when she's really spun." He pushed up from the table. "Oh well. Training is going to be interesting today."

He rose to follow his grandson. "In what way?"

"You'll see it for yourself."

Gunther followed him out into the field and settled onto the sidelines to watch. Jayde's expression was stony. It took determination to a whole new level. Someone that keyed up would either be a danger to herself or a formidable enemy. Gunther kicked back to see which it was.

At first, he was confused by what he saw. As usual, Jayde was armed and Talon wasn't. Talon issued reminders for form and strategy as they sparred. Gunther furrowed his brow and moved forward to watch closer. Jayde was passing up opportunities to strike right and left. *A danger to herself,* he decided.

Finally, Jayde called for time. "What are you doing?" she asked. "Stop opening up like that."

Gunther revamped his opinion slightly. She knew she was passing them up. Jayde was offended that Talon would give her openings instead of letting her find one.

"If that opening comes up in battle, you have to take it," Talon argued.

"You've met many beasts that sloppy?" she asked pointedly.

"A few."

"You wouldn't make that mistake. It's fake. Fight me for real."

"You won't be fighting me," he reminded her.

"According to you, I'm not going to be fighting someone as easy as you," Jayde countered hotly.

"You asked for it. You want my best?"

She smiled a predatory smile. "You won't give me that, but at least an honest effort."

"Agreed, but you take whatever openings you see."

"Any openings?" she asked with a raised eyebrow.

"I don't have a hole," Talon protested.

"If you say so." Jayde shrugged and brought her weapons up.

This time, Talon came in hard. Gunther had seen the young Warrior fight beasts less strenuously. A few minutes in, he landed a blow to her jaw. Talon backed away and gave her recovery time. Jayde nodded as she got her bearings to start again. Talon was right. First night boys were nowhere near this good.

Jayde got inside his defenses. Talon slipped away and immediately opened himself up for an attack, purposely, Gunther was sure. To the old lord's surprise, Jayde faked at the opening far enough to get Talon to react before striking at his groin. She backed off just enough to make the blow count without nailing him like Gunther would have himself for a mistake like that. For a long moment, they all froze as if in shock that she was right.

Talon sank to the ground, cupping himself and turning a deep red. Jayde grimaced, probably unaware that she'd pulled back sufficiently to keep him from more than a few minutes of discomfort. Gunther harrumphed at the knowledge that his grandson would be recovered far too readily for Lord Crossbearer's tastes. A mistake like that was deadly in battle. It should be extremely painful in training as a reminder.

Jayde sheathed her weapons and squatted next to him. "Are you all right?" she asked in genuine concern.

"Sure. Fabulous," he panted back.

"I told you. You leave a hole when you block like that. I'm sorry, but you wouldn't believe me any other way."

"Remind...me to believe you. Damn, that hurts!"

"I tried to be gentle," she protested.

"You were too gentle," Gunther shot back. "Next time, don't pull back, girl. Better you nail him in training than a beast in battle."

Talon glared at him. Already, he was recovering. His breathing had normalized, and his face was returning to a peachy hue. Gunther was sure that most of Talon's distress was the shock of her being right about the hole than an actual injury, per se.

"I want kids someday, Grandfather. If you want the Crossbearer line to continue—"

"If you want children, close that hole," he countered, rising from his place in the grass and striding over to his grandson. "And you," he shot at Jayde, "unsheathe those weapons and face me."

Her eyes widened. "You're kidding, right?" she managed, shrinking slightly toward Talon for aid.

"Why?" he inquired as he pulled off his jacket. "Are you afraid of hurting an old man?"

"Old man, my ass! I'm not afraid of hurting you. On the contrary, I have a pretty damned good idea of what you're capable of doing to me."

"No worse than a beast will," he argued. "Training

Warriors of Crossbearer always face their lord."

"I'm not a Warrior of Crossbearer. I'm a Warrior of Hunter." She looked to Talon for confirmation.

"Grandfather," Talon began evenly, taking up her case on that point of law.

"Be quiet, boy. You know very well that this is necessary. Corwyn demands my assessment of her progress to allow her to stay here. I have to give him a realistic view of her abilities. Jayde knows your fighting style. She won't know the style of a beast she encounters. Trial is the only way to accomplish what Corwyn wants of me."

Talon set his jaw angrily and nodded.

Gunther grunted at him and swung his gaze back to Jayde. She seemed lost in her consideration of what he'd said for a long moment. He needed her agreement for this, and Talon knew it. Jayde might know it, too. Gunther wasn't sure how much of the rules of sanction she'd learned.

Corwyn wanted this, but he hadn't specifically given his leave for a trial. Jayde could refuse. She could demand trial by Corwyn only. She wasn't bound by Crossbearer, even in his range.

Talon understood that he was forbidden to counsel her in this matter, but Gunther could see him aching to do so. What was he so worried about? Surely, Talon knew no one would dare leave a lasting injury on Jayde. She was too important to harm.

Jayde squared her shoulders and rose to face him. "All right," she decided.

Gunther stifled a sigh of relief. Either she didn't know her rights or she'd chosen to throw them away, despite her wish not to face him.

"Frightened?" he asked, glaring at her from under a raised eyebrow.

"Yes," she admitted. "I think that's reasonable."

"Good. You're not a fool. You should fear what I'm capable of, just as you should always be wary of what the beasts are capable of."

He dropped his jacket to Talon and moved several feet away from him. Gunther circled her, watching as she turned with him, keeping him in her sights. Jayde unsheathed her weapons silently, and Gunther smiled that she controlled her fear so well. Most of the boys in training shook when they faced him.

He unsheathed his weapon, and she backed off.

"Armed?" she asked.

"It's an appropriate test."

"The beast won't have a sacred weapon."

"No, he'll have two handfuls of razor-sharp claws," Gunther countered.

Jayde looked to Talon again. "Shouldn't we be wearing some sort of armor?" She furrowed her brow as if trying to remember something he had told her in the past.

Gunther glared at his grandson, and Talon averted his eyes, gritting his teeth.

"Talon doesn't wear armor, and he faces your blades every day," he noted dryly.

"Uh... No offense, but according to what I've heard, Talon is as far above my level as you are above his," Jayde returned.

"Which means I can keep my vow to your father and not maim you, without slowing you down with armor you won't have in battle."

Jayde sighed and nodded in resignation. She

302

moved forward and brought her weapons up. Still, she didn't shake in the face of him. "If I don't have a choice, I should just shut up and face you, right?" she noted without humor.

"Logical as well as intelligent. That's good."

Gunther came in, testing her reflexes and the appropriateness of her responses. Some of her choices surprised him, but they were effective and inventive. Overall, those were good qualities to have in the face of a beast. "Fast," he mused. "You'll need it."

Suddenly, he found her weakness. They always had one. It only amazed Gunther that it took so long to find Jayde's. Unaccustomed to fighting against a blade, her focus left his mid-line and strayed to his weapon far too often. Her attention was being diverted from the center out. That was a dangerous move in battle.

Gunther took advantage of what he saw. The next time her attention wavered, he aimed one of his meaty fists for her ribcage. Jayde saw it coming, but she was too late to avoid it entirely. She took most of his bone-jarring force square in the ribs and crumpled.

She dropped her weapons before her knees and wrapped her shaking hands firmly around her chest. Jayde rocked back and forth, gasping and fighting the spasms gripping her. Still, she didn't cry out, though Gunther knew she was capable of it. She didn't weep, though he was sure she felt the need to. Most of the boys did one or the other—or, like Piers, both—when faced with pain like that for the first time.

"Pain is an effective teacher, Jayde. Don't watch the blade so attentively that you forget to watch the beast wielding it."

She nodded in response, gritting her teeth against

a new wave of spasms. Jayde was a formidable Warrior. It was fitting that she was *Blutjagdfrau.*

Gunther sheathed his weapon and crossed to grab his jacket from Talon's hands. He startled at the fury in the young Warrior's eyes. He wasn't imagining it. His grandson was stamping back *Blutjagd.*

"She did well, Talon, better than you did after a year. You know that. My report to Corwyn will be favorable," Gunther assured him. "Your teaching isn't to blame for this. It's simply a lesson Jayde must correct for herself."

His grandson looked at him coldly and turned his eyes back to his student. There was something dangerous in his eyes, something guarded.

"What's on your mind, boy?" he demanded.

"Nothing, my lord." His voice was flat, emotionless. Gunther had never heard such a voice from Talon. He had a rare wit about him. Only in battle was he so serious.

"Bullshit! What's your problem, Talon? I told you my determination. Speak up."

Talon stood and faced him with a dark flash of mutiny in his eyes. At that one moment in time, Gunther could see the strength of the lord this man would one day be.

"I don't care about your determination. I care even less about Corwyn and what he wants. If Corwyn thinks this is a good idea, you can both eat that damned report for all I care. He's obviously too stupid to see what he's doing to her, and he doesn't deserve her trust."

Talon turned suddenly, closing his mouth before he could say more, and marched away to Jayde. After he sheathed Jayde's weapons for her, Talon helped her to her feet and walked her slowly back to the cabin.

Gunther watched them go. Something in Talon struck a chord in him that he couldn't quite name. If he hadn't seen the blows they'd dealt each other with his own eyes—

He shook his head and started back for the further of the parking areas. Talon knew his duty, and he knew better than to muddle his duty with anything that didn't belong, any sentiment.

Even though Jayde had been granted autonomy, if she did choose her husband, it would be paramount that all the houses be notified immediately. Autonomy or no, she belonged not only to house Hunter but to all of them. She had to, for her own safety.

Surely, it was simply concern he saw in Talon's eyes. Jayde was his duty, after all. Talon wouldn't want to see her hurt, physically or emotionally, in the state she was in. After all, it was his duty to keep her from harm and ease her into this life. He was only doing that duty, and Gunther's actions had been perceived as a threat to it.

* * * *

Talon peeled up Jayde's shirt to get a good look at the rising bruise, grimacing at what lay beneath.

"How bad is it?" she asked quietly.

"Worse than it needed to be," he spat. "Hang on while I get an icepack. We have to reduce this swelling."

She nodded as he sprinted away and closed her eyes in exhaustion. Jayde shivered as the icepack eased onto her ribs and hissed out a deep breath. "What did you say earlier?" she panted. "Damn, that hurts."

"He didn't have to do that," Talon objected.

"I won't argue that point. Will I have to do that with Corwyn?"

"I hope not. No, I know you won't."

"Did he treat you like that when you were training?"

"Worse," Talon admitted. "Believe it or not, he took it easy on you."

Jayde groaned. "Please, tell me I don't have to face him again," she pleaded.

"I doubt it. Gunther can gauge how you're progressing by that encounter. I'm sure he can tell Corwyn much of your fighting style from just those few minutes. Besides, you're not of his house. You could have demanded not to face him. He couldn't force you to, unless Corwyn gave him specific leave to face you in trial."

"Now you tell me."

"He wouldn't let me," he fumed. Talon seethed at that. Gunther had taken advantage of the situation. He'd trusted in her lack of knowledge, and he'd used the threat of Corwyn taking her away, though there was no way he could have known how effective a threat that would be.

Talon grimaced. Gunther might know now. He shouldn't have lost his composure that way. Gunther might suspect now. They would have to do the best they could, if he figured it out. Jayde was much more ready than she'd been even a few days earlier. They could handle a confrontation. They could defend their union. Talon was sure of it.

"So, if he demands another trial, I simply refuse?" she asked hopefully.

"It's not quite that simple. If he tries again, you have to demand trial by Lord Hunter. Even under his care, Gunther has no right to harm you without Corwyn's specific leave to do so. Your trials are Corwyn's right. I have a sneaking suspicion that Corwyn didn't give Gunther specific permission for this."

Jayde opened her eyes and stared at him in horror. "Great. So, I face Corwyn instead? He's even more of a badass than Gunther is. This is the man who took on Ver—that damned elder that killed my mother—three times. He's still breathing, Talon."

"Veriel," he breathed.

"Veriel. I mean, he didn't kill Veriel, but I've heard he's the only Warrior who's ever faced him and lived, let alone won. Corwyn won, dammit! How the hell do I fight him, Talon?"

Facing Gunther, Jayde took with resignation. Facing Corwyn had her shaking, and the man was halfway across the country. Talon wondered how much of that was reputation, how much was the fear of meeting the man who'd sired her, and how much was her fear of losing Talon to him.

"You won't have to," Talon assured her, hoping what Piers and Gunther told him about Corwyn was accurate.

Never a fan of the harsher tactics Gunther was fond of, Corwyn wanted nothing more than to bring his daughter home. It would kill him to do anything to jeopardize that if he could avoid it. Denied the chance to spoil his daughter as all Warriors spoiled their daughters, Corwyn would be wrapped around her little finger—he hoped.

"I don't understand. A trial is a trial, right?"

"You'll have your trial, but Corwyn won't hurt you, not like my grandfather did. You may fall, but it'll be like fighting me."

"How can you be sure?"

"No matter what Gunther said today, I know Corwyn won't be able to... Even Gunther was stunned by your resemblance to Anna. Corwyn doted on her. I don't think he'll be able to look at you and think of her and still hurt you. Printing is forever. I'm sure he loves Anna still.

"Losing both of you in the same night almost killed him. Corwyn dreamed of finding you for years. It was his only reason for living. Just as he had all but given up hope, you got dragged kicking and screaming back into his life, a daughter that had nothing but a lifetime of mistrust for him.

"Worse, he failed you—or he feels he did. There are so many roads he could have taken. Corwyn may not have had any chance of saving you the night your mother died. He was outnumbered badly, but he had a chance to have more help that he passed up. I'm sure he blames himself for that. But, Corwyn was right to refuse the help." He sighed.

"Why? Why would he refuse help if he knew we were in danger?"

"For fifteen hundred years, any Warrior lucky enough to have a daughter freed her rather than train her as *Blutjagdfrau*. Corwyn wanted to do the same. He never wanted this life for you. If Corwyn could do anything for you, he would free you now and visit you often. He can't, so he wants you to be happy. He gave you autonomy against the express wishes of every other house lord except Gunther. A man like that is not going to beat you to a pulp."

Her eyes widened. "Every one of them? I don't understand. What does this have to do with him refusing help protecting us?"

Talon met her eyes. "The other house lords— Every one of them demanded Corwyn train you instead of freeing you when Anna was pregnant with you. He refused. The price of his refusal was loss of support from the other lords. He'd promised Anna to free you if you weren't marked. Corwyn couldn't go back on that promise, and he wouldn't hand his only daughter over to this life if he could free you."

"So, he would have had to break his promise and let me be cursed to get the help?"

"I'm afraid so. Gunther is the only old lord from those days still alive. He— He was the first one to withdraw his aid. He regrets it. I know he regrets it. The other lords probably died regretting it. But, you were marked. Had they helped Corwyn, you would have been safe, and he couldn't have freed you anyway. They would have had what they wanted. It all went wrong somehow."

"Marked? Marked how?" Her eyes widened, and she reached her hand behind her shoulder. "The birthmark?"

Talon nodded. "We call them blood marks. It's the mark of Ani. The Stone chose you. It wouldn't have allowed you to be freed. It wanted you to be *Blutjagdfrau.*"

"If it wanted that, why did it allow me to be stranded? I could have been killed or taken at any time."

Talon shrugged. "I'm not sure. Maybe, the Stone thought you were safer where Veriel couldn't find you. Maybe, It wanted you out of the tension building between the houses. Maybe, it was a punishment on Corwyn for refusing to hand you over. I can't tell you that, but maybe It was protecting you. You said the amulet called to you when you were nearing sexual maturity. Maybe the Stone was protecting you all along."

"Do other Warriors have blood marks? How common are they?"

Talon shook his head. "All the first cursed had them to identify them. Regana had one as the mother of the greatest Warriors. After that, the only Warriors who had them were the ones born with the mark of Syth."

"Does it have some significance to have the mark of Syth?"

"Yes. It marks the next Stone lord."

"What does Ani mean?"

"It means you'll be the mother of the great beast killers."

"But didn't Regana already do that?" she asked in confusion.

"Well, there was no real change in the war after Andris was born. There have been rumors for a long time that something went very wrong there. I guess we'll find out soon enough."

"How?"

"When we have children, we'll know if something

changes. If our children aren't typical Warriors, we'll know we got it right this time."

Chapter Twenty-Seven

June 6th, 2002

Corwyn snapped awake, bolting up in bed. He regulated his breathing and wiped the sheen of sweat from his face. Nightmares! Now that he'd found Jayde, it seemed he'd been plagued by nightmares every time he slept for the last three weeks, worse in the two weeks since the beasts went on their rampage. Corwyn wasn't sure how much longer he could put off seeing her and deciding what was to be done.

Gunther had pronounced Jayde a phenomenal student in training. It was his assertion that she would be better trained than most young Warriors within the month, but he still maintained that she wasn't ready to leave the safety she'd forged for herself in Cross range, the link she had with Talon. The youngest Cross was still her only anchor.

Corwyn's dreams were beyond bad. In them, Veriel was laying over Jayde—Anna with black hair and eyes, the way Gunther had described Jayde to him—while she fought him and bled from a wound like the one the beast had left on Anna the night Corwyn saved her. If any beast came for Jayde, it would be Veriel. Corwyn knew that.

He wasn't even sure what happened between her and Grelden. He'd resolved to ask Talon face-to-face, so he could gauge the young man for the truth.

A voice whispered in his mind...the Stone. {*All will be well, Corwyn.*}

Now you talk to me? And I'm supposed to believe you, I suppose?

{You did not want your daughter pursued. You wished for her not to be pursued, did you not?}

You knew I didn't mean by taking her away from me!

{It was the only way. You could not have both wishes. You know now that she could not have been freed. If she was not set to the wind, she would have died or been taken. I took on her protection myself, as a mother would. This way, she will not even be pursued by your own.}

How do I manage that? The other lords are demanding consideration for their sons. It's been almost a month. I don't know how long I can hold them off.

{You can rebuff them forever.}

How? They'll send their men to her, whether she wishes it or not—whether I do or not. I had to give her autonomy, but giving Jayde autonomy made the men believe I don't need to be considered in forcing her out socially. How can I combat that?

{Go to her. See her.}

Now? Gunther says she's not ready.

{She is ready. She only thinks she is not. Go to her. You must see your daughter, Corwyn. See the woman she is now.}

But what do I do about the men?

{She needs to meet no men at this time. Tell them the Stone decrees that it is so.}

Shouldn't she produce children? The longer she waits, the greater the chance she'll be taken before she produces children. I know you won't allow her to shirk her duty. You never do.

{She needs to meet no men. Go to her quietly, Corwyn. See your daughter as she is. She is strong and

sure. She does you proud—and me. Go tonight.}

Why? What will I find?

{Silence...}

Damn you! What will I find? Why must I see her now?

{Silence...}

Why should I do your bidding, when you've crossed me before?

{Laughter... Go tonight, Corwyn.}

Corwyn cursed solidly then got out of bed and showered. He glanced at the clock. It was just after five o'clock. He could be dressed, packed, and to the airport in Minneapolis by seven.

He could call Amber on the way. Her little five-seater would do the trip to Manchester, NH for him. It was a Saturday, and Amber had most likely planned on a trip east anyway. Corwyn hoped he wasn't ruining any plans for her, but he hadn't called on Amber for anything in a long time. He needed this one. He made a mental note to supply her fuel money and buy her a meal in return. It was the least he could do.

Corwyn was sitting at the kitchen table with a cup of coffee and his duffel when Colin strode in from the night's hunt. Corwyn didn't have to ask how it went. Colin sent one to ground, and he was irritated with himself for it.

Colin eyed the duffel warily. "Something you need to tell me?" he asked.

"The Stone woke me up and told me to go see my daughter today. So, never one to want to piss the damned thing off, I go to see my daughter today. Want coffee? Or do you need sleep?"

"Sleep hell! Don't leave until I get back here."

"Where are you going?"

"To shower and throw a bag together."

"The Stone didn't mention you," Corwyn teased, knowing Colin wouldn't be turned away. His brother had been chomping at the bit to go see Jayde since the night she was found.

"Tough. I'll be down in fifteen minutes."

He was down in twelve. Colin grabbed a cup of coffee for the road, and they were on their way.

Stephen would content himself to wait to meet Jayde. That was his way. Besides, throwing all three of them at her would be overwhelming and would leave Hunter range nearly unprotected. For the sake of their protected alone, Corwyn couldn't do that.

They were waiting for Amber to refuel before Corwyn thought to call Gunther. The old man agreed to meet them at the airport and asked no questions beyond the fact that the Stone had ordered Corwyn to make the trip at this time.

Something about that bothered him. Corwyn had always hated the Stone's riddles. There was a riddle here. The Stone was silent when he'd asked why he had to go and what he would find. The Stone was always silent for riddles, and Corwyn hated riddles.

{Laughter... So untrusting!}

Oh, shut up!

* * * *

Corwyn looked at Gunther, as the old man drove the back roads into the Canadian mountains.

"Does she know I'm coming?" he asked nervously.

"No. She's nervous about meeting you, Corwyn.

She'd be a wreck if I told her ahead of time, especially with you coming so suddenly. They'll sense us soon."

"How soon?"

"Maybe ten minutes."

{Go quietly, Corwyn.}

Corwyn nodded in understanding. That was the second time the Stone had told him to go quietly. "Not if we ghost in," he decided.

Gunther startled. "You want to sneak up on them? Why?"

"I'd like to see her training session, before I make her nervous," he lied. In reality, Corwyn didn't know what the Stone wanted him to see, but he would go quietly and see whatever it was.

"Are you insinuating that Talon isn't doing his duty in her training?" He bristled visibly.

"Not at all. You told me she's a wonder. I believe you. I just want to get an unfettered look at them myself. I'm sure to put her off her game."

The older man nodded curtly. "Agreed. We should go ghost then, just in case Talon's range has expanded."

Corwyn nodded to Colin, letting him know to join them in the tandem.

His younger brother scowled at him but he complied. Colin was tired from lack of sleep, and he was crankier than normal because of it. Considering Colin's typical less-than-rosy attitude, that was saying a lot.

Gunther started speaking again as he parked down the mountain from the training cabin. "Talon says she's progressed even since I saw her last. Her initial problems were in training with his weapons. No more than that."

"Too heavy?" Corwyn guessed, closing the car door and eyeing the steep trail Gunther was pointing out to him.

"The grip is too large for her hands. I've asked James Armen to arrange for some fight-weight blades in training grips for her use. The weight doesn't seem to bother Jayde nearly as much as getting a decent hold when her fingers don't overlap properly."

"Is she so petite?" Corwyn asked in surprise. Jayde was female, but she was a Cursed Warrior. He'd expected her to be of a larger than average human stature because she was a Warrior, just as the men were.

"Much like Anna," the old man imparted. "Except for the coloring, she's her mother all over again. She's shy of five and a half feet and slender. But, don't be fooled. Jayde is much stronger than she looks. You'll see soon."

Corwyn nodded, but his heart sank. The inner vision of Anna running from Veriel with their child in her arms shook him. Surely, someone as fragile as Anna was could be no match for Veriel.

"What is it?" Gunther asked suddenly.

"How can she fight a beast?" he moaned.

"Many hunters are smaller than the prey they take down. Once you see Jayde fight, you may ask how a beast could fight her." He smiled indulgently at the thought.

Corwyn smiled crookedly in response. Jayde certainly sounded like an interesting jumble designed to confuse the beasts—and everyone else.

He eyed Gunther, picking his way over the almost

non-existent trail. "You up to this, old man?" Corwyn teased. "We do want to make it there by nightfall."

"I'll make it. I'm not so sure about your brother, though."

Corwyn glanced back. Colin had been exhausted before the trip, and it showed. He had fallen several hundred yards behind and was still lagging. Corwyn shrugged. He'd catch up eventually.

He looked back to Gunther. "You're in good shape for a man your age."

Gunther offered a snap of his head in acceptance of the compliment but didn't answer. They walked for another fifteen minutes before he motioned to Corwyn. "Just down this slope," he whispered.

Halfway down, Corwyn could already hear the training.

"Again," a male voice instructed below. "Don't drop that elbow. Arm straight."

"Quit shouting commands at me and fight me, dammit," a female voice replied acidly.

Talon laughed in return. "You asked for it," he warned.

They cleared the thick trees, and Corwyn gasped at the scene before him.

Jayde moved fluidly around the open space. She blocked blows rained down on her and attacked with lightning speed whenever the opportunity arose. Jayde's dark hair was pulled back in a thick braid. She wore a Warrior's black T-shirt. The matching headband was soaked in sweat, her jeans covered in dirt and grass stains, and her leather tennis shoes worn and filthy. Her wrists were encased in a pair of training bracers.

He was so rapt on his daughter, drinking in every detail about his first look at her, that Corwyn almost missed the three most important and surprising issues about her training.

The fact that they were both training without armor struck him first. Corwyn almost launched out in fury until he realized that Talon was fighting Jayde unarmed. His blows, if he landed any, would hurt but not maim. The young Warrior was masterful for his age.

{Twenty-nine,} the Stone supplied for him.

The final revelation stunned Corwyn most of all. Jayde was fighting dual-style. The ancient style hadn't been used for at least three centuries that he knew of. Yet, Talon was teaching her to fight dual. It was a brilliant move on his part. No one would expect to see the dead style, but Corwyn had to wonder where Talon learned it himself.

Before he could ask that question of Gunther, Talon faked in to lead Jayde's hand. To Corwyn's surprise, his daughter saw through the ruse and arced one of her blades at his chest instead. Talon threw himself backward to avoid the deadly back slice headed his way. Corwyn smiled at her victory—too soon.

Talon swept her legs from under her, sending Jayde crashing to the ground with bone-jarring force that knocked the wind out of her in an audible blast. The young man launched over her and made to simulate his killing blow, but her blade was already at his throat.

Corwyn held his breath, waiting to see how Talon would handle the mistake. The Crossbearers were notorious for their vicious training practices. That one fact made him fear for his daughter training in this range, but Corwyn had trusted that they would abide by his wishes for training. Now was the moment of truth.

Talon scowled at her and took her wrist, gently leading Jayde's blade to his heart. "Stop thinking human," he reminded her. "You have only one blow when the beast has you like this. You cannot injure him and dance away like you do on your feet. Bleeding him is not enough. The blow you use must kill him in one shot. He cannot have the chance to retaliate. Remember that. He'll kill you, Jayde. Don't give him the chance."

He released her wrist, and she dropped her arms to the ground, trying to catch her breath. Talon pushed to his feet and reached a hand down for her. Jayde sheathed her weapons and took his hand, letting him fairly lift her to her feet.

"Six hours a day," Gunther whispered. "Without fail."

Corwyn nodded his approval. Boys in the change got little more than half that much training.

She stretched her back tenderly. "That's going to bruise," she muttered.

"Better that than dead," Talon replied evenly.

Jayde smiled crookedly. "Such a sweet talker. Is it any wonder I love you so?"

Corwyn raised an eyebrow at Gunther, but the other man had gone pale, his breathing strangled. That alone came as a bad sign to Corwyn. It was obviously not a joke that the older man had ever heard them use.

Before Corwyn could ask if there was any possibility that it was true, Jayde ran a hand along

Talon's jawline affectionately. He bent to capture her mouth in an explosive kiss, pulling her to him possessively. Their weapons clashing punctuated the move, as Talon pulled her up into his arms. Her feet left the ground as he straightened to his full height with her pinned against him. Jayde stroked a hand up his chest suggestively, drawing a groan of pleasure from the young Warrior.

Gunther started to stammer an apology, but Corwyn waved at him for silence.

Talon placed her back on her feet gently and wrapped Jayde under his arm. "Easy on the weapons," he teased.

"Who pulled who?" she asked pointedly.

Talon laughed a husky laugh in response. "Let's get inside and rub out that back," he invited.

"And eat. I'm starving."

"Not cream horns. For the love of all that's holy, no cream horns."

"For dessert?"

"Ugh! If you must."

They stilled, and the smiles disappeared from their faces.

"What is that?" Jayde asked urgently.

Talon pushed her behind him in the standard protective stance a Warrior took when taking an unsealed trainee out into battle. "It's malevolent," he mused. "Stay at my back." His weapon came up instantly.

"It's daylight," she protested. "You said they can't send anything I can't handle until dark."

"Stay at my back," Talon ordered again. His eyes scanned the trees for signs of the being they were sensing.

Corwyn recognized it immediately. It was Colin, and malevolent was an understatement. Apparently, he'd caught up just in time to see Talon's exchange with Jayde.

Jayde wheeled, and her weapon came up for a killing throw before Corwyn even noted the first sign of Colin moving toward them.

Feeling the sudden movement, Talon turned and gripped her throwing arm. "No. Stop. He's one of ours."

Jayde watched Colin's approach uncertainly. She shivered and sank to Talon's back.

Corwyn watched in interest, motioning Gunther to stay out of what was unfolding. Colin may be furious, but Corwyn had his own suspicions about what was going on. He wanted to see how the young couple would conduct themselves before he made his final determination.

Colin stormed to Talon, red-faced and fisting and unfisting his hands constantly as he came. The younger man sheathed his weapon and stood his ground, waiting for the blow he knew was coming. When it came, it knocked Talon to his knees. Corwyn smiled that he didn't defend himself. Talon accepted judgment gracefully.

"Leave," Colin ordered Jayde.

"No." She tried to pull Talon to his feet by her side, but he waved her off, still gasping for breath.

"Fine. Then watch what happens," Colin replied coldly.

He had barely unsheathed his weapon when both of Jayde's were scissored around his throat. Corwyn could see the cold challenge in her eyes. *Blutjagd* was in her manner, burning in her skin like a white-hot cauter. She had printed, and her blood screamed for her to protect her mate. Jayde would choose no other now, and she would bear Talon's children.

{*Perfect. You see? She has no need to meet men.*}

Corwyn ignored the Stone's assessment. He hadn't planned on Jayde printing when he allowed her to stay, but it was a simple answer to all the most immediate problems. She couldn't choose another, so the other Warriors could stay at home and not bother her. Her body would scream to do her duty now. That would please the house lords. Her printing would make her happy, and that in turn would please Corwyn. All he'd ever wanted was her happiness. Overall, it was the best thing that could have happened.

"Throw the weapon away," she ordered Colin.

Colin hesitated, unwilling to give up his perceived right to punish Talon. Corwyn would have to take him to task for that later.

"You are not a vampire—not a beast. You'll die if I do this. Given the choice, I will kill you."

Colin swallowed and met her eyes. "You don't know who I am," he warned.

"On the contrary, you're Colin of Hunter. Welcome to Crossbearer, Uncle. Now that we've settled that, throw away the damned blade."

"You know who I am, but you're refusing my order? Has he taught you nothing? You are a woman of my house," Colin fumed.

"No, I'm not; I am a Warrior of *our* house, and I answer only to Corwyn Lord Hunter, Stone lord and elder hunter. The fact that I'm a female is immaterial. I'm cursed just like you. That affords me all the same rights as you. You've overstepped your bounds, Colin. Stand down."

"This man has taken what is not his to take. He must pay the price. That's our law."

"The Warriors don't ask permission of their houses to marry or mate. He took only what was offered by a Warrior, as is *my* right," she countered. Jayde moved one of her blades to press deeper into his throat as Colin startled.

"Mate?" His face darkened. "You have not permitted that," he thundered.

"I answer only to Lord Hunter," she reminded him.

Colin grabbed Talon by his collar, and Jayde drew a warning cut with her blade. Colin ignored it, but he didn't move his weapon any closer to Talon when he questioned him.

"You answer me. Have you broken our laws and taken her with no permission?"

Corwyn smiled, as Talon met his eyes and said nothing. Jayde took over, as was the way it should have been. Talon couldn't defend himself in any way unless asked by his judge. That was her place.

"Talon has broken no laws, and he answers only to Lord Hunter and Lord Crossbearer. I demand my true judge," Jayde shouted.

"Enough," Corwyn bellowed as he released his ghosting and stepped forward.

Beside him, Gunther did the same thing.

"Sheathe your weapons and stand down."

Jayde started to move, hesitated, and waited for Colin to move first, unwilling to chance Talon's life on Colin's loyalty to his lord.

Corwyn grumbled at his brother's stubborn streak.

"Colin, sheathe your weapon and stand down," he ordered again.

Colin nodded and pushed Talon back onto his heels then sheathed his weapon. Jayde moved immediately to sheathe her own. She helped Talon to his feet and faced her father with her chin raised in challenge.

Gunther stepped around Colin to Talon. "What were you thinking?" he demanded. "I can't protect you now. I must deliver you into Lord Hunter's hands for judgment. You know that."

Talon nodded grimly, his hand pressed over his aching ribs. "You said Lord Hunter had afforded Jayde autonomy, Grandfather," he croaked, offering his first defense to his first judge.

Lord Crossbearer's eyes widened. "I never meant that. By the gods, you had to know I didn't mean that. As *Blutjagdfrau*, her mating—"

"You said all her decisions, any right a Warrior had," Talon reminded him in a clearer voice.

Gunther started to rage, but Corwyn cut him off cleanly. "Explain yourself," he ordered Jayde.

"You heard what I said to Colin?" she asked.

"I did. I also heard what you said to Talon of Crossbearer. So, I'm asking you. What is the truth, Jayde?"

"The truth is that I've exercised my rights as a Warrior. I've made my choice of husband and mate, and Talon made his choice of wife and mate, as is our right. You want children of me within the houses? You'll have them on one condition, the condition *you* agreed to. I choose my mate. Refuse me my rights or take Talon from me in any way, and I will never submit. I'll go to the Warrior's Rest childless. I swear it."

"Blackmail? Why this man and no other?" Corwyn asked in amusement.

"I love him, and I'll accept no less than that. I am not a brood mare. My children will be born out of love or not at all. The choice is yours. I've made mine, and I warn you, I am immovable."

"You love him?"

She nodded resolutely and raised her chin another notch, challenging him again.

"What about you, Talon of Crossbearer? Is her story true?"

"Yes, my lord. If there is judgment to be passed, I'm at your mercy in this matter. I take responsibility for my actions."

"Do you return my daughter's love?" Corwyn asked pointedly.

Talon smiled at Jayde and wound his fingers through hers, prompting a scathing look from Colin. "I do, Lord Hunter. I would gladly give my life for her with no thought of my duty to do so."

Corwyn nodded at the bit of the ancient joining ceremony Talon quoted. He sighed raggedly. "Then, my course is clear. I give my blessing to this union," he decided. "I'll inform the other house lords later."

"What?" Colin asked in disbelief. "How can you give her to that thieving—"

"Quiet," Corwyn ordered. "Female or not, Jayde was well within her rights." He smiled warmly at his daughter. "Let's go inside. We have a lot to talk about."

She looked at him anxiously, still unsure.

Corwyn softened. "You're still demanding cream

horns, huh? HoHos and ice cream too, I'll wager."

Jayde moved her mouth as if to speak then shut it in what appeared to be confusion. She tried again. "If you've had people watching me, why didn't you come for me before the change?"

He laughed. "I haven't. I was basing that on what your mother craved when she was pregnant with you."

Talon swore under his breath as he leaned lightly on her for support. "Is that what gods-damned did it?"

* * * *

Talon winced, as Jayde placed the icepack on his ribs.

"That's going to bruise," she teased, "but better bruised than dead, right?"

He laughed then grimaced in response to the movement. "Yeah. Wait until tomorrow's workout," he warned.

"I wanted to ask about that," Corwyn interrupted. "Talon, who taught you to battle dual-style? It was inspired to teach Jayde the old form."

Talon darkened. "I tried to teach her standard battle. I wasn't going for inspired. I just wanted her able to fight. Simply put, she can't do it."

"I always felt off balance," Jayde admitted. "Even when I lose a blade, I can keep my balance, based on a two-bladed style, now that I've learned what that balance is."

"Felt off balance, hell! You were off balance. Dangerously off. Anyway, when Gunther sent out the training gear for her, I got sidetracked with him for a few minutes while she got her gear on. The next thing I knew, she was gliding beautifully with two weapons and almost perfect balance. I knew then that it was dual or nothing."

Corwyn nodded pensively. "But who taught you?"

"I suppose you could say we taught each other. I started her with the basic movements, right and left. Jayde started with her human training in martial arts and added the blades with my help. After that, we winged it. She came up with whatever felt right in the situation, and we improvised new moves, based on balance and incoming attack. Gunther can tell you that she still improvises well in battle."

"I guarantee you they've never seen anything like it," Gunther concurred. "Not even the first cursed would have fought like this. That alone will make up for those ten lost years of training."

Jayde curled into Talon's shoulder. "I have a good teacher," she yawned, already half-asleep.

"Oh, no, you don't," Talon ordered. "Up. To the shower. You fall asleep like that and you won't be able to move in the morning."

She snuggled further in. "Like you'll be any better."

"I will be, if you don't let me get liniment into that back before you knot up. Then sleep, unless you're still hungry."

"Starving, but I think sleep wins the toss tonight."

"Go get your shower. I'll be in with the liniment and a sandwich when you're done."

"And a cream horn?" she added hopefully.

Talon shook his head, screwing up his face in disgust. "All right. Now, go."

Jayde grumbled but she got to her feet and started for the bedroom.

As the spray of the shower sounded through the main room, Colin eyed Talon suspiciously. "Just what are the sleeping arrangements, Talon of Crossbearer?"

Gunther blushed deeply and looked away. Lord Hunter's eyes glittered in amusement under a raised eyebrow, and he smiled crookedly.

Talon sighed and met Colin's intent gaze steadily. "I suppose you're asking if I'm accustomed to sharing Jayde's bed at night?" he guessed.

"Are you?" he countered.

"Yes, to be honest, I am. The first few days, I prayed Corwyn would come for her quickly. By the time she had her autonomy, Jayde had already made her wishes known and asked for mine. Spending day after day with her, knowing we both wanted the same thing and couldn't pursue it, eating, training, sleeping under the same roof, comforting her when she was upset— It was driving me insane, and probably her too, though she was always better at hiding it.

"When we received news that Lord Hunter would support her decisions, neither of us thought our choices would be condemned. Or maybe we just hoped that the chance of our producing children quickly would outweigh any objections. Whatever the case, we've been sharing a bed since then."

"How long has that been?" Corwyn asked.

Talon met his eyes evenly. After all, the judgment was for him. He had nothing to fear in telling Lord Hunter anything he wanted to know, except that he'd taken pleasure in Jayde before her autonomy was announced. That was something Talon wouldn't divulge unless he was asked directly, and still it would only be a matter of a few blows. Corwyn might even show leniency, considering Talon hadn't pushed to judge Colin for his trespass.

"Two weeks," he admitted. "Once we knew Jayde had autonomy— Waiting had been difficult for both of us."

"Good. Care for her well. When her time is close, don't leave her side for any reason, and don't be the only one to protect her." Corwyn glared at Gunther, and the other man stared at his hands. "I'm sure that every house lord will grant you men from the moment we know she carries and for as long as we feel them necessary."

Gunther nodded without looking up.

"If she does carry, the beasts will stop at nothing to destroy your child, even if it means destroying Jayde as well. Better to wait a thousand more years than to lose outright. Teach her the *Zeremonie der Freiheit* and the *Zeremonie des Schutzes*. She can perform them, and she may have to, if things go badly at the birth.

"You and Jayde are good together, but in accepting her, you've accepted a more solemn oath than any other. You'll no longer be a roaming Night Warrior. You won't travel to prey. The only prey you take, from this day on, will be what comes for you both, and they *will* come for you. You are no longer Crossbearer. Jayde is no longer Hunter. Together, you are *Haus König*."

Talon startled. "A new house? Can that be done?"

"It is done. This is the Stone's idea. When I contact the other lords, I'll inform them. All the houses will be at your disposal. Your range will encompass every range. Whenever Jayde is in danger, you'll find asylum and protection in every house. Your orders, yours and Jayde's and your children's after you, will be law."

"Will the other houses agree to something like that? There's never been a master of all. Even the Stone lord and master trainers only had limited power over the house lords."

Gunther cut in. "For the end of our curse? They'll accept it without question. But, what will become of Crossbearer?"

Talon's heart sank. He had condemned his house. "I'm sorry, Grandfather. I thought Jayde and I would retain our families. I didn't know."

Corwyn sighed. "The Stone is amusing itself again. It only tells me that the answer will be clear in time. I don't understand it. Short of you or Piers producing another heir at this point—" He shook his head. With Talon's mother and grandmother both dead, there was no way either of the men would do that.

Gunther nodded. "*Für die Ausrottung der Biester, die die Nacht durchstreifen, werden wir unser Lebensblut und unsere Leben geben.* For the extinction of the beasts that walk the night, we will give our life's blood and our lives," he quoted from *The Stone's Words* by Gawen. "If Crossbearer dies, it dies."

"You'll be legends," Corwyn assured him. "The Stone has shown me the seal Jayde and Talon will use. *Haus König* will be Hunter-Crossbearers, *Jäger-Kreuzträger.* They'll use a dual seal of the two houses topped by a crown. It's a small consolation, I know."

"I'm honored," Gunther decided.

Talon looked up as the water turned off. He ground his teeth as he pushed to his feet to get Jayde food and liniment before she managed to fall asleep. "Goodnight, gentlemen. If there are no objections, I need to make sure Jayde eats and tend to her injuries now."

Corwyn smiled and shook his head. "You do your duty well, Talon. I would ask a favor of you, aside from your duties." The request had a touch of a plea to it.

Talon turned back to him in surprise. "Yes, Lord Hunter?"

"Protecting Jayde and teaching her are fine. Caring for her physical and emotional state is a good thing. I ask that you keep her happy, as happy as she can be considering what her life must be."

Talon nodded grimly. "That's all I've ever wanted. I can do no less for her. You know that." He started to turn, but Corwyn stopped him again.

"Talon? I must ask one last question..."

He met the lord's eyes uncertainly. Corwyn was in the midst of a great pain. Whatever he was about to ask was hard for him.

"Anything," Talon vowed.

"I know that Grelden laid hands on her," Corwyn managed. Just saying the words tortured him.

Talon's jaw tightened at the memory of the beast's attack then again in the knowledge of what Jayde's father feared most. "Grelden took no pleasure from her, nothing at all. You should be proud of Jayde. When the beast struck, the amulet confused him long enough for her to attack him in return, bare handed but with a blow that would have felled any human man alive. Before I could take his life, Grelden struck her in return—once. He never laid hands on Jayde again. Banish all concerns that your daughter has been abused or taken advantage of, Lord Hunter. She hasn't. Not by anyone."

"I would not suggest that you took her by force or coercion, Talon Lord *König*." Corwyn used the formal address that was his now as a show of respect for the man the Stone had just named his better.

It was jarring to Talon to think of himself as the new Lord of all houses. He put up his hand to stop Corwyn's formal speech. "No. You misunderstood me. Your daughter came to me, Corwyn. She made her choice known and asked for mine. But, she gave me a gift she'd surrendered to no other man. Jayde was intact when she came to me. I swear it to you."

Corwyn looked at him in shock then nodded slowly. "Thank you, Talon. Thank you for telling me."

"Ordinarily, it's not something I would share with you, but I felt you needed to know for your own peace of mind. Good night, Lord Hunter. Sleep easily."

"I will," he replied. "I will now."

Chapter Twenty-Eight

June 7th, 2002

Corwyn watched, as Jayde came to breakfast. Her long, black hair, still damp from the shower, was braided down her back again. His breath caught. An image of Anna, her red hair caught up in a similar style and her green eyes flashing in mirth, assaulted him. A deep sadness made him look away, blinking back tears.

He knew that moment so well. The swell of her pregnant belly had rested beneath his hands as he played with Erin—with Jayde through her skin. Anna had been teasing him not to be late for dinner. She was making his favorite, and he was picking up ice cream for her. The next time Corwyn saw her was his last, because he was too late, because he made the wrong choices, because he allowed himself to be sidetracked from his duty and his love at the worst possible moment.

Corwyn assessed Jayde critically. She may have Anna's features, but the resemblance ended there. Her hair was the color his was when she was born, before the gray took root. Her eyes were almost as black as her hair.

Corwyn had been far too young to be Lord Hunter at twenty-eight, but fate doesn't always choose paths to please the fated. That more than anything had contributed to the mistakes that cost him Anna and Jayde, his youth and inexperience.

And his lies of omission. If only he had prepared Anna for what their females truly represented, for why

Veriel would go to such lengths to have one that was still cursed. He hadn't wanted to frighten her. Maybe if Corwyn had, she would have insisted on the aid that was offered, despite the cost. Maybe Anna wouldn't have begged him to go see Carrick that day.

Corwyn had known Veriel's single-minded course on Anna and Jayde. He should have made choices that took that into account instead of his pride.

He shook his head and returned to his evaluation of his daughter. Her build was deceiving. While Anna was all soft curves, he knew Jayde's curves hid well-trained muscle, enough to make many of their young men ashamed. She was fast and strong. She had a quick, analytical mind.

Moreover, Jayde could temper her sweet smile and easygoing nature with fierce territoriality and determination. When *Blutjagd* was upon her, she was controlled in her fury, and she showed no fear in battle. Light bruises in various stages of healing announced the ferocity with which she trained.

Talon, to his credit, hadn't adopted the Crossbearer style of beating his pupil senseless as a means of teaching. He laid blows, but he trusted Jayde to adjust of her own accord. He lectured but didn't berate her. From what little Corwyn had seen, it was more than effective. She was stunning.

Corwyn smiled, remembering his run-in with Colin late in the evening. His younger brother was still having trouble relinquishing the thought of Jayde as a helpless Hunter-protected girl long enough to see the woman she was. It was something Corwyn would have to work on. Eventually, Jayde and Talon would visit Hunter range, and Colin had to learn the proper respect for them by then. Vow of protection or no, Jayde wasn't Colin's to lord over.

Corwyn found himself listening to the soft sounds filtering from the bedroom into the stillness of the main room with newfound respect for Talon. It was obvious that his tenderness extended beyond his battle training into other areas of their lives together.

He'd always wondered how he would feel to find his daughter grown and fully educated as a woman. The answer, when it came, surprised him. Relief! Corwyn was relieved that she'd bound herself to a man like Talon, who would protect her life and bring joy to it at the same time.

So, when Colin launched to his feet in fury, Corwyn met him toe-to-toe and dragged him bodily to the porch, waving for a red-faced Gunther to accompany them out. The door closed behind them, and he threw his brother to the dirt.

"Stand down, Colin," Corwyn warned dangerously. "I gave my blessing. It's their right to take pleasure in each other."

"He's mocking us," Colin countered. "He's prodding us because he can. Corwyn, see the light. He took her deceitfully, and he can't even claim her a wanton woman. He admits he took her maidenhead."

"I have no doubts that they love each other."

"She's met no one else."

"On the contrary, Jayde has met a whole world full of human men and never chosen one to give herself to. Can any male Warrior say that of human females at her age? What she saw in Talon moved her to commit to him. I respect that. It speaks highly of him."

"Why? Because he's convinced her to open her legs

to him? There's a first time for everything, Corwyn. Any decent rake can accomplish that of a virtuous woman given enough time, and gods know better than most, he had all the time in the world to do the convincing."

Gunther's hand moved to his weapon. "You dare attack the honor of my family?" he asked archly, his blood starting to burn.

"You were quick to attack him this afternoon, I noticed."

"In shock," Gunther admitted. "I hadn't..." He darkened. "No, I did suspect, but I had dismissed it. But...Corwyn is right. They only exercised their rights as Warriors. It wasn't my place or yours to stop them."

Colin's eyes narrowed in the dim light filtering between the parted drapes. "You knew?" he raged.

"I suspected—for a moment. I dismissed it as too far-fetched."

Corwyn put up a hand to still Colin. "What made you suspect?"

"Talon got angry with me. He disagreed with a decision I made regarding Jayde's training. He didn't balk me directly, but prodded, he spoke his mind, and whatever he didn't say was fierce and unforgiving."

"What decision did he disagree with?"

"She faced me in trial. Talon felt I was too harsh in my correction of her mistake."

"That wasn't within your rights," Corwyn protested.

"You wanted my opinion of her training. I can only give you my realistic evaluation by trial. A new opponent, a new situation, and no rules of engagement are the best conditions for a realistic view of fighting skill. It must be like battle in every way possible."

"What did you do, old man?" Corwyn growled.

"A single blow, Corwyn. I drew no blood and broke no bones. If Talon had made that same mistake, even after a year of training, he would have had a scar for his lesson."

"Pray that her story is the same," he warned.

Corwyn was satisfied to see the bastard's eyes widen before Gunther nodded his agreement. He had warned Gunther what he expected. If Crossbearer overstepped his bounds, he would pay the penalty with a fine measure of interest.

"What made you dismiss the idea?" Corwyn asked suddenly. "Did you think Talon so in fear of your wrath that he would be immune to her?"

"No couple lays blows like they did in my presence. She even—" Gunther shook his head in confusion. "I still can't believe she did that, considering what I now know."

"Did what?" Corwyn demanded.

"She showed Talon a hole, a failing of his I thought I had broken him of at sixteen, but bad habits have a way of reappearing if not properly motivated to correct them once in awhile, I suppose. She faked him away to open his stance and took him down by the balls to prove that he was leaving a hole. He was too, pardon the pun, cocksure. Talon denied he was leaving one right up to the moment she used it. Jayde did ease off and prove it as gently as one can and still make it more than painfully clear to a man, but no woman in love would purposely—"

Corwyn laughed in spite of himself, great whooping gales of laughter. "She will if she's protecting her future interests." He sobered slightly. "Listen to me, both of you. However this union began aside, Talon will give *her children that will end the curse for us all. She's printed as we males print. Jayde does share our curse, and you would have to be blind not to recognize the signs of it in her. I will stand for no interference with that. They've chosen this, chosen each other. At the very least, you will both respect it for the salvation it is."*

Corwyn smiled as Jayde's cry of release echoed through the windows followed by Talon's. Gods, it was good that he made her so happy.

"Personally, I hope they give each other pleasure often. Better the chances that the curse will end soon." And, Jayde can be truly free. *They all could be truly free.*

"Breakfast, Corwyn?" Talon asked, breaking him out of his reverie.

"Yes. Thank you." He accepted a plate from the young Warrior's hand. "So, what are your plans for Jayde's training?" Corwyn asked as he sampled the food on the plate and found it superior to his own by far.

Jayde looked up from her half-empty plate and raised an eyebrow at her husband. He smiled in return. It was a private joke, Corwyn was sure.

"We still have to get some blade on blade in, but I need to get her armored for that," Talon answered.

"She won't have armor in battle," Gunther countered.

"That was a lousy argument last time, and it's lousy now," Talon muttered.

"Last time?" Corwyn asked pointedly. "What last time?"

He panned his gaze around the table. Talon's jaw tightened in anger, and he speared at the food on his plate. Jayde rubbed her forehead roughly and stared at hers. Gunther looked at the two of them as if he didn't understand the problem in the least.

Corwyn's blood burned, but he held onto control. He would issue a warning and let them keep whatever secret lay hidden here, he decided. "*Ich habe dir bis jetzt vertraut, Talon. Sie ist immer noch meine Tochter. Wenn ich erfahre, dass du mit ihr Schwert gegen Schwert ohne Rüstung trainiert hast, wirst du mir dafür antworten müssen. Du weißt es besser,*" he warned. Corwyn didn't want to upset Jayde with the warning, but he wanted to make himself clear. Married to Talon or not, he would still protect his daughter from harm.

Jayde moved suddenly. She took to her feet and slammed her open hands down on the table in front of her as she leaned across to her father. "*Du hast recht. Er weiß es besser.* You're right. He does know better," she translated smoothly. "Don't try that shit with me, Corwyn. I speak German." She glared at her father. "You posturing males really are too much," she spat as she scooped up her weapons belt and stormed outside, slamming the door behind her.

Talon pushed his plate away and cursed solidly in the ancient language as he started to stand.

"Haven't you broken her of that foolishness yet?" Gunther grumbled at him.

The young man froze and trained cold eyes on the Lord Crossbearer. "Strangely enough, Grandfather, you and Corwyn always seem to be involved when she decides to get in this mood. I asked you to back down last time. This time, I'm telling you. Stay out of it," he warned.

"Don't balk me, boy. I'm still your house lord."

"Not after last night, you're not. *König*, remember?"

"That's not settled yet," Gunther thundered.

"The Stone decreed it. It's settled, all right. Besides that, Jayde is my *wife*. Even if you were my house lord, you're not hers and you have no say about my dealings with my wife.

"You are counterproductive to everything I seek to do. That little blade on blade between you and Jayde was a bad idea. I said it then, and I'm saying it now. Only, now I have the right to back my protest."

"Wait," Corwyn interrupted. "You're saying Jayde agreed with this unarmored blade on blade?"

"No," Talon exploded. "She asked for armor. Didn't she, Grandfather? She begged, as a Warrior of Hunter, not to face you as trained of Crossbearer. You gave her no options and only promised not to maim her as a *favor*," he spat, "to Corwyn. And when you took her down, what did you say to her? Pain is an effective teacher, Jayde. While she knelt there, wracked in pain and barely able to draw breath, you stood over her and told her that."

Talon turned on Corwyn. "Did you like the blow Colin landed on me yesterday? Pretty piece of work, wasn't it? It was a love tap compared to what the mighty Lord Crossbearer laid on her. She could barely swing a blade for two days after he was through." Talon shook his head in disgust.

If Gunther saw the blow coming, he gave no sign of it. Corwyn stood over him, red-faced and shaking. "Take your time recovering, old man. After I clear up this misconception with Jayde, I expect to take my satisfaction out of your sorry hide." He put a hand up to stop Talon as the young man headed for the door.

"Make sure your grandfather is ready to face me. I need to discuss this with my daughter alone."

Talon looked at him in concern then nodded and backed away. Satisfied that they understood each other perfectly, Corwyn stormed out the way Jayde had gone.

He was pleased to see she hadn't gone far. Somehow, Corwyn doubted that she ever had.

She sat, cross-legged in the middle of the training field, balancing her blade on one finger like a bored child with a wooden play weapon. Jayde didn't look up as he approached, but Corwyn felt sure she knew he was there.

"Up for a little sparring practice?" he asked.

Jayde sighed, her attention still locked on the weapon. "It's your right to demand it. I get my privileges as long as I bend to your will in things like this. So, I suppose I should just shut up and face you, right?"

Corwyn cringed at that. "I didn't demand a trial. I asked for a sparring partner," he reminded her, settling beside her.

She sheathed her blade, a dance of metal over her hand, and looked at him in confusion. "What's the difference? You're still my house lord either way I fight you."

"You've been with Crossbearer too long," he muttered. He could see her firing up for an argument and put up a hand to calm her. "Relax. I meant Gunther, not Talon."

Jayde nodded. "Can't say I'd argue that one," she managed with a tight smile.

"He put you to trial?"

Her eyebrows rose. "Talon was right. You really didn't know, did you?"

"No, I didn't. It won't happen again. I promise you that. He overstepped his bounds on a lot of issues that day. Talon just filled me in. He really gave you no choice?"

Jayde scowled. "And, he forbid Talon to tell me I could demand trial by you instead. I think he was counting on my ignorance of the law."

Corwyn felt his jaw tighten. "That's one more blow he owes me. I'm sorry. Gunther knew what I expected of him. He should never have done any of it."

"Personally, I think he did it because I didn't nail Talon to his satisfaction when I got a blow in. I'm just glad I lasted as long as I did. If not—" She grimaced.

"If not, what?"

"I think he would have taken over my training himself." She shuddered at the thought.

"I would never have allowed it," he vowed.

She smiled an easier smile that time. "Thanks."

Corwyn leaned back on his elbows. "Can I give you a piece of advice?"

"Sure. Why not?"

"If you want children with Talon, don't kick him in the balls too often."

Jayde darkened considerably and looked away. "Guess I can't deny it," she mused.

"Kicking him? Nah. That part of Gunther's story, I actually believe."

"That wasn't— Never mind."

"Ah. Well, that's between you and Talon. Though, from what I saw yesterday and what I heard last night, you've got that part figured out. Do me a favor and do that as often as you can. You never know when you could lose it, so hold on tight while it lasts. Another piece of advice. Sorry. I might do that a lot. I have years of them stored up."

"I never thought I'd be sitting around discussing my sex life with..."

She shook her head and stared at the ground in front of her worn sneakers. Corwyn resolved to have her fitted for a pair of armored boots before he left.

"What's the matter?" he asked.

"It's silly. I don't know what to call you," she admitted.

His heart sank. There it was, yet another reminder that they were strangers. Jayde was talking to him, but it was polite talking. She didn't trust him yet. Corwyn asked. She answered. All very civil.

Corwyn smiled warmly, though he felt miserable. "What do you want to call me?"

"I don't know." She sighed. "Lord Hunter is right out. It's still hard to wrap my mouth around Dad again. I don't really know what I want to call you."

"Tell you what... For now, call me Corwyn. If you ever decide to change that, I won't complain."

Jayde nodded. "Can I ask *you* something?"

That was a step in the right direction. "Of course."

"Well, if anyone was going to slip up and call me Erin, I'd expect it to be you, but you always come out with Jayde. Only you and Talon—"

"Your name is Jayde, right? I mean, it's not the name Anna picked for you, the one that we called you all those months you were making demands and sparring inside her, but it's your name now."

"I guess." She seemed pensive.

"Do you want to be called Erin?"

"I'm not sure I'd remember to answer to it," she joked. "No, I guess not. Are you upset?"

"That you're Jayde now?"

"Or that I'm not the person you expected? Or any of those maddening ideas we come up with?"

"No," Corwyn answered honestly. "I think Jayde is a person I'd like to get to know. Are you disappointed in me?" He waited nervously, while she panned her gaze over him.

"You're different than your picture. No beard. That surprised me at first. I expected the beard. It made you look like a great big bear."

Corwyn nodded and swallowed painfully. "The beard was Anna's beard. I grew it for...your mother because she liked it. When she died—"

Jayde closed her eyes, seemingly pained. "I'm sorry. I didn't know."

He smiled sadly that she was offering her condolences for her mother's death. Jayde had no memories of losing Anna. Still, it had to hurt her, too.

Corwyn only hoped she didn't feel responsible for it. It was no fault of Jayde's that things had gone so wrong, that Veriel wanted her so desperately, that Anna gave her the amulet and gave her life—

"So, other than the beard, what do you think of the old man?" he asked, trying to bury the rest of that thought.

Jayde smiled. "Corwyn seems like a person I'd like to get to know, too. Talon was right about you." She pushed to her feet and offered him a hand up. "Still want a sparring partner?" she offered.

Chapter Twenty-Nine

June 27th, 2002

Jayde groaned, sinking into the corner of the couch. The day's workout had hit her harder than usual. She was exhausted and sore...and she still hadn't mentioned her suspicion to Talon yet.

Jayde grimaced at that. He was going to figure it out soon. He had to. They'd been sleeping together for more than five weeks, and she'd been with him for a week longer than that. At some point, the glaring lack of a period would have to strike Talon as odd. He obviously hadn't noticed it in light of everything else going on or he would have mentioned it by now.

Truthfully, now that it was a very real possibility that she was pregnant, Jayde was scared to death. She barely passed as a Warrior now. If she was pregnant, it would hurt her skills. Her balance would suffer—and her timing. Jayde wouldn't be able to protect herself and her child.

The tandem fighting style she and Talon had been working on, with the help of Piers and Gunther as beast stand-ins, would suffer. Worse, they'd make her slack off on her training. Talon wouldn't give her an honest effort anymore for fear of hurting her or their baby, and the training hours would be cut drastically.

She shifted one of her weapons against her leg and sighed. Jayde would love to disarm, but Talon was taking his shower. Only in bed were they both completely disarmed, and then their weapons were hung within easy reach.

No, Talon would do his final sweep outside while

she showered and meet her in the bedroom where she would undress him slowly. Jayde smiled at the thought, half lost in the daydream and fighting her way back to consciousness lest she actually fall asleep on her watch. She was simply so tired. Still, she kept her eyes closed and let visions of Talon dance in her mind.

The shower turned off, and she glanced at the gathering darkness for a long moment before she gave herself back over to the lovely dreams of slow, soft sex with her husband.

Jayde smiled as Talon's hands dropped onto her shoulders, still hot from the shower and smelling clean and fresh from the greenmint soap Gunther brought them from his last trip into Massachusetts. His hands kneaded her sore neck and shoulder muscles, and she groaned in response.

She stood to give him a better reach of her mid and lower back, and Talon obliged her silently. She weaved on her feet, still half asleep. He moved in front of her, naked and damp from the shower, and Jayde eyed him in appreciation.

Talon planted his lips on the soft skin at her cleavage. "Undress for me," he requested quietly.

Her hands moved to the buttons of her shirt, and he watched her hungrily, hardening as she exposed herself to him. When Jayde tossed the shirt away, he cupped her head to take her mouth in a searing kiss.

She pushed away and assessed Talon warily, unsure of what about the sensation had been wrong. Something just didn't seem right.

"What's the matter?" he asked, moving to nuzzle at her neck in the way he had that melted her knees.

"Nothing, I guess. I thought I felt..."

Jayde shook her head in confusion. What did she feel? The more Talon explored her neck, the less she was able to concentrate on what she'd thought was wrong a moment before.

"Let me know," he murmured as he moved his mouth to an exquisite plunder of her breast through her bra. "What do you feel, now?" he teased. "Undress for me. I want you."

She reached for the clasp on her bra, but Talon's hand brushed by her amulet. "I want only you, with nothing between us," he breathed.

Jayde unsheathed one of her weapons without another thought and struck, knowing Talon would be able to dodge it and knowing this thing, whatever it was, wasn't Talon. As her blade passed through the nothingness of the projection, she uttered a curse and grabbed his weapons belt.

Dream projection. Her father had warned her about this. Veriel had used something similar on her mother. He got inside her unguarded, dreaming mind and made a projection so real that Anna had exhibited a true cut when cut in the projection. Jayde didn't know he could do it through the amulet's protection.

Was it Veriel, then? Was her exhausted, daydreaming mind unguarded enough for him to do the same to her? It must have been.

She bolted for the bedroom door, but stopped short as a beast appeared before her. "Talon, they're here," she screamed in a panic.

Jayde heard a commotion break out behind the door. She cursed solidly again and drew Talon's blade, striding toward the beast guarding the door. She had to get her husband's weapon to him. If that meant going straight through this beast, so be it. She cursed Talon for not taking the weapon with him, despite the steam in the bathroom.

The beast smiled a disarming smile, and his silver eyes seemed lit in amusement. A lock of his rich brown hair fell over his forehead in a very charming and boyish fashion, but whether this was a turned or Veriel, she had to remember that he was a cold-blooded killer who'd come for both her and Talon.

He was dressed in a white cotton dress shirt and jeans, tight jeans that showed the fact that he was semi-erect.

Not what I needed to see. Jayde moved forward again, cursing herself for the split-second her appraisal of him had taken from Talon's fight behind the door.

He laughed lightly. "You cannot attack me," he commented in self-assurance.

"Don't bet on it," she shot back.

"So like your mother," he mused.

His eyes softened, and Jayde stood in shocked silence for another split second. His eyes were disconcerting. She knew this man, didn't she? Somehow, she knew him. But she couldn't, could she?

His hand reached toward her as if in appeal, and she snapped back to the reality of the situation. *Beast!* He was using some sort of trick on her.

"Don't try it. I'm not interested." Jayde swung Talon's blade at the beast's chest, and he dodged just as she'd hoped he would.

She crashed through the door and took in the sight of Talon fighting with an injured beast. *You can fight them with anything...* The broken mirror answered the question of what he could fight with.

The beast she'd attacked reappeared beside her. Jayde brought her blade up to block him and flipped Talon's for a throw. The first and most important thing was arming her husband. "Deck," she screamed to him and let his blade fly, knowing Talon would be out of the way before it struck.

The throw wasn't perfect because of the difference in their blades, but it was close enough for Talon to grab the hilt and drive it home before the beast could react. Talon turned abruptly, his fouled weapon in hand, as Jayde unsheathed her second blade.

The beast beside Jayde made a grab for her, and she brought her blade up to wound him. He moved at the last millisecond and caught her forearm instead. As her arm brushed his chest, the force of her amulet blew them apart, and her blade ripped through the fabric of his shirt without biting skin.

Her arm tingled as if she'd struck her funny bone, distracting Jayde from the fact that the beast wore real clothes. Most beasts clothed themselves in the illusion of clothing. It took a very high level and one who had a fondness for true fabric to expend the energy dematerializing fabric.

The beast trained his silver eyes on her and smiled in a savage glee.

Talon stormed toward her, his eyes widening and his hand tightening on the hilt of his weapon. "Jayde, get away. That's Veriel," he ordered gruffly.

Her gaze locked on the blood mark of Reg, now clearly visible through his torn shirt, and she threw herself to the opposite side of the bed without further delay.

Veriel was an elder. He'd killed her mother. Of all

the Warriors he'd fought, Veriel had left only Corwyn alive. Talon's point was crystal clear. Veriel was too dangerous to her, between his determination to have her and his experience.

Talon positioned himself between them, and Veriel smiled in a mockery of something resembling amusement.

"How appropriate that you choose to face me here, *Kreuzträger*. After I dispatch you, I will claim the Lord *Jäger's* daughter on that bed, in front of your eyes, while she enjoys every touch."

"Over my dead body," Jayde responded evenly, though her stomach turned at the thought. Could he play with her mind again? She couldn't let him. She couldn't do that to Talon.

"Your mother made that same choice. Rest assured, I'll not make that mistake again. Being newly delivered of you would not have saved her from me, but her own hand did. Nothing will save you from me..."

The beast was trying to egg Talon on. Even Jayde could see that.

Veriel's smile spread. "Not even *Kreuzträger's* son. That will be easy to remedy, and the first time will be all for pleasure. I can still take pleasure in you, even if his brat keeps my seed from planting. Once I have ripped it from your womb, you'll be ripe to carry mine in short order, as it should have been."

Jayde stood in shocked disbelief. Why hadn't she told him? Veriel shouldn't have been the one to tell him.

Talon's jaw tightened. "Jayde?" he asked for confirmation.

She couldn't say the words. Talon shouldn't have

found out like this. She should have told him in bed. It should have been a beautiful thing to find out he was about to be a father.

"She hasn't told you," Veriel mused. "How very intriguing."

"Jayde," he demanded.

"Yes. I think so," she whispered. "I'm not sure yet, but I was going to tell..." She stifled a hopeless sob, as Veriel smiled wider, showing his fangs. Her hands moved to the flat span of her stomach.

Talon's nod was barely perceptible. "No matter what happens, you know your duty. That's all this can be. Duty. Promise me."

"Yes. I promise." Jayde knew what he was saying. Even if it meant Talon's death, she could never surrender her amulet. Her duty was to their son, no matter what her heart demanded. "For our child," she whispered hoarsely.

Veriel glared at her over Talon's shoulder. "There will be no child but mine," he spat.

Her husband stepped forward and dropped to a fighting crouch. Jayde held her breath as the battle began. They moved around the cramped space, and she made a mental note to ask Talon to train her for small, enclosed spaces like this. She kept her weapons at the ready in case Veriel decided to turn on her while they circled, but he seemed intent on Talon.

"Yes," she breathed, as Talon landed a crippling blow to the beast's shoulder.

It was a temporary advantage and not a deathblow, but it would bleed him and make Veriel's arm less mobile, for a few minutes anyway. Jayde cheered it none-the-less. Veriel was an elder, and not even

Corwyn had killed him. The best that she could hope for was that they would both survive, and the beast would be sent to ground.

She saw the end coming, but it was over before her cry of anguish left her lips. Veriel seemed to be in two places at once for an instant and materialized solidly at Talon's back. The initial blow sent Talon to his knees, and Veriel dragged his confused form around to face her before Talon could react.

The beast's nails were suddenly the killing claws again, planted on Talon's throat. Talon cried out as Veriel snapped his wrist, then a bone in his hand in quick succession. His blade clattered to the wood floor. He couldn't hold it now.

"It is your choice, woman. I can break each bone in turn," the beast spat. Veriel met her eyes and moved his hand to Talon's forearm, snapping one of the bones with ease.

Talon ground his teeth and bit back his cry of pain for her benefit. He caught her eye and pleaded with her silently. "Leave me," he whispered. He flicked his gaze to the open doorway.

Jayde bolted for it, but Veriel was there first. He was much faster than she was, even while dragging Talon with him. "No escape for you," he promised. His eyes were flat as a snake's. No humor lit the silver. They were like dark gray clouds converging for a storm.

Veriel moved his hand to tease at the other bone in Talon's forearm, rolling it between his fingers while Talon gritted back the pain it caused him to have the already broken arm handled that way. "The next," he said calmly.

Against her better judgment, Jayde's eyes locked

on the movement. With all her training, how could she be so helpless?

"Your amulet," he demanded.

Jayde's hand circled the metal disc, and tears pooled in her eyes. She couldn't do it. Her own life and their son's depended on it. She shook her head, trying to clear the tears while she ran her thumbs over the hilts of her weapons. Why would she want to clear her eyes? So, she could watch Veriel kill her husband without the blur of her tears? She almost choked on that thought.

"Jayde," Talon called softly.

She met his eyes through the haze her silent crying had reduced her to.

"If you love me..."

Jayde released the amulet and lowered her hand. "Never," she agreed.

Veriel snapped the other bone of his forearm in response, and she cried out her frustration.

"No, Jayde. Don't. Better this than that beast's whore," Talon cautioned calmly, fighting the tension in his jaw, sweat running down his temple from the strain he was under.

Veriel released his arm and struck Talon solidly across the back of the head. Jayde flinched as he crumpled in the beast's grasp. She held her breath until she noted the telltale signs of breathing. Talon wasn't dead. He was just out.

Just? He was broken, but at least Talon was beyond pain for a little while.

"I had hoped to have him conscious to convince you," Veriel crooned, "but his words are undoing what his screams would have accomplished. You are much stronger than your mother was, but I'd expected that."

He ran a claw over Talon's throat, drawing a thin line of blood. "It's been centuries since I've fed on a cursed one. Their blood is always so strong. Would you watch if I fed?" he taunted.

Jayde straightened her spine to keep from shuddering at that thought. "You'll kill him anyway. Nothing you do or hope to do can make that worse. You won't turn him. You don't dare."

"If I promised to let him live?" Veriel offered. "Would you take me then? He's unconscious. He wouldn't know you came to me willingly to save him. He might even save you someday and give you more cursed children to even the playing field again."

She shook her head silently. Why was he doing this? He couldn't believe she would buy into this farce.

"I could give you pleasure. So much pleasure you'd never want to return to him. You could be very happy with me. You felt the pleasure I could give you. I could give you that every time."

Jayde grimaced. It hadn't felt right. She knew that. Maybe it was her printing. She'd known somehow that it wasn't Talon, that it wasn't who and what she wanted.

"You won't," she decided. "Neither will the other elders. To hurt my husband and my father—to break me, there will be no pleasure for me. You know that." She whispered it, afraid that her voice would break otherwise.

"I could give you a blood oath, my solemn vow. You would have my word that I would give you only pleasure, that I would grant you my protection, that you would have no mate but me—no other elders and always pleasurable for you."

His voice was husky and—hopeful? Why would he be? Wasn't that a kind emotion? Veriel couldn't feel hope or love. It must be something else. Greed, maybe.

"You have no honor. The blood oath would be broken the first time it suited your purpose. And what about my child?" she countered. "You think it wouldn't be torture for me if you took my child from me?"

"Keep your child. As long as you give me my children, I would grant you that." His eyes burned silver again.

"Why are you bothering with the lies?" she barked. "You can't honestly believe I'd take your word for anything."

Hearing the lies hurt. Hoping she could save them all warred with the knowledge that it was fake and with the knowledge that—pleasure or no, knowing Talon was alive or no—Jayde could never be happy with the beast instead of him.

Veriel growled in annoyance of her stubborn refusal and opened another, slightly deeper track on Talon's neck. The deceiver's gaze locked on the blood running in a thin rivulet down his chest. "I am injured," he mused. "I'll feed while you decide."

Jayde snapped into motion. Veriel moved to avoid her blade as if he'd expected the move. Maybe, he had. After all, the threat had been contrived to draw her out to him and make her disregard Talon's order to stay back.

Jayde hit him with her forearm instead, accepting the force of the reaction that knocked Veriel away from Talon. "You will not," she informed him as he swung out of the corner. She followed him, moving to the side of Talon, but keeping him in easy reach.

Veriel looked at her in cold consideration. "I will have you. If I cannot, I will kill you rather than leave you with him again," he assured her.

"Maybe I'll die, but better that than have you inside me. My mother was very brave in her choice."

"Then we will see which it is," he decided.

"How will you fight me?" she taunted.

He couldn't touch her with his claws, while she refused to remove her amulet. She was trying to put Veriel off balance, to bide her time until Gunther arrived. Maybe if she made the beast think about it, she could buy some more time. By now, Gunther had felt the battle. By now, they knew an elder was here.

Jayde stepped back as Talon's weapon appeared in Veriel's hand from behind his back. When had he grabbed it? How did she miss that?

She shook herself mentally. He couldn't wield it. The beasts were constrained from killing with a sacred weapon. She'd read that in one of the texts. She ducked away from the flash of the blade, but it bit into her throat as she moved, and she cried out in pain.

The beast laughed as he dropped the weapon and took a step toward her. "You are unprotected now, undone by *Kreuzträger's* own blade."

One hand flew to her throat to confirm that the amulet was gone, it's thong cut by Talon's blade. Jayde shook in terror for one long moment before her weapons came up and her mind cleared.

Veriel laughed in something resembling amazement. "You act as if you know how to use those weapons. Why do you pretend? How much training have you had? A month? Not even two."

Jayde cursed audibly. She couldn't even best Gunther. She'd been counting on her amulet to save her, and now it was gone. She was a half-baked Warrior pitted against a fifteen hundred-year-old elder to try and save herself, her baby, and her husband. Talon was ten times the Warrior she was, even without his stronger arm.

She shot at him, determined to do it before she lost her nerve and before Veriel could come for her. The beast's surprise was short-lived, but she wounded him before dancing away. Her next attack was expected. Veriel deflected her blow easily and tried to outflank her as he had Talon. She spun and landed both blades in quick succession before moving away again.

Veriel looked at the damage she'd done him in disbelief. When he raised his eyes to her again, the silver burned like red gold. He screamed in rage and came at her. Jayde was faltering, and she knew it, but she had to fight now. There was only fight or die left for her.

He struck her hard across the face, and she fell, stunned, to the floor. Her left hand was abruptly empty as her grip was broken by the fall. Jayde barely registered the weapon clattering away, tumbling tip over hilt several times from the force of her landing.

The beast's hand closed around her right wrist, but he didn't break the bone as she expected. Instead, he ripped the weapon from her uncertain grip. Jayde looked at the blade with bleary eyes, but he smiled viciously as he tossed it away.

"Not for you. For *Kreuzträger*, after I've taken you in his bed. He won't be unconscious long, not long enough. What I plan to do will take hours."

Veriel grabbed her upper arm and started to drag Jayde toward the bed, compromising her struggle to get her feet beneath her. Jayde closed her hand around something digging into the soft skin of her back as he pulled her toward her fall. Veriel threw her at the mattress roughly, and the hand was trapped beneath her hip as she landed.

Jayde tried to push him away with her knee, but she was uncoordinated, sloppy. Her mind didn't seem able to focus. Veriel pushed the offending leg away in amusement and knelt between her thighs, now spread wide around him. He sliced the button from her jeans with one razor-sharp claw then eased the zipper open slowly, watching its progress with hungry eyes.

"Now, I will show you what pleasure is," he crooned. Veriel met her eyes and seemed to wait for her understanding.

As he reached for her again, she snapped into motion. Jayde's hand came up with Talon's blade, burying it in his chest. "Pull it out with a twist to maximize bleeding," she muttered as she pulled it free.

Veriel looked at her in shock and tried to back away from her, but Jayde locked her legs around him as she would Talon during sex and curled her upper body to slit his throat. The wash of foul, black blood turned her stomach as it splashed over her. She released him and scrambled off the bed as he collapsed where she'd lain a moment before.

Veriel turned his face to lock her in his gaze. His eyes misted with tears and he smiled at her. "*Jäger geboren—*"

A laugh bubbled up, and Jayde shivered at how content that laugh sounded. No kinder emotions, she reminded herself. Then, why did he look so happy?

"Free," he croaked. Veriel furrowed his brow at her, as if she confused him, and the light left his eyes.

Jayde moved to Talon's side, shaking and jerking as she did. She dropped his weapon next to him and collected her own, sheathing them slowly, wiping them on her already ruined jeans with unsteady hands. She zipped her jeans. Jayde considered washing and changing, but she couldn't leave Talon alone that long.

She moved woodenly to retrieve the first aid kit from the main room and scooped up her shirt, almost as an afterthought. Since she couldn't do the buttons with her shaking hands, Jayde left it hanging open over her blackened bra.

She encased Talon's arm in the inflatable splint and somehow managed to fill it with the battery-operated pump and secure it. Next, she turned her attention to his neck. Jayde used rubbing alcohol to clean Veriel's blood from her hands then washed them down with anti-bacterial gel. She wasn't taking any chances with infecting Talon, though she wasn't sure it would work that way. She cleaned out the cuts on his neck carefully and taped a gauze pad over them.

Jayde looked around, and she spied her amulet. "Never again," she breathed. She unbuckled her left bracer and wrapped the thong around her wrist several times, knotting it firmly in place before placing the bracer back over it. There would be no more nonsense of losing the damned thing in battle.

She heard a noise in the main room and focused wearily on the clock. *Nine o'clock... Too many hours 'til dawn.* Jayde stifled a sob and moved between Talon and the door. She unsheathed her weapons and brought them up slowly. They would take Talon over her dead body.

The door swung toward her.

* * * *

"What're their chances?" Piers whispered roughly as they climbed the steps to the silent cabin, casting a nervous glance at the car still in the clearing.

"Against an elder? Probably Veriel?" Gunther shot back in disbelief.

Piers swallowed hard and nodded.

Beasts had died. An elder had been here. Both of them were injured. Beyond that, nothing was clear.

Gunther was distinctly uneasy. The only sense he had was a hazy sense of malevolence and determination. His heart sank. Jayde was gone. Either a seriously injured Talon or a turned was waiting for them behind the door to the bedroom.

The smell of beast blood hung like a poison cloud around them, choking their lungs when they breathed too deeply. Piers bit back a cough, his eyes watering in the effort.

Gunther swung the door open and stepped back in disbelief. "Jayde," he breathed, dropping his hand to his side.

She didn't move or relax her stance, maintaining a rigid crouch though she shook wildly in exhaustion or fear—*probably both.*

"Jayde, it's Gunther," he soothed her. "Sheathe your weapons now. We're here."

She shook her head. "Another trick," she decided. "A projection. Enough. Show yourself," she demanded in a shaking voice.

"Gods alive, Father! What is it?" Piers pleaded.

Gunther scanned her critically.

The button on her jeans was ripped off, and her shirt had obviously been off when she slew one of the beasts. Her own blood was dried in a track from her neck to her chest, but Jayde hadn't been fed upon. It was the nick of a blade. Her amulet was gone, and her face was swollen and purple from an attack on her person. Her clothing, belt and bracers were ruined with the beast's blood. He was over her when she killed him, Gunther realized. Her eyes were wide and wild.

Gunther's attention moved to the beast on the bed again. "Check it," he instructed Piers with a nod of his head.

His son moved in a wide arc around Jayde and dragged the beast to his back. She stifled a sob as his sightless eyes turned to the ceiling, and her shaking intensified.

"Veriel," Piers breathed. "No question. He has the blood mark and the silver eyes. His heart, his throat, his shoulder and chest— Some are battle wounds, but his heart and throat..." His son looked to Jayde, and he offered a jerk of his head in explanation.

Gunther took a step toward Jayde with his hands up and his weapon sheathed.

"Stay back," she ordered.

"It's all right, Jayde. It's Gunther. I need to check on Talon. May I?"

He was counting on her concern for her husband to bring Jayde to some sense of reality, but she was adamant that no one was getting near Talon. "Not again. Your kind has hurt him enough. Don't touch him. I killed Veriel, and I will kill you, too. Name yourself."

Gunther realized that it would take proof to convince her, and they were running out of time. "I'm going to give you my arm, Jayde. Cut me. I'm not a projection, and I'm not a beast. You'll see." He eased his hand toward her, trying not to startle her.

At first, she looked at him uncertainly. She flicked her gaze back and forth between the two Warriors warily. When his arm was too close for her comfort, Jayde hesitated then drew a thin line across his forearm. She retreated out of his reach to Talon's side as soon as she connected flesh. Jayde watched unbelieving as the blood welled up red.

"Real blood," he assured her.

Jayde sheathed her right blade and lunged toward Gunther to grab his wrist, keeping her left blade aimed for his heart. Gunther had no idea what she was looking for, but she seemed satisfied by the results of her test.

He let out his breath in a rush as she dropped to her knees, dropped her remaining blade to the floor, and wrapped her arms around her ribs while sobs wracked her body. "I'm sorry, Gunther," she whispered brokenly. "I'm so sorry. I couldn't take the chance."

He sank to his knees in front of Jayde, not touching her but trying to get a closer look at her injuries. "It's all right," he soothed her. "I understand. I'd rather you be cautious." Gunther met his son's shocked eyes. "Piers," he ordered.

Piers came to his senses and moved to Talon. "I have him," he muttered. "Are you sure his arm is broken, Jayde?"

"Three. No, four times, I think. Veriel..." She looked as if she was about to be sick for a moment and closed her eyes. Jayde tried to stifle more sobs.

Piers pulled the gauze from his son's neck and sighed in relief. "It's all right. He didn't feed." He lifted Talon's eyelids. "Concussion. He'll need medical aid before liftoff in the morning."

"Sylvia." Gunther said it gently, evaluating the need for x-rays on Jayde. There may be need for more invasive procedures, but Gunther wasn't sure if he could broach that subject without sending her into a worse shock.

Piers reached for his cell phone to call the doctor and let her know they would be bringing Talon in when they reached the States again. "What about Jayde?" he asked quietly.

Jayde shook her head furiously. "No doctors. No strangers."

Gunther took her hands gently, noting that she cleaned them—only them. "Jayde, did Veriel take you?"

She shook her head.

"It's all right if he did, but we must know. There are things we can do to keep you from bearing his child. They're painless—"

"No," she shouted in horror. Jayde pulled her hands from his and launched to her feet, sheathing her second blade as she moved. She grabbed clean clothing from the dresser and headed to the bathroom.

"Jayde?" he called after her. "What are you doing?"

"I have to get h...its blood off me. The smell is making me sick to my stomach."

"Five minutes," Gunther agreed. "We have no time."

She nodded and disappeared behind the door.

"Do you believe her?" Piers asked.

Gunther shrugged. "Hard to say, but if there was a chance, I think she'd say so. I hope she'd say so."

Jayde reappeared promptly in four minutes, looking like she had scrubbed herself harshly and dressed in clean clothes. She was buckling her right bracer back on her wrist.

"Leave them," Gunther told her. "We'll get you new ones. The belt, too."

She dropped the right bracer, but the weapons belt and left bracer remained with her.

"Jayde?" he prodded her.

"Not until I have replacements," she commented coolly.

"As you wish. Come on. We have to get Talon to medical aid before we leave." Gunther reached to touch her, but Jayde sidestepped him nervously.

"Where are we going?" she asked.

"For now, your father has a place for you."

She nodded and followed them as they carried Talon between them to the SUV they'd brought with them. Jayde shivered and hesitated before she stepped out into the dark night.

Chapter Thirty

June 28th, 2002

Talon came to consciousness slowly. There was an odd rushing sound surrounding him, and he swallowed to clear his ears. His head ached terribly. He didn't panic until he realized he couldn't move his arm.

Hands held him down as Talon tried to fight his way to sitting. He opened his eyes and tried desperately to bring the image of Gunther into focus. He swung his head, looking for some sign of Jayde, terrified when he saw was no trace of her on Brent's plane.

"She's in the cargo area," his grandfather assured him. "And in much better shape than you are, I might add."

"I want to see her," he managed, holding back tears of joy.

"We need to talk first," Gunther dismissed the idea.

"Thank you." Talon said it before he could forget to say it. He owed them everything, and he wouldn't soon forget that.

"For what?" Gunther asked in confusion.

"Veriel," he spat.

Gunther's confusion melted into misery.

"He's not dead," he guessed. "You drove him to ground?"

He shook his head. "Oh, he's dead, all right, but you didn't see him die," he whispered.

"Well, if you didn't..." Talon felt his blood boil. "No," he protested. "I told her to stay away from him."

"She may not have had a choice, Talon. Veriel was

intent."

"Dammit! She's protected. He can't touch her. Even with those damned claws he has, he can't touch her or her amulet," Talon thundered.

"How about a sacred weapon?" Gunther suggested.

"A beast can't wield it."

"Of course he can. He's only constrained from killing with it. Remember the texts?"

Talon felt a sick swirl assault his head and stomach. "He used my weapon against her after he took it from me. But, she can't have defeated him without her amulet," he reasoned.

"What injuries did you inflict on him?"

"A blow to the shoulder. Why?"

"One? Only one blow? You're sure?"

"Of course I am," Talon growled dangerously.

Gunther shook his head. "Then, she landed three before her killing blows."

Talon stared at him in disbelief.

"You trained her very well," he complimented his grandson. Then, his faint smile disappeared.

"What is it?"

"I was hoping you were conscious for it. I was hoping you could tell us..."

"Tell you what?" he demanded.

"How far Veriel got before she killed him," he admitted.

Talon's mind shut down. Images of that beast— with Jayde— He couldn't think straight. He had to see her. He had to know. If Veriel had, no beast would be safe from him, not that they were on a daily basis, but...

Gunther could see his confusion and pain. "She

denies it, Talon, but she was so shattered when we got there, she was convinced we were projections, until I offered my arm to prove we weren't. We know he was over her when she killed him."

"He may have downed her," Talon protested weakly. *Please, let it be that simple.*

"He did. He took her down pretty hard. I'd be surprised if she stayed conscious, though she swears she did." Gunther shook his head. "You don't understand what I'm trying to tell you. He was over her when she killed him—on your bed." The older man restrained him as Talon tried to launch to his feet. "Even if Veriel didn't succeed, he tried to take her. We need to know how far he got."

"What does Jayde say?"

"Not much. Only that he didn't. How she armed herself and killed him when he had her unarmed is a complete mystery. Every time we try to talk to her, she says he didn't and leaves it at that." Gunther sighed raggedly. "She scrubbed herself raw before we left. She said she had to get the blood off. It was making her sick."

"That's understandable. She'd just made her first kill. She was in mortal danger. Plus, the stuff reeks."

"Jayde won't disarm, though her bracer and belt are soaked in that same blood, and we can't find her amulet. It's not anywhere, and she refuses to accept a replacement. We looked the entire time she was in the bathroom. It's just gone, and every time we try to offer another—"

"It may have flown behind a piece of furniture," he replied distractedly. "What else made you think he may have succeeded?"

"Her jeans were—" Gunther chopped off the comment as Talon tensed. "She went ballistic when I told her there were things we could do to keep her from having Veriel's child, if he..." he whispered.

Talon groaned. "Has she seen a doctor?" he asked.

"She refused."

"And you let her get away with that?" he demanded.

"I thought you could talk her into it. We have time. If I radio ahead, Corwyn can have one waiting for us."

"Dammit! Time isn't my largest concern here. Radio Corwyn. She's seeing that doctor. Where is she?"

"Blowing off steam."

"How?" he asked suspiciously.

"Training. Piers tried to be sedate with her, but somewhere around the fourth time she damn near took his head, he stopped slacking off."

Gunther's indulgent smile disappeared, as Talon pushed to his feet and stormed unsteadily toward the empty cargo area of the plane.

"Are you crazy?" he seethed. "Let me guess. Jayde hasn't said anything about anything that went on at that cabin, has she?"

"Talon, what's wrong?"

"You'll figure it out. Right now, I need to have a talk with my wife." He knew he was growling. He should calm down before he talked to Jayde, but it was hard to convince himself to back off. Distraught was one thing. She was being reckless.

Talon opened the door and gaped at the sight of Jayde beating Piers back to the bay wall. She pinned him with a chest thrust. Then she nodded and backed off.

"Again," she demanded.

"No. You're done," Talon ordered.

Jayde spun to look at him, and he grimaced at her battered face. *He took her down pretty hard...* Talon softened as his gaze wandered to the cut at her throat. *He used my weapon against her...*

She'd worked herself to the point of shaking, and she was bathed in sweat.

His jaw tightened in anger. Talon crossed to her and wrenched the weapons belt off of her hips. He took the blades from her hands and dropped them on top of the belt. "Until this whole thing is settled and you're healed, you do not train. Do you understand me?" he growled at her.

Jayde nodded slowly, her entire body quaking hard. "Are you all right?" she asked in a tremulous voice.

"Better than you will be if you disobey me. I can still tie you hand and foot," he warned. Talon pulled at the single bracer she still wore. "Take that off," he ordered when he realized he had no hope of working the tiny buckles with only his left hand.

She pulled her arms to her chest and shook her head. "No. Not until I get a new one," she countered with a cold, calculating look.

"It stinks to high Heaven," he complained.

"No," she thundered.

"Why not?" he demanded.

"I'm not losing it again."

"Losing what?"

"My amulet! One of them ever tries to touch me again..." Her voice broke. "Have to take my damn arm off first," Jayde whispered. The fight seemed to go out of her, and her eyes pleaded with him for understanding.

Talon ran his hand over the bracer and nodded as he encountered the disc through the thick leather. He wrapped his good hand around her neck and pulled her to his chest. "Keep it," he whispered. "It was a good plan. I wish I had thought of it earlier. I didn't know there was a way—"

Her shaking intensified until her knees buckled and she sagged against him, sobbing into his shoulder.

Talon crooned to her, trying to calm her upset. He had never seen Jayde this upset, including her first day with him. "I'm here. From now on, we'll have more protection. I swear it."

"Never again, Talon," she pleaded.

He held her, afraid of what that comment meant and afraid to ask her what it meant. He sensed her fearfully. Jayde's body wasn't on cycle, but she was also in shock. Even if Veriel had kept his word, Talon wasn't sure her body would show signs of it yet.

"Come with me," he said gently. "Grandfather, get a cold drink for us. I'm taking her back to the pallet."

Once Talon had her snuggled into his lap, Jayde's sobbing subsided. She was still hitching when Gunther returned.

Talon scowled at his choice of red wine, half-wondering where he got it in the first place. "Non-alcoholic, please," he requested.

"I think she could use a stiff drink. Stiffer than this, but it's the best we have available."

"And, I think that's a lousy idea," Talon asserted.

"As you wish," Gunther replied with more than a hint of sarcasm. He came back with juice.

Talon thanked him before sending him away. Gunther glared at him, but he did leave. Talon sighed at his retreating back. Getting the other lords to take his orders was going to be difficult, especially those who were accustomed to ordering him around.

He handed Jayde one of the bottles of juice. "Now, drink that slowly and start at the beginning. I need to know everything that happened before you delivered my blade and after I got knocked out."

She started off slowly, and Talon understood immediately why she was convinced that Gunther and Piers were projections. Though Jayde didn't say it, he could tell that the projection of himself, though not perfect, had unnerved her quite a bit.

Talon agreed with her that Veriel's promises were empty ones and found it amusing that the beast had bothered to attempt it. Jayde didn't find it amusing at all. The thought tortured her on some level that he couldn't quite grasp, but she was too muddled to explain it properly.

He wasn't surprised that the beast drew her out by threatening to feed. The thought chilled him, but it amused him that she'd used her amulet so effectively while she had it. And, some part of Talon thanked her for not letting that damned thing feed on him while he couldn't defend himself.

Her description of her battle with Veriel and his attempt to force himself on her had Talon walking the edges of uncontrolled *Blutjagd*. "Never again," he promised her solemnly. "I swear on my life that they will never lay hands on you again." Talon kissed her forehead and pressed the juice to her lips. "Drink some more," he invited.

He was stunned at how she managed to secret his blade to the bed and take her killing blow when the beast was—otherwise occupied. The spike of fury resurfaced with a bang at that image.

Jayde knew Veriel was dead when she took his heart. His throat was cut, not to speed his death, but to inflict pain and fear on him in retribution for all those Veriel had injured.

The fact that Jayde killed Veriel with Talon's blade and that she got that blade out of the beast's sloppy handling, even she found funny. It was the only thing Jayde found funny about the encounter, and he couldn't fault her for that.

When Gunther and Piers had arrived, her nerves had been shot. Jayde was sure more beasts had arrived, and she was far too tired to protect them for long.

Her tears started again. She was in a state beyond exhaustion. While Talon lay unconscious all night, she hadn't slept at all. Jayde had paced, trained, and cried, anything and everything she could think of besides giving in to the urge to sleep. Baby or no baby, she still required sleep for her own sanity and healing.

At his insistence, she finished both bottles of juice and curled onto the pallet with him. Talon covered her carefully with the heavy blanket. Now that she was done training, Jayde was soaked with sweat and shivering in the cool plane.

Talon crooned to her and ran his hand in soothing circles over most of her body until she was lost in much-needed slumber. When he was sure Jayde was deeply asleep, he went in search of Gunther and sent Piers to stand guard over her with orders to get him immediately if she woke.

Gunther was on the air phone to Corwyn when Talon found him.

"Yes," Gunther answered some question the Lord Hunter asked. "He's right here. I'm sure he'd like to speak to you as much as you'd like to speak to him." He shrugged as he handed his grandson the phone.

Talon settled next to him and stretched his legs. "Yes, Corwyn?"

"How is she?" he demanded.

"Physically, not bad. Emotionally, she's spent. I finally got her to sleep."

"I'll ask you directly. Did that bastard Veriel lay hands on my daughter?"

"He didn't take her, but he did lay hands on her. He would have taken her, and he damn well tried, but he didn't succeed. Jayde will need to see a doctor we trust when we arrive, a woman preferably."

"How could this happen?" Corwyn raged. "She has her blessing. Gunther told me she had your blessing."

"He used my weapon to break your amulet from her. We've remedied that temporarily, but unless you want to smell beast blood for days, we'll need some supplies when we arrive."

"For instance?"

"A set of training bracers. A boys' weapons belt with sheaths that will fit two standard blades. Clothing. Jayde showered, but she reeks of them because of her bracer and belt. I'm still in what I fought in. A fresh blade for me, unless someone grabbed mine from the floor?" Talon looked to Gunther hopefully and was disappointed to see him shake his head.

"We were more worried about clearing the hell out of there," he explained.

Talon sighed. He truly hated breaking in a new blade and did it as seldom as possible. Then again, he'd have to do intensive left-handed training followed by recovery training once the cast came off anyway.

"I heard it," Corwyn answered. "Jayde needs to see a doctor? What should I tell the doctor to expect?"

"I'm only concerned with two things. First, is her cheekbone broken? And second...is she pregnant?"

Gunther's eyes widened.

Corwyn sucked in his breath audibly. "You said," the Lord Hunter started to rage.

"Not by Veriel," Talon snapped. "Veriel told me she was, and she admitted it was a possibility that she hadn't confirmed."

"Then, why do you sound so concerned, *König*?" he asked pointedly. "Why not just sense her?"

"Veriel made a threat that upset both of us greatly. That was his intent, of course. I want to make sure that bastard hasn't done it."

"Done what?"

"Ripped my child from her womb to make her ripe for them," he answered quietly. "My sense says she's off cycle, but I can't be sure that's accurate. It's too soon if he's..." Talon glanced at Gunther then away from the pain he saw mirrored there.

"Gods alive," Corwyn breathed. "If she's not?"

"Jayde knew she was. I know she did. If she's not, she'll know Veriel was the cause of it."

"How far along was she? Is she? Gods-damn it!"

"In all the time she's been with me, Jayde hasn't had a monthly. That's six and a half weeks. I haven't asked her when she would have been due, because I don't want to make this more painful for her."

"She had one," Corwyn exploded. "Gunther said—"

"Piers saw blood and assumed. It was the evidence of her maidenhead he actually saw."

"You didn't realize? You didn't mention this?" he fumed.

"I was distracted with training and keeping her safe," Talon replied miserably. "It wasn't until Veriel made his threat that I realized it." He sighed. "Jayde realized it, though. I'm sure of that. When I asked her if Veriel was telling the truth, I could smell her fear. Jayde knew the threat was valid. When she's recovered, I have to find out why she never told me."

"Training," Gunther shot back in annoyance.

"What?" the other two asked in unison.

"The first thing you did was take away her training. Jayde knew you would. She's afraid she won't be able to fight one off, and she's afraid she won't be able to train to do it. We have to find a way to let her keep training without jeopardizing her or her child."

Talon stared at him in amazement. Gunther was right. How was it that his grandfather saw it when Talon missed it? "She's already more dangerous than an elder," he quipped, seeking for the mental equivalent of stable ground beneath his feet.

He shook his head and looked away from his grandfather. "If we step it down, we may be able to keep her from backsliding, at least until she starts to show. Regardless of that, I've promised Jayde more protection. I have a basic plan for that, but we can't allow her to be unprotected again. Veriel's move was entirely too bold.

"Right now, we're a sorry bunch to look at. Jayde may be carrying a child. That hasn't slowed her down yet, but she's emotionally unable to deal with another attack for a little while. My arm is broken in—" He looked to Gunther again.

"Five," his grandfather supplied.

"Ouch. I only remember three— No, four. Five places?"

Gunther nodded, and Talon shuddered at the thought. Had the beast broken another bone after he was unconscious or gotten two with one attempt?

"How the hell did that happen?" Corwyn asked.

"Torture. He was trying to convince Jayde to give up her amulet to *save* me. I also have a pretty decent concussion. I guess my talking her out of it while he was busy breaking bones irritated him a little."

"Jayde stood up to that?"

"That and much more. He tried projection—one of those ones you told her he used on Anna. He tried tempting Jayde with his false promises, torturing me, forcing her, threats against us both— She's been through the mental wringer. Don't be surprised if Jayde's a little skittish."

Chapter Thirty-One

Corwyn led the detail to pick up Jayde himself. When she stepped down onto the tarmac, his gaze slid from Talon's shattered arm to his daughter's face.

Laid hands, hell! The beast battered her, body and soul. The bruise that covered the entire side of her face from cheekbone to earlobe blended into the purple circles beneath her eyes in an incredibly pale face. Even from ten yards away, Corwyn could clearly see that the brown of her accessories was almost universally stained black. Jayde must have been fairly bathed in Veriel's blood at the end. Her weapons belt was slung over Talon's shoulder, though he looked as though he'd rather not touch it.

Corwyn still couldn't believe that Jayde killed Veriel. Even he hadn't managed that. Perhaps, Gunther and Talon were right about her skill being worth a decade of training. It had to be worth more than that if she killed Veriel. Fourteen years of training certainly hadn't done Corwyn any good that he could see.

He went to her cautiously, trying not to spook her. Jayde touched his arm before throwing herself at him for his comfort. Corwyn met Talon's eyes in shock as he wrapped his arms around her.

At their last meeting, Jayde had permitted him several hugs and a peck on the cheek or two, but she'd made it clear that she wasn't comfortable with Corwyn. He would have given anything for this response the last time, given in love. This time, knowing it signified her desperate need to trust someone, it was heartbreaking.

Corwyn led her to the van he'd arranged for and tried to direct Jayde to the front seat, but she shied away and stubbornly ducked into the center seat, pulling Talon in after her.

Gunther sighed then took the front seat. "She's feeling exposed," he explained, as if Corwyn needed him to lay that one out for him.

Corwyn remembered how exposed facing Veriel could make a person feel. He'd seen it in Anna and in himself. He nodded sadly and closed the sliding door behind them.

He wrinkled his nose as he took the driver's seat. Talon wasn't kidding. The fetid smell of beast blood hung like a pall over the vehicle.

"I think I've just changed plans," he announced. "We'll have to stop at the manor house and get cleaned up before we seek medical aid. Our doctor's a sensible woman, but..."

Talon nodded. "I wouldn't complain."

"Food and showers it is," he decided brightly. "Sound good, Jayde?"

There was a long pause.

"Asleep," Talon confirmed. "She's only had two hours down in the last thirty. I'm not surprised she didn't last long."

At the manor house, Corwyn pulled straight into the main garage, past the small band of guards he'd hired to protect the estate today. By nightfall, he would have a veritable army of Warriors to do the job for them, but Corwyn had to take human minions into account when planning the day. Luckily, any well-trained human could handle human minions, and the Warriors themselves could handle up to twenty on their own.

Corwyn nodded to Joseph on his way past. Even into his seventies, Joseph was their most skilled and trusted human guard. Corwyn had saved the man's family from three high-level turneds when he was little more than a first night. All Corwyn had to say was that his own daughter was in danger to get the man here on a Sunday with several loyal men.

Joseph had three daughters of his own, and he still bore the scar of the beast that was trying to drain him dry when Corwyn arrived. Corwyn hadn't been able to stop all of the damage. The man's oldest had been raped before he arrived, but considering what could have happened, what Joseph knew could have happened, the man had been one of his most loyal from that day on.

Corwyn pulled into the parking space closest to the underground entrance to the house, exited the vehicle, and opened the sliding door.

Talon sighed. "I hate to wake her. Ordinarily I'd carry her, but I'm not capable, and she still won't let Gunther or Piers touch her."

Corwyn smiled sadly. "She'll let me. I only got the chance to carry Jayde once in her life, and she was much smaller then, but I'd like to give it a try," he offered.

Talon nodded his thanks and ducked past Corwyn's shoulder out of the way.

Corwyn cradled his daughter to his chest and turned to find Joseph giving him a smile and a tentative nod. For all those years, Corwyn had had no real understanding of what the other man had felt that night, but he did now. Joseph was a strong man. He bit back his emotions and nodded his thanks in return as he swept her past Colin and Stephen to the room he'd had prepared for them, Talon close on his heels.

As he laid Jayde on the bed, Corwyn considered what Gunther had told him about her condition when they'd found her guarding Talon. If it was possible, he would let her sleep as long as she needed, but time was an issue. "Two hours," he decided. "She has two hours before we absolutely must take her to Laura."

"Your doctor?" Talon guessed.

"Yes. Our best."

He looked up at his son-in-law. "There is a change of clothes on the dresser and more in the dresser. You're about my size, so they'll do for now. The bath is through that door. There's plastic to wrap your cast. If you need anything else, someone will always be close by."

"You gave us the lord's chambers?" Talon asked in surprise, scanning the simple but comfortable space.

"Of course. Where else would I allow you to sleep?" Corwyn rose to leave.

"Wait. Would you watch Jayde while I shower—in case she wakes? I promised her..." Talon blushed at the admission, as if a little coddling would be frowned upon in her situation.

Corwyn sat on the edge of the bed again. "I would be honored. She should have someone here in case she wakes."

Talon's shoulders relaxed. "Thank you, Corwyn. It will mean as much to her as it does to me."

The young man wasted no time. He looped Jayde's belt over the headboard. Something in his manner led Corwyn to believe that it wasn't a random move, but rather very deliberate. Talon touched her unblemished cheek lightly then ambled away to the dresser.

He pulled off his empty belt and dropped it on the dresser next to the clean clothes then added the sling supporting his cast to the pile. Talon pulled off his armored boots with his good hand and strode to the bathroom, nodding his thanks again as he went.

Corwyn sighed as the door closed behind him. He could only imagine Jayde's anguish, watching the beast crush the man she loved, the man that was willingly trading his life for hers and that of his child.

Corwyn would have willingly done that for Anna and Jayde. He sighed at the thought that giving his life for them might have been easier than living without them, but who said the fates were easy on a man?

He could imagine—though no one gave him a blow by blow of the situation—the proud, young Warrior pleading with her to accept his sacrifice. Talon wouldn't simply issue orders to her. Their relationship wasn't that type.

Corwyn wrinkled his nose as the shower turned on. Jayde really did reek of the ancient beast she'd killed, killed while he tried to force himself on her. Corwyn clenched his fists at the thought of that beast over Jayde as he had been over Anna. He grabbed her weapons belt and moved away, stamping down his anger painfully.

Blutjagd would alert the other Warriors. It might snap Jayde awake. If it didn't, the stampede of Warriors on a hair-trigger surely would.

He dropped the belt into a garbage bag he'd brought in for the fouled gear. Once something made of leather was stained, there was no way to take the smell out. Clothing, at least, could be laundered several times to do the job. Once the smell was in the leather, it would alert any beast you approached, and the element of surprise would be lost. It seemed a waste to discard supplies that way, but there was no alternative. Besides, the blood would eat away the leather—and the skin it touched like an acid over enough time.

Corwyn added Talon's boots to the bag and made a mental note to pick up another pair for him when he picked up Jayde's. In the meantime, Corwyn had already procured him a pair of steel-toed hiking boots and her a pair of tennis shoes to hold them over, at Gunther's urging. He added Jayde's shoes to the bag, smiling that she was overdue for a new pair anyway.

He cleaned Jayde's blades carefully and sheathed them in her new belt, making another mental note to get her some *Jäger* blades while he had *König* ones made. Corwyn had no problem with her using Crossbearer blades. Jayde was married to Talon, after all, but perhaps one of each might be more appropriate for her.

Corwyn hung the belt over the back of the door, and went on to inspect Talon's belt. Since it wasn't in need of replacement, he sheathed one of his own blades, with the lord's seal, in it. Any decent Warrior had spare blades. Talon had simply been forced to leave his behind. At any rate, Corwyn would see all their new blades made with the *König* lord's seal, as they should be.

His gaze fell to the single bracer Jayde wore, and he grimaced. It was wet with a mixture of water and Veriel's blood. Though Corwyn wouldn't have a replacement until the morning, he had to remove it. The blood was probably already causing severe irritation to her. Corwyn's surprise that she kept it on almost outweighed his surprise that Talon would let her keep it. It smelled horrible and had to be causing Jayde pain. He sighed. Whether she liked it or not, the bracer had to come off.

Corwyn was working on the buckles when Talon emerged from the bathroom wrapped in a bath sheet.

Talon's smile disappeared and his eyes widened. "Do you have a replacement?" he asked urgently.

"Not yet, but—" he began.

"Leave it," he ordered.

"Talon, be reasonable. You don't need to indulge her every whim. You know what this will do to her."

"No. It stays."

Corwyn looked at him, trying to gauge what brand of madness this was. "It stinks of Veriel. It's wet. It's probably eating her flesh away. Why would she want it?"

Talon sighed and moved to the bed. "Veriel took her amulet once. With guards, even with me, there is always going to be a chance of a beast getting his hands on a sacred weapon again. Jayde won't chance that, and neither will I. Never again, Corwyn. I gave my vow."

"I don't understand the connection."

He took her hand from Corwyn and outlined a circle beneath the leather with his thumb. "Her amulet," Talon explained, laying her hand back on the bed gently. "It was brilliant. I can't believe no one else ever thought to do it. I was down. She was exhausted. The amulet was all she had left."

Talon crossed to the door and removed her belt from the hook, hanging it above her head again. In her sleep, Jayde raised her hand to grip the edge of a sheath as it scraped the headboard then wrapped the arm around her head.

Corwyn grimaced. Was this what her life had become? Living with weapons, even in bed?

"She has to know how it's hurting her," he prodded without conviction.

Talon shrugged as he turned to the dresser and pulled a T-shirt off the pile of men's clothing. He looped it around the cast expertly and drew it over his head.

He's had a high cast before.

"She came up with that? The bracer idea?" Corwyn asked quietly, looking at his daughter's face, troubled even in sleep.

"She was desperate, Corwyn. She'd lose her arm before she'd allow them to lay hands on her again. Jayde is very much like her mother. Even Veriel commented on that." Talon dragged a pair of jeans over his hips one-handed.

Corwyn's head snapped up. "What do you mean by that?" he demanded.

Talon looked at him in surprise then blushed and nodded. "I'm sorry, Corwyn. I must be more tired than I thought. I didn't think before I spoke," he apologized.

"No. I mean it. Tell me what you know. What made you say that?" he insisted. His heart ached at what might be said, but he had to know.

"I only know what Veriel said, and he's The Mad Deceiver. You know that."

Corwyn tightened his jaw, a silent demand for the answers the young Warrior had.

Talon nodded in resignation. "When Veriel threatened to take Jayde, she assured him it would be over her dead body. Veriel— He claimed Anna took her own life to stop him from taking her. He admitted that he'd underestimated her resolve. He swore it was a mistake he wouldn't make again. Not with Jayde."

Corwyn nodded and stood to leave. "Thank you, Talon. Thank you for telling me," he whispered as he headed for the door, feeling every day of his fifty-three years.

"Corwyn...it wasn't your fault. Anna gave her amulet and her life to save Jayde, just as you or I would give our lives for Jayde. Would you really consider your duty before you did it?"

He met his son-in-law's eyes miserably. "My daughter chose well, Talon."

* * * *

Talon eyed Laura Briony as critically as she eyed him. The honey-haired doctor with the piercing blue eyes evaluated everyone in the company as if the scene was foreign to her.

She curled her nose in distaste. "What is that smell?" she demanded. "Corwyn, did you drag a carcass in with you?"

Okay, not so foreign after all.

The Lord Hunter smiled crookedly. "A smell you never forget, Doc. I apologize, but this was necessary. Until I get a new piece of equipment..." His lips quirked in amusement that spoke of a private joke between them. "My daughter has to use a stained one."

"Your daughter?" Laura stared at him, her face

pale, then panned her eyes to pick out Jayde, half hidden by the wall of men surrounding her. Her smile widened. "You finally brought Erin home. Anna would be so proud."

Talon looked at her in shock. This doctor was obviously very trusted. None of the Warriors had confided the existence of the *Blutjagdfrau*, even to the most trusted humans. If Corwyn trusted Laura with foreknowledge, it was obvious why he trusted her to see to Jayde's needs now.

Her eyes narrowed as she glanced at the weapons hanging on Jayde's hip. "I thought there were no female Warriors," she noted.

"She's the only one, Laura. The only one there's ever been."

Laura nodded sadly. "Not in time," she mused. She motioned Colin aside with a stern look and reached a hand to Jayde. "But, I am truly honored."

Jayde eyed her suspiciously, and Laura nodded in understanding. The doctor scooped a Hunter amulet from her neckline and let it fall to her shirt, a lord's amulet. She was highly prized. Talon calculated what level of service a professional would have to offer to be that highly prized.

"She's safe, Jayde," Corwyn assured her. "Any doctor we trust you with will be protected. Our most trusted people are protected, and it's safe to say that Laura is the most trusted doctor our ranks have, bar none."

"Because we owe the Warriors our lives," Laura was quick to add with a sidelong glance at Colin—who was inexplicably red-faced.

Talon bit back a smile. Whatever else she was, it

would seem the lady doctor had also been someone's playmate. Talon looked away from Colin, sure that he knew which Hunter had the pleasure of Laura's company while it lasted.

"We continue to owe them our lives." Laura patted the amulet. "In return, we render service where we can."

The urge to laugh was nearly overpowering. Talon rubbed his stubbled cheek to hide the proof that he was holding back that laughter.

Jayde nodded and clasped the hand Laura had extended to her a moment earlier. Talon smiled his approval. Aside from Talon and Corwyn, this was the only person Jayde had allowed to touch her since her encounter with Veriel.

"Thank you," she whispered hoarsely.

"Come in," Laura invited.

The entire company surged forward at once, an honor guard protecting Jayde.

Laura laughed warmly. "Corwyn, call off your men. You'll be sufficient guard, I think."

Jayde wound her fingers through Talon's and met the doctor's eye silently.

Corwyn stepped back into the group and wrapped an arm around his daughter. "And her husband," he supplied for her.

Laura blew out an exasperated breath. "Nothing can ever be easy with you," she teased. "Let's go." She led the way down the closest hallway.

Jayde looked around the deserted office, and Laura smiled.

"If it were a weekday, this would be more difficult. Either I would have to come to the house with no heavy equipment or falsify paperwork and do some serious sneaking or wait for night when the clinic closed and sneak in then."

Laura startled, as Jayde shuddered at that thought and sank closer to her husband. She snapped an accusing look at Corwyn.

"It's a long story, Doc," he warned.

She nodded and opened the door to an exam room. "I chose a Gyn room, because your father thought it might be a good idea. How late are you?"

Laura tried to catch Jayde's eye, but the younger woman looked away and blushed, locking her gaze on the pictures on the walls of the exam room, settling on one in particular.

Talon followed her gaze. The picture was one of Laura with a teenaged girl. His eyes narrowed as he took in the black hair and eyes on the laughing girl. He glanced at Corwyn and saw the fleeting motion of him redirecting his eyes.

Surely not! No Warrior had children except with his mate. None of them would ever chance such a thing. *Not to mention, the Hunters couldn't have had two daughters. Females were too rare for that.*

It had to be coincidence. Laura's daughter must have had a dark-haired, dark-eyed father. Of course, Corwyn would know the child. If the mother was protected, the daughter might be, too. Maybe, the father was lost when he saved the other two. Talon shook his head. No, she couldn't be the freed daughter of a Warrior.

Jayde broke the spell entirely. "Um... Almost a month late, I think," she offered. "Please, don't ask for the date of my last menses, because I'll admit that the last few weeks have been a mess. I don't even know today's date, let alone the date I had a period last."

Corwyn set his jaw angrily, and Talon resolved to have a long talk with his wife about her duty to protect their child later. She should have told him the first day she missed.

Talon sobered. He'd known the possibility was there. He should have realized when she didn't bleed. He should have checked. Of the two of them, he was the one who knew *how* to sense for it. They'd set out to have a baby. Talon should have known they'd succeed immediately. Most Warriors did.

"You haven't thought of checking before now?" the doctor asked.

"At first, I thought it might just be stress. When the possibility became clear to me—"

"When was that?" Corwyn asked in a controlled voice.

Jayde glanced from him to Talon and swallowed a lump in her throat. "About a week ago, I realized just how long it had been. Like I said, everything was a whirlwind for a while there."

"And?"

"Well, I wanted to be sure, and I didn't want to get every Warrior in perdition up in arms for a false alarm. If word went out that I even suspected it, every Warrior and beast in the Northern Hemisphere would have converged on me."

Corwyn nodded, and his eyes softened. "I see. You didn't want to cause the apocalypse until you absolutely had to?"

She nodded silently. Still, Talon owed her a talking to for this one.

Laura set her clipboard down. "You're not going to continue to hunt them, are you?"

"I don't hunt," Jayde countered as she removed her long, leather jacket, a gift from Corwyn to replace her beloved suede that got left behind—and part of a Warrior's wear. Little by little, her life was being converted to that of a Warrior.

Her boots had been made for her especially. The craftsmen who typically supplied them had never made them for a woman's smaller foot and leg before. Where Talon's were stock for them, Jayde's had to be hand-made to her stature.

Laura took in the black button-down shirt, the weapons belt, and finally the stained bracer. "So I see," she answered sarcastically.

"No, you don't see," Talon countered. "Jayde doesn't hunt. She's hunted."

Laura took her hand and looked at the bracer critically, lifting the edge to peer beneath. "You have to take this off."

"No," the three Warriors answered in unison.

"Will you take it off and let me treat the damage if you put it back on when I'm done?"

Jayde shifted her eyes to Talon and bit her lower lip. "How many hours 'til dark?" she joked weakly.

He nodded. Humor was a good sign. "You're safe here," Talon soothed her.

Jayde took a deep breath and peeled off the bracer, groaning as it left her skin, dropping it on the exam table by a two-fingered grasp.

Talon grimaced at the sight of the raw skin that had been hidden beneath it. He knew it would be bad. He hadn't expected that it would be this bad. It had to be torture to let that thing keep touching her. The skin left was red and abraded, covered with weeping and bleeding sores that might once have been blisters. Jayde would heal, he reminded himself. In a few days, there would be no sign of the damage. Still, it hurt to look at.

Laura eyed the amulet in confusion. "I won't ask you to remove that," she joked.

"Good, because I won't," Jayde replied.

Laura cleaned the area with alcohol swabs, coated it in an antibiotic gel, and wrapped it lightly in gauze before nodding to the bracer. "You should come up with some sort of a soft liner if you intend to do that long term...and always keep spares. Leaving beast blood on your skin is a little like leaving gasoline on there."

Laura pointed to a door opposite the exam table. "Specimen cups are in there. You know what to do with one, I'm sure."

Jayde did what she'd been instructed, and the doctor set up a test while she examined her cheek.

Laura returned to the counter. "Oh, baby! I think it's definite. You have a baby in there, Mama."

Jayde blushed deeply. "Is there any way to tell if he's okay?"

Laura looked around in confusion.

Jayde pointed to her cheek. "Bad encounter," she managed weakly.

She nodded in response. "I was just hooking up the ultrasound to check on that cheekbone anyway. Since you're pregnant, I don't want to resort to x-rays. We'll do a check on the baby afterward."

Jayde nodded her thanks, and Laura motioned her

up on the table. She set up the machine, while Jayde divested herself of her weapons belt and scooted up. Jayde winced a little at the wand on her cheek but settled for the examination.

Laura worked quickly. "Cracked. With your Cursed Warrior healing— You do have that, don't you?"

"Yes. I do."

"Good. Then, you know you'll be fine in a week or less. Tylenol for pain. From now on, *only* Tylenol for pain."

Jayde nodded. "Actually, I didn't know it would be that fast, but thanks for telling me."

Laura smiled tightly. "Well, I have quite a bit of experience piecing Hunters back together. I think I've finally gotten used to their peculiarities in healing. I just wish you Warriors would stop biting off more than you can chew safely." She sighed in exasperation.

Jayde paled. "I take it you've patched Corwyn up from a battle with Veriel, too?" she asked quietly.

The doctor turned with a horrified expression on her face.

Corwyn moved to plant a steadying hand on her shoulder. "Once or twice, but luckily no one else's life is ever going to get ruined by that particular beast," he soothed them both.

"He's dead?" Laura asked breathlessly.

Corwyn nodded.

Laura let out a ragged breath. "Thank you, Corwyn."

"Thank Jayde," he replied gruffly. "She's the one who ended him. I would have if I could have. You know that."

She looked at the younger woman with newfound

respect. "Time to leave, Corwyn. I have to see a lady about a baby."

"But, I've seen—" he began in confusion.

"Transvaginal," she stated.

"Oh." Corwyn dropped a peck on his daughter's unaffected cheek. "I'll be in the hall, if you need me," he told her on the way out the door.

At Laura's request, Jayde stripped from the waist down and settled back on the table.

Laura palpitated her abdomen first. "Definitely pregnant," she decided.

Talon brushed the fingertips of his injured hand over Jayde's jawline, as she squeezed on the other hand, keeping it locked in her death grip.

"It's all right," he crooned next to her ear. "I'm right here with you."

He knew her fear. Just because the baby was there didn't mean he was safe. With Veriel, anything was possible.

Jayde closed her eyes as the wand went in, but she didn't seem to be in pain. Talon kissed her forehead, lingering on her skin while he waited for Laura's determination, but she seemed to take forever. A stream of paper flowed from the front of the machine, but the doctor stared at the screen, ignoring it.

Finally, she turned the screen to them. "Healthy," Laura assured them. "There is your baby's heartbeat." She ripped off the wide tape from the front of the machine and handed it to Talon. "And here're baby's first pictures, Daddy."

He looked at the images in surprise, little more than a curl of baby inside a sac of fluid. Talon tried to show them to his wife, but Jayde was locked on the screen, on that faint fluttering that announced their baby was alive. Her eyes were wide and her smile remained long after the monitor was turned off and she was dressed again. Jayde pored over the pictures with Talon, pressing his hand to their son in contentment that seemed to grow with each passing second.

Laura followed them out into the hall and passed a small bag into Corwyn's hands. "Samples of vitamins and a prescription for more," she explained. "I'd tell them, but I think I've lost them to the lure of a baby. Remind them that she needs to take them. Healthy Warrior babies or not, proper nutrition can't hurt."

Talon laughed. "No more HoHos and cream horns," he decided.

Laura smiled. "No more than one a day," she qualified, chuckling at his scowl. She handed Corwyn a slip of paper. "Take her for lab work tomorrow morning," she instructed.

Corwyn nodded. "Another change of plans," he muttered. "Looks like you're spending the night at the manor, after all."

No one had to ask what Laura's tests showed. One look at the grins on the three Warriors' faces sent a titter of laughter through the waiting room. In the van, Jayde slipped back into a deep sleep, despite the excited roar that seemed never to end. This time, Talon and Corwyn agreed that she should sleep as long as her body and mind required of her.

Chapter Thirty-Two

There was still much to discuss, so they delivered Jayde to bed and left Stephen to stand guard over her. The rest of the men retired to the library where the congratulations started again.

"That didn't take long," Piers teased his son.

Talon blushed. "I won't justify that one with an answer," he decided.

Corwyn laughed and clapped a hand on his shoulder. "I'm sure Jayde will appreciate that."

"I'm sure you're right."

Gunther puffed up his chest. "What's to be offended by? Just because Crossbearers are potent men—"

Colin laughed heartily. "I think quantity rather than quality may be at work here."

Gunther smiled in return. "Okay, so we're virile men, too. Either way, he's sure to be a strapping boy."

Talon felt his ears burn. "Enough of that. We have important things to discuss."

"What's more important than the *Blutjagdfrau* being pregnant?" Colin queried happily.

Talon scowled at him. "It's my wife that's pregnant, Colin. The important thing is making sure she stays that way, delivers safely, and that we keep our baby safe.

"I've promised Jayde more protection, and I think we're going to need it. Veriel knew she was carrying my son, which means they all know. Jayde fights like a tiger, but even if our baby doesn't slow her down, we can't take the chance of her being hurt by them in a fight. Yesterday proves it's possible for them to get past even an amulet—

"Which reminds me... We need to devise a soft liner for the bracer, so it doesn't irritate her to have it on constantly. It has to be comfortable and breathable. Suggestions on any and all of the above will be accepted now."

Their jovial attitude disappeared somewhere around the mention of Veriel's name.

Corwyn spoke first. "As far as the liner, I'd suggest wool for winter and cotton for summer. Natural fibers will absorb sweat and irritate least. In time, we can work on making a padded bracer for comfort, maybe lined in flannel."

"Agreed. We'll take care of it tomorrow when we get that new bracer." Talon nodded as he considered it. "We need someone to fashion child-sized bracers."

"Why?" Colin asked in confusion.

"They know how to get an amulet off now. Our baby has to be protected immediately and always. In addition to the amulet, we have to have a padded bracer ready to place over it. Not leather...something soft but durable."

Corwyn nodded thoughtfully. "The *König* form of baby booties," he noted. "Denim might work well."

"Unfortunately, the bracers are the least of our problems," Talon continued. "We'll have to move often—all over, but Jayde will still need proper medical care. That means routing all her care through one doctor who—hopefully, will deliver her when the time comes. Jayde can't stay in one place like most Warrior wives and see the same doctor every month. That means picking a place and a doctor soon."

"Here," Corwyn decided. "Laura can deliver her."

"I think Jayde should make that decision for herself. She has to be comfortable with the doctor she chooses. If she likes Laura, I think Hunter range is a damn good idea."

"What if there are problems?" Piers cut in.

"Then, we're in a world of hurt. You know she can't deliver in a hospital. Bedrest would be about the worst we could juggle with ease. Beyond that, this becomes almost unmanageable. Luckily, Warriors seldom have problems like that, and I'll wager it's damned near impossible with Jayde being a Warrior, too.

"Pray to whichever gods you favor, folks. Jayde is strong and healthy. I don't think this is a problem, so let's focus on the problems we know about for now."

"You said you had an idea for extra protection," Gunther noted. "What do you suggest?"

Talon paced the floor while he talked. "We set up three safe houses in each North American range. I don't want to take her further than Canada, unless we have to. We never spend more than three weeks in any one place. We travel from range to range with no advance notice. We carry one or two Warriors with us and pick up another one or two from whatever range we're sheltered in."

Corwyn nodded thoughtfully. "Who is your permanent complement?"

"I want Jayde's input on that." He glanced at Gunther and away again. "I want people she's comfortable with, and I don't think it should be you, Corwyn."

"Why not?" he demanded.

Talon winced at the hurt in his eyes. "Couple of

reasons. First, the beasts are going to be all over this range, hoping that you can lead them to us. No offense to Stephen and Colin, but you are the best. We can take out a lot of beasts if we just let them come to you."

"And?" Corwyn prodded.

"I want you as extra muscle when delivery approaches—Grandpa." He smiled crookedly.

Corwyn laughed in response. "Thank you, Talon."

"For what?"

"For trusting me to get it right this time," he answered seriously.

Talon clapped a hand on his shoulder. "It's a mistake you only make once, Corwyn. You won't make it again. Trust me."

"Well, I guess I have some phone calls to make," Corwyn decided.

"To get the house lords busy setting up those safe houses?" Talon guessed.

"That too," Corwyn sighed. "Actually, I just want to spread the news that I'm going to be a grandfather."

* * * *

Jayde stretched out toward where Talon should be in the bed next to her, but there was empty space. She groaned in dissatisfaction and opened her eyes. She knew there was much to do. Jayde shouldn't have counted on Talon being in bed with her, but she was bereft at his absence regardless.

"You okay?" a voice asked softly.

She identified the voice without turning. The gentle voice with a touch of amusement could only be one person. "Yes, Uncle Stephen. Where's Talon?" she half-grumbled at him as she rolled to face him.

"Strategy meeting with the other men. Would you like to go down?"

"Any chance of getting food on the way? I'm starving." She was. Jayde hadn't had anything but the juice and half a sandwich that she forced down, at Talon's insistence, when she woke the first time.

Stephen's eyes crinkled in restrained laughter. "Sure. We'll gladly feed you," he managed with almost a straight face.

"I bet," she teased. "You guys just want to feed the baby. Well, tough luck. Mom is going to enjoy herself a little." Jayde pushed up from the bed slowly. "I might even find where Talon hid the HoHos and cream horns." She smiled at the thought. He had threatened to do just that as they were leaving the doctor's office.

Her uncle chuckled. "How did you know your father stocked up on them for you?"

Jayde raised an eyebrow at him before she grabbed her belt from the headboard and headed for the bathroom. *Let him wonder*, she decided.

"Umm... Jayde, you really don't have to take your blades in with you," he assured her, his voiced laced with something she would identify as sadness.

"It's a long story, Stephen. I'd feel more comfortable taking them." Jayde glanced at him sheepishly. "If yesterday has taught me anything, it's that nothing and nowhere is sacred to a beast."

"Whatever you need," he decided.

She relieved herself, leaving the door unlocked in case Stephen needed to reach her. Next, she went to the sink to clean up. Jayde yawned as she started the water, trailing her fingers in the sink while it heated.

She froze, searching the room with her eyes and senses. Her senses were a blank slate, but she hadn't sensed Veriel and his cohort until they'd unghosted.

Jayde closed her eyes and forced her heart to slow. "Paranoid," she muttered. She turned back to the sink and splashed warm water on her face, trying to clear her head.

"Jayde..." The voice was a ghostly whisper with no apparent location. It seemed to surround her.

Startled, she wheeled around, settling her back in the corner between the sink and the wall, her right blade in hand. Jayde groped for the belt, but it was just outside her reach, so she decided to abandon the second blade for the moment. If the beast did touch it, she would at least have a direction to strike.

Her mind spun in the reality of the situation. How could she fight something she couldn't see? How do you land a killing blow on something invisible? A killing blow was necessary in so enclosed a space. Jayde knew that.

"Be nice, Jayde," the voice chided her.

She arced her blade where the voice seemed to be, but nothing caused resistance.

The voice came again, with a new direction and distance. "I just came to deliver a message, Jayde. I learned my lesson a long time ago. Never tangle with an elder hunter. I can smell his blood on you."

"Name yourself," she whispered in challenge.

Jayde couldn't alert Stephen until she knew for sure where he was. Stephen would walk right into the ambush, if she wasn't careful. She was safe for the moment. Between her amulet and position, he couldn't touch her. Jayde was suddenly thankful that the running water would hide his words from her uncle until she could get a bead on him.

"Don't seek to hurt me, *Blutjagdfrau*." His voice sounded tired and resigned. "I was sent to deliver a message. That is all. My word—" He stopped, knowing she couldn't trust his word even if, by some stretch, it was sincere.

"Name yourself."

The disembodied voice sighed. "I am called Polero, an old acquaintance of your father's. He is a great man."

"What do you want, beast? Why the compliments?"

"I ask only to deliver my message and leave in peace. Promise me that."

Jayde shook her head. "I can't. You know I can't."

"I thought not. Your kind never can. Perhaps—" He sighed again. "Perhaps, it was best that I came then."

"What's the message?"

"You carry a child. The elders know it. You killed Veriel. They know that, too. Though they're thankful for it, killing an elder doesn't put them at ease with you, even if the one you killed was Veriel.

"They want you to know that they aren't as affected by you as Veriel was. There will be little attempt to use you for their breeding now. You're too dangerous to them, because you're an elder killer. You are hunted now, Jayde."

"That's hardly news," she grumbled through gritted teeth. She had always been hunted.

"Open the door, Jayde. Open the door and let me leave now. My duty here is done."

She grasped at that. If Polero really needed her to

do that, he wasn't that high a level, after all. If he couldn't dematerialize while maintaining his ghosting at the same time— Of course, it could just be a trick to get her to open herself up to attack. Right now, she could see what was coming at her.

"No, you won't. You just want my guard down."

"I want to escape you. My beast wants—"

"You want me dead," she countered, raising her voice suddenly.

"They want you dead. I just want to leave this place."

A knock came at the door, and Jayde started. *Stephen!* She forgot Stephen when she called out.

"Jayde? Are you all right?" he asked, rattling the locked door that she hadn't locked.

She had to warn him what he would be walking into. Jayde started to yell out that warning. Polero's hand moved to cover her mouth. The blast pushed them apart, and she grunted as she hit her head on the tile behind her. Jayde struggled to clear her vision, noting something that flickered in the mirror. Without thinking, she used it for relative placement and struck.

Polero howled and lost his concentration. He was suddenly, clearly visible. Stephen started pounding on the door and yelling for her, as she backed away from the beast. She grabbed her second blade, and he met her eyes.

The pale blue of his own shone with a deep need that Jayde couldn't comprehend. His blond hair fell across his forehead in boyish disregard, leaving a rakish curl lingering above those expressive eyes. He looked at the weapon in his chest in shock. It was only eight inches or so from a killing blow. His gaze panned back to her face, his eyes filled with desperation.

"Finish it," he implored her. "Please, end it now."

Jayde nodded uncertainly and plunged the second blade through his heart, pulling them both out with her backward movement. "I free you," she whispered, as they slid back with her hands.

Stephen resorted to trying to break the heavy door off its hinges, but the fact that it was meant to open out into the bedroom was a detriment.

Polero sank to his knees. "Thank you." He laughed in relief.

Jayde nodded and backed toward the door. As she laid her hand on the knob, he spoke again.

"I wanted this, Jayde. I asked to come. I knew you wouldn't let me leave alive. There are others like me, who must fight but do not wish to. Be ready for them."

"I will." She opened the door before he could collapse and pushed past Stephen into the bedroom beyond.

Jayde wasn't sure if Stephen walked away from her, though she theorized he must have checked on Polero.

When he returned, he ran his hand over her cheek. "Jayde, talk to me," Stephen pleaded.

"I think I've lost my appetite," she whispered, dropping her gaze to stare at the drops of Polero's blood splashing onto her socks and the rug around her. Jayde vaguely registered the thunder of Warriors coming from the opposite wing downstairs before Corwyn and Talon burst through the door.

Chapter Thirty-Three

February 13ᵗʰ, 2003

Jayde paced the floor, running her hand in soothing circles over the mound of her son.

It had been a long eight months, moving from place to place. She'd often wondered if her children had nothing at all to do with the end. The turneds who wanted freed had come first, and word had it that the elders had killed even more they suspected were the same sort of mistakes, beasts who hadn't truly wanted to be turned but had been turned anyway. More had met their end at Hunter home base, and still more had died trying to get to Jayde.

In the early months, several had made it to Jayde herself, and she'd never failed to make her kill. When the elder Draden showed up at six months into her pregnancy, she'd been much less able to fight. Talon had become an elder killer that night, one of the true elite of the Warriors, above even Corwyn and equaled only by Jayde and Pauwel first Lord *Kreuzträger*, Talon's revered first-cursed ancestor.

The only other elder foolish enough to take them head-on was Carstol. He'd attacked only a month ago, and it had taken the combined efforts of Talon, Stephen, and Piers to subdue him. Talon had taken the killing blow again, though he joked that the other two men had the assist, trying to raise them to elder killers with him. Ultimately, they chose to stay elder hunters, and the legends of Talon as the perfect mate for the elder killer *Blutjagdfrau* grew. The beasts were becoming desperate as her pregnancy progressed, and with two elders left, Jayde was afraid of what would come next.

She ambled to the dresser and pulled out some more supplies they'd need tonight. Jayde tossed them into the box on top and looked at the clock.

Four thirty, almost four long hours until dawn and safety. She wasn't going to make it that long. *Dammit!* Her luck never changed. It was as unbelievably lousy as ever. Except where Talon was concerned, she reminded herself.

As if the thought of him summoned him forth, her husband woke and started as he realized she wasn't in bed with him. Jayde watched, as he swung out of bed and stalked to her, gloriously naked but still looking dangerous in his annoyance that she was padding barefoot around the chilly room instead of getting rest.

Talon glanced at the snow falling in the darkness of the frigid February night and scowled at the detriment to their movement it represented. If they had to run tonight, the snow would make it more difficult.

"Jayde, what are you doing?" he asked quietly.

"Can't sleep," she admitted.

He moved behind her and ran his hands over the tense muscles in her back. "Nightmare?" Talon asked, laying a kiss on her shoulder tenderly.

She shook her head slowly. "No." Jayde groaned the word, half in pleasure and half in discomfort.

Talon's hands moved to caress her womb, but he stilled on contact. "What the hell..." His breathing sounded harsh next to her ear.

Jayde let out a measured breath as her muscles relaxed beneath his hand.

"Is that what I think it is?" he whispered in awe.

"Yes, it is," she confirmed.

Talon swore fluently; he launched across the room and came up with his cell phone.

"What are you doing?" she asked, rubbing her hand under her baby again.

"Getting Laura here. What do you think?" he replied urgently.

"No, Talon. We can't. Not 'til daybreak."

He looked at her in shock.

"She'll lead them in."

Talon stared at the phone and closed the connection in resignation. "Will you make it that long?"

"I don't know," she admitted. "I'm kinda new at this." She smiled weakly.

He crossed to her and led her back to the bed. "Lay down. Maybe we can stall this off a little."

Jayde nodded and crawled back under the covers.

Talon dragged on his jeans.

"Where are you going?" she asked fearfully. He couldn't intend to bring Laura in himself. Talon couldn't leave her now.

"Just down the hall to wake the others. Are you shielding your emotions?"

"Always, when it's important. You know that."

"Your weapons are above your head. I want everyone up and moving. When you slip, you may not even realize you have." Talon planted a quick kiss on her lips that she enticed him into deepening for one delightful minute. He smiled and traced a fingertip along her lower lip. "I'll be right back. Try to relax."

Jayde nodded, and he bolted from the room.

Control— She had learned to mask emotion. It was a theory of Corwyn's that the beasts were often drawn to her by the deep emotions that major life changes caused for her. Their plan was to hide the birth as long as they could—if they could.

The problem with this, as with most new things they tried, was that their theories remained largely theories until proven in battle. The Stone was notorious for not offering aid when it would benefit them that way.

Jayde took a deep breath and picked up the amulet their baby would wear from the nightstand. It would be done quickly. It had to be. No matter what, the beasts would be all over them when her baby was born. All she needed was four hours. Would those ancient gods grant her four measly hours? With her luck, there was no way.

She sucked in a cleansing breath like Laura had taught her to and prayed yet again that she wasn't as far along as it felt. Laura had trained the men to deliver Jayde in an emergency, but it wasn't something she cared to try if she could avoid it, even with Gabby's help.

Stephen's wife had joined the group from time to time while they traveled, and she was here through delivery now. She had delivered two children of her own. Now aged nineteen and sixteen, they had been delegated to stay behind with Colin's three boys as a fallback and to guard the Hunter-protected in case something went wrong. Gabby's experience should have made her feel better, but it didn't. Jayde wanted Laura, but bringing her out was too dangerous.

Corwyn came through the door first, his face a mask of concern. "How are you?" he asked, taking a seat on the bed next to her and scooping up her hand.

"Been better, Dad," Jayde admitted. She looked past him at the hallway, hoping Talon was behind him somewhere.

He smiled at the endearment she'd fallen into the habit of using four months earlier. "Talon's waking Stephen and Gabby next. She'll be here in a few minutes," he soothed her, pushing her hair back from her forehead.

Corwyn watched her as she sucked in another breath and ground her teeth. Jayde could see him counting the seconds under his breath as the contraction rose and fell. When she let out the breath with a groan, he checked his watch.

"Bad?" he asked.

"Let's just say Gunther's blow has gone down in my estimation in the last hour. Maybe your pound of flesh should have been less painful," she joked weakly.

"No wonder women make such fine Warriors," he teased.

"I'd trade places right now—for training purposes, of course," she offered.

"If I could," Corwyn began.

Jayde smiled at the honesty she read from him and dragged in another breath. Corwyn glanced at his watch in surprise, and she closed her eyes and waited for it to end again.

"Likely—story," she panted out with the breath.

Gabby came in with Talon close behind. Her short blond curls and pixie stature and features belied her forty-two years, even with the uncharacteristic scowl on her face. "Couldn't do this at a decent hour, could you?" she said seriously.

"I'd kill to do this in daylight. You know—" A

particularly strong contraction shot through her womb, down through her vaginal walls and into her thighs. "That," Jayde finished in a strangled voice.

Talon replaced her father at the edge of the bed. He placed her hand in his own. "Squeeze," he invited as the pain increased. "Come on. I know you can do better than that. Don't worry. If you break my hand, it will heal in a week or two."

A tear ran down her cheek as she released the first breath and took another.

"Relax. It will ease slightly if you relax." Talon wiped the tear away with his thumb, soothing her tenderly.

"Relax and it will ease," she panted in the last downswing of the contraction. "You were right last time. I hope—" The pain spiked back up again, and she cried out in surprise.

"Staying or going, Corwyn?" Gabby asked abruptly, surging toward the bed.

"Now?" he demanded. "Jayde, how far are you?"

"I don't know," she repeated hopelessly. *Why does everyone seem to think I'm the expert here?* "Stay if you want. We'll need the extra help."

"Staying or going?" Gabby repeated in annoyance as she sat on the foot of the bed and accepted the anti-bacterial gel from Talon.

"Staying," Corwyn barked back.

"Good. Then stay out of my way." Gabby pushed the blanket and sheet up to Jayde's hips and removed her panties from beneath her trapeze-style top. "Do you feel pressure?" Gabby used the gel on her hands.

"What kind? All I feel is—" Jayde grunted in frustration as another contraction gripped her.

"Like you need to use the bathroom?"

Jayde shook her head and gripped Talon's hand tight enough to make him wince.

"Like the baby is forcing his way straight down and out of you?"

That time, she nodded her agreement.

"Okay. Put your knees up for me while I check. You'll be sore," she warned.

Jayde nodded her understanding. *Sore is news? Since when is sore news? I've been sore to exams for a month.* She closed her eyes and squeezed harder, as Gabby's hand made contact with the tender tissues inside her. Sore took on a whole new meaning.

A sharp knock sounded at the door, and Gabby pulled back her hand as Jayde shifted.

"Talon," Stephen called. "Everyone's awake. May I come in?"

"Not yet, Stephen," Gabby barked. "Towels and blankets. Fresh sheets. Now!"

"Gods alive," he breathed through the door. He bolted away, shouting orders at the top of his lungs.

"Okay. I'll finish that check, now. Hold onto Talon. It doesn't get much worse than you've already felt."

Jayde bit back a scream, as Gabby's hand prodded at her again. *Not much worse, huh?*

"How long until dawn?" the older woman asked. She eased her hand out and used the sheet to wipe it. She used more of the gel while she waited for an answer.

"More than three and a half hours," Corwyn informed her in a tense voice.

"Christ! She's not going to make it that long. No way."

Jayde groaned and degraded to trying to ignore the almost constant contractions. *Dammit! You couldn't just give me a couple of hours, could you?*

"Are you sure?" Talon asked.

"I'm sure. I should have trusted my instincts and called Laura to stay here overnight, but when Jayde fell asleep... I could never sleep in labor, so I assumed it was false labor."

"How far is she? How much time do we have?"

"The top of the baby's head is already past the cervix. Even if Jayde keeps suppressing her urge to push, which she has obviously been doing, the baby's not going to be stopped now. He's going to deliver. Sooner if she helps, later if she doesn't, but he's coming, whether we're ready or not."

"What can we do now?" Talon asked, seeking options with a desperate look on his face.

"Corwyn, get the supplies Laura left ready."

"On the dresser," Jayde panted. "The box has everything in it for delivery and the baby."

"How long were you awake?" Talon asked in accusation.

"Two hours, but I kept hoping I'd make it 'til daybreak," she managed miserably.

Talon's jaw tightened as it always did when he was angry with her for not telling him something. "We're discussing that one later," he promised.

A sound that could only be Stephen kicking at the door startled her. Corwyn opened the door for him, and Stephen placed the stack of linens on the bed next to the box of supplies Corwyn had set down while they talked. Everything in Gabby's reach, the two older men paced nervously. Gabby worked quickly, making a nest of some of the linens and positioning it under her for delivery.

Talon's irritation with Jayde momentarily forgotten, he set about trying to keep her relaxed. She was aware more of the soft sound of his voice and the soothing touch of his hands than the words he was saying. Discussion in the room seemed very far away as she sank herself into rising above the pain as Corwyn taught her for use in battle. Jayde dimly noted that Gabby was setting out supplies she thought she'd need immediately. She closed her eyes to the world.

A hand cupped her face. "Jayde, look at me," Talon ordered.

She opened her eyes in exhaustion. Had he been talking to her? It seemed he might have been.

"You have to push."

Jayde tried to shake her head, but he held her firmly, keeping her eyes locked with his. "No. It's too early. Not daybreak," she argued, pushing back another wave of the pain threatening to crush her into the depths.

"Push, Jayde. What you're doing isn't good for the baby."

"Beasts aren't good for him," she whispered, trying to let her eyes slide shut again.

"They're coming now. If you push, we'll have him protected before they arrive. Work with me. If we meet them while you're still laboring, we lose," Talon finished hopelessly.

The force of what he said dragged Jayde back to reality, and her senses confirmed what he'd said. She screamed in a combination of the jarring sense of danger headed for them and the sudden return of the pain she'd been blocking. Jayde pushed desperately, trying to make up for whatever time she'd cost them.

"That's better," Gabby urged her. "Push like that, and he'll be born in no time."

Voices faded away around her again. Only the beating of her heart and Talon's hand clasped in her own existed for her between the pain and the rising sense of danger.

Jayde panted and shook as the siege abruptly abated. *How long? A minute? Ten? An hour?* She had no sense of how much time had passed, only that it was still deadly dark.

Through bleary eyes, she saw Gabby hand her baby into the towel in Corwyn's hands.

Talon cried out in a panic. "The amulet! Where is the amulet?"

Jayde raised her hand slowly, staring at the metal disc dangling from its thong, still clasped in her fist, in confused amazement. "Here," she breathed.

Corwyn pushed the box aside with his knee and leaned to cradle her son in her arms while Talon retrieved the amulet and wrapped it around the baby's wrist, tying it securely. *Close.* They were too close. Corwyn placed his hand under the baby's head, Talon on his right cheek, and Jayde on his left.

"Now," Talon breathed. "Just as we discussed it."

In unison, the three Warriors started reciting the *Zeremonie des Schutzes*. If any were interrupted, the others—or the one—could finish. Jayde bestowed her kiss as the door exploded in. Corwyn kissed the baby's forehead and wheeled toward the movement with his blade up. Talon crowded in to drop his own where Corwyn's had been then ran his hand over Jayde's cheek. He slapped one of her blades into her free hand with a smile.

He turned away to face the enemy with a sigh that Jayde echoed. Family time was later. Battle was upon them.

Jayde laughed weakly as Gabby cut the baby's cord. "Play nice, boys," she teased.

"Easy for you to say," Talon replied. "You get to lie down on the job."

"I did my part. You do yours."

Gabby laughed as she packed the tear the baby made with sponges, as Laura had instructed. "I will never get used to the idea of a female Warrior." She pulled the blanket down over Jayde's legs and snuggled another around her from the pile, as the battle began. "That will have to do until the doc gets here," she decided. She launched over the box to the headboard next to Jayde and her baby. "What do you need?"

"Get the denim bracer from the box and get it over his amulet," she ordered. That accomplished, they lay back against the headboard to watch the battle unfolding around them.

It was almost impossible for Jayde to keep her mind on the potential dangers and keep from staring at the perfect little bundle in her arms. He was beautiful. He yawned widely and looked at her with questioning eyes.

"It's okay," she crooned, fingering the mark of Ori, the sun, that stood out in stark relief in the center of her son's chest. They got it right this time, she decided. Andris didn't have a blood mark. Anything different was good. "The noisy beasts will be gone soon." *Very soon. Today followed by forever.*

The baby screwed up his face and clawed at her shirt.

"Hungry already," Gabby noted. "Typical Warrior baby."

Jayde considered her situation for only a moment before passing her weapon to Gabby. "Just for a minute," she explained as she peeled up her shirt and got the baby latched on to eat. Then, Jayde took the blade back and nestled it behind her son as she pulled him snug into her chest.

She handed the blade back to Gabby long enough to burp him and settle him to the opposite breast. The baby placed a tiny hand on her breast as he ate and sighed in contentment.

The baby? That has to stop. She and Talon hadn't named him earlier to ward off bad luck, but he was here now. He had to have a name. "Hunter," she breathed.

* * * *

"What?" Talon asked in shock, without taking his eyes off of the beast he was fighting. *She can't be considering not giving my son my name. Just because we haven't been able to arrange a legal wedding between her listing as a missing person and moving so often...*

His heart sank. If she wasn't legally Jayde Marie Cross, what could he expect? It was within her rights to name their son whatever she chose.

"Hunter," she repeated. "Hunter Jonas Cross. Do you like it?"

Talon dealt a killing blow and pushed his opponent away in giddy elation. He cupped Jayde's head to plant a fierce kiss on her lips before drawing his hand along his son's forearm and turning to strike a blow on the next beast advancing on him. "I love it. Just keep presenting them to me as Cross babies, and you can name them whatever given name pleases you."

"Good, because if we have a girl, she's being named Erin Anne Cross."

"You're already thinking about another?" Talon teased.

Jayde murmured a response that was lost in the din around them.

Talon chanced a look at her. His smile spread at the sight. If ever there was a picture of their *Blutjagdfrau*, that was it. His fierce Warrior woman was nursing a newborn, cradling him tenderly with her blade nestled behind him, prepared to defend him to the death. Corwyn met his eyes, and his smile said that he saw it, too.

Talon's senses were humming. While he, Stephen, and Corwyn fought in the bedroom; Piers, Kord Maher, and Tristan Armen fought in the living room and library. As the beasts filtered in, so did their own people.

Colin joined the battle shortly after it started, reporting that the representatives of the houses who had come to Hunter range to help were in flight of the bumblebee mode to get to the site. So far, word had filtered up to them that David Farmer, Joshua Smith, and Reece Kaufmann had taken up the fight in various parts of the house. They were all strong, young Warriors—the best in their houses, except Kord.

Kord was the house lord of Maher and an old fighting mate of Corwyn's. For him, it was a family matter. He claimed that no other Warrior of Maher would have the honor and duty of protecting Corwyn's daughter and grandson.

As the siege wore on, Jayde finally surrendered to her body's need for rest. Heedless of the ongoing battle, Talon ordered Gabby to check her bleeding, worried that she was losing too much blood before Laura could tend to her. To his relief, the older woman decreed that she was faring well.

At a break in the fighting, Talon went to her. He sighed in relief as he kissed her forehead. He brushed a single finger over his son's hand, laid comfortably on his mother's breast. Then, he tucked the blankets closer around them to keep them warm.

"They're coming in again, Talon," Corwyn interrupted him.

"I know it." Talon looked at the clock in exhaustion. "Damn! Still more than an hour," he complained.

"Understand why she let you sleep now?" Stephen asked.

"Yeah. I think I do." Talon moved quickly, while he knew he had a few minutes, to pull on thick socks and his armored boots. It was a damned miracle that none of the beasts had used that advantage yet.

A head popped in the doorway. "How's it going in here?"

Talon nodded. "Good, Tristan. Everyone all right out there?"

"Joshua needs stitches, but we've been facing turned so far. An elder is on the way."

"I feel it. We just have to hold on until daybreak." Talon moved to the dresser and pulled out a T-shirt. He didn't need it to keep warm while he battled, but there was a decided chill in the air at rest.

Corwyn chuckled. "If you're covered out there, why don't you hold down Daddy's back?" he suggested. "It's been a long night."

Talon looked at him in disbelief. "I don't need your babysitters, Grandpa," he shot back.

Tristan laughed the boyish laugh that Jayde thought was so charming. "What you need is to put your shirt on, *König*," he teased. "I think Corwyn just wants you to survive long enough to produce more children."

Talon smiled. "It would be nice, but he really wants me to keep my promise to him."

He dragged the shirt over his chest and flexed his arm experimentally. Even months later, his right arm still weakened after continuous use. Talon sighed and switched his blade to his left hand.

The move wasn't lost on the other Warriors in the room. "*König*, maybe you should back off," Tristan suggested quietly.

"Not until Jayde's safe," he vowed. "My left may be slower, but it's stronger."

Corwyn nodded slowly. "Have you considered fighting dual? I've never been able to understand the nuances of it, but you trained with Jayde. If you led with your left..." He shrugged.

Talon raised an eyebrow and smiled. He strapped Jayde's weapons belt on, large enough because of her pregnancy. Corwyn stared at him in confusion as he tucked the remaining sheathed blade behind his left hip.

"What the hell are you up to, *König*?" Tristan asked in confusion.

Talon laughed lightly. "My wife improvises often. This was one of my favorite tricks. Watch and learn, Tristan."

"Veriel?" Stephen asked.

Talon smiled widely and nodded, and the other Warrior let out a hoot of laughter.

Corwyn sucked in his breath. "He's here."

Talon nodded and brought his weapon up in his left hand.

When the elder solidified, he put up his hands in a calming gesture to still the advance of the Warriors. "I would speak with you, Talon of Crossbearer, Lord *König*, elder killer," he requested formally.

"Name yourself, beast elder," he countered.

"I am Cerran, my lord." He pulled his shirt back from the hollow of his throat to expose the mark of Fih—war, proof positive of his identity.

"Explain yourself. Why the false praise?"

"It is not false praise I offer," he stated simply.

"What do you offer?"

"Peace. This is ridiculous. Can we not reach an accord?"

Corwyn barked in laughter. "You must have learned lessons from Ditrich first lord *Jäger*. He was Dobler, the twin peace bringer and diplomat, as I recall. That would make him your opposite marked."

The elder darkened slightly. "Yes, your great ancestor, so well you know his mark."

"What kind of a deal could you possibly offer us that we would accept?"

"You slaughter us for a woman we have no use for. Those of us who would take her are dead. They have faced you already—and lost. Those few left are tired of fighting. Veriel spread this madness. For want—for love of a lost woman, he created this mess. Can we not come to an agreement to stop it now that he is gone?"

"Anna," Corwyn breathed. His face was drawn tight in pain.

"Veriel in love?" Talon spat. "Impossible."

"Yes, it was," Cerran admitted, "but he coveted love. He drove himself mad with the wanting."

"I am supposed to do what?" Talon asked.

"Let us live. In exchange, no more turned. We will enjoy the bare minimum to survive. We only wish to be."

Talon shook his head. "You know we can't agree to that. As long as your kind exists, our children will be cursed. Even if I could turn a blind eye to your human victims— Even if you ceased the slaughter, fed minimally, and refrained from taking your urges out on them, I couldn't ignore my descendents that way."

Cerran sighed. "Must it always be war with you?"

"It's your kind who are coming to destroy us," Talon countered. "We're slaughtering you in defense."

"You hunt us."

"We defend those who cannot defend themselves against you. It is the sacred trust you yourself were trained to and turned your back on."

"Semantics. To live, we must live as we are. If you recall, we are damned because we chose it to save your ancestors. We gave up our humanity for you."

"Then, be martyred already," Talon fumed. "No human lives even a tenth as long as you have, even considering your half-life. You chose to be damned for certain victory rather than face dying. Nothing has changed in fifteen hundred years, Cerran. You still choose your damned half-life rather than face death as every being on Earth does."

"Is it so easy for you? Is facing death really so easy for you?" he asked in something resembling amusement, but which was cold and hard.

"Compared to the alternative? Absolutely."

"That is your last word? You will never consider peace between us?"

"It is. We are what we are. Our curse ends with you, and your damnation ends with us. I cannot change that fact. No one can." Talon saw Corwyn nod his approval out of the corner of his eye.

"You will raise that child to destroy us?" Cerran asked, motioning to the bed behind Talon.

"He's *Krieger der Nacht*, like all who came before him. You know it's my duty to train him," Talon answered simply. Time— If he could keep Cerran talking a little longer, he'd run out of time for the night.

"I cannot allow that," the elder decided.

"You'll have to fight through all of us. Are you prepared for that?" Corwyn warned.

Cerran shrugged. "I will not waste time trying to coax an amulet off a woman. I will not try to take her to bed. I will not hesitate to kill each of you instead of sparing you for revenge or as a means of swaying your *Blutjagdfrau*. I fight a simple fight, unlike my brothers you've met so far."

The other men moved into a rough vee between Talon and the elder, waiting for a sign to lay on. If

Cerran wanted a *König*...any *König*, he would literally have to go through all of them first or resort to some trickery to pass the line. From the look on his face, Talon was sure he would choose the former option.

A commotion broke out on the floor below, no doubt orchestrated by the elder to cover his attack. Cerran burst forward. What followed was a game of cat and mouse in which Cerran materialized and dematerialized over and over, striking once and moving on before anyone could retaliate. The energy Cerran was expending had to be considerable, and his feeding would have to have been deep to allow him to do it. The feeding he would require to replenish himself would be even more so.

Talon grimaced. The sight of three battle-hardened Warriors having rings run around them would have been amusing were it not so deadly serious.

Stephen fell first. The blow wasn't fatal, but he wouldn't be able to continue battling with the three claw punctures Cerran left through his right shoulder. Gabby's eyes widened and she launched off the bed, dragging her husband past the beast bodies littering the floor to the hall. Gabby worked furiously, convinced that his wounds were worse than Talon knew them to be.

Tristan went next. Tossed across the room after only a few tight exchanges, Talon knew the sickening snap meant a broken leg before the younger Warrior howled out his pain. The beast swept Tristan's weapon from his hand expertly, as he tried to crawl toward the battle to offer further support, and buried it in the wall high over Jayde's head.

Cerran met Talon's eyes with a shrug. "Too bad I

am constrained," he growled. "Using a Warrior's blade on them would be such sweet justice."

The elder moved to Corwyn smoothly. "The great Lord *Jäger* and father of the *Blutjagdfrau*," he mused. "You would fight to the death for her and her bastard?"

"Try me, beast," he challenged in response.

"You are old, Corwyn. You survived Veriel three times, but you were young and lucky then...and Veriel had other plans for you. He only wanted to make you suffer for taking his woman from him. I do not make mistakes like that."

"You've left us alive so far," he noted, stalling for time.

"Expediency. After I finish them," he motioned to the bed, "I will finish off all of you."

Cerran moved suddenly, and Corwyn dodged and landed a solid blow to the beast's arm before backing to lead him away from the *Königs*.

Talon had to admit to himself that he was impressed. He knew Corwyn still had it when he took on Gunther. Unlike most penalties for trespasses the house lords took, Corwyn had encouraged the older man to defend himself in a barehanded match. The sole purpose, of course, was a public and painful lesson not to presume to raise Corwyn's daughter for him. Overall, while more barbaric than Talon typically preferred personally, it was one of the most effective lessons he'd ever seen taught. Not to mention, Gunther had been unable to leave bed for the entire three days of Corwyn's stay.

Cerran looked at the wound in shock, and his eyes hardened. His second attack ended much the same way, and Corwyn smiled in a self-satisfied way at the howl of pain that shot from the beast's lips.

You're winning, Corwyn. Don't get too cocky. Stay in control and you have a chance to bleed him out or delay him until the sun comes up.

Talon knew it was over before Cerran's next move. Something subtle changed in the elder that just didn't feel right to him. Cerran dematerialized as Corwyn's blade swung at him; for a long moment, he was nowhere. Talon's warning came too late. The beast materialized with his hand around Corwyn's throat and dealt the blow that knocked the Lord Hunter unconscious before the Warrior could react.

The beast turned to Talon and smiled viciously. "Only the great *König* elder killers left," he mused. "And I have nearly an hour to deal with the three of you. Will you be more of a challenge than your guards? Of course you will; you have the blood of three elders and the hearts of two on your hands."

Talon took a single step toward him. "Even if you use me as bait, Jayde will never remove her amulet or my son's. She can wait you out for half an hour if she has to."

"Their protection only prevents me from touching them directly. They are hardly in condition to run from me, and while it is a cowardly way to kill a largely defenseless woman and child..." Cerran shrugged. "I have no honor, as you are so fond of pointing out. So, the idea of using some neutral tool as a means to kill them, while not my usual style and not as clean and satisfying a kill, is well within my power."

Talon was still reeling from the probability that the beasts had come up with a new and completely possible scenario, when Cerran attacked. Even left handed, Talon held his own initially, but the beast landed a blow that knocked Talon hard against the wall, and his weapon was yanked away and thrown.

Cerran's hand came up to his throat; he willed his claws to form and extended his fangs.

Fed on or with my throat ripped out— Either way, I have nothing to lose.

Talon startled, more at the piercing shriek his son sent forth than in the knowledge that he might die in the next few seconds. Cerran smiled as Talon tried to get one last look at his family. Talon moved his hand to his back quietly, as the beast's eyes followed the progress of his own to the bed.

Cerran's smile disappeared and he bowed forward, Jayde's blade planted in the elder's back.

"Off center," she screamed hopelessly. She reached for her belt and found it gone.

Jayde looked at him in dismay, but Talon was smiling. That throw was the final straw. Cerran couldn't escape now. His tricks were on ice, because of the weapon lodged in him. Jayde had provided Talon with the opening he needed.

Her other blade came from behind his back for the killing blow. He pushed the beast away and took an unsteady breath as Tristan crowed in victory. Talon nodded his direction and moved to Jayde's side. She was wrapping Hunter in a clean towel, but he drew her face up for a kiss.

"Thank you," he whispered.

"Guess Hunter and I get the assist on that one," Jayde teased.

"Gladly. Sunrise is coming, and I'll need Colin. We'll need a full medical complement soon, and I need him to call in the troops."

"For me and who else?" she asked quietly.

"Your father is out. Stephen has a few stab wounds. Tristan has a broken leg, and Joshua needs stitches—unless there've been more injuries I don't know about."

She nodded in exhaustion. "Get Colin to make the calls then give me a hand dressing our son. After Laura has us patched up, we'll have to move to a new safe house."

Talon nodded at her sound logic. "The good news is that there's only one elder left."

Jayde smiled at Hunter, as he yawned widely. "Not for long, in the grand scheme of things. There'll be another elder killer in this family someday. If it's not Hunter, it'll be another child of ours."

Talon leaned in to plant a lingering kiss on her lips. "Still talking about another? Shouldn't you discuss this with me?" he teased.

Jayde ran her free hand up his thigh suggestively, making Talon take control of his raging need for her.

"Weeks," he groaned. It would be weeks before Jayde was ready for him again. Talon shuddered at the thought of such a wait and hoped Hunter would be adequate distraction to him in the interim.

She smiled warmly at him. "I'll heal soon enough. We don't want to shoot for another right away, of course, but if you're trying to convince me that you'd balk at the idea—"

"Shut up and agree with her, *König*," Colin snapped at him from the doorway. "Sun's almost up, and the others have left to go to ground." He crossed to the bed to smile down at his great nephew. "Just agree.

Don't make me hurt you."

Talon laughed harshly. "Now, he's going to hurt me for not taking you. The last time—"

"I can do math, Talon," Colin shot back. "I know she was expecting already when I threatened you." He glared at the young lord.

"All right," Talon stated, laughing. "I agree. After all, I did agree to keep Jayde happy."

"And?" she prodded.

"It would make me happy, too," he admitted.

"Good," Colin asserted. "Now kiss her, while I go make some phone calls."

Jayde watched her uncle's retreating back, giggling uncontrollably until Talon captured her mouth in a heated kiss.

Talon smiled as Hunter grabbed his fingertip. "Guess you give a whole new meaning to Hunter born," he teased his son.

The End

Excerpt from The Stone's Words

By Gawen first Lord Schwertträger,
Stone lord and master trainer
505 AD

For the extinction of the beasts that walk the night, we will give our life's blood and our lives. Such is the curse that we were born to. Such is the duty we swear to. Such are the lives we lead.

Father to son, the curse will pass. Cursed born, our daughters may be freed, but never our sons. The Ceremony of Freeing is a sacred trust. Performed at birth, in the first unguarded moments of his daughter's life, a Warrior takes a blood oath to accept her curse unto himself, freeing her from the duty of a Warrior.

To perform the ceremony, the Warrior must draw a cut as if for a blood oath on himself and paint the mark of Syth, the symbol of the Stone's trust, upon her brow and breast as he would in the blood of a beast at a young Warrior's first kill.

Placing his hand over the mark at her brow, he must say the following: "By the gods who forged us all, I ask that this one be transformed unto Human form for the protection of all. Blood of my blood, be free of my curse, for now and all times."

Then placing his hand over the mark over her heart, he must say the following: "I free you from the obligation of my curse and accept back into myself the duty that would have been yours. It is my oath that I shall fight in your stead and for your honor, until the day that I join the Warrior's Rest."

Freed from the curse, his daughter must be protected from the beasts. The freeing must be completed first. If a Warrior completes the Ceremony of

Protection without freeing his daughter first, she will be cursed with no hope of freeing. The Ceremony of Protection will seal the child onto his or her path forever.

The Ceremony of Protection must be completed for all Warrior mates and children, Warrior born and taken into his household alike. In addition, innocents saved of a beast who fed upon them shall be granted such protection if they wish it. Other victims may be offered protection if such a thing will prove beneficial to the Warriors.

Among those others, human sensitives should always be protected, if they will accept such protection. A human sensitive is a rare and precious find. A Warrior will know the sensitive by her ability to know the beast whether ghosted, cloaked in illusion, or as a mist. A sensitive who can mark all three is a jewel beyond compare. Sensitives should always be offered a place in the household of a Warrior when found. While it is beneath a Warrior to place such a woman in service as payment, he should offer personal protection to her in respect of the curse she shares—human but pursued by the beasts always.

To complete the Ceremony of Protection, the Warrior must place a sacred amulet on the person he is to protect. He then places his hand somewhere about the face or head of the person to be protected and recites the following: "By the gods who forged us all, I grant you the protection of the House (of the Warrior giving his blessing). Any and all of our kind and kin shall lay down life to preserve yours from the evil that walks among us. Walked blessed among us, now." The ceremony should be sealed with the Warrior's kiss anywhere about the face of the protected.

The blessing, once given and sealed, is with the person always. While neither blessing nor amulet alone is effective, any sacred amulet may take the place of an amulet given at blessing, which is lost, taken, or otherwise removed. A new blessing is not required, nor will it add to the protection of an individual.

More than one amulet or blessing given will not increase protection. Still, it will not cause injury to Warrior or protected to give a blessing when in doubt if the Ceremony has been completed or as a symbolic gesture of a Warrior taking a woman already protected by another house to mate and offering his protection to her accordingly.

From the time of a Warrior's first kill, he will remove his amulet as a sign of his blood seal. From the time of his first night through his first kill, he will remove the amulet while he hunts, under his lord's or father's protection, as a sign of his curse and duty. Even his first kill must be taken without benefit of the amulet's protection. Only *Blutjagdfrau* may keep her amulet always to safeguard her from use by the beasts.

Excerpt from Early Histories

Section One
By Gawen first Lord Schwertträger,
Stone lord and master trainer

Know you now that I set ink to paper in the year 535. The Stone, as always, amuses itself at our expense. When I took my place as Stone lord, I believed this war would be short as the last beast war was short. I thought that stories could be held as knowledge only to those few first cursed and taken to our graves with us. With the passage of time, I find that I will soon pass from this realm into the Warrior's Rest, and there are things I would tell before the gods take me.

Some are those tales known only to those first cursed, but with the deaths of many of the first lords and more importantly of my beloved nephew Andris, they are truths I would have future generations know for the protection of all. Those most affected, my dear sister and her family, no longer live to be harmed by these truths.

The Warriors are strong, but the end hinges not on the strength of men but rather on the strength of a woman.

Born to my household and given to me as my own in the Stone's trust, Regana was strong and bold as any Warrior ever was. Known for her importance only to Sibold, she was raised in battle play with the young Warriors and educated as a lady by Kethe, sister of Pauwel.

Though her coloring was that of the Stone-Chosen, the gods hid her blood mark well. Not even I saw it as I cared for her as she grew. Not even Pauwel saw it as he took her to his bed as wife. Beneath her hair lay the symbol of Ani, and Regana was granted protection of the Stone as befits a mother. It was not until long after Sibold's death and my succession as Stone lord that this was made clear to me.

In retrospect, such a thing should have been clear, even to the blind! Her coloring aside, Regana could have been naught but the Stone-Chosen mother. From her earliest days, she was never one to follow commands, as much to my dismay as Sibold's. A Warrior's heart beat in her chest, but untamed as any woman's soul.

Raised with the young Warriors, she knew them all well; but she knew myself, Pauwel, and Jörg best of all. Jörg was as her brother. Only half a year separated them in age, and to my great shame, the young pup was raised by me in place of his dead father. Many a year, I have been tortured by how I might have done different by him, but in the end, 'twas his curse that undid him.

When Jörg began his training, our number was complete. Sibold partnered us for battle: Wilhelmus with Olbrecht, Cunczel with Dado, Ditrich with Geldric, Gerhardus with Bertolf, Tilbrand with Redulf, and Pauwel with Jörg. I, as leader, partnered no one.

Sibold matched the Warriors to complement each other in battle. Pauwel and Jörg were our strongest, named by the Stone as such and proven in trial with the others. Marked by the symbols of *Ori* and *Reg*, they burned bright as their symbols foretold. Pauwel with his cool grace and Jörg as a fiery berzerker complemented each other well, as if born to fight side by side instead of head to head. Closer than brothers in many ways, they knew each other's fighting styles like no other could.

But the stronger the Warrior, the stronger the curse. While the other elders went to the Stone in greed or fear, spurred on by Marclef's promises, Jörg was lost to madness. It was the only likely way for him to circumnavigate the Stone's protection and deliver up the ancient beasts, earning his title of The Mad Deceiver.

NOTE: In the original text, there is a section here scratched into unreadability, presumably by Gawen's own hand.

Pauwel succumbed to his own form of madness, reaching *Endspiel* and pursuing Regana for his own. Whether he fell because of his stronger curse or because the object of his printing was Regana was never clear. Either way, Raga went to the lord elder slayer, as was right.

That transgression might have cost Pauwel his life, not by Sibold's hand but by my own and the hands of our cursed brothers. Safe from my hand by virtue of Regana's love for him, his need and love for her, and the fact that Andris slept in her womb; it fell to me to keep peace as master trainer.

Pauwel was the lord elder slayer. While none of our brethren had any more knowledge of what Pauwel and Regana represented together than I did, still none matched him in battle, and this they knew well. It was better to have him fallen but fighting than dead by a blade, whether that blade be my own or Sibold's.

Those Warriors who remained after the beasts were released chose their mates as the Stone intended for them, none interfering with another. The elders, now beast, knew only one drive. Drawn to Regana by some unnamed force, they sought to possess or to destroy her, each in his own way. Veriel came for her the first time the night after he went beast, but he was driven off by her amulet and my blades.

I thought at the time that it was strange that the beasts were granted this knowledge denied the Warriors themselves. Or perhaps, they knew not why they pursued, as Pauwel knew not why he burned for her so. Still, they pursued.

The beasts fought the battle on the basis of Marclef's lies, lies that ultimately cost the leader his life for his treachery. Veriel turned the leader and left him to me to kill. Thus, I became the first beast killer of the new war. The fact that Marclef faced the same fate he enticed others to embrace seemed to amuse The Mad Deceiver. In this case, I could almost agree that The Destroyer of Lives had only obliged one who sought to destroy his own life with his underhanded ways. Veriel and Resten left immediately from the battlefield to accomplish this task once they learned they had been lied to...and to try for Regana as their prize.

Resten tried for her first, killing Sibold in his bid to gain access to her within the Stone's keep. Veriel sent him to ground and returned to claim Regana for himself.

But, Regana was never one to accept a man's rule. While the elders had been gone in their battle, she had left the protection of the Stone to save Sibold. Veriel came for her before she had the master trainer inside the stronghold, but Regana did not accept his claim on her lightly. Taking Sibold's blades from his dying hands, she threatened to plant them in the beast if he remained in her sight.

The idea seemed laughable. Regana had played at battle with wooden weapons and even found herself in her share of barehanded matches with the older and much larger boys, but she was not a trained Warrior. She was half the size of the beast she faced and human, with only my amulet and blessing to protect her from his wrath. Moreover, unknown to any of us but herself, Regana was with child. Still, she refused to yield Sibold to the beast. She placed herself between Veriel and his prey, oblivious to the fact that she was the beast's true prey.

In truth, Veriel laughed at her attempt, but he left her regardless. Whether he left to play another night—admitting some time later that she amused him with her threats and her stubborn spirit—or something about her unnerved him was unclear even to the end. He left her without incident, and she brought Sibold into the safety of the Stone to wait for daybreak.

In the end, her valiant efforts could only delay Sibold's death long enough for me to reach them and take my place as Stone lord properly. In the intervening hours, the master trainer gifted Regana with his blades for her own protection and the protection of the innocents in their midst.

The fact that she nearly took Pauwel's head as he entered the stronghold in the weak pre-dawn light was simply the final blow for us all in a very trying night. Perhaps, the fact that Regana was to be trained should have been apparent to us then, but without Sibold's word or the Stone's comment, we could not know such a thing was in store for her.

Still, I had no idea of the secret vows that lay between Pauwel and Regana. As the choosing night approached, Regana became withdrawn and unsettled—volatile on a scale that disturbed me, but I had no clue of the origin of this strange upset, save the beasts' interest in her.

In reality, she became afraid, realizing that Pauwel

could face death when her baby's arrival proved their crimes. In a panic, Regana refused her place in the choosing, hoping to take dishonor alone and spare his life.

Pauwel was a printed man and could not choose another. In desperation, he confided his indiscretions to me and begged my mercy in judgment, begged for the one woman who eased his pain.

My shock was overcome by my anger, but I was calmed by my choosing of Bavin and that she would have me as her own. In truth, had his confession—or my discovery by other means—come at any other time, I might have taken a deathblow without letting my mind rule my curse.

Reserving my judgment until they could face me together, we returned to my lands to find Resten and Veriel vying for Regana yet again. NOTE: Again, there is a section destroyed by Gawen, as he wrote.

Pauwel killed Resten in her defense, and Veriel fled our combined strength. That in itself nearly sealed my decision to take my single blow and give Regana to him. Surely, I could not kill the first lord elder slayer nor lose him to the madness of losing one he was printed to.

The announcement of Regana's gravid state shocked me, but it was even more of a shock to Pauwel. Regana had not told him of her condition out of concern for his reaction to their inattention to the details of checking her cycle of late, fear that Pauwel would come to me with a confession at a time when I would not be capable of showing mercy to either of them.

Still, Pauwel held his ground, waiting patiently for my judgment before accepting his blow gracefully and scooping his wife to him in joy for his son in her womb.

Thorald joined them formally the very next day, though my Stone duty to protect her meant she retained my personal protection even in her married life. Pauwel did not question why he could not give her his amulet. It was a small boon to ask of him in return for Regana, his son, and his life.

Even with this new information about her, there was a puzzle about Regana that the Stone intended us to solve. In the end, Regana solved it herself.

Rumors abounded about Regana—dangerous rumors because of her coloring and unladylike actions in the face of Veriel. Complicating matters were the jealous streak Riberta bore Regana for capturing the love of the Warrior she wanted for herself and the half-mad stories Eberhard told, stories that proclaimed Regana an evil omen.

With Sibold dead and Eberhard a madman, Regana went to the last remaining person with memories of her birth, Emecin, the midwife. Breaking her oath to Sibold at last, Emecin confirmed for Regana that she was Raga, the mother.

That fact was not enough to sway the villagers. Bermer, the oldest son in the family of blacksmiths, tried to kill her, in the belief that her death would send the beasts away. Regana felled him, though Bermer was almost the size of a Warrior and she large with Pauwel's son. She ran from him, but he gained on her quickly and attacked her bodily and with intent to slit her throat. Bermer would have killed her were it not for the boy healer, Landric, who took the man's life in her defense and brought her back to her lord for comfort and care.

Finding his game with Regana threatened and never one to blithely accept an interruption to his play even before he went mad, Veriel used and killed the fair Riberta, Wil's sister, for spreading the dangerous rumors that almost cost him his prey. Then, Veriel orchestrated a full beast war on the village. Spanning days, the battle sought to destroy every villager who harbored thoughts of injuring Regana before Veriel played out his game. The people were executed in the most gruesome manners imaginable.

Intent on his game, Veriel came for Regana again. His threats to her and to Pauwel stated clearly, he left her presence, amused by Kethe's threat to use blades on him in defense of Pauwel's wife and son. To protect her from villager and beast alike, Pauwel and I undertook formal training for Regana, as any Stone-Chosen would.

Desperate now to minimize the effects of the sons of Raga, Veriel sought to use Pauwel in his plan. He defeated the strong young lord in battle and fed from him deeply until he controlled his will. His will not his own, Pauwel was forced to drink of Veriel's foul blood, turning him to a beast.

Veriel brought Pauwel to Regana, believing that she would choose to let him kill her husband when posed the choice of accepting him as he was or death for him. To Pauwel's dismay as much as my own, Regana tore off her amulet to cradle her husband to the babe growing within her. Undone by his own game, Veriel learned that turning Pauwel was a mistake he would live to regret.

As a printed Warrior, Pauwel was not the puppet the elder had hoped for. Rather, Pauwel retained his love and all things that made him husband and Warrior, even as he was turned beast. Veriel lived to regret that night, forced to ground again and again and thwarted at almost every turn. By turning Pauwel, he did naught but create a more powerful barrier between himself and his prey. He could not hope to touch Regana while Pauwel lived as beast, and Veriel lacked the ability—perhaps because Pauwel was a Warrior beast—to kill his adversary.

Still, the elder was determined enough to plague Regana at her son's birth with threats of ending the only son of Raga. With Pauwel as beast, there could be no more sons from him, and so he protected his son fiercely, if anonymously.

Only the first cursed, Kethe, and Bavin shared Regana's secret of her beast husband. To the rest of the world, he was dead and Regana a widow. So it came to pass that at his birth, I granted Andris the amulet of his father's personal protection and my own blessing, one of the many things Pauwel could no longer give his son as beast. Still, never a more doting father had I ever seen—in the early days before Andris was old enough to repeat what he saw, and Pauwel was still able to hold him and care for him as a father would.

In the meantime, Pauwel became the ultimate Warrior, killing turned whenever he encountered them and sending elders to ground for up to a week at a time. The reservations the other first lords had with this strange arrangement were set aside quickly as the irony of the beasts' folly became ever clearer.

Veriel tried to take Andris three times before he was a man and finally—on the young man's first night.

NOTE: Yet again, Gawen destroys a portion of what he has written and begins again.

Driven to ground by one of his many turned, one of the many who did not wish damned by him, Veriel lost his opportunity to kill Andris before he claimed the seal of Lord Kreuzträger. The young Warrior freed the injured high-level and won his seal, a most noble bit of generosity and caring that he showed the beast who had no wish for his damned life.

Knowing his son was lord and Regana safely in the care of myself and Andris, Pauwel came to me when next he was seriously injured and begged me to free him. With a heavy heart, I did as he bid me. Regana wept for him, as the other first lords and I gave her husband a Warrior's burial.

It was our only chance to free Pauwel, the only chance we would likely ever have to defeat him and give him peace, while Regana still lived to stabilize him and keep the Warrior in him alive and in control of the beast in himself. Pauwel knew this sad truth, and so he sought death before the time when Regana could die and leave him a danger to all.

Had I known the results his death would have on Regana, I might have chanced the beast in Pauwel and denied him his respite still. My beautiful sister fell into a deep melancholy without Pauwel's love. Andris claiming Ger's daughter, Berna, as his bride cheered her but hours. News of their coming child barely touched her in her grief.

Little more than a year after her husband's death, Regana could stand her isolation no longer. She slipped into the dark night with her weapons, and with nothing left to lose, she searched out Veriel.

She fought him as a Warrior fights, without an amulet to protect her, seeking to find Pauwel in the Warrior's Rest at her death. Skilled beyond even my comprehension, Regana sent The Mad Elder to ground for three days, but her own life was forfeit in return. Veriel fed on her and left Regana to bleed to death in the spot where once they played together as children, the ultimate show of disdain for the one he once called sister.

I failed in my Stone duty to Regana. She was gone. I should have been able to stop her—or to save her. Still, I have no concept how that beast could feed on my own lands and not have me know that he was there. Perhaps, the Stone was taking some measure of pity on Regana by letting her join her lord with no interference from me. I can only hope that is the case, though I fear it is not.

Regana was given a Warrior's burial by her lord's side, together in eternity as they could never be in life.

With the wrath of Andris and myself looming, Veriel wisely backed from his assault on Raga's family. After all, his own death would not come at the hands of a Schwertträger or Kreuzträger. Veriel turned his attention to the young Warriors of Jäger. His death was slated at the hands of that house, and so his brutality moved to them.

Excerpts from The Kaufmann Histories

The lost page
As penned by Rober Lord Kaufmann in 1497

When my brother, Etienne, was struck down, I rushed to his aid. One beast had died by his hand that night, but another had escaped judgment. In the midst of a scene of fierce battle where Veriel left my lord to die in a growing pool of his own blood, a wailing servant girl tried to keep him alive, but it was not for the dying house lord that she wept.

Jacquine had been the lady's maid to Caitrina de Leon. The fair Caitrina had been betrothed to her lord Jörg der Schmeidt, a man of German descent but powerful, wealthy, and a noble gentleman who won her father's agreement to the match. Her tears were for Caitrina, mortally wounded in error by Etienne's blade as he sought to free her from the beast Veriel.

The Mad Deceiver, using his forbidden human name, had enchanted the beauteous maid to him so completely that she fought my lord with a sword in hand to remain the beast's alone. Never had Etienne seen such dogged determination for such a thing. It unnerved him to see such devotion to so foul a creature.

The young miss believed Veriel the perfect young lord, attentive and courteous, deep in his love and regard for her. He called his lady by German endearments—*Geliebte* and *Regana,* in his tender moments alone with her.

The maid knew not the import of such things, but we were chilled by the implications. Had this Caitrina been chosen and we lost our chance at an end yet again? She had not the look of a Stone-Chosen, but Veriel had not the look of a true Warrior either, though he bore the mark. In fact, her deep brown hair and sparkling blue eyes might well be compared to the anomalous appearance of The Destroyer of Lives. The only truth was in the marking, and that was something beyond our power to check, as Veriel had stolen his lady away with him before my approach.

Etienne mourned the woman's loss, chosen or not, for his part in her exit from her human life, though I know it to have been honest error and not negligent loss. Worse, he cursed his inability to stop Veriel from feeding the lady on his foul blood and turning her from the light and goodness of her soul.

The Stone has long foretold the dangers of a female turned. In his final tortured cries to the gods, Etienne begged forgiveness for what his action and inaction hath wrought on the world.

I only pray, as I bury my brother and take my seal, that the name of Kaufmann is not forever synonymous with the heinous crimes the once virtuous Caitrina de Leon will surely commit in her altered state of being.

Having seen the foul deed and what her lady has become—and her lord always was, Jacquine has accepted my personal protection. Pray Veriel knows, if he ever dares come for her, he will find my blade ready to protect the girl with my life.

Excerpt from The First Book of Texts

By Gawen first Lord Schwertträger,
Stone lord and master trainer
"The Rules of Sanction"
Part One (penned in 510 AD)

A Warrior must be mindful always of the humans around him. More than human, less than damned; the cursed have the potential to do great good. Inherent in that potential is the ability to do great harm.

A Warrior will have enemies, and to protect those humans bound by the Stone's sacred trust, the Warrior will kill in honorable battle those enemies.

A child is never truly an enemy. He may be disarmed and even rendered unable to continue the present battle, but though the child of today may grow to be the enemy tomorrow, today he is naught but a boy.

A woman may be slain in battle only as a last resort. If she raises her blade against a Warrior, he will first treat her as he would a child. Remember always that a woman battles most fiercely for child and home. Whenever possible, a Warrior should seek his true enemy elsewhere and leave her to protect what is hers from less honorable men—and less dangerous.

In battle, unforeseen events will occur. In battle, innocents will often die. The Warrior should never carry a battle to innocents that can be fought elsewhere. When there is no choice, the Warrior must be mindful of the innocents in his midst. An innocent life taken in honest error is lamentable. One taken in negligence is unforgivable.

More than human, less than damned. The Warrior must never forget that humans are powerless before him. This is not a reason for pride but rather a warning.

The Stone made a pact in its wisdom. One of the foundations of that pact is the Warrior's promise to do no harm. Those under a Warrior's protection and innocents all, the Warrior must protect to death.

Humans are fragile things in that they are frail and unable to heal as Warriors do as much as in that they fear and attack any perceived threat. Warriors possess the power to be perceived as a threat.

As the chain is only as strong as its weakest link, so the pact is only strong as the trust imparted by its weakest to its strongest. For the safety of Warrior and mate, no Warrior may threaten that trust and live.

Warriors are cursed. Stone-Chosen or passed from father to son, the curse manifests in the same fashion, generation after generation. Akin to the damnation of the beasts, never doubt the curse for what it is.

Blutjagd, the blood lust, comes first and foremost. Where the beasts are driven only by darkness, the darkness in a Warrior's soul will be very strong. The urge to kill the beasts is at its heart, for dark knows dark, as the Warriors and beasts each sense the other and seek each to destroy the opposing dark.

Blutjagd in its purest sense is naught but good, but that is not only how it will make itself known. The gift of *Blutjagd* is also the ability to protect what a Warrior holds dear to him and what he has a duty to protect, but there is a fierce streak in him that rivals his love and loyalty.

When a wrong is done by a human to him and his, a Warrior must not allow darkness to rule him. Capital offenses require the ultimate price. Of that there is no doubt, but the price must be exacted on the one who has wronged him alone. Revenge is not something a Warrior indulges in. The ones who have not acted against him are innocents. The pain of their loss is more punishment than they deserve.

If the offense is injurious but not capital, retribution should be taken in kind. If no injury is sustained, no blood may be spilled in return, unless the guilty attacks in earnest.

A Warrior must ever be mindful of the nature of the crime against him. He cannot allow his pain to rule him. Capital crimes involve grave harm and disregard of innocence. Murder or rape or the attempt of either, an unprovoked attack on a Warrior's mate or child— In such a case, the interloper must pay the ultimate price, as the pact demands. The Warrior who exacts the ultimate price for a crime that is not capital or not in defense will face death himself from his true judge, having proven himself lacking in control and respect for the fragile sanctity of life.

Likewise, the Warrior must gauge his punishment of Warriors who wrong him by the rules of sanction. A Warrior has the right to face the Warrior he has most wronged as judge—or his house lord, as case the may be when the injury is to his own house or to a human not of a Warrior's household. One who acts as judge in another's stead faces sanction by both the true judge and the Warrior he judged out of place—or the Warrior's lord if he is incapable of judging for himself.

The drive to print can lead to madness in *Endspiel*. Printing can make a Warrior the most stable of men, unless his mate or children are endangered, but the time of printing is the most dangerous and unstable time of all for a Warrior.

Warriors are not lawless soldiers. A Warrior must

rule his curse, lest the curse rule him. The sanctions in taking women are understandably rigid because of the great danger printing poses.

The beasts take women brutally, without care and concern. Until a Warrior finds his mate—or after he loses his mate, he will require release with women aside from his mate. While he has a mate, she will provide the only true release he will find. She is a balm for his soul, calming his *Blutjagd* and appeasing his sexual appetite as no other woman can while she lives. He will have no need and no wish to perform with another, as long as he has her.

But, a Warrior who cannot control his curse is no better than a beast. A Warrior may not take an unwilling woman, even if she is the woman of an enemy or an enemy herself. Neither shall a Warrior use his whiles to sway an unwilling woman to some form of willingness to bed her. Such a move is dishonorable in that it exploits her innocence and does her injustice.

A lover must always be treated kindly and with respect. It is the Warrior's duty to repay the peace a lover grants him with pleasure. If she gifts him with her maiden's blood, he must ease it from her and repay her tenfold for her sacrifice.

A Warrior must never take a child to his bed. A woman shy of fifteen years, though she bleeds, is not a woman for the taking. Her body is not adequate to carry a Warrior's child until she matures, and her innocence is still largely intact.

If the woman of a Warrior's desire is the freed daughter of another Warrior, she may not be taken without her father's consent or that of her house lord, if her father is dead. The Warrior protecting his child is a dangerous man, and the interloper may be perceived as a threat to that family. For the safety of all, this rule must be adhered to.

The Warrior who takes simple pleasure without permission from her keeper owes a solid blow for every instance to the one who would give his permission. Judgment of whether or not the Warrior is worthy of the woman will then be rendered by her judge.

If the Warrior takes his satisfaction in her in such a case, he must submit to that same man as judge. It is within his judge's rights to exact one of three punishments. If he deems the Warrior without either honor or control, he may take his life for it. He may take him to trial and forbid his interaction with the woman again. Or, he may take a single blow and give his consent—with any reasonable restrictions he deems fit the situation, from the question of when children are appropriate to loyalties in repayment for his trespass.

In any case—satisfaction taken or no—the judge has the right to strike the woman a single open-handed blow if he feels she is without honor in her actions.

A Warrior who cannot control his curse is no better than a beast. A Warrior who returns to a forbidden woman a second time faces the certainty of death.

A Warrior must always submit absolutely to his judge. If he raises a hand in his own defense to any Warrior—judge or no—or does not meet and live by his punishment gracefully—even unto a sentence of death, he will face death, as he has shown himself without control. If the Warrior lies to his judge to hide his misdeeds when asked for the truth, he will face any penalty up to and including death, as his judge wishes, for he has shown himself lacking in honor.

If the woman wronged is human not of a Warrior house, the house lord of the Warrior who wronged her will sit as his judge. If the accused is a house lord, the

Stone lord will stand as judge. If he is Stone lord, a council of the lords will stand as judge. In the case of the house lord, he will no longer be deemed worthy of his position and shall forfeit his place as house lord to the next in line to hold the seal. The Stone will take care of its own succession as It always has.

Taking any woman—human or of a household—unwilling or attempting to do so, automatically warrants a sentence of death, as would attempting her murder or the murder of a child. The body of the Warrior would then be presented to the woman and her family and personal protection be granted them in repayment by the house lord.

If the Warrior is come upon in the act, the woman's safety is paramount. If he can be restrained and presented to his true judge, it should be done despite the fury driving the Warrior who comes upon the scene. If such a thing cannot be accomplished without the threat of further violence to his victim, the criminal should be executed as he is. She should then be tended to medically and returned to her family with proof of the attacker's state.

If a human family wishes to exact their own punishment on a Warrior, they will be permitted the right of inflicting their own beating, with the protection of the Warrior guard, before the judge passes his own sentence. Remember always that when a Warrior breaks the pact, the safety of all depends on restoring the peace with the humans injured.

Only in a challenge of trial is the Warrior to defend himself physically. Only to his true judge, at the appropriate time, is the Warrior to defend himself in words—if such is the case that there is any excuse or explanation for his actions—or to plead mercy for the woman involved. A Warrior should never plead mercy for himself, as his actions are his own, dishonorable or honorable, and honor demands he take responsibility for them.

The Warrior may demand his right of his true judge and no more of the Warrior who places him in custody. If he raises a hand to that Warrior, he will be restrained or killed as the situation unfolds. Should he survive the punishment of his true judge for his first crime, he still faces death at the hands of the Warrior holding custody for his lack of control. If the Warrior taken into custody attempts violence against an innocent— In such a case, no move will be made to restrain him. His life is forfeit.

The Stone Alphabet

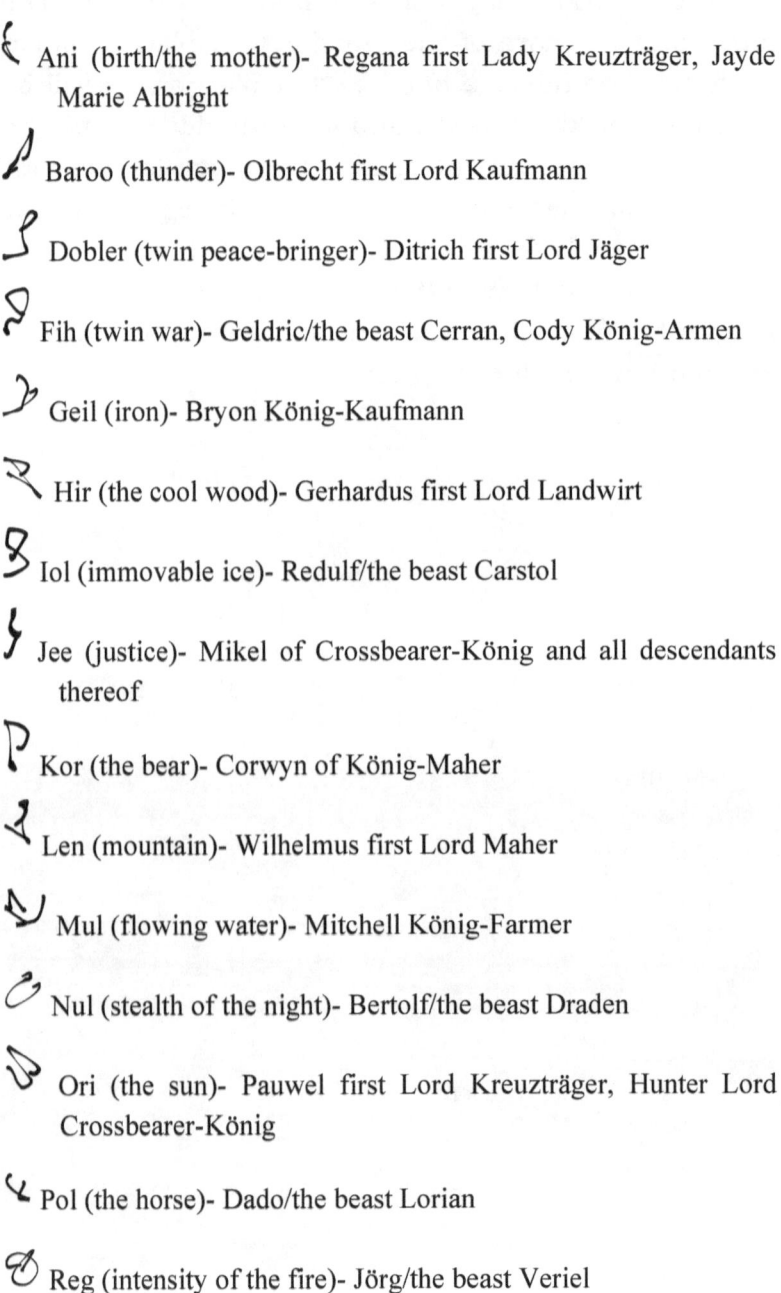

⌇ Ani (birth/the mother)- Regana first Lady Kreuzträger, Jayde Marie Albright

⌇ Baroo (thunder)- Olbrecht first Lord Kaufmann

⌇ Dobler (twin peace-bringer)- Ditrich first Lord Jäger

⌇ Fih (twin war)- Geldric/the beast Cerran, Cody König-Armen

⌇ Geil (iron)- Bryon König-Kaufmann

⌇ Hir (the cool wood)- Gerhardus first Lord Landwirt

⌇ Iol (immovable ice)- Redulf/the beast Carstol

⌇ Jee (justice)- Mikel of Crossbearer-König and all descendants thereof

⌇ Kor (the bear)- Corwyn of König-Maher

⌇ Len (mountain)- Wilhelmus first Lord Maher

⌇ Mul (flowing water)- Mitchell König-Farmer

⌇ Nul (stealth of the night)- Bertolf/the beast Draden

⌇ Ori (the sun)- Pauwel first Lord Kreuzträger, Hunter Lord Crossbearer-König

⌇ Pol (the horse)- Dado/the beast Lorian

⌇ Reg (intensity of the fire)- Jörg/the beast Veriel

✦ Syth (the Stone lord)- Master Trainer Sibold, Gawen first Lord Schwertträger, Etienne Lord Kaufmann, Joseph Lord Armen, Carrick Lord Armen, Corwyn Lord Hunter, Lewis of Maher

✦ Tes (stars and moon)- Kevin König-Smith

✦ Vin (wind)- Cunczel first Lord Schmied

✦ Wul (the wolf)- Tilbrand/the beast Resten

✦ Zel (ending/death)- Erin of Crossbearer-König, Kaitlyn "Katie" of König-Maher, Skye of König-Armen, Victorious Ellen "Vick/Vicky" of König-Smith, Margaret Elizabeth "Maggie" König-Farmer, Colette "Lettie" Kong-Kaufmann

About the Author

Brenna Lyons wears many hats, sometimes all on the same day: former president of EPIC, author of more than 100 published works, owner of Fireborn Publishing, columnist, special needs teacher, wife, mother...and member in good standing of more than 60 writing advocacy groups.

In her first ten years published in novel-length, she's won 3 EPIC e-Book Awards (out of 15 finalists) and finaled for 3 PEARLS (including one Honorable Mention, second to NY Times Bestseller Angela Knight), 2 CAPAS, and a Dream Realm Award. She's also taken Spinetingler's Book of the Year for 2007.

Brenna writes in 26 established worlds plus stand-alones, poetry, articles and essays. She's a bestseller in indie/e fantasy and horror, straight genre and cross-genres thereof. Brenna has been termed "one of the most deviant erotic minds in the publishing world...not for the weak." (Rachelle for Fallen Angels Reviews) Milieu-heavy dark work is practically Brenna's calling card, with or without the erotic content.

She teaches classes in everything from POV studies to advanced editing, networking to marketing. Brenna enjoys hearing from people who read her work and can be reached by e-mail.

Website: http://www.brennalyons.com/

Facebook: http://www.facebook.com/brenna.lyons

Email: brennalyons4168@live.com

Also by this Author

Available from *Fireborn Publishing*

KEIF'S DEN AND PACK
Keif's Pack
Mother of the Keif
Keif's Den (Coming Soon)

PROPHECY
Prophecy: Revelations
Prophecy: Rapture
The Prophet's Mate
Prophecy: Rampage - Meet Gavin
Prophecy: Rampage (Coming Soon)

THE FANTASY CLUB
The Consort

Beyond the Veil
Fairy Wishes (Coming Soon)
Mine for the Night
Once in a Blue Moon
Overtime Pay
Stay With Me
The Fire God's Woman
The Punishment of Phoebus Apollo
Werewolf U

Available from *Phaze Books*

ANGEL-WING SAGA
Sons of Heaven: Beldon
Daughters of Man: Prize Match
Sons of Heaven: Unexpected Mates
Daughters of Man: Claiming a Princess

BRIDE BALL
Bride Ball
Poison, Lies, and No-Win Choices

COLOR OF LOVE
The Color of Love

FIRE AND ICE
Magmon's Hunger
Magmon's Lover

INSTINCT SERIES
Animal Instincts

KEGIN SERIES
Conquest
The Last of Fion's Daughters
Last Chance for Love
Rites of Mating
In Her Ladyship's Service
Matchmaker's Misery

KIELAN SERIES
The Lady's Lowborn Lover
Time Currents
Cubed

NIGHT WARRIORS
Night Warriors
Will of the Stone
Bearing Armen
Hunter's Moon
Maher Men
Choosing a Mate/Starting a War
Raised to Be His Own
Veriel's Tales I: Crossbearer Turned
Veriel's Tales II: Losing Regana
Blutjagdfrau Lost
The Warrior's Man
Damsel in Distress

STAR MAGES
The Master's Lover

XXAN WAR
Daahan Rising
Crossbred Son
Raashh Decisions

Enslaved
All I Want for Christmas is You
Fates Magic
All's Fair...
Black Sail
Mama's Tales
Dream Walk
Unexpected Daddy
Phaze in Verse
We Shall Live Again
May the Best Man Win
Nevermore
Marked
And It Was Good

Available from **Mundania Press**

STAR MAGES
Written in the Stars

Fairy Dreams
Monsters of Myth Anthology

Available from **Under the Moon**

RENEGADES SERIES
TYGERS
Renegade's Run
Max Sec

URBAN GRIMM
Catch Me, If You Can
Three Wishes
Temptation of Eve

With Great Power
Undead in Blue
Evil Overlords Union Issue #1 Anthology
Undead Embrace
"Playing Games" in *Forbidden Love: Bad Boys*
"Marked" in *Forbidden Love: Wicked Women*
"The Master's Lover" in *Forbidden Love: Sacred Bands*

Available from **Logical Lust**

"Mine for the Night" in *The Cougar Book* Anthology

Available from **Coming Together Charity Anthologies**

INSTINCT SERIES
"Foundling" in *Coming Together: Into the Light* Anthology

"Claim Mate" (available separately and as part of the *Coming Together: Against the Odds* Anthology)
"The Fire God's Woman" in *Coming Together: Under Fire* Anthology

Available *self-published*

KEGIN SERIES
Earth-Born Lord
Graham: Training the Earth-Born Lord

NIGHT WARRIORS
Claiming a Lady

Stone Lord
Mother's Son

COLOR OF LOVE
A Safe Heart

Snapshots from a Poet's Life

Award-Winning Books

EPPIE/EPIC eBOOK AWARDS WINNERS
Coming Together: Against the Odds- 2010
Time Currents- 2010
Coming Together: Into the Light- 2011

EPPIE/EPIC eBOOK AWARDS FINALISTS
Fion's Daughter- 2004
Collected Poems: Book One- 2005 (now titled *Snapshots of a Poet's Life*)
Renegade's Run- 2005
Rites of Mating- 2006
All I Want for Christmas- 2006
Phaze in Verse- 2008
"The Fire God's Woman" in Coming Together: Under Fire- 2009
Three Wishes- 2010
Matchmaker's Misery- 2010
The Cougar Book- 2011
The Master's Lover- 2011
Bride Ball- 2011

DREAM REALM AWARDS FINALIST
Last Chance for Love- 2003

PEARL HONORABLE MENTION
Night Warriors- 2004

PEARL FINALISTS
Schente Night- 2003 (now included in *The Last of Fion's Daughters*)
König Cursebreakers- 2004 (now titled *Will of the Stone*)

JOYFULLY REVIEWED BEST BOOKS OF 2010
Written in the Stars- 2010

SPINETINGLER'S BOOK OF THE YEAR 2007
NOBODY: An Anthology of Dark Fiction- 2007 (Brenna's pieces of the anthology can be found in *Beyond the Veil*)

TRS's CAPA FINALISTS
Ultimate Warriors- 2004 (Brenna's portion is now available as
With Great Power)
Written in the Stars

LOVE ROMANCE AND MORE CAFÉ BOOK OF THE YEAR
RUNNER UP
Last Chance for Love- 2008

ROAD TO ROMANCE REVIEWERS' CHOICE AWARD
Prophecy: Revelations- 2004

LOVE ROMANCES REVIEWERS' CHOICE AWARD
Black Sail- 2003

ROMANCE JUNKIES BOOK CLUB STAFF PICK
TYGERS- 2003

FALLEN ANGELS ROMANCE RECOMMENDED READ
Devon's Price-2005 (now available in *Bearing Armen*)

JOYFULLY RECOMMENDED READ
Fairy Dreams- 2008
The Last of Fion's Daughters- 2009

TREBLE HEART FINALIST
Prophecy: Revelations- 2003

www.ingramcontent.com/pod-product-compliance
Lightning Source LLC
Chambersburg PA
CBHW031051260626
47172CB00001B/25